TWOPENCE PRESS books are published by
Twopence Press, LLC
P.O. Box 1753
Leonardtown, Maryland 20650

All Twopence Press titles are available at special quan-
tity discounts for bulk purchases for sales promotion,
premiums, fund-raising, educational, or institutional
use.

Cover Design and Interior Format by
The Killion Group, Inc.

The Cedar Point Affair

Heart of St. Mary's County
Book Three

CHRISTINE TRENT

DEDICATION

In memory of the servicemen who trained at Solomons Amphibious Base in Solomons, Maryland, and subsequently perished during the invasions at Guadalcanal, Normandy, and other far-flung locations.

And in memory of
Captain Walter Francis Duke
August 6, 1921– June 6, 1944
St. Mary's County Hometown Hero

Diane Ruth Yonker Townsend
December 17, 1943 – May 7, 2023
Greatly missed friend

Frances Darden Carpenter
May 14, 1914 – March 14, 1981
My grandmother, World War II home front survivor

Growing up during World War II certainly affected my whole view of life, but I hardly know how, it goes so deep. What's hard to explain now is that, though we were never invaded, and bombed only once and ineffectively on the coast of Oregon, everybody in the country was in that war. Everything we did was influenced by it—eating, traveling, dressing, thinking— everything in daily life.

~Ursula K. Le Guin
American author, 1929-2018
Winner of the National Book Award, seven Hugo Awards, six Nebula Awards, and more

PART I:
DIANE ALVEY

Patuxent River, Maryland
Present Day

CHAPTER 1

A MOUSE SKITTERED ALONG my office's dented pine baseboard, no doubt thinking it was very cleverly getting past me.

The mouse was right, of course. Leila was never going to permit me to take care of it with the finality it required.

Mice were only part of the exasperation I experienced daily. Fortunately, I was able to withstand their little squeaks and scampering without having to stand on my chair every time I thought one passed by.

The strangest thing about working at Patuxent River Naval Air Station is the bizarre juxtaposition between cutting-edge modernity and relative antiquity.

I might start my day photographing a new piece of sophisticated aircraft gear, surrounded by the brilliant engineers who developed it, then end the day inside my musty office within my tired, dilapidated old administration building, writing an exciting article for the station newsletter about how said gear was going to revolutionize the way the U.S. Navy fights—and wins—wars.

Meanwhile, it was nearly impossible for most of us to even get new desks and chairs.

My own desk had a mouse living somewhere

inside of it, but the behemoth metal piece weighed as much as a polar bear, so it was hard to move it to search in and around it for tell-tale nesting materials.

Not that it mattered. Leila, our department's personnel representative, had such a soft spot for all animals, no matter how verminous, that you couldn't set a real trap for their demise. She would set up little plastic boxes that trapped the critters inside, then take the boxes outside and release them.

My situation wasn't unique. Many buildings on the air station, which we all referred to as Pax River, or just Pax, were beleaguered with mice, asbestos, mold, and some truly horrendous decor that was surely left over from the building's construction in the 1940s. Conditions were challenging to say the least, and because of bureaucratic red tape, procurements and contracts for renovations took years to come to fruition.

Leila's flaming red hair poked around the corner before I could actually see her ever-smiling, freckled face. "Hey Diane, I'm running into Lexington Park for a couple of errands during lunch. Want some coffee?"

Leila loved coffee as much as she adored the squeaky little creatures in my desk and would drink it all day long. She had the pep of The Energizer Bunny, which amazed me. Her husband regularly headed out on extreme sport weekends, leaving her with their three kids, whom she was perpetually ferrying off to every extracurricular activity their school and church offered. Yet she was always bouncy and vivacious.

"I probably shouldn't…". In contrast to Leila, I lived in a modest home, enjoyed puttering around in my flower beds, had a peaceful—if unexciting—relationship with my boyfriend of two years, Gus, and was relatively successful in my career. Oh, and I had a decrepit old cat named Tobias who loved me with abandon and loathed every other human being on the planet.

All in all, I suppose my life wasn't bad for a twenty-eight-year-old.

I sighed and glanced at the old, electric, brown metal Westclox hanging on the wall, another relic from the past. It was almost one o'clock. A little late for coffee for me. However, I hadn't had any lunch yet, and I had a long way to go to wrap up for the day.

"Sure," I said, contradicting myself. Coffee counted as food for office workers, right?

"The usual? Large peppermint-mocha-extra-hot-skim-milk-no-whip?"

I laughed at the rapid way Leila spoke my order. "Perfect, thank you."

"You public affairs officers are so predictable," she replied before saluting me and leaving.

I wondered if I should have called her back and told her to get me whatever she was having so I could grab a little of her vitality, but she had already disappeared from the long hallway by the time I reached my doorway.

Martin Kessler, one of our department's financial managers, poked his gray hair covered-head into my doorway. "Did you let Leila talk you into afternoon coffee again, Diane? You know you're going to come in tomorrow without having slept a wink tonight."

"You're right as always, Marty. But those peppermint mochas are irresistible." I winked at Marty, who was the proverbial lovable curmudgeon of the office.

He shook his head dolefully. "I've run the cost-benefit analysis on buying and drinking those things every day. They don't make good sense." He winked back at me before disappearing back into his office.

Yes, there were many disadvantages to working for the federal government, but I did love my working environment, which was warm and relaxed. I was very lucky as I knew some administration buildings could be pretentious and stuffy.

I was not only fortunate to have good camaraderie with my fellow employees, but I also had considerable independence in deciding what I wanted to work on, particularly since my job encompassed a full range of communications duties, not just public-facing communications. As long as I kept up with newsletter production, dealt with public inquiries, and wrote communiques that my boss needed, I could be as creative as I wanted to be elsewhere.

Knowing I had close to an hour before Leila returned, I decided to stop working on my current station newsletter to spend a little time on a new history project I had been planning. It was a project I'd not yet revealed to most of my colleagues as I was still unsure of the direction I was taking, but I was quietly doing a lot of research in the one place where the most information could be found.

I rose, stretched, grabbed my iPad and a pair of earbuds, and went to the Morgue.

CHAPTER 2

I VENTURED DOWN THE long, narrow space upstairs to my destination. The Morgue was a library of sorts located at one end of the building, shaped more like an old military barracks than anything else, although I know it had never been used in that manner. Everyone had access to the space to rifle through whatever they needed for whatever project they were working on, though I was one of the few who ventured up here.

My understanding was this area once housed the communications department in the 1940s. It was where the typing pool sat, spitting out letters and propaganda on their Underwood typewriters. I gazed down the airless room, which was probably twenty feet across, seventy-five feet long, and maybe fifteen feet high. A bank of windows was inset into the wall to my right.

To my left, the wall was lined with stained pine "Navy-grade" bookshelf planks anchored firmly against the paneled wall. They were ugly as sin but could probably hold the weight of an aircraft carrier. I could imagine a series of desks and chairs, placed in a military line down the center of the room, each attended by a young woman with cherry red lips and hair placed in fashionable waves.

I self-consciously reached up and touched my own loosely worn hair. It was a color I referred to as Tween. Somewhere *between* blonde and brown. And with glints of red if you caught me in the sunlight. I often considered coloring it some exotic color, like platinum blonde, but I always lost my nerve before my stylist could lay a squeeze-bottle tip to my hairline.

My mom had had strikingly blonde hair. I remember always thinking that my mother was very glamorous, even as I became a rebellious teenager. When I was around thirteen, a friend of my mother's came over to play cards—a euphemism for gossiping about the neighbors—and while I set out a box of Lorna Doone shortbreads and a pitcher of lemonade for them, the friend asked slyly, "Shirley, is your hair getting blonder?"

No doubt the friend thought she had tripped my mother up, but the woman just did not understand Shirley Alvey. Mom had leaned forward, cupped a hand around one side of her mouth as if to share a secret, and said loudly, "Of course it is."

It was one of the funniest memories I had of Mom, who had been gone seven years now after a shockingly brief bout with cancer. But Mom looked elegant and smart to the end, even in her casket.

I tried to make up for my lack of hair flair by dressing somewhat stylishly. Or in my own style, anyway. I favored blocky jackets in bold geometric patterns over wide-legged pants and solid tops. Finding fun costume jewelry at thrift stores was a favorite annual activity with my best friend, Mary. I guess you could categorize my style as moderate bohemian.

Much unlike the women who would have inhabited this room long ago. No doubt they would have been required to wear a uniform of sorts, or would have at least had a clothing requirement to keep things regimented. What would they have thought of today's "casual Fridays"?

Today the room was called "the Morgue" for good reason. The bookshelves were filled with boxes and heaps of papers, records, and ephemera from the past, no doubt decades of old documents that had remained there because management was fearful of tossing something that might one day be requested in an audit.

The floor itself contained old tables, mimeograph machines, rotary dial telephones, and other office equipment that had suffered obsolescence long ago. Nothing was arranged or ordered, but merely dumped in whatever open spot had been available at the time.

My only improvement to the situation had been to drag the least-wobbly table to the middle of the room a few weeks ago as my workspace.

I walked to a spot at the center of the bookshelves and approached the ladder leaning against the left wall. It was one of those old-fashioned, rolling type things made of oak that hooks into a metal bar at the top of the bookcase or along a wall so you can slide along, picking out what you want.

I grabbed the ladder rails, one in each hand, and climbed up until I was about eight feet off the ground and staring at an old banker's box tied up with twine and marked "1944, The Incident–DO NOT DESTROY" in faded black magic marker.

"You look interesting," I said aloud. My voice reverberated throughout the hall.

Maintaining my balance, I reached for the box and carefully brought it down the ladder with me, happy that it wasn't particularly heavy. I placed it on my worktable, where it joined several other, specially selected boxes that I intended to use as part of my new project.

With my boss's blessing, I had initiated a "History Hall" to document the history of Pax River via museum-type wallpaper along both sides of the main hallway at the building's entry. I planned to strategically hang various artifacts to punctuate the write-ups of important people and events that had occurred since the station's commissioning in 1943.

I worked for Lieutenant Commander Patrick Barry, the station's director of communications. He looked as Irish as his name sounded, and he had gladly mentored me in my role as a public affairs officer.

"Fabulous idea, Diane," he had said when I suggested it to him. "You'll need to visit the Morgue for what you need."

I was taken aback by the suggestion, not realizing that a set of doors at the end of an upstairs hallway hid the cavernous room that lay before me now, full of any historical artifact one could want. Provided one was willing to dig through hundreds of boxes for the pearls among the oysters, of course.

I was so excited about my project that I was willing to dig.

To date, I had found sheafs of papers concerning the initial construction of the base, including lots of procurement documentation. I would have to whittle that information down to a few paragraphs for my History Hall.

I had also discovered photographs of previous commanding officers that I planned to have restored and placed in the hallway.

There were also various yellowed newspaper articles concerning the base and old newsletters stored in binders that were full of interesting facts and pictures. I had even found a couple of yearbooks from the first few years of the base's founding. In perfect condition, they were chock full of photographs of sailors eating, working on aircraft, taking smoke breaks, and even dancing with young women in front of a brass band.

Today there were few actual sailors at Pax River, as the base now consisted mostly of civilian and contractor employees. It was fun to glance through the yearbooks and imagine the story behind each individual gaze on me from its little rectangular picture.

The artifact I had found that I couldn't wait to hang in the hall was an old **WELCOME TO NAVAL AIR STATION PATUXENT RIVER** sign. Hand-painted in blue and gold, it must have hung at the main entry gate many decades ago, and I planned to make it the entry sign to the History Hall.

Before I got too far ahead of myself, though, I needed to make sure I collected everything I could find so that I could decide how to tell the story of Pax River in a way that would be fun and engaging to visitors.

Neither I nor the Lieutenant Commander had ever been involved in such a project before, so it was a challenge in addition to being fun.

"So, let's see what treasures you hold," I said aloud, popping in my ear buds to continue listening to a cozy mystery novel featuring a murder-solving pink flamingo as I started to untie the string wrapped around the box. It was so old that as soon as I started fiddling with it, the string crumbled within my fingers.

I brushed it away from the top of the box and opened the flaps. I frowned at the contents as I pulled each item out. There were a few eight-by-ten, black and white photographs of young men in Marine Corps uniforms. The photographs had crease marks horizontally across the centers, so they must have been folded at some point. Each of the handsome, fresh-scrubbed Marines wore a serious expression, but I wondered what else I was seeing behind their gazes. Hope? Fear? Determination?

Which of them hadn't survived the war?

There were also other formal portraits of men and women in U.S. Navy uniforms. I turned all of the photos over individually to see what might be on the flip side. They each had the same thing written on the back in tight, precise cursive.

1944
Just before it happened

Just before *what* happened?

Only two of these formal photos had names inscribed on the back, Master Sergeant Roger Douglas and Sergeant Kenneth Campbell. As with all the other portraits, the men were handsome and staring intently at the camera.

There was one other photo, this one smaller and more casual. It showed a group of women in smart-looking uniforms standing in front of a bus.

I put the photos aside and reached back into the box.

Also inside the box was a silk neckerchief, wrapped in old, brittle tissue paper. It looked like it belonged to a Marine Corps dress blues uniform. Unfolding the neckerchief, I found a gold button tucked in the center of it. Again, this appeared to be from a Marine Corps dress uniform.

I gently laid the items aside. Right now, I could only assume they belonged to one of the men in the photographs.

More items in the box included a combat knife in a leather sheath—the leather in nearly perfect condition except for a little green mold on it. I slid the knife out. There were dark rust stains on the blade that I didn't want any details on. I slid it back in and laid the sheath aside.

My hand touched a small leather presentation

box. Inside was an old Navy-Marine Corps medal that appeared to have never been worn. I recognized it because I had had a distant uncle who had received one of these medals during the war.

I tried to remember what Uncle Billy had done to earn the medal. Wasn't it for the rescue of fellow troops? I would have to talk to my Aunt Poppy. She was the family historian and would instantly remember.

I gently lifted the medal out of its box, holding it in my palm and examining it. The top ribbon consisted of three equal, vertical stripes in navy, gold, and red. Beneath this was an octagonal bronze medal, depicting a globe overlayed with an eagle holding an anchor. The word "heroism" was inscribed beneath the globe.

I presumed it belonged to whomever owned the neckerchief, button, and knife. I wondered why they were in an old box of office goods instead of stored with someone's family memorabilia.

Next in the box was an old, World War II-era gas ration sheet. I'd heard of these but had never seen one. This one was labeled as an "A" ration. The coupon's owner, according to the handwriting on it, was a Sophie Russell. What was an "A" ration worth? Three or four gallons, I imagined.

The coupons had not all been used. This was interesting, as I imagine they were as valuable as gold during the rationing of the war era. Maybe the war ended before all of the coupons could be used.

I laid the coupon book next to the neckerchief,

button, knife, and photo. Ah, here was something that might be interesting for the History Hall. I lifted out an old, yellowed edition of the *St. Mary's Beacon*. The date was Monday, June 19, 1944, and the headline was enormous.

DROWNED BODY FOUND OFF CEDAR POINT

The body of a man wearing a U.S. Marine Corps uniform was found washed ashore at Cedar Point on Friday, June 16.

Capt. Milligan "Sparky" Nickerson, the executive officer for the Marine barracks security department, stated that, "We have accounted for our detachment members. Therefore, we are investigating where this body may have come from, whether he's an actual Marine or someone who was simply wearing the uniform. Regardless, we offer condolences to the family of this man, whose life was cut short by this terrible accident in the Patuxent River."

The Navy has taken possession of the body for an autopsy and will release further information as appropriate. The public is requested to avoid circulating unfounded rumors while the investigation takes place.

Slashed across the entire article in red ink was the word, "LIES."

I popped the buds from my ears. Flo the pink flamingo would have to wait. I had to fully focus on this, which I had to presume was the aforementioned "incident."

I had been a public affairs officer long enough to know that this was a carefully scripted press release, not an article written by a newspaper reporter. Why did the Navy feel the need to control information about an accidental drowning? Curious.

Cedar Point still existed on the northeast end of the base where the Patuxent River met the Chesapeake Bay. There had once been a lighthouse there, but erosion, time, and neglect had ravaged it, and the lighthouse had been dismantled in the 1990s. The light itself had been removed to the Pax River Naval Air Museum, but there was nothing left of the lighthouse building.

If I recalled correctly, the lighthouse had not been in use by the 1940s but would have still sat a short distance offshore. Maybe this Marine had been curious and attempted to swim out to it and been caught in a current? The Patuxent River was not a body of water to be trifled with and had viciously claimed more than one soul over the years.

I felt a pang of sadness for the drowning victim's family. Had they ever had resolution to the man's death?

I re-read the article. It didn't actually say that the man had been swimming. It didn't say much at all about what had happened to him. I would have to see if I could find out anything else about it. Maybe it had been a significant enough event in the station's history to include in the History Hall.

I glanced at the digital watch on my arm. Gus had given it to me for my birthday last year. The watch did nearly everything except cook dinner, but I used it for little other than telling time.

It had been a thoughtful gift, but was really something Gus had liked, not something with great appeal for me.

I chastised myself for the disloyal thought. Such a nice man, and here I was mentally insulting his gift. It did have a cute pink watchband.

It was two o'clock. I had plans to meet my friend, Mary, for after-work drinks, and I needed to finish my current newsletter so that Lt. Cmdr. Barry could review it.

With my stomach rumbling over how long it was taking Leila to return with coffee, I spent another hour making trips up the ladder for more World War II ephemera but came up empty. Now it was nearly three o'clock, so I forced myself to return to my office to work on the newsletter, which didn't hold nearly the interest for me that the Morgue did.

I wasn't prepared, though, for Mary's reaction that evening when I told her about my findings.

CHAPTER 3

"OH MY GOSH, you've got a gen-u-wine mystery to solve!" Mary said, pushing aside her margarita and reaching for a tater tot from the platter we were sharing at the Greene Turtle. The tots were deliciously slathered in cheese, bacon, and homemade ranch dressing.

I shrugged, unsure what to think.

Mary, though, was quite excited. "If someone wrote 'lies' across the article, it must mean that someone died at Cedar Point, but not accidentally. You love mystery stories. You could figure out whodunnit. Imagine the headline. 'St. Mary's County Woman Solves Decades-Old Murder.' You'd be a celebrity down here."

"As fun as that sounds, I'm guessing that any mystery was solved long ago," I said. I took a sip of my own margarita through its green plastic straw. Frozen strawberry, my favorite. "I suppose I could do some online research, find digitized copies of old news–"

Mary paid no attention to me. "Ooh, here's a thought. I bet the Morgue is full of old documentation about unsolved happenings on the base." Mary was warming up but stopped for another tot. "You could carve out an entire job just cleaning up old mysteries from the base."

With it swallowed, she continued. "There could even be a television show about you! Imagine that."

I moved Mary's margarita further out of her reach. "I think you've had enough."

She tossed her curly blonde hair and laughed good-naturedly—she was always good-natured about everything, even her mostly-unemployed boyfriend—and it made me realize something important.

I needed to take myself less seriously.

Mary changed the subject. "Hey, we haven't gotten together with the guys in a while. Want to double date soon? Maybe on the next first Friday in Leonardtown, we could walk around, have dinner and ice cream, maybe walk down to the wharf."

"Sure, I'll talk to Gus," I said vaguely, knowing Gus wouldn't be interested, and I would end up going by myself. Gus was a sweet guy, intelligent, and very mild-mannered, but also not very sociable. He much preferred staying locked away in his home office, developing online games, than going out with friends. I'd learned over the past couple of years to only invite him out if it was important to me or my career that he be present. Otherwise, I flew solo. It could be a little lonely, but I suppose it wasn't that big a deal.

As we tossed money down for the bill, Mary's phone buzzed on the table next to her. She glanced down to read a text, and her expression became uncharacteristically sober.

"Not again," she said. The words were severe, but her tone was mild.

I shut my purse and put it back down on the booth next to me. "What's wrong?"

Mary wrinkled her nose. "Brad lost his job today."

"Really? Didn't he just start there a few weeks ago?" I didn't have enough hands to count the number of jobs Brad had been through since Mary had started seeing him three years ago.

"Yes. He says they weren't willing to let him apply for his own patents while he worked there if the patent was in the company's field."

I shrugged. "I think that's common. They don't want their employees competing with them."

"True. Brad has so many patent ideas that I don't know where he *could* work where he wouldn't have some sort of conflict of interest. And this is St. Mary's County. Once word gets around enough, he could become unemployable." Mary furrowed her brow.

I reached across the table and put my hand over hers. "But he doesn't have to work on all of his patents at once, does he?"

Mary bit her lip. "No, I suppose not." Her expression cleared, and she became sunny again. "I'm lucky to be with someone so smart. He really is, you know. He talks at a level that most people can't even understand. Me included." She laughed her infectious laugh that could be heard across the room. A couple at a nearby table smiled our way. Mary had that effect on people.

I refrained from saying anything else negative

about Brad. "I'm sure he'll find something else soon. There are plenty of technical jobs here in St. Mary's County." I rose from the table and Mary joined me.

"You're right," she said as we walked to our cars, which were parked together. "Brad is too bright and valuable to be left on the street for long. See you next week."

I waved as I got into my car. The last of the sun's rays was dipping below the horizon and there were billowing dark clouds quickly approaching from the distance.

I sat in my car, thinking, as Mary drove away. Was Mary throwing her lot in with Brad because she was nearing thirty and thought her prospects were narrowing for finding a mate? Was she settling for someone less than satisfactory to avoid being alone?

Rain started spattering my windshield. By the time I started the engine and put the car in gear, it was coming down in torrential sheets.

As I slowly drove away, I felt a pang of discomfort shoot through me. Was I doing the same?

No, of course not. Mary's situation was much more disagreeable. Wasn't it?

⁓⁓

After a fitful night of sleep, I rose early and prepared for work, reaching into the back of my closet for a Barbie-pink and white jacket I hadn't worn in months. Putting that over a white blouse and black pants, I pored through my jewelry box until I finally found an old ebony, Bakelite bangle bracelet I'd found at a yard sale. Pleased with my outfit, I slipped out of the house without waking Tobias from his feline slumbers. I arrived at the office at six o'clock, chastising myself for having forgotten to bring along a cup of coffee. I was the first one in the communications office, even beating Lt. Cmdr. Barry in, so I took my time setting up a communal pot of coffee for everyone and scanning through overnight e-mails while I waited for it to brew.

The government was relentless in its daily e-mail avalanche. On any given day, I would get multiple e-mails from my work unit, from N.A.S. Patuxent River, from the Secretary of the Navy, from the Department of Defense, and from any of a number of ancillary agencies. It was tempting to just delete them all unread in order to stay on top of things, but as a public affairs officer, or P-A-O as we were commonly called, I had to know what was going on everywhere so that I could react appropriately should something happen on base that required an immediate response to employees or the press or, heaven forbid, Congress.

Today was just the usual round of don't-forget-your-time-sheet-come-to-the-base-theatre-for-a-family-movie-remember-security-is-our-highest-priority type e-mails.

With my in-box cleared out, I got up and poured more coffee, then returned to my desk. "Time to learn who you were, Mr. Marine," I said to the screen. "Are you worthy of my History Hall?"

I performed various web searches on news events of the period, including terms like "Marines," "drowning," and "Cedar Point" in my searches.

I did eventually find the newspaper article I'd read by digging through a *St. Mary's Beacon* digital archive. The archive also held various captioned photos of U.S. Marines who had been stationed at Pax in the 1940s. One interesting photo was from an old Pax River newsletter and showed a uniformed man holding a rifle in front of a guard shack with a German Shepherd sitting obediently next to him.

Master Sgt. Douglas and his faithful companion, Gunney, are fierce protectors of Patuxent River Naval Air Station.
U.S. Navy photo, 1943.

This looked like the same Marine I had seen in the Morgue archive, Master Sergeant Roger Douglas. This particular photo was interesting, but only marginally illuminating about life at Pax so long ago. However, I saved the photo to a file for future reference.

Didn't I have binders full of old Pax River newsletters put aside in the Morgue? I needed to go through them to see if there might be other photos—or perhaps articles—from which I might at least be able to get more information on the Marines' service at Pax during the war, and from there decipher who else was in the other photos. Maybe that would somehow lead me to whatever had happened at Cedar Point.

It was time to return to the Morgue. I drained the coffee in my cup, picked up my phone and key ring, tossed them in my jacket pocket, and headed down the hall.

It was still early in the day. I saw a couple of office doors open, and light filtered into the hallway. Lt. Cmdr. Barry wasn't in yet. I waved good morning to people without stopping for chit-chat as I made my way to the Morgue's double doors.

I inserted the old, tarnished brass room key into the lock, amazed that the room had never had its lock upgraded to something keyless.

I entered the room, shutting and turning the old-fashioned deadbolt behind me. I took a deep breath. The air was permeated with the mustiness that all airless, abandoned room seem to adopt.

"Concentrate on old newsletters," I said to no one, hearing my voice echo around the room.

I dug out the dusty, black-bound binders that were organized by date in cramped, faded writing atop cards stuck in metal label holders on their spines.

The old, yellowed newsletters were put together with staples that were rusty and weak. I had to flip the pages carefully to keep them together.

However, someone had done an admirable job maintaining a complete archive of them in perfect date order. I soon stopped flipping idly through them and intentionally dug down to the 1940s era.

I soon had the very first station newsletter in

my hand. Dated May 1943, it was a blend of information on base construction, war news, and employee achievements—including a member of the WAVES noted for having rigged a record number of parachutes in a month's time.

The front page was a letter from the station's commanding officer, Capt. Aaron P. Stricker III. In it, he praised employees for the progress being made on winning the war, with admonitions about continuing to set an example for other Americans by proudly sacrificing wherever possible, including buying war bonds at an upcoming rally.

The newsletter even contained ads for local businesses—the Bell Motor Company, the A&P grocery store, and a hardware store. I shook my head in amusement. Such ads would be a complete no-no in today's government environment, where sensitivities were high about the Navy maintaining an arm's length relationship with businesses, particularly defense contractors.

But I could imagine that with the base's startup, the Navy was likely anxious to have as good a relationship as possible with the townspeople, especially given that many of them had been displaced from homes, farms, and businesses as a result of the Navy's arrival.

I scanned the other newsletters for the remainder of 1943. Except for an article about the newly arriving civilian workers and the Pinkerton agency being replaced by U.S. Marines as station guards, nothing else stood out to me.

I had no idea the Pinkerton agency had existed

into the World War II era. I remembered from history books that they were a detective agency hired to protect President Abraham Lincoln. They were a forerunner of the U.S. Secret Service.

There had been a cloud over the agency, though, following Lincoln's death. I searched my memory banks. Something about Pinkerton using unorthodox means to help the government in strikebreaking against labor unions.

Interesting that Pinkerton agents had been used to protect the base. I wonder why they were replaced by Marines, given that so many of those men were needed to fight overseas at the time.

Well, the Pinkertons had no bearing on my tasking, and thus far, I wasn't having much luck with digging up information on the Marines, so I decided to switch gears and perform other World War II era research for my History Hall.

I had recently learned about the Women Accepted for Volunteer Emergency Service, or WAVES. The WAVES were like a Naval Reserve for women, and I wanted to ensure they received adequate credit in the History Hall.

What could I find on the WAVES contingent at Pax River?

I returned to the bookcase ladder, slid it down about six feet, and climbed about halfway up to better scan the shelves.

I reached forward to push aside some old banners emblazoned with long disused logos—government agencies are forever reorganizing and developing new branding—as well as some small recruitment posters that appeared to be from the late 1970s. "Navy, it's Not Just a Job, it's an Adventure." Each showed sailors in what looked like exotic ports of call.

On second thought…I grabbed both the banners and posters and climbed down the ladder to add them to my collection table.

Back up the ladder I went, continuing in my ongoing needle-in-a-haystack search for memorabilia for the History Hall, now with an emphasis on WAVES.

I found a recruitment brochure for them, explaining how the Naval reserve system worked for women and what they could expect in terms of pay and benefits.

How many WAVES had worked here? The area was mostly farmland back in the 1940s, so I imagined the women assigned here had predominantly come from other places.

In that moment, I had a stroke of inspiration for the History Hall. What if I developed a fictional WAVE in order to tell a "story" about the life of women newly inducted into the Navy?

I liked it. In fact, I could develop several storylines across the deadlines told from various Naval personnel viewpoints. Maybe I could even—

What was this? I tilted my head to one side.

No way. It wasn't possible.

With my heart hammering in my chest, I reached out a finger to touch a place on the wall behind the shelves.

It was subtle but I could see a crack line in the

wall. Not just a random settling crack, but a line that seemed to indicate a deliberate cut in the wall.

I felt a slight movement beneath my finger as I pressed the wall to the left of the crack line.

I muttered a four-letter word to myself. Going down two rungs, I shoved aside everything on the shelf below where I had been. There was the crack again. I reached out again and got the same spongy sensation.

If I wasn't mistaken, there was a door behind these shelves.

CHAPTER 4

I SCRAMBLED DOWN FROM the ladder, holding a hand to my chest. My heartbeat was so wild and erratic I was afraid I might have a cardiac event while locked up in here and no one would find my body until Lt. Cmdr. Barry noticed that I hadn't submitted my time sheet for approval next week.

I calmed down as I stood next to the ladder, my left hand still on a rung and my right hand patting my chest.

What was I to do next? I needed to verify that it really was a door hidden beneath layers of white paint over old wood grain paneling, but there were long shelves full of items in front of it.

I had no choice but to dismantle the shelves and the vertical brackets upon which they hung. I briefly wondered what Lt. Cmdr. Barry would say to that. He likely wouldn't be enthused. After all, what did some old door in an equally old building have to do with our mission?

I checked the Morgue doors again to ensure that they were locked. As I returned to the bookshelves, I saw movement on the floor out of the corner of my eye and yelped when I felt something run across my open-toed sandals.

A mouse sprinted across the carpet beyond me and disappeared into a tiny hole in the molding at the bottom of the shelves.

He was no doubt yukking it up with his friends right now, telling them how he had frightened the cowardly human again.

Stupid rodent.

Maybe it was time to explain to Leila that the mice really were becoming a menace.

My more important task, though, was getting behind the shelves.

Knowing I shouldn't destroy government property, I headed back to my office to retrieve the petite hammer I kept on hand for hanging pictures.

I was just about to go through my own door when Lt. Cmdr. Barry appeared out of nowhere with a carafe-sized coffee thermos in his hand. "There you are," he said. "Chat a minute about the newsletter? I know you're anxious to put it in production."

I was anxious about it yesterday. Today I had forgotten all about it.

I followed my boss back to his office and sat patiently while he went over changes he wanted to the newsletter. Move an article to the lede, use a different photo for "Sailor of the Month," and so on. All minor changes that my graphic artist, Natalie, could whip out in no time.

An idea popped into my mind as I attempted to pay attention. "What would you think about putting a 'Back When' feature in the newsletter? A look back at the base in its earlier days? I've been finding some interesting information about life in St. Mary's County and on the base back in the day."

My boss nodded his head. "It's a good tie-in to your History Hall, too. How's that coming?"

"Well, I have quite a bit of ephemera now, but I need to develop the end-to-end story I want to tell. The wall space I have is plentiful but not infinite, so I need to condense everything and figure out what gets put up and what goes back into the Morgue."

"Let me know if you need assistance. Anything else I should know?"

I liked that my boss let me run with projects and just offered help if I needed it. "I'm good."

With our conversation thankfully over, I returned to my own office and dug out my little hammer from a desk drawer. Its handle was covered in a comfortable, teal-colored silicone grip. I'd hung many a picture in my office and throughout the building with it.

I was once again derailed, this time by my phone buzzing in my pocket.

"Hi, Gus," I said, wondering if there was a problem. He had a busy job on base as an engineer for a secret program and didn't often call me at work.

"Hey, Diane. Um, was just thinking—wondering—if you'd like to go to the movies tonight. We could see something new, or they're also doing a special showing of *Casablanca*. You've never seen that one, right?" Gus spoke haltingly. I think that even after two years of dating, he was still nervous around me, as though I might bolt at any minute.

Casablanca was the World War II flick about an American cafe owner who can't decide whether or not to help his former lover and her husband, a Czech resistance leader, escape the Nazis in French Morocco. The movie starred luminary film stars of the time–Humphrey Bogart, Ingrid Bergman, and Paul Henreid, and was one of several 1940s classics that I had never seen except in snatches. I also had *The Maltese Falcon* and *Mildred Pierce* as tops on my list of old flicks to eventually watch in their entireties.

"Right. I've been wanting to see it. Might be fun on the big screen."

We agreed on a time for Gus to pick me up, and I clicked off the call. It was thoughtful of him to remember my desire to see these old pictures when he probably had no interest in them himself.

Back into my jacket pocket went the phone for safekeeping, although I was determined not to answer it if another call came through. No more interruptions to what I was doing.

I locked myself back in the Morgue. Tossing the hammer onto my artifacts table, I stood a short distance away from the bookcase and contemplated it. Then I went to the ladder and rolled it off to one side. That was when the door outline became much more apparent.

How had I not noticed it before?

Rolling the ladder back into place, I climbed up and laboriously removed everything from the shelves that blocked the wall cracks. Up and down I went, stacking everything in a pile on the floor.

I should have been tired when I was done, but instead, I was pumped with adrenaline. The outline in the wall paneling was so obvious now.

I got to work on removing the shelves, a tricky operation because they were long and, having sat in place for years, were "stuck" to the wall. Working carefully with a combination of brute force and using both the head and claw parts of the hammer, I was able to dislodge the shelves and stack them against a wall.

So far, so good. It didn't appear as though anyone had heard me. At least, there wasn't anyone banging on the doors and asking if anything was wrong.

Fortunately, none of the vertical support brackets covered the door, so I didn't have to deal with removing them.

Time for the reality check.

I put the hammer back on the table and rolled the ladder completely out of the way. Standing in front of the area I had just cleared, I pressed along the wall's crack before me. It was spongy all the way down. I attempted to press in with my left hand to create an opening while inserting a couple of the fingers of my right hand into the crack.

It wasn't working. The door wasn't giving enough to let me hook my fingers inside.

I retrieved the hammer. Using the claw end, I gently inserted it into the crack as I applied pressure with my left hand.

"Gotcha," I murmured as I felt it start to give way. I added my left hand to my right in its grip around the hammer handle to add more weight to the pull.

The door creaked and protested, but eventually gave way, separating enough that I could toss the hammer down and get my two hands around the door to pull it completely open. I should have been concerned about whether I was permanently destroying government property, but my curiosity had overridden my common sense.

Buried inside the building as it was, I couldn't see inside. I grabbed my phone from my pocket and switched on the flashlight function to illuminate what was behind the door.

I gasped. What lay before me was impossible.

⚯

My heart beat rapidly. This was just crazy. It was the interior of an old print shop, frozen in time.

I took a tentative step into the room. Moving the flashlight around, I noticed a light switch on the wall. I flipped the switch, but of course, nothing happened.

I scanned the room with my phone's flashlight again. Printing equipment sure was enormous back in the day, taller than a human being and as wide as a small car.

I stepped further into the room. It smelled of neglect and disuse. Cobwebs thick with dust swung from ceiling corners and within machine crevices. There was a faint odor of oil or grease that hung in the air, too. That was surprising, given how long the room had likely been sealed up.

When *had* it been closed off?

I lifted my free arm. My smart watch glowed as it showed me the time. I had been in the Morgue for over an hour. Someone was going to notice my absence soon.

I approached a piece of equipment that seemed the most complicated, with large, exposed wheels and gears supporting a long, covered bed.

How spoiled I was with today's operationally simple printers.

On the bed was a browned sheet of paper lying face down.

Feeling a wee bit sacrilegious for even touching it, I pulled it from the surface. It required some gentle tugging since, like the bookshelves, it was aged in place and reluctant to be removed.

However, the sheet gave way far more easily than the door had.

I held it up and shined my phone's flashlight on the brittle piece of paper.

It was like holding a monumental piece of history in my hand. The paper was a D-Day announcement to Pax River employees.

A MIGHTY ENDEAVOR HAS BEEN WON!

June 7, 1944

Attention Sailors, WAVES, and other workers aboard Patuxent River Naval Air Station!

As many of you may know, yesterday saw the tremendous victory of our troops during their invasion of Normandy. It took time for accurate reports to be released, as the news media outlets were suspicious of it being a German trick.

But the Allied forces have been triumphant, and you may rest assured that the tide has turned against the Axis of Evil.

The country's efforts, including the endless invasion preparations conducted locally, have resulted in one of the most important victories in the course of human history.

Transcriptions of the president's prayer in his address to the nation last night have been printed and are available in the administration building.

The flyer also contained grainy photographs of President Roosevelt and an aerial view of a P–38 Mustang in flight.

The endless invasion preparations conducted locally. What did that mean?

I gently laid the promo piece back on the printer and continued looking around the room. Except for the flyer, I could see no other printed materials in the room. It was as if the room had been cleaned up and then shut off from the world.

I left the print shop and pushed the old door shut again. Eventually, I would let the facilities people know what I had discovered, but to do so now would likely result in caution tape over everything and a banning of everyone from the Morgue.

"Not until I'm done with my History Hall," I murmured.

The door no longer fit as seamlessly as it had before. I was struggling as I continued trying to close it when I noticed an object that had partially dislodged itself within the wall next to the door's opening and was now preventing it from completely closing.

I gently tugged on it and within moments I was holding an old tattered, thick black volume with a broken brass lock on it and the word "*DIARY*" embossed in faded gilt lettering across it.

Inside the cover was written, "*Property of Frances Parker.*" I quickly thumbed the pages, which were printed with faded blue lines. The script written on those lines was tiny, cramped, and difficult to read.

As I continued riffling through the pages, various dates from the 1940s flashed before my eyes. I realized that I had just stumbled upon a very precious artifact.

I replaced the shelves and shelf contents, then searched around until I found an old, wheeled chair, its leather cracked but the stuffing only poking out minimally. Good enough. I rolled it next to the table containing my ephemera collection and plopped down to determine who Frances Parker was and if she might have something interesting to say.

PART 2:
FRANCES PARKER

Patuxent River, Maryland
August 1943

CHAPTER 5

THE BUS SQUEALED to a halt in a cloud of belching smoke in front of a sign propped up haphazardly against a guard shack that read, **WELCOME TO PATUXENT RIVER NAVAL AIR STATION**. Another, smaller, sign indicated that they were entering on Cedar Point Road.

Frances Parker jostled with the other thirty women to debark the bus. Once they were all on the ground in the blazing sunshine, a photographer with a giant camera asked them to all group together around the sign so he could take a picture.

She stood as tall and proud as she could among the others, all of them dressed exactly alike in their new uniforms. They had just completed several weeks of basic training at Hunter College in the Bronx, New York. There had been so many women at the training center that Frances didn't know anyone currently aboard the bus being sent down to Patuxent River Naval Air Station, one of many stations that were now employing women for emergency war service.

Her training had been both terrorizing and inadequate. Her daily routine included waking up every day at 5:30 a.m., followed by breakfast at 6:30 a.m., then classes and drills all day with breaks for lunch and dinner, then bedtime at 10:00 p.m. Once per week they were reviewed in formation.

Frances now knew how to identify every class of ship and aircraft from every military, Allied or Axis, in addition to having absorbed many of the Navy's copious and tangled rules and regulations.

She had also learned how to function well on very little sleep. But it was over now and all worth it because she had finally arrived for her first assignment. It was truly the start of her adult life.

"Complete your uniforms, ladies," the photographer said as he gazed through his lens.

Despite the heat, the women all readily reached into their pocketbooks—the only variation in their looks other than the styling of their ebony, glossy Oxford pumps—to withdraw black gloves.

Their uniforms consisted of a pale gray jacket with black buttons and pockets at the breast and waist, with a matching skirt that fell below the knee, a rounded collar white blouse, and a black kerchief.

What made Frances feel the proudest she had ever felt in her twenty-one years, however, was her hat. It was white with a black brim and felt so…official.

She was among the latest batch of the U.S. Navy's Women Accepted for Emergency Volunteer Service, or WAVES. They were part of a new naval women's reserve force, created to take on shore duties while regular sailors were off fighting in Europe and Japan.

Frances had been the first girl in Louisa County, Virginia, to venture away from home to join the WAVES. Most were still collecting scrap metal to be recycled into planes and tanks, or growing victory gardens with their parents, or selling war bonds. Daddy had been proud to the point of weeping, believing that his girl would go on to be a pilot or admiral one day.

Her mother had also wept, but at the thought of Frances being so far from home for an undefined amount of time, particularly with her brother already gone and currently serving in the U.S. Army somewhere overseas.

Mama had wept a lot over the past year or so, especially when she opened or shut their front curtains and saw the white flag with a red border and a single blue star in the middle of it, which had hung in their window since her brother had shipped out in 1942. Most families had a blue star flag in their windows, indicating by the number of stars how many men had left the household to join the war effort.

When that flag was replaced by one with a gold star, your neighbors knew that you had lost someone.

The photographer held up his hand for the girls to hold their poses. Frances resisted the great urge to shield her eyes with her gloved hand, so strong was the sun's beam. She hoped she wouldn't appear to be crying in the developed photo.

They re-boarded the bus, waved in unison

to the guard through the open windows, and were driven onto the air station, which, to Frances's surprise, wasn't much more than a dusty, deafening construction zone. Machinery seemed to be moving earth everywhere. It was good to have a window seat to observe all the work. Hundreds of men moved like ants as far as the eye could see as the bus drove down Cedar Point Road amid mounds of red earth and excavators and men in coveralls plying spades.

"Such language!" exclaimed Sophie Russell from the aisle seat next to her. Sophie had picked the seat next to Frances when they had boarded in New York five hours ago and had been a bubbly seatmate ever since. "Do they talk like that to their girlfriends and mothers?" She tossed her blonde curls. "Such disrespect to the troops. I wonder what they will have for us for dinner? I'm starved!"

Sophie was already proving that she could have multiple thoughts at one time. However, she seemed fun so maybe Frances would have to learn to keep up. After all, they had both been assigned to the same work location so they would be spending time together.

The new WAVES were not all as young as Frances. In fact, some seemed to be at least twice her age. That was comforting. Perhaps there would be someone to look up to during her time here.

She unsnapped her pocketbook and drew out her orders once more to review them.

...you have been assigned to the TYPING POOL in the ADMINISTRATION BUILDING for a pay rate of $30 MONTHLY, plus a uniform allowance of $8 MONTHLY. You will also have the benefits of the finest medical and dental care, special tax exemptions, low-cost Government life insurance, free mail, and reduced rates on transportation, theater tickets, etc.

The bus will depart Hunter College on Sunday, August 1, 1943, following chapel services, and will take you to your new quarters in the WAVES barracks aboard Patuxent River Naval Air Station. Please confine belongings to a single suitcase.

As BREAKFAST and DINNER, in addition to LODGINGS, will be provided to you, no quarters allowance and no further supplemental income will be forthcoming.

You are employed by the U.S. Navy for the duration of the war plus six months.

Frances had typed a few times before but was by no means proficient. She had also attempted the shorthand method promoted by Mr. Gregg a half century ago and was even less expert in that. But she had somehow passed the Navy's typing test, so if the Navy wanted her in the typing pool, she would do her best for the cause and hope she could improve her skills before she irritated anyone.

Doing a good job was the least she could do for her brother, Freddy. He was two years older than she, but they had always been close. In fact,

Francis was the only person he would allow to call him Freddy. With everyone else, he insisted on the more formal, "Frederick."

The bus once more screeched and belched smoke as it came to a stop in front of an unmarked, long, two-story, dormitory-style gunmetal-gray building that seemed to have been dropped out of the sky as it sat completely finished amid other construction.

"Hey, driver," Sophie sang out. "No welcoming committee? Not even a sign on the building?"

The driver, who fit so snugly behind the wheel it seemed as though he had been molded into place, lumbered up and faced the women. "No sign. Men working on base don't need it advertised that there are a bunch of pretty women living together in one place."

"As if they wouldn't notice with their own eyes," someone said from behind Frances.

The passengers all laughed.

With their luggage disgorged from the storage under the bus by the driver, each woman picked up her own case and walked in a single file line to the barracks.

CHAPTER 6

INSIDE, ENORMOUS FANS were set everywhere to keep air flowing and cool, but they could barely keep up with their work. However, the fans were a luxury compared to basic training conditions.

Except for a small reception area near the front door, where a matronly woman sat behind a desk and checked in the new WAVES, the cavernous room in which she stood was full of tiny compartments against the two long walls, curtained to provide a modicum of privacy. A few of them had their dark blue end curtains pulled, revealing an iron bedstead, a drab green blanket with a striped pillow on it, a metal chair, and a small chest of drawers that served as both nightstand and clothing storage. An adjustable mirror sat on the dresser, and there was a high window inset into the wall overlooking each compartment, keeping the barracks well lit.

At each end of the hall were forbidding double doors, tightly shut.

However, the building smelled new, a combination of the white paint on the walls and fresh wax on the linoleum floors. Those strong odors were being blown around by the noisy fans. Best of all, no bunk beds. Combined with the luxury of a curtained-off space, it was as though Frances had entered a palace.

The room was nearly empty except for the bus group. Presumably, most of the other WAVES were out on personal errands since it was a Sunday and a day off from work.

Sophie elbowed her. "Grand quarters, ain't it?" she said over the whirring of the multiple fans. "I'm surprised we have metal chairs and beds. I'd a thought they would have gone in for the war effort."

Frances frowned. "I guess this *is* part of the war effort."

Sophie considered this and laughed. "Right you are, Francie."

"SHHHH." The matron working at the desk offered Sophie a stern glance. "We maintain decorum in our work for the Navy, ladies."

Sophie should have been cowed, but clearly wasn't, offering Frances a wink and broad smile.

Francie. No one had ever called Frances that before. Did it make her sound more sophisticated?

Frances finally reached the matron's desk. The woman, whose desk plate read, "Lt. Delores Wallace," glanced at Frances's proffered orders then flipped through a large ledger in front of her.

"Bed twelve, along the opposite wall. You will eat dinner at eighteen hundred in the cafeteria at the end of the hall." The lieutenant pointed at the set of double doors to her right. "Showers and toilets are at the other end of the hall. You may call home twice a week on the dorm phone. A doctor comes in once a month to address any ailments you may have. Report to the administration building at oh-eight-hundred sharp tomorrow morning to learn your duties."

"How do I get to—'"

"Next!" Lt. Wallace said, looking beyond Frances. Her gaze fell on Sophie, offering Frances's new friend a withering glance. Sophie bowed her head respectfully, but she was smirking as she approached the WAVES matron.

Frances walked along the long row across the hall from where Sophie was now standing before Lt. Wallace. Each of the curtains had a small number printed on a card safety-pinned to it. "Nine. Ten. Eleven. Here we are," she said softly to herself.

Frances swept open the curtain. Her cubby looked like all the rest of them. A bed, green blanket, chair, small chest of drawers.

She heaved her suitcase up and laid it on the chair. Might as well start making herself at home. She began unpacking what few clothes she had brought with her. There wasn't much to buy these days, what with rationing on nearly everything, so her bag was sparsely packed.

Frances had just put away the last of her cotton underthings and was setting out a framed picture of Freddy next to her Westclox chime alarm clock on her chest of drawers when she was startled by a "Hiya!" at the open curtain.

She turned around quickly. Before her was a stunning woman, maybe five years older than she was, with glossy black tresses held back in a snood. She wore lipstick the color of a McIntosh apple and had matching long nails.

Hitler was reputed to despise red lipstick on women, so any woman who could afford it had lipstick in patriotic shades, such as Fighting Red, Montezuma Red, and Victory Red. Matching nails made a girl feel like she was being extra rebellious against the German dictator.

Realizing that Frances was admiring her nails, she brushed the talons of her right hand along her left arm. "I'm Lillian Harrington, I'm in number eleven. Who are you?"

"I'm Frances Parker. Are you in the typing pool, too?"

"No, I'm a telephone operator and message courier, but I think we'll be working in the same building. I came in yesterday, but they told me I needed to wait for today's new arrivals and then I'll start work with you tomorrow. I can show you the ropes. At least, what I've learned so far. I'm sure Lieutenant Wallace offered you as much direction as an angry wasp would."

Frances nodded, pleased by Lillian's offer of friendship.

"That your beau?" Lillian asked, lifting her chin toward the frame.

"Oh, no, that's my big brother, Freddy. He's in service in Europe, I think."

Lillian nodded knowingly. "We all have someone somewhere. My fiancée was captured by the Japanese last year in Bataan, just before he was scheduled to come home on leave for a month. We were going to get married while he was here. He was shot during a forced march to a prisoner-of-war camp." The woman paused and took a deep breath. "Frank and I both had dreams of being teachers. Anyway…"

Lillian's statement hung between them. So tragic, yet so many women had the same story. Frances had barely been old enough to start going out on serious dates when Pearl Harbor had been bombed at the end of 1941, and every eligible bachelor went racing to the recruiting station. Thus, she hadn't gotten as far as even a steady beau to have suffered a tragedy like Lillian's.

Frances shivered, silently praying that wherever Freddy was, he was safe.

Lillian seemed to recover quickly. "So, where are you from?"

"A tiny place in central Virginia. Truthfully, I've never been away from home before, but I wanted to help, and this opportunity came along."

Lillian smiled. Her teeth were as straight and white as Chiclets, Frances's favorite chewing gum. "As did I. I'm from the Eastern Shore of Maryland. Talbot County. My family has been there for generations although some of us break out on occasion. With Frank gone, I just needed something valuable to *do*. Something not involving weeping or dwelling on how he might have suffered. So, I signed up for the WAVES. Maybe one day when the war is over, I will find a teaching job." Lillian frowned and looked down at her nails, as if suddenly unhappy with them.

"I'm sure you'll be able to do that," Frances said. "It won't be long until–"

"Old Wally is going to be a tough ol' harridan, isn't she?" Sophie appeared at Frances's compartment. "Boy, I'm hungry. Hello, I'm Sophie, who are you?"

Sophie held out a hand to Lillian, who shook it. Frances made introductions.

Sophie continued talking before Lillian could say anything. "I'm across the way in number fifty-seven. You'd think they'd keep the typing pool girls together or something. I could use some freshening up, how about you, Francie?"

Lillian offered her brilliant smile once more. "I was just about to show Frances around. We can start with the women's toilets and showers."

Lillian led them to one end of the hall and through a set of double doors. Behind the doors was a bank of ten curtained compartments, each continuing a toilet, sink, and mirror. Anyone could see that that was never going to be enough for the slew of sleeping compartments out on the main floor.

There was also a row of curtained showers with large, forbidding shower heads protruding from the ceiling for each one. Along another wall, a long bench was positioned under a panel of five tall windows. The windows let in great light…and heat. Fans spun futilely in here as some of the newly arrived women entered and turned on shower knobs, creating steam on the walls. The air quickly became heavy with damp and mustiness, but nearly all the newcomers had expectant smiles on their faces. After all, they had been accepted into volunteer work to support victory in the war and had completed the very big hurdle of basic training.

"Welcome to service in the U.S. Navy, where you will find none of the comforts of home," Lillian said, sweeping an arm out in presentation.

It was fine with Frances. "It makes me think that I'm doing what Freddy is doing. As if we are somehow connected right now."

"Imagine the stories we will have for our friends back home after just a week here!" Sophie exclaimed.

Once Frances and Sophie each spent a moment in a toilet compartment, Lillian led them back across the barracks to the dining hall.

This was an even larger area obscured from the open sleeping quarters. Rows and rows of wood tables and metal chairs filled the center of the hall, and on the far wall was a cafeteria-style serving setup.

All was quiet here except for an area along another wall containing several shelves and tables full of goods. A woman in regular clothing—a simple belted dress and low-heeled pumps—was there, folding clothing items and rearranging other products.

"You'll need to get to know Maisie," Lillian said, leading them over the stand.

"Maisie, these are Frances and Sophie, just arrived on the bus. We will be working together. Take good care of us."

Maisie immediately struck Frances as a woman who had experienced a difficult life. Her skin was weathered and leathery, although she couldn't be more than forty. Yet, she seemed exceedingly cheerful.

"I take care of all the girls, Lil," said the woman named Maisie without stopping what she was doing for even a second. "Need somethin'?" she asked. "Girdles? Lipstick? I have the color that the Marine Corps Women's Reserve get in their makeup kits. Letter-writing paper? Hair pins? Whatever you need, I have it. Good prices, too. Cash on the nail, though, I don't wait until payday."

"Maisie has been authorized by the Navy to set up a sundry store for us. I hear that for the most part, she doesn't cheat us."

Maisie grinned broadly, exposing several gaps in her teeth. "C'mon now, I'd never cheat the girls. At least not the ones I like." She winked with exaggeration.

Lillian shook her head, but it was clear to Frances that her new friend already had affection for Maisie.

"Dinner should be in a couple of hours," Lillian said, "so we have the luxury of some time to ourselves. We should take advantage of it, because I imagine we won't get much once we start working."

Sophie grabbed Frances's hand. "Isn't it wonderful that we have our own separate compartments? It's like heaven. Do come and see mine."

With a wave to Lillian, who disappeared into her own compartment, Frances followed Sophie, who dramatically pulled open her curtain. It required moments to take it all in.

Sophie had already decorated her space in a style that could only be described as Hollywood Rampage. She had movie magazines strewn on her chair and bed, with titles such as *Modern Screen*, *Screenland*, *Silver Screen*, and *Photoplay*. Certain pages had been torn from the magazines and were in frames crowded on her dresser. Among them were posed pictures of Nelson Eddy, Robert Taylor, and Victor Fleming, all handsome leading men.

Taped to her mirror was a photo of Clark Gable with his wife, Carole Lombard. Lombard had died in a plane crash last year on a flight home to California after attending a war bond rally in her home state of Indiana. Everyone knew Gable had been utterly devastated by his wife's death.

Sophie's pillow had a magazine still of Errol Flynn lying across it.

"Isn't this just dreamy?" Sophie asked, clearly proud of what she had done.

"You carried all of these magazines with you in your suitcase?" Frances instantly regretted her insensitive comment.

Sophie didn't seem to care. "I did. There was nowhere to put them out during training, what with us only getting bunk beds and foot lockers. Now I can look at them whenever I want."

"Very pretty," Frances said, unsure what else to say.

"Hey, would you like a copy to read in your compartment? Who do you like? Bogart? Olivier? What a dreamboat he is. Oh, how about Tyrone Power? Doesn't he have eyes that could melt you into a puddle? He's in the Marine Corps now, you know." Sophie began shuffling through magazines, eventually pulling out a dog-eared copy of *Movieland* and handing it to Frances.

"Boy, I'm just so hungry I could eat my mattress. Aren't you hungry, Francie? Maybe I should just take a nap between now and dinner to pass the time."

Frances took the magazine. "Why don't you come down to my compartment at six o'clock and we can go to the dining hall together?"

With that agreed on, Frances dropped the magazine off in her compartment, tossing it onto her dresser, changed into more comfortable shoes, then checked out with Lt. Wallace before going for a walk.

It was still August-hot outside, and the misery of the heat was compounded by the construction dust everywhere and the clanging and roaring of equipment and men. There were no finished walkways or side streets other than Cedar Point Road. Well, if this was the only road on station, surely it wouldn't take long to find the administration building.

She headed further down Cedar Point Road, staying out of the road as much as she could while also avoiding rubble and building materials.

As she came around a curve, Frances came upon what must have been the administration building. It resembled the WAVES barracks in that it was two stories and long. But this was no metal building. This was gleaming white with gorgeous blue awnings over every window.

The parking lot was freshly paved, and both trees and grass had been planted around the area. It was an oasis of serenity in the middle of construction chaos.

She moved closer. Several large, sleek Chrysler Town and Country wagons with exotic wood side panels and American flags attached to their antennas—both vehicle luxuries—were parked in the front of the building.

Frances had seen these at Hunter College on important inspection days. They belonged to important Navy personnel, most likely admirals.

Was she, Frances Parker, going to be working directly with admirals?

Her heart both swelled with pride and raced erratically.

She returned to the WAVES barracks, as lighthearted as she had been the day she received notification that she had been accepted into the naval workforce.

She joined Lillian and a freshened-up Sophie for dinner, which consisted of meatloaf, boiled potatoes, and peas, followed by a slab of yellow cake with white icing.

Frances felt guilty about the meatloaf, knowing that her brother was likely eating Spam for most of his meals.

There was to be a showing of last year's *The Talk of the Town* in the dining hall following dinner. Sophie chattered on about the careers of both Cary Grant—such a dream!—and Jean Arthur—such unconventional looks!—and how exciting it was to see the film, but Frances was exhausted by the day's events. She made her apologies, visited the women's bathroom—which was crowded with other women preparing for either bed or the movie—for a shower, and settled into her compartment.

After changing into her long cotton nightgown, which would soon need some repair along the hem, Frances kissed the picture of her brother and set her chime alarm clock. Her mother had given it to her—with tears, of course—saying that it would ensure Frances was punctual and thus she would make a good impression on the Navy. She hadn't needed it before now, since during basic training she was always awakened with a bugle trumpeting.

Instead of a loud buzzer for an alarm, the clock made a gentle *ding-ding-ding* sound. It also didn't *tick* across each second. It had been a wonderful gift. Frances set it for six o'clock the next morning and slipped beneath the sheet and rough blanket, too exhausted to worry about whether she was comfortable. She quickly fell into dreams.

Frances never had the opportunity to wake to the sweet alarm. Instead, she was woken in terror by a deafening clanging.

CHAPTER 7

SOMEONE WAS BEATING on a large piece of metal with what sounded like a hammer. The blowing fans seemed to be absorbing the noise and spitting it back out into the room twice as loud. Frances hadn't realized that her life on the air station might be just as intense as it was during training.

But within seconds, that basic training permeated her brain, and she jumped right out of bed, throwing off her nightgown and grabbing underclothes from a drawer and her uniform from where it was draped over her chair. Within two minutes, she had dressed, raked a brush through her hair, and was standing outside of her compartment.

All the other WAVES were outside of their compartments, too. Next to her, Lillian looked as glamorous as she had yesterday evening, as if she hadn't even been in bed. Her lipstick was perfectly applied, and she didn't have a single hair out of place. It must be the black, netted snood that kept her hair tamed and untousled.

Did Maisie sell snoods?

Lt. Wallace was in the center of the room, holding a large aluminum kettle and, indeed, a hammer. "Some of you need to be more presentable when you make your morning appearance," she said.

The lieutenant herself was as put together as Lillian, if only a little more severely so.

"You will have the opportunity to visit the bathroom, then you will have a nutritious breakfast, then you will be taken to your respective workplaces." Lt. Wallace carried herself like a drill instructor, marching back and forth and occasionally tapping the kettle, as though to remind them all to pay attention. "Those of you who are new will be boarding the bus to your work locations for the first time today. Once you are there, you will follow the instructions given to you politely and without fail. The bus will pick you up again this afternoon at five o'clock sharp to bring you back here, and then your time is your own until tomorrow morning. Understood?"

"Yes, ma'am," Frances said in unison with everyone else.

Everyone else except one. Sophie was across the room, dressed but yawning. That earned Lt. Wallace's withering ire. "Yeoman Russell, have we interrupted your morning ablutions? Is what I'm saying of no interest to you?" The matron approached Sophie and blocked Frances's view of her new friend.

"No, Lieutenant. I just didn't get to sleep until–"

"I wasn't asking you to make an excuse. I am attempting to shame you into being punctual and professional looking. You did, after all, just complete basic training, and readiness was part of that training, was it not?"

"Yes, ma'am," Sophie said, straightening up but sounding unrepentant.

"I am utterly shocked that you passed basic training. All I can imagine is that you must have passed written tests with flying colors."

How *had* Sophie passed basic training?

"Yes, ma'am—I mean, no ma'am, I mean—"

Lt. Wallace's upbraiding had finally discomfited Sophie.

"That's enough. Be more prepared tomorrow morning."

"Yes, ma'am," Sophie said with a salute. She'd found her footing again.

Lt. Wallace resumed her pacing. "I cannot emphasize to you girls enough that your quarters are luxurious compared to those of the station's construction workers. You have privacy curtains and furniture for your belongings. You also have food provided to you. All this on top of your wages. Moreover, you are being given unheard-of employment opportunities, and your work will be significant in the war effort. For these considerations, you owe the Navy your gratitude and respect."

Frances remained still and gazing forward as she considered how true everything Lt. Wallace said was. Not that Frances had seen the workers' quarters, but it wasn't hard to imagine that they were less than comfortable.

The lieutenant walked away to chastise another WAVE for her skirt being askew. Sophie glanced across at Frances at winked.

Frances shook her head at her new friend. Sophie was going to get into real trouble one day, she just knew it.

The women were given time to use the bathroom with Lt. Wallace beating against the pan as they marched there, and then got a hammering against the pan to guide them to the dining room for breakfast.

Ah, the pan beatings had different rhythms, much like how reveille and taps did during basic training. This wasn't going to be difficult to learn.

As Frances marched with the others to the dining hall, she heard the faint *ding-ding-ding* of her chime alarm.

CHAPTER 8

THREE BUSES AWAITED the WAVES outside after breakfast. The new girls were each directed to specific buses and climbed aboard. On Frances's bus, yesterday's driver was wedged into the seat again.

Surprisingly, he drove past the administration building and on to another facility further down Cedar Point Road. It was a large structure with a curved, barrel-shaped roof.

"Oh, that must be the airplane hangar!" one of the other girls said. "This is my stop for learning how to perform cockpit training for pilots." She and several other girls disembarked the bus.

Near this structure was the framework for three other large buildings. Compared to the completed hanger, they looked like wood skeletons next to a voluptuous body. Dancing around the skeleton buildings were various shacks, presumably where supplies were stored and construction managers kept their offices.

A short drive further put them in front of a newly constructed tall, square edifice with a long runway in front of it. "That must be the air traffic control tower!" another WAVE exclaimed. "I'm going to be directing air traffic on and off the station."

The driver must have heard her, for he said, "They just started flights on and off the base, so you'll catch up nice and quick. Sounds like you're in a war zone yourself when they go overhead, flying so low you can just about read their tail fin numbers and them sounding like a thousand storm clouds crashing at once."

The atmosphere in the bus vibrated with excitement despite more passengers leaving.

Had Frances made a mistake in accepting a typing job? Should she have pushed for a position more thrilling and technically challenging?

The bus made a couple more stops, then turned around and made its stop at the administration building. Only Frances, Lillian, and Sophie were left on the bus.

There was only one fancy automobile parked in front of the building today. The other important men must be on business in Washington. Or maybe they had flown to some other naval air station for a secret meeting.

Sophie elbowed her, interrupting Frances's vivid imaginings of where the air station's brass might be at the moment.

"Can you believe we are finally here? This is going to be a snap-your-car sort of a day, for sure."

The three women stepped off the bus. "Remember, be back here to board at five o'clock sharp," the driver said before cranking the handle to shut the door and moving off, leaving them in a cloud of exhaust.

"Well, isn't he a stinkeroo," Sophie said, tossing her head.

Frances heard a low rumble that grew into a steady thunder. Into view came two Corsair aircraft, flying over them. She held up a hand of greeting to them, as did Sophie and Lillian, until they had passed out of sight.

Frances headed into an open door at the end of the building where the driver had dropped them, excited to start the day. The lobby was notably cool with no sound of fan blades whirring. How was that possible? What was this magical place?

"Why, I think I feel a chill," Lillian said.

"It's like an October day in a pumpkin patch in here," Sophie observed, also looking around in wonder.

The lobby was square-shaped, with a tall reception desk opposite the door. The entire room was paneled in new, oak paneling. The carpet even smelled fresh. Two large, gold-framed, oil portraits dominated the wall behind the reception desk, one of President Roosevelt and the other of Secretary of the Navy Frank Knox.

There was a hallway to the right behind the receptionist desk that was so long it reminded Frances of a runway. It, too, had beautiful new carpet and gorgeous woodgrain paneling on the walls and name plates on doors. There appeared to be more portraits and photographs lining the wall. They were presumably of naval leadership and heroes of yore.

Frances's heart swelled once again. *No one back home would believe where I am right now. I'm part of something tremendously important.*

The receptionist, wearing a WAVES uniform

with a navy and gold scarf tied jauntily at her neck, greeted them warmly and asked that they wait. She pressed a wide button at the bottom of a microphone in its stand. "Sir, the new yeomen are here."

Appearing shortly was a man in a crisp khaki uniform. He didn't seem to be much older than Frances but carried himself with ease and confidence.

"Welcome to Patuxent River Naval Air Station," he said. "I'm Ensign Maynard Porter. Which of you is Yeoman Lawson?"

Lillian stood straighter and saluted. "I'm Yeoman Lawson, sir."

"You'll be downstairs in the switchboard room. Yeomans Parker and Russell, you'll be in the Communications Department, near the commanding officer's suite upstairs."

A tremor shot through Frances. *Working close to the most important man on station.*

Another woman in a WAVES uniform came out and led Lillian down the endless hallway.

Ensign Porter escorted Frances and Sophie to a door—cleverly paneled and set within the lobby's walls so that it wasn't noticeable—and up a set of rough, wooden stairs that lay beyond. The stairwell bore no resemblance to the beautiful lobby, including the fact that it was much warmer here.

Make a good impression. Mama's words echoed in her head. Frances had no idea if she was being impertinent but gripped the stair rail and asked a question anyway as they made their way upstairs.

"Sir, if I may ask, I noticed that the interior here is very cool. Refreshing, really. How can that be?"

"We have air conditioners in many of the windows here. We have our own print shop in here, and the paper must not suffer too much heat or humidity. The Navy deemed it an imperative to control the air temperature and moisture in the administration building. I trust that it does not bother you?"

Frances had definitely chosen the right job. What unbelievable luxury. Air conditioners, which were big metal squares bolted into the windows presumably costing upwards of $10,000. Only the richest Americans could afford such a thing. And, apparently, the Navy.

"Oh, no, sir! It's quite nice. I–" Was she already making a bad impression?

The ensign stopped on the landing between the first and second floors. He turned to Frances, grinning.

"You're joking with me," she said in relief.

"Yeoman, we are doing dead serious work here, but sometimes we have to laugh to ease the load. Here we are."

Ensign Porter pushed open a door that led to a replica hallway over the one into which Lillian had disappeared.

"To the end of the hallway," he said, pointing.

Frances walked resolutely, determined to keep in step with the man, glad of the calisthenics she had performed every morning for the past eight weeks. Sophie breathed heavily behind her but didn't fall back and had actually stopped chattering for a few moments.

The doors along both sides of the hall—which was as richly paneled as the downstairs hall—were emblazoned with name plates, too. Lieutenants, lieutenant commanders, commanders…it was a cornucopia of ranks working behind the doors.

"There's a small canteen on base but there tend to be roughnecks gathered there most days. You'll want to work out provisions for your meals," Ensign Porter advised. "Also, you may end up doing shift work. Shifts are mostly used for air traffic control and testing work, but it sometimes happens in administration. Depends on what the enemy is up to at any given time and what the demands are from Washington."

So much to think about and remember.

A woman pushing a mail cart came out from behind one of the doors and nearly collided with Frances. From behind the open door, it was apparent that people were busy like bees back there already this morning, buzzing back and forth from one desk to another.

"Oops, apologies," the woman said dispassionately and kept going to the next room.

They reached the end of the hallway, which terminated at a set of double doors. "We call this the Nursery," he said, pushing the door open, which had a large sign on it reading, **N.A.S. Patuxent River Communications**. "Because this is where ideas are born." He laughed at his own joke.

Frances was amazed by the condition of the room, which was cavernous with its high ceiling and tall, partially open windows. Metal air conditioning units were secured into the openings of the windows and held in place by brackets on the wall. Yards and yards of brightly colored cloth were stuffed into the windows surrounding each air conditioner.

It was remarkable. No ineffectual fans, just pure coolness, although the units were at least as noisy as fans.

Two lines of drab green desks ran down the center of the room. On each of several desks was a gleaming black Underwood typewriter, a Parker fountain pen, and a stack of carbon paper next to the typewriter. Other desks were heaped with papers, hastily folded maps, and half-filled coffee mugs.

The remainder of the hall—for it was so much more than just a room—was haphazardly set. A coffee mess was on the wall beneath the windows next to a mimeograph machine whose crank was being turned rhythmically by a uniformed young man no older than Frances herself.

A bank of clocks set to multiple international times hung on the wall across from the windows, and an oak wood radio blared a rerun of a comedic *Fibber McGee and Molly* episode from atop another table beneath the clocks. As near as Frances could tell, Fibber was learning the benefits of rationing but not without his usual exasperating exaggeration and verbal sparring.

Other available wall space was covered with maps, marked with pins and string, presumably denoting troop movements and enemy lines. Two men with coffee cups in their hands stood at one of those maps, gesturing emphatically at somewhere in the far east.

Whirring and clanking sounds rose above everything else but were coming from somewhere unidentifiable.

Beyond the young man at the mimeograph machine, which was spitting out pages full of purple text, were other people in uniforms conferring in groups with sheafs of papers and ledgers in their hands. Some stood around the messy desks talking earnestly to one another, but no one was seated at any of the typewriter desks.

Which of those will be mine?

CHAPTER 9

"FOLLOW ME, LADIES, to meet your new supervisor." Porter led them through the chaos to a door set to one side of the rear wall. The door had a very large plaque on it.

Lieutenant Commander Edward Mackey
Officer-in-Charge, NAS Patuxent River
Communications Department

Ensign Porter knocked and opened the door, ushering Frances and Sophie in. This was a lobby space that ran the entire width of the hall behind them but was perhaps twenty feet deep. The decor here was lusher than in the downstairs entry, with large potted plants on the floor and decorative lamps placed on a credenza flanked by two leather guest chairs.

Also, here was another WAVE at a desk positioned outside yet another door that presumably led to Lt. Cmdr. Mackey's inner sanctum. Her short hair was pulled up in a tight wave closely plastered to her head. She reminded Francis of a Kewpie doll, except the woman wasn't nearly as charming. She also didn't sport the patriotic red lipstick so many women did, instead showing off thin, compressed, bloodless lips.

She stood. "Good morning. I am Lieutenant Barbara Hall, Lieutenant Commander Mackey's assistant. Please wait here." She turned and went into the other interior room.

Frances continued to stand in place, not daring to sit down without being invited to do so. Soon, Sophie nudged her. "That Lieutenant Babbles looks like she'd skin you alive for giving her the cross-eye. Like Bette Davis in *Jezebel*. Wouldn't want to get on her bad side or else—"

"Shhh," Frances cautioned. Sophie was fun, but didn't know when to be quiet.

Sophie silenced herself for about two seconds. "Nice digs here. Maybe one day I'll be head of the Communications Department and sit back here."

"Sure, maybe." Frances was hardly listening as Sophie chattered on. Lt. Hall had been gone an awfully long time for just announcing that she and Sophie had arrived. Was anything wrong?

At that moment, the inner door burst open, and Frances jumped. Even Sophie squeaked next to her.

Out charged a bear of a man, so big and muscular he looked as though he could pick up an F-4 Wildcat fighter plane and throw it across a runway.

Yet, he also had beautiful cerulean pools for eyes and long, dark lashes framing them. Unfortunately, his intriguing eyes were overshadowed by the caterpillars he had for eyebrows and the dark hair sprouting wildly from his head and hands. Those hands were balled into angry fists.

What sort of man was this?

Lt. Hall was on his heels, her colorless lips curved up as she returned to his desk while the man, presumably Lt. Cmdr. Mackey, lumbered up to them.

Maintaining his fists, Frances's new supervisor folded his arms, standing so close that Frances could practically see up his nose, given how far over them he towered.

The supervisor frowned at them, the furrows in his brow deepening as he took in what Frances was sure was Sophie's saucy expression. Frances didn't dare move to look at her friend.

"I was told I was getting older, more experienced WAVES. You two look like you're barely out of high school. And you–" He looked directly at Frances and her heart revved violently like a propeller. "Your typing test was abysmal. I don't know how the chuckleheads at the Bronx facility thought you would be of help to my department."

Although momentarily cowed by this very intimidating man, Frances found her footing and calmed her hammering heart. She was, after all, a genuine member of the U.S. Navy. It was her duty to take orders, but not to be berated to death on her first day.

She even grew angry. She was here to help the cause for victory, to honor her brother's service, and to be of credit to the nation.

"Sir, my initial test may not have been of the best proficiency, but I assure you that in all other areas I was rated as excellent, and I am prepared to offer my all to—"

Mackey's expression was withering. "You're a child, and you think you know what hard work is after a few weeks at a women's day camp?" He laughed, which was a cross between a huff and a snort.

She prayed Sophie would also stay quiet, and, thankfully, Sophie was. For the moment, anyway.

Frances remained silent, knowing that she would not help her cause by arguing with this man. She was already reconsidering applying for an air traffic control job. Or maybe she could pack parachutes. Or perhaps even become a codebreaker. She'd heard about women training for that.

Of course, that would mean the brute in front of her would have conquered her. Squashed her like a June beetle before she'd even sat behind a desk for the first time.

But Mackey wasn't done.

"Can you even begin to understand how important the work we do here is? We maintain station morale with our newsletters, issue messages regarding Navy brass, and ensure that communications with every single entity outside of this base are addressed immediately without fail. No failures can be tolerated or Hitler wins the war!" Mackey held up a fist to emphasize his point.

"And if Hitler wins, I'll never see another promotion in my career. Do you intend to be responsible for that?" he roared.

Even brash Sophie was quailing under Mackey's onslaught.

But Frances was getting madder. It was an emotion that didn't come to her often. However, Mackey reminded her of her cousin, Dickie, who had a red-hot temper. Dickie would immediately shout "Weisenheimer" at anyone who dared challenge his perpetually changing rules over their childhood kick-the-can and Simon Says games they played during the muggy, hot summers in central Virginia.

Frances had once slapped Dickie across the face in the middle of one of his tirades about someone cheating when it was apparent that Dickie himself had been the cheater. Dickie still ranted during games after that, but neither accused Frances nor even looked in her direction ever again.

Lt. Commander Mackey was a Dickie. Except she couldn't slap him.

"Yes, Mr. Mackey," she began. "I—*we*—understand the importance of all work here on the air station. We've spent many weeks learning as much as possible about the Navy, and we are very anxious to use that knowledge and prove ourselves to you if you will just give us the chance." Frances hoped her measured tone would serve to ease his mind.

Mackey's features softened for a moment. Perhaps she had soothed the savage breast.

In fact, she hadn't. He screwed up his face in rage again. "This won't do," he was bellowing again. "This won't do at all. Get out." He pointed to the door.

Sophie started to scramble away but Frances put a hand on her shoulder to calm her and kept it there as they went through the doorway to make the endless walk through the staff, who had surely heard the tirade even over the cacophony of noise.

No, Mr. Mackey wasn't a Dickie. Mackey held an authority she couldn't challenge.

Her last glimpse of Lt. Hall suggested that the other WAVE was quite pleased to see the backs of Frances Parker and Sophie Russell.

As they made their way out of the hall, Frances felt like a condemned prisoner on her way to the gallows, with the townspeople having gathered around for a glimpse of her demise. She kept her hand on Sophie's shoulder, staying a step behind and guiding the other girl who, for the first time in twenty-four hours, had been completely stunned into silence.

Several faces among the employees held sympathetic expressions, other people shook their heads. The sailor at the mimeograph machine had stopped his work and turned to witness their departure, offering them a quick salute.

Good heavens, this has happened before.

Frances had no idea what to make of that realization. In that moment, she noticed that on the wall to her right, which was largely covered in pinned maps, a hidden door concealed in the wall paneling opened and a man wearing earmuffs and a black-stained leather apron exited, shutting the door behind him as he made his way out of the hall.

However, Frances caught a glimpse of what lay behind the door, and she realized that was where the great noise emanated from. The room was full of what appeared to be printing equipment, being operated at a velocity that kept them shaking and banging as though they might come apart at any moment. A worker fed paper in, cranked handles, and removed the resulting printed pages at breakneck speed.

This was the print shop that required the air conditioning the ensign had mentioned. The secrecy of the print shop suggested to Frances that sensitive materials were being produced here. Or would be in the future.

PART 3: DIANE

Present Day

CHAPTER 10

I FELT AS IF I was coming out of a dream state as I tucked one of my business cards into the diary to mark my place and walked dazedly back to my office. It was as if I had become so immersed in Frances Parker's diary that I had actually experienced the events of her life that had gone down on paper.

Leila checked in on me at some point, offering to make a run for afternoon coffee but immediately frowning and pursing her lips at me. "Are you okay? You look like you're floating somewhere around Pluto."

Leave it to Leila to bluntly—but accurately—describe how I felt. Thinking quickly, I reassured her that I was fine by saying that I had been working in the Morgue and that maybe there was a little bit of mold in there affecting me.

"We need to let the facilities people know there's a problem in there," she said, her expression full of concern.

"I've already taken care of it." I hated lying to her, even if she was the impediment to handling the office mouse problem, but I wasn't ready for anyone else to find the print shop I had uncovered. It felt like a secret I needed to keep for now. Hopefully, I could prevent others from finding it. I'd have a difficult time explaining myself if the facilities people stumbled upon it.

I never returned to the Morgue that day as I got caught up in meetings and deadlines. Annoyed that I would have to resume the diary tomorrow, I placed it inside my top desk drawer, then immediately reopened the desk drawer.

"Can't have Mr. Mouse chew you into a nest," I said to the diary, glad no one was there to hear me talking to a book. I thought about how Frances' story affected me. Something like a good novel where you could visualize the setting, characters, and emotions, only it was more than that.

I dug out a manila envelope from my desk, tucked the diary in it, then went to the bookcase across the room from my desk. Reaching up on my tiptoes, I put it upright on the top shelf between two acrylic awards I had received for various public relations campaigns I had conducted for the base.

I left the office with barely enough time to shower and get ready for my date.

Gus picked me up at my house that evening. He nodded his head toward Tobias in acknowledgement of the cat's presence on top of the kitchen cabinets and was rewarded for his effort by Tobias's particularly effective growl and hiss combination that the goofy feline reserved for nearly everyone.

Except for Mary. Tobias seemed to have a soft spot for her and could curl up in her lap for hours.

Gus drove us in his gray sedan to the movie

theatre. Gray was his color. His car was gray, his home's carpet was gray, the drapes were gray, the furniture was gray. Even his blue eyes seemed to be taking on a tinge of gray over time and I teased him endlessly about it.

Now that I thought about it, he had a fish tank full of freshwater fish that were striped, speckled, and solid, all in black and gray. Not a splash of color on any of them.

That's what was comforting about Gus. He was reliable in all things. You always knew what you were getting, and he was kind to a fault.

I loved *Casablanca*, despite the overwrought dialogue. No wonder they called that period the "Golden Age" of movies.

"What did you think?" I asked my boyfriend as the lights went up.

"Yeah, it was good," he said, rising. Numerous popcorn kernels were stuck to his charcoal gray polo shirt.

"Is that it? What was your favorite part?"

Gus shrugged. "I don't know. Maybe when the Nazis shut down the bar for gambling while at the same time the one who shuts it down receives his gambling winnings."

That occurred in the movie right after a stirring part where the Nazis are singing in the bar and the other patrons drown them out with a stirring rendition of the French national anthem, "La Marseillaise."

But Gus was moved by a far less impactful moment of the movie immediately following that. I shook my head. "Okay."

Gus drove me home and walked me to the

door, kissing me as we stood in the glow of my front porch light. Like Gus overall, it was a reliable kiss. My toes had never curled over his attentions, but I always felt traitorous at those thoughts. He was so nice and kind, willing to do anything I asked. What did it matter if I didn't hear explosions overhead when he took my hand, or kissed me, or–

"Goodnight," I said. Yes, Gus was reliable, and that was important. After all, I could be stuck dating someone like Brad Maddox, Mary's boyfriend.

With the door shut and the sound of Gus's engine fading into the distance, I realized that I had never even mentioned my interesting experience to him. I had just been exhausted from the day's events, was all. I would make sure to do it next time we got together.

I was still too tense from the day to settle into pajamas and go to bed. I watched an episode of a silly reality television program I had been following, then flipped open my laptop to see what wonders the Internet could show me.

I searched on the Pinkerton Agency, which I had only had a vague notion about, but which had been mentioned in one of the old newsletters as having been replaced by the Marines here at Pax River. To my surprise, I found that they still existed, although, like many organizations, they had experienced some unsavory press— predominantly surrounding their involvement in late 19th-century strikebreaking. Reestablishing themselves as a personal security and risk management firm in the 20th century, they were now part of a Swedish corporate entity.

However, although still involved in security for defense contractors, it appeared that they were no longer involved in presidential or military base security.

The information, while interesting, wasn't particularly revealing. I should have brought home the WAVES recruitment brochure to read in more depth.

I yawned and stretched, the computer session having finally relaxed me to the point where I could go to sleep.

My last thought as I hit the pillow was that I couldn't wait to jump back into the diary again.

CHAPTER 11

BY FIVE O'CLOCK in the morning, I had given up on sleep after a terrible night, waking up every hour on the hour. The diary wouldn't let go of my psyche. I rose and got ready for work, ensuring I poured a thermos of fresh, hot coffee to keep me going for the day.

Tobias sat on the counter with his orange-striped head tilted to one side as if judging me while I got the Thermos prepped. "Look, you," I said, giving him a scratch behind the ear, "you've got a full dish of food. Don't worry about my caffeine intake."

He rose and presented me with his rear end before jumping off the counter, undoubtedly on a mission to find a good napping spot.

I was once again in the office before anyone else. I was already starting to like the peace and quiet that came with being the first one in on the second floor.

After the usual task of e-mail scanning and sorting, I settled in to finalize the base newsletter by implementing Lt. Cmdr. Barry's changes and adding in my "Back When" feature. I used the photo of the women—presumably WAVES—standing in front of the bus.

With my *Back When* feature done, I sent the

newsletter to Natalie for final layout. She would then process it through the contractor print shop off base to have copies run. Employees generally got the newsletter via e-mail, but I insisted on a small print run each time, both to have a physical archive of them and because those in the upper ranks liked to have copies in their waiting rooms for guests to read.

There was no longer a real print shop on base. Everything was contracted out to local printers by a weird dictate of the Defense Logistics Agency, whose purpose in military printing escaped me.

This meant that if leadership discovered that hidden print shop in the Morgue, it would likely be demolished faster than you could say, "Have a great Navy day."

I checked my watch. Ten minutes until the weekly staff meeting. I grabbed my notepad to doodle on for the meeting, dropped my cell phone into my jacket pocket, and headed down to the conference room, which was down the hall from me in the opposite direction of the Morgue.

The meeting was run by Pax River's commanding officer, and it was a chance for him to hear from all of us about the status of projects we were working on. To my surprise, Lt. Cmdr. Barry spent extensive time talking about my History Hall project and praising me for the work I was doing on it.

I admit I was flattered by the recognition.

I was also surprised to see someone new in the meeting, whom the CO introduced as Benjamin

Tennyson, our new operations officer. I'd had no idea the position, which had been open for months, had finally been filled.

After the meeting, I approached Tennyson and invited him to come to my office for a chat. He was warm and friendly, and I estimated him to be around my age. He invited me to call him by his nickname, "Ben-Ten."

"I transferred up from Webster Field," he told me, referring to an "outpost" of Pax River about ten miles south. I knew from research that Webster Field had been constructed as an auxiliary landing field for Pax River while the naval air station was being built. Today, employees there work on cutting-edge defense technologies.

"Let's do a piece on you for the next newsletter, Ben-Ten," I suggested. "Have the base employees get to know you."

He frowned. "I don't think I'm that interesting."

"Everyone is interesting," I assured him. "People want to know their co-workers at a personal level, not just what their career accomplishments or certifications or professional awards are. We can talk about your hobbies, community involvement, the fact that you, say, breed ferrets or have climbed Mt. Everest, or have sailed on twenty-seven cruises to the Bahamas or—"

He laughed and held up his hands as if to ward me off. "Okay, okay, got it. Probably the most interesting thing about me is that we are standing on property that my family used to own."

I was intrigued. "What do you mean?"

"My family used to be farmers here in what was once called Jarboesville until the Navy took it over."

I stilled. My interview with Tennyson was about to take a turn. "Really? You heard in the meeting that I'm working on a History Hall for the building, starting with the base's construction during World War II. Maybe you have information that would help me. Or perhaps photos?"

He nodded. "Yeah, I'm sure I can dig something up for you. Mind if we talk about this off base and off Navy time? Maybe just over coffee somewhere?"

I was puzzled over the request, as work on the History Hall couldn't be construed as "personal" work but agreed to plan a coffee date soon to give him time to collect some photographs for me.

As for me, I was excited to have additional material for the hall and attacked the rest of the morning with enthusiastic ferocity.

As part of my "attack," I met with Natalie in my office and together we worked on the overall physical layout of the History Hall—where we had to worry about door openings, how far down on the wall we would allow text, where we would leave spacing to attach ephemera to the wall, that sort of thing.

Before I knew it, Leila was popping her nose into my office. "A bunch of us are going to Solomons for lunch to welcome Ben Tennyson to the team. Wanna come?"

I checked my watch. Noon already? As PAO,

I should have enthusiastically agreed to a social event like that, but the thought that most people would be out of the office for a while made me want to visit the Morgue while I had relative privacy. "Thanks, no. I have a lot to catch up on and will be meeting with Ben at a later date for the newsletter, anyway."

Natalie signaled that she wanted to attend the lunch, so as Leila gave me a thumbs-up and moved on to the next office down the hall, Natalie took her leave. I heard Leila offering the invitation to someone else, and soon people were drifting up the hallway toward the stairway.

Fortunately, Leila seemed to have forgotten about my claim on mold in the Morgue and was no longer questioning me on it.

Once I was confident that the new-employee lunch crowd was gone, I retrieved the diary and made my way to the Morgue. For some superstitious reason, I was hesitant, not sure whether to go straight to Frances's book or to further explore the walls of the Morgue. I finally opted to explore the cavernous room more before continuing my read of the diary.

I walked to the rear of the Morgue, the location of Lt. Cmdr. Mackey's office in Frances's diary. If the print shop still existed behind a wall, maybe his office did, as well.

I exerted effort in moving aside the mass of tables, boxes, old lamps, equipment, framed pictures, and chairs that were in the way. I was sweating profusely by the time I was done. I explored the entire rear wall, which was covered in the same ugly old brown paneling as the other walls. I pressed in at various points, hoping for a spongy feel that would indicate an opening.

Nothing.

I was confused. The diary had seemed clear regarding the print shop along one wall and Lt. Cmdr. Mackey's office back here, but only the print shop still existed?

There was nothing to do but to put everything back. I did everything in reverse, this time trying to at least bring a little order and neatness to the situation. I was pleased with how the rear wall looked by the time I was done.

In fact, I was so inordinately pleased with how it looked that I decided to attack a portion of the wall to the right, opposite the bookcases, to clean it up a bit.

That's when I found something that made me gasp.

It was an old typewriter, exactly the kind Frances had received her first day on the job. Of course, no doubt Frances had received one that was shiny and new and this one was old and covered in dust. It was a heavy beast, but I hefted it up and carried it to my ephemera table, setting it down with a loud thud next to the "incident" box.

The machine looked as if someone had been typing on it one minute, then shoved it off to the side the next. There was even a ribbon still inside the machine. I didn't touch it, fearful it would disintegrate if I did. I knelt to eye level to look at the ribbon. I could see where the keys had struck the black ribbon and made imprints.

> *By the order of CAPT. Aaron P. Stricker III, Comm—*

From there, the ribbon disappeared into a spool.

If I were able to dislodge the ribbon and unwind it, I could see more. But I knew that was likely a futile task. I brushed my fingers against the keys. Had a WAVE sat before it for countless hours, typing out memoranda and announcements regarding the war? Had this belonged to Frances herself?

The typewriter had obviously not been used since the war. Likely, some newer model had come out and replaced this one, so this unit had been tossed into a corner. The Navy was famous for warehousing old stuff until it became functional and desirable again, as it was much easier to simply keep an item than to go through the paperwork to formally dispose of it.

The military was the original "retro" pioneer.

Stepping away from the typewriter, I peered once more into the ephemera box, removing all the items and placing each one in its own spot on the table. I scanned the front-page newspaper article again, but this time I laid the paper on the table when I was done and opened it, scanning the pages and advertisements inside. I had my doubts that the paper's scant few pages would give me any real information.

I was wrong.

Although the advertisements for a 1942 Oldsmobile B-44—*with Hydra-Matic Drive!*—and for a victory garden cookbook which was apparently free with the purchase of a can of Lysol, were interesting, it was what lay between pages four and five that was the pot of gold.

Staring up at me invitingly was an envelope, nearly as yellowed as the newspaper, "*Received June 18, 1944, after the incident*" scrawled across the front.

I picked it up, turned it over, and gently slid a nail under the flap. The glue had long ago lost its adhesive properties, and the flap lifted right up. I removed the single, brittle sheet of paper, the writing on it in straight rows atop the faded blue lines running horizontally across the page.

The pencil lettering was small and cramped like in Frances's diary, but perfectly legible and covered both sides of the sheet.

June 1, 1944

My dearest sister,
Thanks for your last letter. I am doing fine, just preparing with an endless line of men for an imminent mission.

Everyone's spirits are good. The brass tell us that the Germans are close to being smashed, at which time the war will nearly be over. There is nothing we want more. Although, for me, I'd also be happy to never eat another can of spam ever again. I miss Mom's home cooking.

We recently had a large contingent of jack tars and lobster backs visit from Britain, wanting to observe our training methods.

The British troops are friendly enough, but I believe you would laugh to see how shocked they are by the Americans. They have a strict hierarchy, I guess because of their history of kings and queens. They are formal to a fault and punishments for infractions are swift and severe.

To them, we are appallingly relaxed, although we don't see ourselves that way at all. We were all finishing up a group meal in the barracks the other night. Someone had lost his lighter and said to Sgt. Bemis, "Hey, Sarge, got a light?"

Of course, the sergeant offered up his lighter, offering the flame not only to the private asking for it but to some others sitting around him who produced cigarettes from their pockets.

I thought the Brits would lose their minds. "How can he talk to his superior in such a crass manner?" they wanted to know. "Why isn't he punished for insubordination?"

I wish you could have been there; you would have had a belly laugh.

I'm so proud of your work. Don't let the other jealous girls back home cause you to waver in your duty and devotion to our country. Your efforts will ensure we boys get home sooner.

The letter closed with, *"Sorry I'm such a lousy letter writer, but I still remain your devoted brother, Freddy."*

Freddy. That was the name of Frances Parker's brother.

Of course, Freddy wasn't an uncommon name and could have referred to anyone of the time. I should concentrate on what was important, which was that the letter provided a fascinating insight into relations among Allied troops.

I folded the letter up reverently and placed it back in the envelope.

Had it been the last letter Freddy had ever written? Or, had he returned home and led a long life?

I was torn. What a treasured memento from the war. It would be a significant piece for the history wall. Yet was I intruding on a real person's most private moments?

I was sure most people in the 1940s had an expectation that their correspondence was private, unlike today's world where anything digitally written could be plastered across the Internet in seconds.

Although both parties would be long gone by now, would it be disrespectful of me to include this letter on the History Hall as a peek into the station's history? What would Freddy say about it if he stood before me right now?

I tucked the envelope back inside the pages of the newspaper. I'd think about it later.

I sat down in the creaky old chair I'd obtained for myself, placed the diary in my lap, and opened it to the page where my business card held my place.

PART 4:
FRANCES

November 1943

CHAPTER 12

ON A MONDAY morning, Frances looked up from where she was typing an all-hands announcement to the base. Ensign Porter was escorting a new girl—who appeared to be in total awe—into the Nursery.

Frances hadn't noticed the girl at roll call this morning, but there was always so much else to focus on that it wasn't surprising.

Frances turned and glanced over her shoulder at Sophie, who raised her eyebrows.

The new girl reminded Frances of her own horrifying first day, before she had learned that Lt. Cmdr. Mackey put every new employee through "the Mackey Terror," as it was commonly known, then had the individual called back the following day. Mackey apparently thought it instilled a healthy dose of fear in his employees that helped him maintain order.

Since that day, Mackey had been reasonably polite to her and Sophie, although Lt. Hall had remained cool and distant. It was perfectly fine with Frances, for she had been so busy mastering her typing skills that she hadn't had time to consider whether she was popular in the office.

Although Mackey was ostensibly the office head, he mostly hobnobbed and curried favor with those above him and issued broad orders. It was really Lt. Hall who ran things day to day, particularly where the typing pool was concerned.

Frances had studied her typing manual assiduously, disciplining herself to always start with her fingers on the middle—or "home" row of keys, and memorizing where all the keys were without having to look at them.

She was now timing herself at around forty-five words per minute. It was nothing like Sophie's blazing speed—the woman's hands passed over the keys in a blur—but Frances was making good progress. She prided herself on making few errors.

Ironically, Lt. Hall found little fault in her, but Sophie—a whiz at the typewriter—was perpetually drawing Hall's ire. Initially intimidated by their new office circumstances, Sophie had quickly recovered to her old self. Lt. Hall was not impressed, as evidenced by the disdainful glances she shot at Sophie when passing down the aisle past their desks.

"You're too pert," Frances would tell her friend, who would toss her hair and insist that that old Harridan Hall wasn't going to cow her. But Lt. Hall was working hard at doing so, and Frances worried that Sophie might eventually be dismissed for real. Not only because Sophie was bold and flirtatious, but because she kept her desk drawer full of movie star magazines and not only read them repeatedly while eating her lunchtime sandwich, but chattered about how actor Jimmy Stewart—so dutiful to the country!—had been promoted to captain over the summer, and how divine the pictures of Rita Hayworth's recent wedding to Orson Welles were, and even how successful Bob Hope's latest USO appearance had been.

There were now five girls in the typing pool, all of whom had survived the Mackey Terror. Frances hoped the new girl, a mousy little thing who wore glasses and a beige button-up sweater that was at least two sizes too big over her uniform, was already a competent typist... and had no obsession over Hollywood.

As Ensign Porter led the girl past her desk, Frances impulsively reached out and grabbed her hand. "It will be fine, I promise," was all she could get out since the girl wasn't permitted to stop. The poor young woman's expression went from awe to apprehension as she continued toward Mackey's office.

"Let's invite her to go with us to the dance," Sophie whispered. A dance was planned for Friday evening at the new officers' club on station. All the girls at the barracks were excited about the opportunity, not only to meet some of the sailors and Marines on base, but to forget about the raging war—which seemed to have been going on for decades—for a few hours.

Frances nodded and returned to what she was typing.

ALL HANDS ANNOUNCEMENT: JARBOESVILLE TO BE RENAMED

From: CAPT. Aaron P. Stricker III, Commanding Officer, November 8, 1943

To all Patuxent River Naval Air Station Personnel:

Henceforth, the town of Jarboesville, located immediately outside the air station's main gate, will be known as Lexington Park.

The town is being renamed in honor of USS Lexington, the aircraft carrier tragically lost in May of last year during the Battle of Coral Sea and struck from service the following month. This naming pays tribute to the 715 Allied souls lost in the battle.

Another carrier currently being built at Fore River Shipyard will be renamed from Cabot to Lexington, as per direction by Secretary of the Navy Frank Knox.

Additionally, under construction in Lexington Park are 150 dual-family housing units to address what the Navy acknowledges is a severe housing shortage. Current plans are to name the streets after battles in the Pacific where the Allies have been victorious, including Coral, Shangri-La, Salamaua, and Tulagi.

The proximity of the housing to the base should be particularly pleasing to employees, given current gas rationing.

It is anticipated that the housing will be completed by this time next year. Further guidance will be issued by the Federal Housing Authority with regard to eligibility and applications for these units.

When she was finished typing up the instructions that had been hand-written by the base's second-in-command, known as the executive officer, or "XO," she rolled up the long cylinder to release the onion skin sheet from the typewriter, read through the document and, finding no errors, she rose from her desk to take it to Lt. Hall.

Nothing left the office without Mackey's review, although Frances suspected it was his assistant doing the actual reviewing.

As she was about to walk to Mackey's office, the door to his suite opened, and out came the new girl, her face blotchy and her lips trembling. Frances glanced at Sophie, who shook her head in disgust.

Frances tried to murmur something comforting to the girl as she walked past, but the girl brushed her off, clearly intent on making it out the door before bursting into tears.

Frances resolved to find the girl as soon as she got back to the barracks this evening.

She walked down to the place that the girl had just left and knocked softly on the door before entering. "I'm finished with this assignment, Lieutenant Hall."

Mackey's assistant took the proffered sheet of paper without looking at it, placing it in a wooden tray marked "IN" on a white label glued to it. "I understand a lot of girls are planning to go to the dance this Friday," the senior WAVE said without preamble.

"Yes, ma'am, we're looking forward to a night out." Frances wondered if the woman disapproved of the dance and might do something to prevent them from going, like insisting they needed to work late.

Lt. Hall's lips compressed even tighter than usual. "You should be careful. There will be inebriated young men carousing there. You don't want to be a young woman in trouble and bring dishonor to the Navy."

Frances blushed at the implication. "No, ma'am, I don't. I'll be careful. We will all be careful."

The WAVE harrumphed. "I'm sure you'll be alright, Yeoman Parker. As for Yeoman Russell, one can only wonder what trouble she might encounter."

"Yes, ma'am." Arguing with a superior could bring up charges of insubordination and be fatal to one's career. Sophie did seem to have a penchant for ruffling feathers.

Lt. Hall looked at Frances thoughtfully for a moment and then, to Frances's great surprise, took a red pen from her top desk drawer, then lifted the typed correspondence out of her in-box and began reviewing it.

With a few minimal marks, Lt. Hall handed the sheet back to Frances. "I'm sure you can retype this before the end of the day. If your work continues to be this high quality for the remainder of the week, I'll authorize you to leave a couple of hours early on Friday to get ready for the dance. Who knows, Yeoman, maybe you'll meet someone. Wouldn't that be a humdinger?"

Why was Lt. Hall suddenly being friendly?

CHAPTER 13

BACK AT THE barracks that evening, Frances suggested to Sophie that they immediately seek out the new girl. To Frances's surprise, Lillian was already with her in the dining hall. The girl's face was still blotchy, and Lillian appeared to be comforting her.

"This is Dorothy Morgan," Lillian said as Frances and Sophie sat down. "She's from Johnston County, Oklahoma, and she went to the naval training center in Stillwater."

"Oh!" Sophie said. "Gene Autry, the singing cowboy, grew up in Oklahoma, did you know that?"

"Yes," Dorothy replied. "He graduated from my high school—years before me, of course—and he still returns to town to visit family. I've seen him at a local diner there on occasion."

Frances sensed Sophie falling into a near-swoon next to her. Not wanting to spend the evening discussing the movements of movie stars, Frances immediately changed the subject.

"I have an idea what Lieutenant Commander Mackey put you through today. Please be assured that he does that to everyone who comes through the Nursery doors, and you will be called back to work tomorrow."

"Really?" Dorothy's face cleared instantly. With a smile on her face, she was quite pretty, with dark hair set in waves around her face and long lashes framing emerald eyes behind her wire-rimmed glasses. The boys at the dance were going to fall hard for her. Hopefully, there would be so many of them that it wouldn't matter so much if Dorothy had the attention of several of them.

"Really. Sophie and I were called back the next day. He may be a barking dog, but he doesn't have rabies."

"But keep an eye out for Lieutenant Babbles. She'll chomp your hand off and *she's* who you really work for," Sophie said, biting out in the air for emphasis.

At that, Dorothy laughed. "Thank you for making me feel better. And my friends call me Dottie." She grew pensive again. "The war has been so…difficult. I was hoping that joining the WAVES would help me forget the bad and cause me to feel like I have purpose."

Lillian put an arm around the other girl's shoulders. "Dottie's brother was killed at Midway last year."

Now Frances understood how the two women came to be in close conversation.

"Well, there's a dance this Friday at the new officers' club. You should join us," Frances said.

"I don't know. I'm so new here. Maybe I should just stay in my compartment and write letters home to my–"

"Nonsense and stuffing," Sophie exclaimed. "Writing letters is for Sundays after chapel.

Friday nights are for dancing and meeting men. Speaking of dancing, I need my strength for that and I'm starving. Let's get some chow."

All four women got in line for dinner. Tonight's offering was pot roast—which looked suspiciously like sliced Spam covered with gravy—mashed potatoes, and green beans, with slices of apple pie and coffee for dessert.

Sophie devoured her food in an instant and launched into chatter, gossiping about another employee she'd met in the building lobby, complaining about Lt. Hall's latest insult, and wondering if the handsome sailor she had seen walking outside the office would be at the dance on Friday.

Frances responded to most of what Sophie was saying with an occasional, "Really," until her friend mentioned an opportunity she wanted to pursue.

"I learned today that the station needs photographers. For filming aircraft takeoffs and landings, as well as happenings on station." Sophie took a sip of coffee. "I'm going to apply for one of the positions."

That startled Frances. "You don't enjoy working together in the typing pool?" she asked, putting down her forkful of potatoes.

"Oh, you're great fun, Francie, but photography is a new world. I'll be able to work on my own and not be confined to a building. I might even get to drive a staff car and—" she lowered her voice dramatically, "—have a 'C' gas ration card. Stick with me and we might be able to escape this place for new adventures off-station."

Frances was impressed. Since early 1942, gas had been rationed in the country, since so much of it was needed to fuel airplanes, tanks, ships, and jeeps. Average citizens were granted "A" level rations, or roughly 240 miles per month in gas. If you even had a car, of course. Rubber was also rationed for the war effort, and it was nearly impossible to replace tires on a car if they wore out, even if you were among the privileged who could have higher gas rations.

"B" rations provided for a supplemental amount of gasoline, up to 470 miles per month, provided the driver carried three or more passengers at a time. The coveted "C" rations were for single drivers up to 470 miles per month, whose work was considered "essential." The government, of course, decided who was essential or not.

"Are you worried that you don't know anything about photography?" Frances asked.

"You didn't know anything about typing. But you learned, didn't you?" Sophie raised a perfectly manicured eyebrow at her. Sophie was far more willing to join the daily jostle for mirror space in the bathroom than Frances was, and it showed.

It was going to look like cheetahs fighting over a pack of gazelles in there Friday afternoon.

Maisie would be doing great business this week. Frances glanced over to where her stall was. There were already girls crowding around Maisie this evening.

Frances self-consciously raised a hand to her own brow. How long had it been since she'd plucked? A sweep of an eyebrow pencil couldn't hurt. And surely she could afford a new red lipstick.

Sophie followed her gaze. "Let's visit ol' Maisekins later."

Frances nodded.

"How did you hear about the job?" Dottie asked Sophie, returning their attention to the table.

"Babbles told me. Pretty nice of her, given how crusty she's been up until now. But she said that my interests clearly aligned with what was needed in a photographer and that I might go on to be famous. Like a female Carl Mydans or something."

Mydans was already famous for his gripping pictures of war-torn Europe and Asia, and their suffering citizens. Sophie was much more likely to want to photograph Frances Langford on a USO tour.

But this explained why Lt. Hall had been kind to Frances today. She knew she was getting rid of Frances's friend and wanted to ensure Frances didn't follow Sophie.

"Taking pictures on the flight line will be hot and dirty work, maybe even dangerous," Lillian suggested. "Are you ready for that?"

"Of course I am!" Sophie retorted with a pout. "I've been through the same training that you have, you know."

Frances wasn't sure herself about Sophie as a photographer, but Lillian's concern seemed outlandish. "It's not like she's picking up a rifle, Lillian, or working in a bomb plant."

"And I have an eye for pictures, too." Sophie

placed her white coffee cup in its saucer and pushed it away from her. "Particularly if they will contain handsome flyboys." She winked at Dottie.

Frances couldn't criticize Sophie for wanting to try something new. After all, they were already being offered tremendous opportunities within the military. Why not try for more?

"I'll look forward to seeing your pictures, Sophie. But you know you'll have to make room in your compartment to hang any you take of pilots."

Sophie considered this. "Perhaps I should buy a scrapbook with my next paycheck. Then I can hold all my boys' photos together in one place." She put a hand over her heart and looked upward, striking a movie star pose.

Sophie will get us all in trouble one day, echoed in Frances's head.

CHAPTER 14

THE LOUDSPEAKER POSITIONED in a ceiling corner screeched, then Lt. Wallace's voice boomed over them. "Please finish your meals in the next fifteen minutes. We will be presenting a half-hour film on proper social etiquette in anticipation of Friday night's dance."

Loudspeakers were positioned both inside and outside of the barracks to ensure that it was impossible for a WAVE to claim she hadn't heard an announcement.

Sophie rolled her eyes. "What do they think we're going to do? Follow the boys back to their barracks?"

"I think that's exactly what they think," Lillian said, taking a last forkful of apple pie and placing the fork neatly across the center of the dish.

"Following the etiquette film, we will be doing a showing of 1941's *Sergeant York*—"

"Ooh, Gary Cooper and Joan Leslie," Sophie breathed.

"—Do not stay up too late and risk waking up overtired and yawning in the morning." With that final admonishment, the intercom screeched off.

Frances took the last bite of her apple pie. The canned apples were nothing like those she picked out of the Winesap trees on her family's homestead, but they filled the belly.

Maybe they should start a victory garden behind the women's barracks as a way to supplement their daily food rations. Frances would talk to Lt. Wallace about it in the morning after roll call.

"How are things in the telephone office?" Frances asked Lillian.

To her surprise, Lillian became very serious. "It's well. It's much harder than it looks. When I receive calls from certain...locations...I have to be very prompt in finding the receiving party. It's not always easy. And I think the phone calls are..." Her voice drifted off.

"Are what, Lil?" Sophie said. "You're not arranging calls between a man stepping out on his girl and his latest fling, are you?"

"Don't be a stupid little girl," Lillian snapped and immediately became contrite. "I'm sorry. I shouldn't have said that. No, the calls aren't between paramours. They are between men of...power. I can't say any more."

Sophie clearly took no offense, for she was chattering with Dottie in seconds.

Lillian, however, was pensive from that point forward, even though the etiquette film was so badly acted and condescending that most of the WAVES laughed uproariously at it. When the movie started, she said her goodbyes and went back to her compartment.

Frances was nodding out about halfway through the movie, so she left Sophie and Dottie, who were so enthralled by Cooper plodding through a torrential rainstorm on his horse that they hardly acknowledged Frances's departure.

She perked back up on the walk to her compartment and, knowing that the bathroom would be in low use this late and with a movie playing in the dining hall, she took the opportunity for a long shower and some much-needed personal grooming.

An hour later, feeling much improved, she returned to her compartment and changed into her nightgown, a yellow, ratty thing that she had patched a few times. It still served its purpose. After all, it wasn't as though there was a husband on the horizon to see her in it.

She kissed her brother's photo and tumbled into bed, but sleep eluded her. What did Lillian know that troubled her so much?

⁓

By Thursday, the recent cool snap had receded, so Frances, Sophie, Dottie, and the other girls in the typing pool decided to walk back to the WAVE barracks from the administration building when the workday was done. They were joined by Lillian as they stepped outside.

Taking advantage of the pleasant weather, the construction crews were all working even harder. None of them even looked over at a gaggle of women walking down the street.

The construction sites were like beehives of activity, with men moving back and forth in seemingly random ways, yet the progress was undeniable. Surrounding each actual construction location were various temporary huts and sheds, presumably containing material storage and offices.

Frances wondered if those small buildings got moved from site to site.

At one of the sites, a group of men was busy spreading out wet concrete over a large area. There were clearly three more adjacent areas ready to receive the wet, gloppy mix. The men moved in almost dance-like movements as they quickly slid their trowels across the concrete, smoothing the surface into perfection. One man stood off to the side, barking orders to the men holding the trowels.

"I wonder how well they are paid," Frances mused aloud, thinking that it must be exhausting work to push concrete around.

Lillian snorted. "Paid? Those men may or may not be getting paid. The foreman is, though. He's a member of the Cullison family. I understand the Cullisons have quite a few concrete contracts here on station. Those workers who belong to the Cullisons are getting paid. The civilian service members probably aren't."

Frances stopped in her tracks, causing Sophie to bump into her.

"Wait. What? What do you mean some of them aren't getting paid?" Were the men volunteers?

Everyone else stopped, too, and they formed into a small circle on the side of the road.

"You know about conscientious objectors, don't you?" Lillian asked.

Frances nodded. "They don't believe in killing other people under any circumstances, that it is against God's law to do so. Quakers, in particular, are conscientious objectors." Freddy hadn't been happy when his best friend, Joel, had backed out of enlisting. They were going to enlist together, but when Joel's parents had discovered their son's plan, they lectured him day and night over the impropriety of it, so Joel had informed Freddy the day before they were to sign up together that he wasn't going to do so.

Frances's brother had been devastated by his friend's betrayal of sorts, but in his usual cheerful way, told Frances he would find a new buddy in the Army to help him ferret out the Krauts.

Sophie sniffed. "Yes, they're cowards, the lot of them. It's an excuse to avoid service, and it's shameful. To think of all our American boys over there risking their lives, and they just sit by the radio listening to casualty reports and drinking beer. Shameful," she repeated.

Lillian shrugged. "Some may be cowards, some may hold true convictions," she said placidly. Frances wondered how much older Lillian was than the rest of them. She carried herself so… regally.

"Nevertheless, for most of them, a refusal to carry a gun doesn't mean an avoidance of the draft. So many choose civilian service rather than jail time for not answering the call. The civilian jobs tend to be the worst of the worst, though. Smoke jumpers putting out forest fires, trail building, even serving as subjects for medical experiments. That sort of thing. I imagine there are plenty of conscientious objectors supporting the construction contractors here at the station."

Sophie wasn't convinced. "Well," she said as the group began walking together again toward the barracks, "they wouldn't have to do lowly jobs if they just did their duty to the country to begin with."

Her words hung in the air around them as they walked past a site with a small structure under construction. Perhaps it would eventually be something helpful to the WAVES, like a store or post office.

A tall, thin worker wearing denim overalls, a stained blue chambray shirt, a denim cap doused in sweat, and worn boots, looked up from where he was clearly performing site cleanup, tossing all manner of refuse into a large bin. He smiled at the sight of them. Frances felt like he had seen right through her, so penetrating was his gaze.

He dropped a chunk of mangled metal into the bin and crossed the road to them.

"Good afternoon. I thought WAVES were supposed to be hideous spinsters, but by the looks of you ladies, I see that I was completely mistaken. What an improvement you make to this place." He grinned, his cheeks dimpling. He appeared to be a little older than Frances and seemed completely at ease with himself and his charms.

Sophie, however, was unimpressed. "Are you with the construction company or are you in civilian service?" Her tone was unmistakably frosty.

But he didn't seem to catch that tone. "I'm in civilian service, doing my part to help the war effort. I'm Ira Reed, but they call me Reedy. What's your name, miss?"

Sophie tossed her hair, which seemed to be her signature movement. "I don't know you well enough to give you my name, sir. And I certainly don't give my name to cowardly weasels."

Her words hung in the air. Frances held her breath over her new friend's crassness.

For his part, Reedy stared at Sophie in disbelief. After endless moments, he flushed. "Nice to meet you, ladies." He turned and stalked off without another word.

Frances was mortified.

She went to bed that night, completely unsettled from the interaction with the worker and wondering what Joel, Freddy's friend, was doing right now.

CHAPTER 15

THE NEW OFFICER'S CLUB was full of freshly scrubbed men in dress uniforms and women clad as prettily as possible, given ongoing rationing and shortages of nearly everything.

The hall was awash in dark blue and gold paper streamers, which were draped from the ceiling and from every available surface. A punch bowl full of something candy apple red—and likely powerful and intoxicating—sat on a corner table with people standing in line to slosh ladles full of the drink into cut glass cups.

Tables and chairs were placed around the perimeter of the room. Completely opposite the punch bowl table was a makeshift stage on which sat a ten-member band of mostly older musicians. Among the instruments, Frances counted two trumpets, two trombones, a saxophone, a guitar, a piano, drums, and an instrument she didn't recognize. The band, which denoted itself with "The Andy Vaughn Orchestra" on a sign hanging from the ceiling behind it, was already in full flower as Frances and her friends arrived. Standing at the front of the group was the tenth band member, a balding man in a suit who directed the players and occasionally added commentary for the audience.

The current song ended, and the bandleader announced they were taking a short break and would return soon with some great dance songs. The band members all stood and disappeared through a curtain behind the stage.

Frances felt a shiver course through her. She hadn't danced since the end of high school. Would anyone ask her to dance? Would she even remember how?

Several couples had been doing the foxtrot in front of the stage. That was easy enough. But if they started to jitterbug—

"Hey, Francie," Sophie elbowed her and pointed across the room. "Look at that little group over there. I see some men who are greatly in need of me. And you."

"I don't know if I'm ready yet—"

"Nonsense and stuffing. We didn't spend two hours in that bathroom battleground to stand here like wallflowers. You need to put that new Montezuma Red lipstick and brown mascara to use and give a man some pouty lips and coy glances."

About a hundred women had attempted to pile into the bathroom three hours earlier, jostling for the showers, the toilets, and, most importantly, the sinks and mirrors. They had resembled bees buzzing their way into a cluster of succulent flowers in hopes of attaining the best pollen.

But they had all survived the bathroom episode,

thanks to Lt. Wallace eventually taking charge and making the girls all get ready in shifts. They were now ready to meet men and enjoy life for a few hours without thinking about Hitler's shenanigans and Japanese perfidy.

Frances now stood in the Officer's Club in a mint-colored tea-length dress and her hair done up in her best attempt at a full pompadour style.

Sophie had gushed that it was actress Greer Garson's favorite style.

Regardless, Frances hoped the full skirt would look fancy while dancing and would also hide the small tears she had sewn closed.

Sophie had done her best imitation of Carole Lombard, with her hair styled in gentle waves around her face and donning a chiffon gown topped with a long duster. Perhaps tonight, Sophie would find her Clark Gable.

Sophie grabbed Frances by the elbow and led her across the room, where a group consisting of three men in dress uniforms and another young woman stood. "Hiya. I'm Sophie, and this is Francie. We're WAVES working in the administration building. Who might you strapping fellows be?"

"I might be Kenny Campbell," said the tallest, most handsome man in the group. He held out a hand to Sophie, and she flashed him a bright, camera-bulb smile.

"And *who* are you, Mr. Campbell? Not a civilian worker, I presume?" Sophie asked as she shook his hand.

Kenny was not just tall, but a man confident in himself. He bowed in a courtly manner over Sophie's hand, and his cheeks dimpled charmingly as he rose, grinning at her.

"Of course not. I'm a sergeant in the U.S. Marine Corps, part of the security detachment here on station. Let me introduce you to my friends," Kenny said, dropping Sophie's hand slowly, as if reluctant to do so.

"This is First Lieutenant Walter Duke of the Army Air Corps and his sweetheart, Verja Graham," Kenny said, sweeping an arm toward the woman and the man standing next to her. Verja tucked her hand into Duke's elbow. "Lieutenant Duke is home on leave to marry his girl, and then he's shipping off to India."

Verja dislodged her arm from Duke's elbow as he slid that arm around her shoulders.

"She's been my best girl for eight years," Duke said, grinning broadly. "It's about time we made it official." The two must have been childhood sweethearts. Neither of them could have been more than twenty years old. Verja reminded Frances of a little painted China doll, petite and fragile with molded dark hair and eyes, as she curved into her fiancé's embrace.

"And this weak specimen is Master Sergeant Roger Douglas," Kenny said. "He's also part of the Marine security detachment. Our job is to keep you ladies safe from any invaders on station." Kenny's gaze was only for Sophie, though, and his cheeks dimpled again as Sophie fluttered her new Max Factor lashes at him.

Master Sgt. Douglas didn't appear to be a weak specimen at all to Frances. Although he was perhaps a few inches shorter than the very tall Sgt. Kenny Campbell, he was blond-haired, trim, and wore his uniform well. His expression behind his pale blue eyes was as serious as Kenny's was light. Was he perhaps dour?

The band members returned and took their seats, causing everyone to focus their attention on the stage. "Ladies and gentlemen, before we get started again, I'd like you to meet the members of the Andy Vaughn Orchestra. On trumpets, we have Frankie and Clarence."

The two men blasted out a few notes, and the audience clapped. "Frankie and Clarence are both veterans of the Great War and stepped up to take the place of our regular trumpeters, who are now fighting the Axis devils in the Pacific."

The audience clapped with enthusiasm.

"In fact, everyone here is a Great War veteran. On piano is Ralph–"

The piano player stood and briefly banged on the keys.

The band leader recognized all of the veterans on the stage in this way before announcing, "And now, it's time to get those feet moving. Ready to jitterbug? A one, a two, a one-two-three!"

The band struck up the telltale drumbeats of *Sing, Sing, Sing,* a fast tune made popular by Benny Goodman. It was ironically named, since Goodman's version was a big band tune with no words.

Without hesitation, Kenny grabbed Sophie's hand. "Let's cut a rug!" he exclaimed as he led her to the dance floor where they started furiously dancing together. Lt. Duke led Verja out behind Kenny and Sophie.

Master Sgt. Douglas gazed at Frances with intensity. It was unsettling. "Would you care to dance, Miss—?" He stood close and raised his voice to be heard over the horns and drums.

"Parker. But please call me Frances. Sophie calls me Francie, and I don't know why."

A hint of a smile appeared on his face, like the sun breaking through clouds. "I suspect Miss Sophie is a girl who does whatever she wants. Frances," he added. "And you should call me Roger."

Roger offered his elbow to Frances and led her toward the stage. She appreciated the courtly nature of his action. Surprisingly, Frances not only remembered how to dance, but lost herself in the pure joy of it. The band was loud enough that no serious thought could possibly penetrate her mind as she jumped, twirled, and shook with Roger, who was quite competent on the floor.

Perhaps not as good as Sgt. Campbell, who was practically twirling Sophie as if she were a baton. Sophie's long duster had been carelessly tossed across the back of a chair. So much for her Carole Lombard ensemble.

Frances herself was immensely happy in the moment with her dance partner.

The band concluded *Sing, Sing, Sing* and jumped right into another popular tune, Irving Berlin's *Alexander's Ragtime Band*. Roger quirked an eyebrow, and Frances nodded, so they launched straight into more furious dancing.

Damp and exhausted at the conclusion of a second fast-paced song, Frances held up a hand to indicate she had had enough, so Roger led her from the dance floor. She waved to Sophie, who was still dancing with abandon and hardly acknowledged her.

"Would you like some punch and perhaps to spend a few moments on the patio, away from the noise?" Roger asked, cupping his hand around his mouth and leaning toward her ear while pointing to a set of doors opposite the entry doors. "The punch line is a little long so I could be a while."

Frances nodded and went through the doors, which exited onto a concrete patio. Another project by the Cullison family, she assumed.

There were several other couples outside, some laughing and some nuzzling one another under the night sky.

The evening was clear and breezy. Near perfect, considering that it was November. Frances quickly cooled down from the frenetic dancing while she awaited Roger and the cup of punch. She glanced up into the sky, which was so littered with stars that she could hardly detect the black background of the universe. The moon was a sliver off to her right.

What is Freddy doing right now? Does he see the same stars or does the sky look different where he is?

Frances closed her eyes, willing her brother to know that she was thinking of him.

"Are you seeing Pegasus, too? Or perhaps Cassiopeia there in the Milky Way?" came a female voice from behind her.

Frances started and turned to see that Verja Graham had joined her on the patio. With her raven hair and tiny frame, it was difficult to see her, despite the tremendous starlight.

"Sorry, I didn't mean to frighten you. Walter is getting me some punch and suggested I wait for him here."

Frances smiled. "Master Sergeant Douglas is doing the same."

She was becoming more accustomed to the dark and could see that Verja nodded.

"I'm fortunate to live in St. Mary's County and to have known Walter for so long. It's not as easy for the WAVES who are coming to a strange place and building their lives, don't you think? Where are you from?"

Frances briefly outlined her background from Virginia and the fact that Freddy was stationed far away while she was at the naval air station working in the typing pool as her part for the war effort.

"I suppose that makes a second reason I am lucky. I do not have a male relative away in the war. But I do so worry about Walter. He is a pilot and a good one. But he is brave to the point that I worry about him being reckless." She sighed. "But I am not the only girl worried about someone. I know you worry about your brother, too."

This was getting too serious for Frances. This was a single evening to be carefree and joyful. "I wish you great happiness in your marriage," she said. "You must be very excited to become Mrs. Duke."

Verja sighed again. "Walter will only have a week here before he's shipped off. However, by getting married now, he can arrange for us to have married housing, and I will wait there for him. I hope it's not for long. I want to start a family as soon as possible."

"I guess you won't be able to have a proper honeymoon if he's shipping off so quickly."

"No." Vera's expression was wistful. "That will have to wait until he returns. May this dratted war end soon."

Frances considered this. "Perhaps you need a new friend. Especially once you'll be alone in married housing. I could be that friend. We could get together and have cups of what passes for coffee these days and talk about Walter and Freddy."

Verja perked up considerably at this suggestion. "Truly? I would really like that. I'm so glad I met you this evening, Frances."

Roger and Walter appeared together, carrying cups of punch. Wordlessly, Walter led Verja off to another area of the patio, leaving Frances alone with Roger.

"What do you do as part of the Marine security detachment, Roger?" she asked, taking a sip from her cup. "If you can tell me."

"A little more than just protecting women from invaders," he said. "We protect the entire base from trouble. We're surrounded by water, and it would be quite easy for our enemies to attempt a small craft landing at night. Not to mention that hooligans of all types attempt to come in through the gate. And, of course, I helped clean up the Pinkerton mess."

Frances frowned quizzically at him, the punch cup now resting in the palm of her left hand. "The Pinkerton mess? I haven't been assigned to the air station for long, so I'm afraid I don't know what you mean."

Roger downed the rest of his punch before speaking. Frances imagined it was too sweet for him and the other men, but, to his credit, he didn't make a face over it.

"The Pinkerton Detective Agency used to run security here on station. The FBI did some background checks on the guards, and it turned out that most of them were worse criminals than those they were supposedly protecting the base from. Once the Navy realized what was going on, it established an intelligence and security department on station, and I was brought on board to help once I was sent home from a Pacific tour. Would you like more punch?"

Frances shook her head no and he continued.

"I was part of the investigation that dug out that rat's nest. You can't imagine the amount of bribery, thievery, and intimidation against workers that was occurring when they were here. Once they were discharged of their duties, they, of course, didn't want to leave and put up quite the resistance. We Marines cleared them out in short order. I was happy to knock a few heads together."

"Oh," Frances breathed. "That must have been very dangerous work."

Roger shrugged. "I'm sure I will one day be

shipped back out to duty overseas. That's when it will get dangerous again."

Refusing to let her mind wander to Freddy, Frances quickly smiled. "And Kenny helped you run out the Pinkerton guards?"

"Yes. He and others from the security detachment. My main help, though, is Gunney."

"Gunney?" She wrinkled her nose out of habit but quickly stopped. Her mother would not have approved of such unladylike behavior.

"My German Shepherd. He does walking patrols with me. Several of us have them."

"How nice to have a companion like that. The most we have at the WAVES barracks is a pair of squirrels who sit outside and hope for scraps each day."

Frances also finished off her cup. Roger took it from her and held both of them in his hands. The band had stopped playing, but moments later picked up another tune, again providing background noise to their discussion.

"What about you? What do you do as a WAVE?" he asked.

"I'm in the communications department's typing pool in the administration building. It's not nearly as exciting as being part of security, but I like feeling as though I contribute to the effort. My mother was none too happy about my coming here, since my brother was already away in Europe. At least, that's where I think he is. I haven't had a letter from him in four months."

Roger gazed at her with concern. Was she wrinkling her nose again?

"He'll come back just fine, Frances. Meanwhile, you're doing your part to make sure of it."

Frances smiled, and it was genuine. The master sergeant did have a way of making her feel better.

He glanced at the ground. "Er…umm…" He seemed to be having difficulty finding words.

Finally, he looked directly at her. "Would you like to do this again?"

Frances wasn't sure what he meant. "Certainly, but I don't know when another dance will be scheduled, do you?"

"No, I mean, have punch together. No, what I really mean to say is–" Roger sighed and shook his head. "Perhaps a boat ride with a picnic on Sunday, two weeks from now? It's my next full day off."

Had she just been asked out on a date? Frances felt the heat creep up her cheeks and knew for certain she was flushed. "Yes, I think I'd like that."

They returned indoors and danced together for several more songs until the band finally quit for the evening. As they joined the crowd leaving the building, they caught up with Walter Duke, Verja, Kenny, and Sophie, as well as Lillian and Dottie.

They walked as a group toward the WAVES barracks, their path illuminated by several men standing outside directing them with flashlights.

Sgt. Campbell was bragging, this time about having caught someone prowling near the air station's secret gasoline storage.

Frances had no idea where gasoline reserves

were stored on station, but she did know that it was a scarce commodity and surely required the Marines to be on constant guard over someone attempting to locate it and siphon it out.

"Kenny," Roger interjected, his tone stern. "That's not talk for a social event with ladies present."

"What? Oh, sure. It's boring stuff, anyway. Hey, who's seen *The More the Merrier?* Two men and a woman sharing an apartment in Washington, with the older man playing cupid. I hear it's a humdinger."

"Oooh," Sophie squealed, taking Kenny's arm. "I hear that, too. And it features Jean Arthur and Joel McCrea. He's the dreamiest. Maybe the base will offer it for us, and we can have a big screening party."

Kenny grinned. "I bet I can arrange it," he said.

Frances leaned toward Roger and said softly, "He shouldn't be saying those things about gasoline storage. I don't understand much, but I know we should keep any knowledge to ourselves, even if we know we are surrounded by our fellow workers and friends."

"You're right about that." Roger kept his voice down, as well. "It's stupid and risky. He's going to create a problem one day. I worry that he will end up drummed out of the Marines—or much worse."

CHAPTER 16

"YOU'RE VERY HAPPY these days, aren't you?" Dottie asked, sitting back from her crouched position as she brushed her hands together to remove some of the soil staining them. She had her glasses secured to her face with a piece of string tied around each end of her eyeglass arms then tied at the back of her head. It was both funny and cute.

They each wore floppy hats and coveralls that Maisie had somehow procured and offered for a reasonable price. It was best not to question Maisie's methods.

Frances stopped humming *I Had the Craziest Dream*. It was a popular song recently published by British singer Vera Lynn and was so full hope and joy that it was hard to resist playing it over and over in her head. Then again, Frances was probably humming and singing regularly these days.

"I suppose I *am* happy. As happy as anyone can be until the war is over." Roger Douglas had invited her out for a boat ride and picnic that would occur next week, Lt. Wallace had not only approved a victory garden behind the barracks but had ordered winter vegetable seeds and supplies from a local hardware shop, and

Frances had recently timed her typing skills, pleased that she was up to sixty words per minute without errors.

She pulled at a stubborn weed. How remarkable was it that earth that had just been churned could already be overcome with crabgrass and other undesirable growth?

Frances had measured out a ten-foot by twenty-foot plot and marked it with string, then created a sketch of where they would plant kale, broccoli, and turnips. Come spring, she would re-draw the plot for summer vegetables and maybe even expand the bed.

Now they were turning the dirt and getting rid of weeds to prepare the ground for planting.

Sophie had spent around ten minutes in the garden before declaring that she would return to do her work during the harvesting of the crops. Sophie was too focused on Kenny Campbell to care about the garden, anyway.

Lillian had helped some, too, but her gaze was far away these days. She seemed unable to concentrate on much and spent many extra hours at work.

Other WAVES in the barracks had pitched in, too, but it was Dottie who seemed as devoted to getting the vegetable bed ready as Frances was.

Frances couldn't blame the others. Many of them had exhausting jobs on station. It was understandable that in the evenings they wanted to eat, smoke, gossip, primp, and walk off nervous energy.

Especially since the days were getting shorter. Not only was there little daylight left for gardening, but there was also little left for taking walks after work.

"May I tell you something?" Dottie asked, her voice low.

"Of course." Recognizing the seriousness in her friend's voice, Frances also sat up with her legs resting under her, wiping her arm across her brow. It might be getting cooler outside, but gardening was still hard work.

"Do you remember when…when we came back from the administration building and that civilian worker approached us?" Dottie was rubbing her hands together, but now it seemed to be a nervous gesture and not for the removal of dirt.

"I do. I'm afraid Sophie wasn't very kind to him."

"No." Dottie cast her gaze downward as if gathering her courage. "Umm, remember when Lieutenant Hall asked me to take a memo to Major Canavan at Hangar One?"

Frances nodded her head. The major was the first U.S. Marine aviator to fly a jet. It was difficult to imagine a plane with no propellors. It was also difficult to keep this new, modern aircraft a secret. Frances had typed a memorandum from Capt. Stricker that included hushed instructions regarding the covering of the nose of the aircraft while on the ground so that its lack of propellor could not be detected.

Dottie swallowed. "I met him—Mr. Reed— again while I rode the bicycle to the hangar."

Administration now had a bicycle stored under

a lean-to next to the building so that anyone could jump on and run errands around base.

Frances waited as Dottie dug some dirt out from under a fingernail.

The other girl looked up at Frances. "And, umm, I accepted a date with him."

Frances nodded, knowing that was likely where Dottie was going by bringing him up. Dottie seemed to take it as encouragement.

"He really is ever so nice. And much smarter than you'd think. He wanted to enter the service but his parents were terribly against it." Dottie was speaking rapidly now. "He was deemed One-A when his town's draft capsule was chosen about a week after his older brother was killed in action during Operation Torch."

Frances drew in a breath. Everyone knew about that campaign, which had enabled the British to secure victory in North Africa while giving the United States an opportunity to begin directly fighting Germany and Italy.

"Mr. Reed's mama nearly went out of her mind at the thought that she would lose her remaining boy. She went into hysterics and begged him to run and hide in Canada or somewhere, but he refused to be a coward. So, instead, he told the government he was a conscientious objector so that he would be able to serve while keeping his mother out of the asylum. That made him a One-D, normally assigned to students, instead of the demeaning Four-F."

Frances wondered how often that story might have played out across the country.

"He wishes he could don a uniform, but he wants to keep his mama happy. He says he meets people like Sophie all the time. Please, Frances, don't tell her—or anyone—about this." Tears welled up in Dottie's eyes.

Frances well understood Dottie's desire to keep this information from Sophie. "Your secret is safe with me, Dottie. But it won't be safe for long. Someone will see you two together and will blast it through the barracks like a howitzer. You'll have to decide how much Sophie's—and perhaps others—opinions mean to you."

Dottie nodded. "What is *your* opinion of Mr. Reed, Frances?"

Frances sighed. "I don't know whether Sophie is right, or Lillian is right, or what. All I know is that happiness is in short supply. I think I might have found some and I want you to have some, too. If one day you find yourself humming the *Trolley Song* from *Meet Me in St. Louis,* then I think you'll be doing something right."

Dottie smiled, sat back on her legs, and uncharacteristically belted out lyrics.

Clang, clang, clang, went the trolley
Ding, ding, ding, went the bell
Zing, zing, zing, went my heartstrings
For the moment I saw him I fell

With that, she giggled and returned to the dirt with gusto. Frances was inordinately pleased to see Dottie happy.

They worked until the evening dinner bell rang. Lt. Wallace announced over the intercom that tonight would feature a short "Private Snafu" cartoon called *Spies*, followed by a showing of *Here Comes Mr. Jordan*, starring Robert Montgomery.

Sophie's whoop of delight could be heard outside.

CHAPTER 17

IT WAS NICE to have dinner without the fans humming and blowing like airplane propellors, forcing the WAVES to shout at one another across the long dining tables.

After a long day at work, followed by working in the new garden and then cleaning up, Frances was ready to settle down with Sophie and the others in a movie after dinner. Tonight's offering was canned ham with a sticky glaze, likely made from molasses since sugar was in short supply. The meal was rounded off with round, boiled potatoes and carrots that had the same sticky glaze on them.

Tonight's dessert was miniature fruit cake bars. Sophie picked hers up and rapped it against the table. "I call order in the court!" she exclaimed, eliciting laughter all around.

But Maisie was selling slices of a moist, golden cake with chocolate frosting. Most of the women lined up to pay for a slice of it, and the fruit cakes ended up in piles on the tables.

"Well worth it," Frances murmured as she put her fork in her mouth.

Lillian sat to Frances's left this evening, while Dottie and Sophie sat across from them. For once, Lillian seemed relaxed, her expression serene. She even laughed at Sophie's joke.

"Everything well in the telephone office?" Frances asked her in a low voice.

"It's better," Lillian said. "But I've learned something truly wonderful. Did you know the Navy is planning to build an elementary school?" She picked through her potatoes, eventually spearing one of them, swirling it in the glaze over the ham, and popping it in her mouth. Lillian tended to be the slowpoke at the table, which was ironic given how brisk and professional she was in everything else.

Frances didn't know that, although with the overwhelming influx of workers and their families into the area, it was of no surprise. "Where?"

"Outside the entry gate. Not sure yet when construction will begin. But it will serve all the military personnel's children in the area."

"And that...is interesting to you?" Frances licked the final bit of chocolate frosting from her fork. It was a wonderful treat.

"It is. Don't get me wrong, I'm happy in my work for the Navy—well, mostly, I am—but I would love to be a teacher. It has always been my dream. I wonder if I could shift into teaching at the school as a WAVE."

Frances frowned. "Do you want to get married someday and have a family?"

Lillian sighed. "Yes, of course. Not that anyone special like Frank has come along yet. And I know that a teaching career would be over as soon as I said, 'I do.' No husband would want me leaving our home and children every day. But what about between now and then? It would be so much more fulfilling as compared to what I'm doing now. All those bright young minds to fill with history, civic duty, mathematics..." Lillian stared off wistfully.

Frances was sympathetic. So many women now were starting impressive careers. What was to happen when the men came home and wanted their jobs back? How were women going to transition back to their previous roles?

"I think you could find a man who appreciates that women have taken on working careers. Why, you could even tell him you'll be so rich together you can afford a live-in housekeeper and nanny!"

Lillian laughed, her disposition sunny again. "That's a brilliant idea. I should—"

"Whatcha talking about?" Sophie had turned her attention to them.

"Just men," Frances said.

"Now that's a fun topic," Sophie said with a toss of her head. "Personally, I think men are like chocolates. Fun to unwrap and try, but you don't want too much of the same type. And you certainly don't want the ones filled with coconut. You know, the undesirable kind." Sophie giggled prettily.

Dottie went rigid across from Frances.

The Private Snafu cartoon reel started. It featured the popular cartoon Army private, an affable but stupid character, who slowly leaks classified information until the enemy finally pieces things together, attacks Snafu's transport ship, and blows it up.

Kenny could learn from this film.

"Hey, how's your jobs?" Sophie asked but plowed on without waiting for an answer. "You should see all the photography I'm already doing. A coupla days ago, I staged some WAVES fixing an aircraft engine. Got dirt smudges on their faces for it and everything. My boss wants me to submit it to *Life* magazine. Can you imagine if my photo made the cover?"

Sophie was more animated than Frances had ever seen her. "Oh, and tomorrow I'm working on a series of photos documenting all the buildings that have been constructed so far. It's funny, did you know they number the buildings in the order in which they are constructed and not according to how they are located? Imagine if our own home addresses were irrationally done that way."

Sophie took a final sip from an iced tea glass next to her and pushed it aside, then dropped her voice to a theatrically dramatic stage whisper. "I'm going to take pictures of all those civilian workers, too. I think it would be smart to have them on record. You never know when they might be valuable, right?"

Dottie's lip trembled, but she said nothing. Sophie's attention was on Frances and Lillian across the table, so she didn't notice Dottie.

"Guess what else?" Sophie said, raising her voice once more.

Frances shook her head. "I can't imagine that there's more."

"There is." She was down to a stage whisper again. "Kenny is taking me out on Saturday night. He's going to borrow a car to take me over to Solomons Island."

Solomons Island was a tiny strip of land in Calvert County, across the Patuxent River from the air station. It was as rural and dotted with farms as St. Mary's. Frances knew there was naval activity going on there, but no one really seemed to know what it was.

"Why?" she asked.

"He says he's going to show me a secret."

Frances's heart plummeted. This couldn't be good. "What kind of secret?"

Sophie shrugged. "He says it's a war secret and I won't be able to talk about it."

This sounded like a terrible idea. At the very least, anything deemed a military "secret" would be heavily guarded, so the two of them were likely to be arrested. "Sophie, you mustn't go. You don't want to be witness to any secrets that the Navy has not invited you to see."

Next to her, Lillian was also shaking her head, although her ever-present snood prevented her hair from tossing about like Sophie's did. "What he is suggesting to you is dangerous. You could get hurt."

But Dottie was now smiling. "Sounds interesting and fun. You should go."

<hr>

Frances's date with Roger was still over a week away, but in the interim, the station had announced an outdoor movie screening on

Friday night, open to everyone who worked on the base, including all civilian workers.

Dottie was quiet around the barracks, but her expression was one of joy at the prospect. Frances was quite happy, too, knowing that she could spend time with Roger as he had dropped a note with the administration building receptionist to let her know that his superiors were letting nearly all the Marines off to attend the movie.

"They're showing *Wuthering Heights*," Sophie gushed on Friday morning as they walked as a group to their respective workplaces. Walking had become simpler and faster than loading up on buses and being choked by the vehicle exhaust to travel what was ultimately a few hundred yards.

"It stars Laurence Olivier, David Niven, and Merle Oberon and was nominated for best picture in 1939, but of course lost to *Gone with the Wind*. Olivier and Niven might be British, but they are just so handsome, aren't they? Did you know that Merle and David had a passionate affair when they filmed *Beloved Enemy* in 1936? I read that she wanted to marry him, but, alas, he was not faithful to her. So sad. Too bad they aren't playing the film at the new theatre in Leonardtown—inside would be so much more comfortable than outside—but I suppose then we wouldn't have as many fine military men around us, would we?" Sophie chattered on until Frances, Dottie, and Lillian broke away to enter the administration building.

Fortunately, Frances was busy all day, so she didn't have too much time to be overly excited about the evening's prospects, although Lt. Hall had taken a keen interest in the dance.

"Sounds like you ended up on a cloud after the dance," Hall said when the two women ran into each other in the bathroom. "And the master sergeant sounds like a dream. Tell me about the other fellas there, too."

Frances proceeded to tell Lt. Hall about Kenny, George, and the rest, amused to see that the lieutenant hung on her every word about what had happened that night. It had never occurred to Frances that perhaps Lt. Barbara Hall was lonely, too.

Later that morning, Yeoman Blake, who managed the print shop, had pulled her aside and asked if she would like to learn how to operate the Vandercook letterpress. His regular employee had come down with the flu and wasn't going to be in for several days, but Blake had several important jobs that required immediate production.

Frances had readily agreed and, with Lt. Hall's approval, entered the print shop to assist Blake.

First, he had her clean the print cylinder, which involved rubbing beef fat on the black metal, then hand cranking it around dozens of times so that the fat spread on it before wiping it off with rags. To her surprise, after wiping it down, the roller proved to be a shiny silver metal. Blake then gave her a bottle of mineral spirits—the odor of which nearly choked her— and instructed her to apply it to everything on the bed of the printer and wipe it all clean.

Frances had to put serious work into it, but

by the end, she was pleased with the gleaming results of her efforts. Blake was, too. "Well done, Yeoman," he said. "Now let me show you how to roll paper through for some hygiene posters we need to put up around the station."

It was tricky work, setting up the various guides and gauges to properly align the paper so that it accurately fed through the cylinder and made proper contact with the inked bed, then feeding the sheet in, rolling it with the right amount of speed, then whisking the paper out to dry on a table next to her and immediately replacing the printed sheet with a new one.

However, within a couple of hours, she was reasonably proficient at running copies, to the point that the machine was in near continuous motion. It was surprising how interesting the work was, even if it was noisy and reeking of oil and ink, the latter of which had to be constantly re-filled inside the machinery's fountain.

Blake praised her output. "You're very good at this. I could use you more often. Next time I'll show you how to do some typesetting."

Coveralls would be much better attire than her skirt and pumps, for sure.

With the print shop supervisor's praise of her work dancing in her head, Frances left with Dottie at the end of the day to head back to the barracks to prepare for the evening.

Again, the women had to use the bathroom in shifts, as nearly all of them wanted to attend the movie in hopes of meeting someone.

Frances carefully donned a button-up navy-and-white pinstriped dress with a sash belt and a simple pair of pumps. The shoes were a little scuffed, but they were comfortable. She added a red, button-up sweater—borrowed from Lillian—to protect against any chills. Once the sun went down, the unusually warm temperatures would go with it.

Frustrated with her hair, which desperately needed a hairdresser's attention, she borrowed a snood from Lillian and tucked her hair into the black lace netting, letting it drape along the back of her neck.

It felt elegant. Would Roger think so, too?

CHAPTER 18

FRANCES GRABBED THE blanket from her bed to spread on the ground and joined the other girls heading over. They all had their blankets rolled up under their arms, too.

The movie screen was set up on an old farm field, one of the few locations that was not undergoing some sort of construction. The Navy had even ordered all other construction to stop early for the perpetual dust clouds on base to settle for a few hours before the outdoor gathering.

As Frances and her friends approached the site, where an enormous screen had been erected, propped up against a crisscrossing of boards—no doubt construction scrap—she saw Roger and several friends already there, including Kenny Campbell.

Her heart leapt a little. Roger Douglas was still the handsome man she remembered from the dance.

"Yoo hoo!" Sophie called out, waving to the men.

"Sophie, really," Lillian said. "That's so unladylike."

Sophie waved a hand at Lillian. "You need a man, my dear, to unstuff you. Sometimes you can be a bit of a prig." She strode ahead of them to join the men.

Once Frances, Dottie, and Lillian had arrived, introductions were again made for newcomers to the group, Dottie and two more military men.

After Frances introduced Dottie, Roger indicated that his other friends were both fellow Marines in the security detachment. One of them was introduced as Billy Alvey. Billy was a hulk of a man with an enormous grin that exposed a wide gap between his two front teeth. He had been at Midway in the Pacific and shot down numerous enemy aircraft. After suffering a non-lethal wound, had been sent to Patuxent River to work security.

Billy grinned and held up his left hand, which had three fingers partially removed. "The Japs got me good but I'm lucky compared to some who didn't come back. Plus, I'm from the county, so I'm serving near home." He didn't seem bothered at all by his injury.

"You just care about being able to carry a Betsy," Kenny teased.

Billy nodded solemnly and placed his damaged hand across his chest. "I do love my rifle. And being able to walk Lucifer on patrol. And because I am brilliant, I can do both with one hand."

The other man, George Somerville, was one of few dark-skinned men Frances had seen during her time on base.

"I'm also one of the lucky ones," he said to Frances. "Joined the Marines five years ago to improve my life. Did a coupla tours and ended up right back home where my mother can keep an eye on me." He smiled widely, suggesting he was joking.

"Do you live on station?" Frances asked.

"Of course. Have to be ready when Sparky starts shouting so that I can take my licks with the rest of the boys. I might be lucky, but I'm not privileged."

The other Marines laughed and clapped him on the back, their camaraderie obvious and genuine. George must have made an inside joke about how difficult it was to be in the Marine Corps.

A makeshift canteen had been set up for the movie, offering candy and bottled pop.

"Would you like something?" Roger asked. Frances's instinct was to tell him no, so that he wouldn't have to spend money, but he was making a generous offer to her. "A Coca-Cola would be nice," she said. President Roosevelt had declared that Coca-Cola would be available to all American troops for just five cents per bottle, so the purchase wouldn't rob Roger's wallet.

Billy, George, and Kenny also volunteered to get snacks for the other girls at the canteen. Dottie declined, but Sophie and Lillian accepted. "Buy something as sweet as we are," Sophie said with a wink, which Kenny found uproariously funny.

While they were gone, Dottie's gaze was darting around constantly.

Frances went to her. "Maybe you should go look for him," she whispered.

"Wouldn't it be rude?" Dottie whispered back.

"*Go.* I'll make excuses for you. And hopefully I won't see you again until after the movie concludes." Frances winked at her friend, hoping it would encourage her.

It worked. Dottie hugged her and slipped away without a word to Sophie and Lillian.

The men returned with small sacks of candy and pop bottles as the sun began to sink on the horizon. They all dug into the goodies as a thin young man with a prominent underbite and wearing an ill-fitting theatre usher's uniform wandered about with a tray full of holes, each hole containing a paper cone stuffed with fragrant popcorn.

"Have piping hot popcorn, only five cents," the usher called out, holding out his tray for all to see. "A movie isn't the same without hot, buttery popcorn!"

George Somerville approached the usher and held up a nickel. The usher glanced at George's dark skin with disdain and continued to call out, "Who wants popcorn, made fresh at the canteen?"

George shrugged and started to drop the nickel back into his pocket, but Roger stayed his hand, approaching the usher with an expression Frances could only describe as steely.

"We all bleed blue here, boy," Roger growled, clenching a fist. "He asked for some popcorn and you will give it to him."

The usher stared at Roger. "He can get it at the canteen."

"He will have it from you!" Roger roared at the usher, who shrank back nervously, causing a couple of his popcorn cones to fall from his tray and to the ground. Billy and Kenny went and stood to either side of Roger and George.

George held up a hand. "Hey, don't worry about it, fellas. Some folks are good, some aren't. I'm not bothered."

Roger glanced back at his friend. "You deserve better," he said before turning his full fury on the usher, who was shaking his head no.

"Blow it out your barracks bag. Is his nickel not made of silver?" Roger demanded, towering over the young man. The usher grabbed a cone and thrust it at Roger before quickly walking away without taking any money.

"Where does the Navy find these cracked eggs?" Kenny said as Roger handed the cone to George, who seemed embarrassed by his friends coming to his rescue over the situation.

Fortunately, the situation was forgotten when a loudspeaker set up on a pole crackled as a male voice came over it. "Please find your places. The movie will begin momentarily."

There was rustling among the crowd as people sought to spread their blankets out. Frances's group had several blankets among them, and they spread them out into one contiguous patchwork over the ground.

It was difficult to sit comfortably in a modest fashion on her blanket, but she did her best. She caught Roger glancing appreciatively at her legs and felt heat on her neck from the hidden thrill that was. Suddenly, the cooling temperature didn't bother her.

The group sat haphazardly across the blankets. Roger was on one side of her, and Billy Alvey was on the other. To distract herself from Roger's glances, she said to Billy, "Do you have a sweetheart here?"

To her surprise, her comment caused a complete change in his happy-go-lucky expression. "I did. Her name was Rosie. She didn't wait for me."

His manner was suddenly doleful. "She heard that I'd been injured and, without waiting to hear what had happened, decided she needed a man who was, in her words, 'completely whole.' She found some Army chump and abandoned me for him last year."

"I'm so sorry," Frances said. She refrained from any silly platitudes about how he would find someone else. "Rosie made a huge mistake."

Billy withdrew a billfold from his pocket, opened it, and pulled a folded piece of paper from it. "This is how I remember Rosie," he said, proffering the paper to Frances.

Did he really want her to read his intimate correspondence?

She gently unfolded the page, which had clearly been unfolded and refolded dozens of times. The sun had dipped below the horizon but there was still enough light by which to read.

Darling Billy,

I hope you are safe and well and that the weather isn't too hot wherever you are. My family's victory garden is in full bloom, and we have cucumbers and tomatoes galore. I know you think that I am too delicate for such hard gardening work, but I do actually enjoy it.

I'm helping Mama can spaghetti sauce from the tomatoes. You would be impressed with how much I am learning about cooking, which I hope to put to good use one day with you!

I volunteered for a scrap drive, and you should see the heaps of rubber and aluminum we've collected in the town square. It helps me pass the time while you're gone. I worry for you every day, and every night I look up at the sky and wonder if you see the same stars that I do.

Hurry home, my love.
Ever your—
Rosie

There were hearts drawn around the edges of the page.

She glanced up at Billy. He looked so sad.

Funny how accustomed one could become to seeing in the dark. With the only illumination now the stars and the faint light from the canteen's lanterns, Frances could see everything around her as though it were daytime.

"There was one more letter, of course," he said, "where she let me know that she had found someone else, but I choose to remember her this way, when she still loved me. Before she thought I wasn't going to be man enough for her."

Frances carefully folded the letter and offered it back to Billy, who promptly replaced it in his wallet.

"Hey," Billy's manner brightened. "Maybe one day I'll find a gal who is as beautiful as one of the movie stars we'll see tonight." He cast a furtive glance at Lillian, who leaned back serenely on her arms, her gaze upward as she seemed to enjoy the night air.

Frances smiled. "Anything can happen."

The loudspeaker screeched again. "Ladies and gentlemen, please tune in first for a news broadcast."

The screen glowed white, then a series of images—planes dropping bombs, planes landing on aircraft carriers, soldiers laughing together and eating canned meals—appeared while a newscaster intoned war news in the background. The most recent occurrence was what was being hailed as "Black Thursday," a second strike on German ball bearing factories in the city of Schweinfurt that had occurred back on October 14th. The Americans had lost six B-17 bombers, plus many others had been damaged. Worse, the casualty rate topped six hundred. Still, the United States was declaring success because of the raid's deep penetration into German territory.

The newscaster finished up by telling listeners that the tide of the war was turning, and everyone must continue to pitch in and do his or her part to beat the Axis enemy so that all the boys could come home.

The news broadcast was less than five minutes, but it did its job well. The mood over the crowd was palpably patriotic and hopeful.

"And now," the loudspeaker barked, "our feature presentation, 1939's *Wuthering Heights*."

As the opening credits and music began rolling, George Somerville said to no one in particular, "They used the Mitchell blimped noiseless camera for filming this movie. It's special because it's so quiet. I think all movies will eventually be made with it."

Sophie, who had been leaning flirtatiously toward Kenny, sat up straight. "What? Really? Did you know that Vivien Leigh was quite upset that she wasn't cast opposite Laurence Olivier for this movie. They are quite the item, you know. But then she went on to do *Gone With the Wind*, so I suppose that was alright for her."

George frowned. "Can't say as I did know that. I'm mostly interested in how they technically make the movies—camera angles, set design to fool the eye, that sort of thing. Filmmaking is fascinating from that perspective. I'd like to be a director one day."

For Sophie, it was as though an air raid siren had just sounded, so much at full alert was she. "Films *are* fascinating. Do you read *Screen Guide* or *Movie Mirror*? There's so much to learn from them."

"No, never heard of them."

"Oh, I will loan you some copies. I have loads of them. I'll look for some issues that have articles about the directors and the producers. I think I even have a special issue all about Victor Fleming and his movies." Sophie was highly animated.

This made George effervescent, as well. "He's been a pioneer in using Technicolor to colorize movies. *The Wizard of Oz, Gone with the Wind.* Color movies are the future, for sure, if they can get around the expense of them."

"Hey, Sophie, the movie is starting," Kenny interrupted. "Maybe focus on your popcorn a little more. And me." He squeezed her shoulder and shot George a glance of daggers. The Marine Corps camaraderie of a few minutes ago was gone.

Sophie giggled. "Aw, come on now, we have a date tomorrow, remember? To go to Solomons Island."

Roger immediately sat erect. "What do you mean, you have a date to go to Solomons?"

Kenny waved a hand at Roger. "Nothing to worry about. Just going to take Sophie over to see the sights."

"What sights?" Roger demanded. He seemed as angry as he had over the usher refusing to serve George Somerville. "There are no sights over there to be seen. Just farms and marshes."

"Hey, buddy, don't get worked up." Kenny offered his easy-going smile to Roger. "There are gorgeous sunsets to be taken in with a gorgeous woman."

Sophie preened at Kenny's flattery.

"There are gorgeous sunsets elsewhere." Roger

was clearly unhappy with his friend's planned date.

Frances was pained. Should she tell Roger about Sophie's claim that she would be witness to a secret at Solomons, or keep her mouth shut and protect her friend?

The movie itself finally started, and the group settled down to watch as Mr. Lockwood made his way through a blinding snowstorm to the front door of the forbidding Wuthering Heights manor house.

To Frances's delight, Roger put his arm around her shoulder. She leaned toward him to encourage him to keep it there.

By the time the final credits were rolling, the air was chilly, and Frances had been so focused on Roger gently stroking her arm that she couldn't have recited the first thing about what had happened in the movie. They walked together as a group toward the women's barracks, it being understood that the ladies should be accompanied to their front door.

Dottie had reappeared out of nowhere and joined them for the return walk.

There was a great deal of laughter and teasing among the group, particularly on Sophie's part, as they walked toward the WAVES' quarters. She seemed to be flirting with George to rankle Kenny, and it was working. Kenny's shoulders were hunched as he walked along, not taking part in the chummy atmosphere.

Roger shook his head, and Frances could tell that he hated this sort of unnecessary personal strife.

As they continued on toward the WAVE dormitory, Frances slowed her steps. It had the desired effect of separating her and Roger from the rest of the group.

"Is everything alright?" he asked.

"I'm not sure. I know something and I'm not sure if I should repeat it…" Frances was still hesitant, despite deliberately creating a quiet space for them to talk.

"What is it? You can tell me. I promise I won't say a word."

She bit her lip. Sometimes you had to trust your instincts. And her instincts told her that Roger Douglas was completely worthy of her trust.

"I–I'm mostly worried about betraying Sophie," Frances said quietly, staring toward the ground as they walked behind everyone else. "She's my friend."

"Would what you know get Sophie into legal trouble?"

Frances stopped and looked at him. His statement had pierced her soul. "I think it might."

"This must have something to do with Kenny," he said. "That dumb, stupid–" Roger stopped, no doubt biting his tongue on an epithet that he would have tossed about freely among his fellow Marines.

Frances nodded. Roger took her hand, causing her to face him directly. He waited a few moments while the others put more distance between them.

"Frances, it's always best to be up front and honest in all dealings."

"I know," she said, her voice quiet and pensive. She cast her gaze down one more time, then looked up at him, holding back tears. She swallowed, and the hint of tears disappeared. "Kenny told Sophie that he plans to show her a secret—a war secret—when they go to Solomons Island for their date tomorrow night."

Roger blinked several times but made no other reaction. "Did he say what the war secret was about?"

"No. And he made it sound as though once she knew the secret, she wouldn't be able to talk about it, either."

Roger took a deep breath. "I will hold what you've told me in the strictest confidence," he said. "I can't let Kenny show Sophie any so-called 'secrets', but I can probably get him detailed onto a project tomorrow so that he can't take her out. From there, I'll figure out what to do. Okay?"

Frances nodded. "Thank you. I want Sophie safe, but I feel terrible talking about her in this way."

Roger placed his roughened palm against the side of her face and she leaned into it. Strange that this hand, which held rifles and combat knives with ease, could be so gentle against her own feminine skin.

"Frances, I like you very much. I-I–" Frances smiled up at him, hoping he would kiss her, but Roger seemed to falter.

"I'm glad you told me about Kenny's plan. You're a good girl."

Had she completely misread his intent? She was puzzled, but nodded. "Thank you for holding it to yourself."

Roger started walking again, this time quickly, with his hands shoved into his pockets. Frances kept up with him as best she could, and they caught up to the rest of the group as they neared the women's barracks.

"I'll see you next Sunday for our boat ride," he said. "There's much to do between now and then."

CHAPTER 19

FRANCES CONTINUED TO be confused by Roger's actions, so certain he had been about to kiss her, but then he hadn't. Maybe she had somehow disappointed him by talking about Sophie?

That was ridiculous. He must have been preoccupied with how to handle it. He certainly still seemed committed to their date.

She had little time to think about it as she prepared for bed, and Dottie came to her compartment, practically bristling with electricity as she talked softly about her secret meeting with Ira Reed.

"Ira—we are on a first-name basis now—bought me a popcorn and a Fanta drink. We sat way off to one side where no one could see us—he understands that women like Sophie cannot possibly understand men like him—and we ended up just talking and talking and talking. Honestly, I don't even know what the movie was about. Ira loves to hunt deer and ducks. Says there is no one like him with a rifle. He says that one day he will fill me a freezer full of food. Isn't that romantic, Frances? We are going to have a real date, too. Isn't that the bee's knees?"

Frances could hardly believe this was the quiet, introspective Dottie standing before her, pacing back and forth across the eight feet of space in the compartment as she babbled on about her new beau.

"I'm happy for you, but…how long do you plan to keep this a secret?" Frances asked with equal quiet.

Dottie waved a hand. "It will all come out in due time and people like Sophie will just have to accept our happiness. But–" Dottie stopped for a moment. "You won't tell her just yet, right?"

"Of course not." Frances had revealed one secret, she wasn't going to do another.

Dottie rambled on about Ira for several moments, which served to help Frances forget what she had to admit was a bit of disappointment regarding Roger.

What would his lips against hers have felt like?

But between Dottie's overwhelming excitement and what happened the following Monday at her job, Frances had little time to think about Roger.

Lt. Cmdr. Mackey and Lt. Hall were already barking orders at people as they arrived at the Nursery, and the place was in upheaval. The typists' desks had all been removed except for two, and those had been moved to the end of the room on the other side of Lt. Cmdr. Mackey's office. To be closer to Lt. Hall for some reason?

A large table full of maps that were stuck with pins and held down by coffee cups dominated the center of the room.

Lt. Cmdr. Mackey came striding out of his

office area, his demeanor more gruff than usual. "Yeoman Morgan, you'll be at the desk nearest my office today. Many important memos and instructions going out today, and you're our fastest typist. Hop to it, my girl."

Dottie literally jumped as she obeyed his instruction, moving rapidly to the other end of the room.

"Yeoman Parker, can you take dictation?"

She had taken a class, but she hadn't written any shorthand since arriving at Pax River. "Yes, sir, of course."

He nodded gruffly. "The Nursery is to be used as an important planning room for brass. Expect to see admirals floating around. You'll be continuing to assist Yeoman Blake in the print shop, but I also want you ready to take notes and make reports of decisions being made."

Lt. Hall had emerged from her office and joined Frances and Lt. Cmdr. Mackey. "I'll show you the format for the reports. You will keep a cover sheet over them at all times, and you will only give them to me. If I am not available, you will put them in a safe in my office. I will provide you a combination to the safe, which you will tell to no one at the risk of charges being brought against you. All of your shorthand notes will be incinerated in the burn barrel at the conclusion of each day, no exceptions, ever. To fail to burn them will result in dismissal."

Frances's supervisor was gesticulating quite a bit—at Frances, toward her own office, at the windows—telling Frances that the woman was quite agitated by whatever was going on.

Frances knew instinctively that she should not ask for any details but should just remain silent and salute.

Mackey nodded his approval at what Lt. Hall was saying. "And since you live here in St. Mary's, lieutenant, I'm going to see about having you made into an air raid warden for your neighborhood in Dameron. We must all be particularly careful now."

It had never occurred to Frances to inquire as to where the lieutenant lived. Certainly, she was never in the barracks. Lt. Hall had gotten awfully lucky, like Ira Reed and George Somerville, to have been stationed near home. It probably saved the Navy money and valuable space to let her return home each night.

With a final dismissal from Lt. Cmdr. Mackey, Frances got to work.

Men in uniforms with a variety of stripes and insignia on their jacket sleeves began piling into the room, demanding coffee and circling around the large conference table. They played with the pins and drew red circles in various locations.

Frances withdrew to the print shops, where Yeoman Blake was in the process of running some information posters. *They Do It...So Can We. Do With Less...So They'll Have Enough. Dig On for Victory.* Words like this were firmly imprinted in every American's brain.

Frances silently began helping him, removing the fresh prints and clipping them to a string hung across part of the room so that they could finish drying.

She knew it was ridiculous to consider, yet she still wondered if this new batch of posters had somehow been ordered because of Kenny.

Frances shuddered to think it. *No, that's silly. Nonsense and stuffing, as Sophie would say.*

Throughout the day, as both the printers and the officers clanked along, Frances was pulled back and forth from print shop to table, eventually finding a stool and setting it unobtrusively at one corner end of the table so she could sit with her notepad and pens and capture proceedings, despite how erratic and prone to arguments the men were.

By the middle of the day, it was clear that a secret invasion into Europe was being planned. Her heart pounded at the thought of what all of that entailed.

What wasn't so clear yet was why so much discussion was being held at Pax River instead of at the Pentagon, which had just been completed a few months ago to house the War Department. That construction had been finished even faster than Pax River and reportedly had four million square feet of temporary space that would be turned into a large hospital or warehouse once the war was over.

After all, what would America need with so much military office space once it was no longer fighting this war?

She banged her ballpoint pen in frustration against her notepad. Maybe she should return to using her fountain pen. Refilling the chamber was messy and repetitive, but these supposedly new ballpoint pens the Navy had purchased constantly leaked and skipped, making a disaster of her work. She wasn't even sure she could go back and translate what she had written.

She quickly ran to the back of the room to her desk, opened the top drawer, tossed the offensive pen in, and withdrew her faithful Parker fountain pen and a jar of black ink.

Dottie stopped only momentarily from her frantic typing to nod a hello at Frances.

Back at her spot at one corner of the table, Frances continued to listen and write. By the end of the day, she knew it all. And what she knew frightened her.

Now Frances was the one with a secret to keep.

CHAPTER 20

EVERYONE WAS PENSIVE at dinner. Frances suspected that they were all keeping secrets and pretending like nothing had happened. Was Lillian patching calls from the Pentagon? Was Sophie creating fake photographs that would be used as propaganda to fool the Germans into thinking Americans were doing nothing? Or might she be doing something else entirely?

Frances hadn't breathed a word to Dottie about what she knew, but surely the other girl had overheard plenty. In fact, they had said nothing to one another about the day except to comment on how busy it had been.

After dinner was over, Frances decided to retreat to her compartment to write a letter to Freddy. She had just finished filling up the back side of the page and was folding the sheet when Lt. Wallace cleared her throat outside the curtain.

"Yeoman Parker, there's a visitor for you."

A visitor? At the barracks? That was odd.

To Frances's surprise, it was Verja Graham, or, rather, Verja Duke, in the barracks entryway.

Verja was dressed primly in a plain dark blue jacket and skirt with faded brass buttons. On her head was a matching blue straw hat with a white veil and a red feather jauntily placed across the top of it. She also wore navy blue gloves that had been expertly sewn–the repair patches on them were barely noticeable.

"Hello, Miss Parker. I hope you don't mind my intrusion. When we met at the dance, you said you would be interested in being friends and…well, Walter left yesterday for India, and I sure could use that friend right now."

Frances had many thoughts, and unfortunately, blurted out the first one that came to mind. "How did you get on station?" Married housing was in trailers located just off base. With what Frances knew was going on, surely security was tighter than usual. How could the Marines have let any regular citizen on board?

"Oh, that kind Sergeant Campbell recognized me. He said that now that Walter and I are married, I have free access to the station." Verja seemed oblivious to what she was saying.

Frances bit her tongue. Verja Duke didn't automatically have privileges simply for marrying an armed forces pilot.

"Congratulations on your wedding," she said, changing the subject. "I trust it all went well."

Verja sighed. "Except for the lopsided wedding cake my aunt made, it was beautiful. I planned an old-fashioned morning wedding with breakfast afterward. So much easier to procure eggs, tomatoes, and potatoes than dinner meats."

Verja was right on that count. Walter Duke had married a clever girl.

"Walter was able to secure some parachute silk, and my mother and I made a dress from it. So meaningful, don't you think? Of course, Walter wore his dress uniform. My bridesmaid wore a dress with a black bodice and an ivory skirt, and Walter's groomsman wore a black jacket and ivory pants. So elegant, don't you think?"

"It all sounds lovely," Frances murmured. "And you were able to have your ceremony here in your hometown before he shipped off."

Verja shook her head. "We married here, but I'm not a local girl. I'm originally from Washington, D.C., but attended St. Mary's Academy in Leonardtown. I met Walter at a music recital. He was trying so hard to become proficient at the violin. I had to laugh watching him, a gawky young boy with his tongue poking out as he concentrated on pulling his bow across the strings." Verja gazed into the distance, smiling.

It was funny to hear Verja referring to Duke as "gawky" and "young," when she looked to be barely out of her teens herself.

"I had taken piano lessons from an early age and had some proficiency on it, so I volunteered to be his accompanist. We've always shared a love of music, even if Walter's talents lay more in the direction of guiding an airplane, not a violin."

"Which I'm sure he is doing most expertly as we speak."

Another sigh, but this time Verja clamped her lips together as if to bite back a comment and changed the subject.

"As soon as married housing on base is built, we will move into it. Right now, our trailer outside the base is tiny, just barely enough room for two people to pass one another inside, but it's ours. I'm planning to plant the smallest victory garden you've ever seen, in addition to a few flowers to spruce it up." Verja again had that dreamy look. "Hey, would you like to see it? It really isn't far to walk."

Frances agreed. Grabbing a flashlight from the vestibule, which always had a collection of umbrellas, flashlights, and rain ponchos in it, she joined Verja on a walk to her trailer, which, as she had said, was not actually that far a walk. Or maybe Frances had just become accustomed to walking everywhere.

As far as she could tell in the dark, the trailer was a gunmetal color. Rounded at both ends, it was probably twenty feet long and sat amid numerous other trailers.

The interior was indeed tiny and cramped, but in her few days of marriage, Verja had done an admirable job. There were white curtains on the two windows in the trailer, parachute silk again, if Frances wasn't mistaken. The icebox, range, and sink were practically dollhouse-sized, but the Navy had ensured they were new.

The only furniture was a tiny table for two, a bed barely large enough for one, and a chair next to an end table featuring a lamp on it.

Two small doors at the far end of the trailer presumably led to a bathroom and a closet, although they each couldn't have been more than a couple of feet deep. The ceiling hung low over them—it must have been uncomfortable for a tall man like Walter Duke to walk through here.

But it was cozy. Way better than barracks.

"Please sit down," Verja invited Frances, indicating the table and two chairs.

Frances placed her flashlight on the table between them. "Thank you for inviting me."

"I would like to offer you some coffee or a snack, but I've used up nearly all of my ration cards for the month to ensure Walter was sent off with a full belly..." Verja's expression was pained.

Frances held up a hand. "Think nothing of it. I've already eaten dinner and couldn't possibly fit another thing inside me."

With Walter gone, Verja would have his pay, but it likely wasn't much. She'd need every bit to survive on, and then she would need money to set up her new household once she secured on-station quarters.

Verja flashed a grateful smile. "Walter's been gone only a short time, but I already miss him dreadfully. I don't know how I'll survive until this war ends. It just seems to drag on and on, don't you think? Why don't I get us some water?"

Verja rose, walked a few steps, drew two mismatched glasses from the lone cabinet above her tiny, white enameled stove, and filled them from the faucet. As she placed the glasses on the table and sat back down, Frances's innards clenched.

The war might not go on too much longer, she knew, but she couldn't offer any hint of encouragement in that direction. "It really does. But now you have a new friend to help you pass the time." She reached across the table and took Verja's hand.

The other woman smiled. "I'm glad of it. I do so worry about Walter. He's very smart and brave, you know. He graduated at the top of his flight training class in the Army Air Corps before he was assigned to a fighter group on Long Island, New York. He was flying a plane called a P-47, but with this move to India, he will be flying a plane called a P-38. He said they call it the 'Lightning,' which, I confess, frightens me, especially because of how excited he sounded to fly it."

Frances could well understand that a plane referred to as "lightning" did not sound as if it would be conducting tame excursion flights. "But you say he is smart and brave, and they would only ask the cleverest pilots to fly such craft, knowing that they would always fly them safely and easily return them to their airfields."

"Yes, I'm sure you're right." Verja didn't sound convinced. "Before he left, Walter told me he would name his P-38 the 'Miss V,' for me. That's very romantic, don't you think?"

Frances nodded. "I think you have a handsome, brave, romantic husband. You are the envy of all women."

Verja seemed pleased at that. "You and Master Sergeant Douglas seem to be getting on well. He's very handsome, too."

Frances fluttered. She had done a good job until now of putting her upcoming date out of her mind. She took a sip of the lukewarm water to settle her stomach and didn't respond.

"That Sergeant Campbell is handsome in a roguish sort of way, don't you think? He seems to be..." Verja paused, as if considering her next words. "He seems to be very taken with Sophie. If you don't mind my saying, Sophie doesn't behave very..." Again, a pause. "Very cautiously. I worry for her."

There was much to worry about where Sophie was concerned.

But Frances wanted to be loyal. "Sophie is high-spirited but means well. I hope that Kenny is a good match for her. As good a match as Walter is for you."

At that, Verja blushed and was ready to move back to the topic of her husband. "With so much happening in the Pacific, I'm up every night worried that Walter will be amid heavy fighting. An airplane is so very vulnerable, don't you think? What would I do without him? Surely God wouldn't take my brand-new husband away from me this soon?"

Tears welled up in Vera's eyes, and Frances realized that as cozy as it must have been to have her own place for the first time in her young life, it was probably also terrifying to be alone all the time.

Surely Frances could offer some comfort without revealing secrets. "I don't think the Pacific is cause for concern. The area is not the focus of the war right now, as far as I can tell."

Verja gripped her glass without raising it to her lips. "Where do you think the focus is?"

Frances shrugged, hoping it appeared casual. "I don't know. But I'm not seeing much naval communication regarding movements in the Pacific."

Verja was suddenly very inquisitive. "That's wonderful to hear. But if not the Pacific, then the Atlantic? Is there a concentrated effort in Europe? What do you think might be happening?"

No good deed goes unpunished. Wasn't that what columnist Walter Winchell said about diplomats in Washington? Frances should have kept her mouth shut and let Verja remain in doubt.

Offering vague explanations and a promise to get together again soon, Frances finally extricated herself from Verja's trailer and headed back to her barracks in the dark, swinging her flashlight wide to avoid stumbling into or over any leftover construction messes.

As she finally tumbled into her bed, Frances found herself tense with worry. Had she just made her own mess with her words?

She had to be more careful. Not only because of the risk to all of the troops and everyone's great desire to end the war, but because Freddy might be in Europe somewhere and thus in danger's way.

CHAPTER 21

ALL HER FRIENDS gathered around her prior to the start of Frances's Sunday afternoon date, fussing over her appearance and offering advice.

Sophie, in particular, was full of adages about what to do and not do to keep a man attracted. Most of her advice seemed attached to an article in a tattered old *Modern Screen* magazine featuring Mae West, who had been famously open about intimate matters.

Sophie's date with Kenny on Solomons Island had seemingly gone well, although Sophie had been surprisingly tight-lipped about whatever she may have seen, just flippantly saying that Solomons Island was just full of old farms, old boats, and old coots.

In any case, Roger must have avoided a confrontation over it, because it wasn't as though there had been any sort of arrest or disturbance. At least not anything that had made it to Frances's ears.

It was Lillian who finally nodded approval on Frances's appearance, which consisted of a simple red and blue plaid dress borrowed from Dottie, a gorgeous scarlet scarf from Sophie, who had tied it artfully around Frances's head, and her own plain work shoes. Lillian had helped Frances apply makeup. "Beautiful red lips are everything, don't worry so much about the rest of your face," was her advice.

Lillian had also provided her with a thickly knitted, button-up, camel-colored cardigan. "It doesn't match, but you'll appreciate having it."

Despite all the preparation, she was still nervous and jittery as she stood in the windowed vestibule, waiting, when Roger arrived at the barracks. To her surprise—and that of the other girls based on their *oohs* and *ahhs* behind her—he pulled up in an automobile.

Frances turned to Sophie, who winked at her and said, "It's good to know people who have access to a car. Especially people with access to a car and extra gas rations."

Could Sophie get in trouble for having helped Roger in this way? Frances had to admit, in the moment, it didn't matter. She was about to go on a date in a nice automobile.

Roger exited the car with a small bouquet in one hand. He was dressed in casual clothing, consisting of tan wide-legged trousers, a wide-collar, button-up sky-blue shirt, and a pair of cinnamon-colored loafers. As he neared the building, it was obvious that he was freshly shaved, and his close-cropped military haircut had been given an extra bit of attention.

Fortunately, the other women melted away as Roger touched the doorknob. His face lit up at seeing Frances, letting her know that she had dressed well for the occasion.

"These are for you," he said, handing her the small bouquet. "I'm sorry they are sparse. Not much available in the fields this time of year."

Frances was surprised. "You picked these yourself?"

Now Roger looked puzzled. "Of course. Who else would do it? I promise they will be better next time."

It could have been a wad of sticks for all Frances cared. "They are lovely as they are. Perfect, even."

Roger grinned and escorted her to the car, a huge Buick that may have been several years old but had been well-maintained, no doubt on a schedule of military precision.

He opened the passenger door, and she slid onto the tufted leather bench seat. As he shut the door behind her, she knew that the other WAVES were watching in envy from various windows.

Was this what it felt like to be a movie star?

To Frances's surprise, there was a dog seated in the back seat. A German Shepherd, his tongue lolling out and looking for all the world like he was smiling and happy to see her.

"Hope you don't mind, I brought Gunney with me," Roger said as he got in on the driver's side. "He loves boat rides. And he's always good protection."

Gunney leaned forward and sniffed at Frances, then gave her a quick swipe across her cheek with his tongue. The dog was large, even for a German Shepherd, with thick, dense fur and dark black markings.

Compared to Sunny, the little golden cocker spaniel her family had at home, this animal was a beast.

"I don't mind at all, as long as he doesn't believe that you need protection from me," Frances said.

Again, she received an appreciative look.

"Gunney is very good at sensing my moods and knowing when there is danger around. More than once he has run a trespasser to ground for me." Roger put the car in gear. "I thought we'd go for a drive first if that suits you."

Frances nodded. The luxury of leaning against the leather made her want to giggle but she refrained from it. "Sure. Are you and Gunney taking me somewhere in particular?"

Roger drove away slowly and Frances knew the other girls would be sighing as they pulled out of view. Gunney stuck his head out the rolled-down window of the rear seat behind Frances to pant and enjoy his own doggie vista.

"I'd like to go see construction of the new off-site Navy housing. It's supposed to be quite nice for military quarters."

Frances agreed to the idea. The housing was so close to the air station that they were there in under five minutes.

As with the base, this area was under a cloud of construction dust, and they were only permitted a short way into the building compound. At the northern end, there were multiple units in various stages of completion, and a few looked to be almost done. They were all the same, in that they were small duplexes of white-painted concrete with strangely angled roofs, which made the tops of the homes appear to be nearly flat.

However, each unit had numerous cut-outs for windows and a brick fireplace chimney at one end. There also appeared to be room for a short driveway to each unit, as well as a tiny patch of ground that would work well for a garden.

The southern end of the housing complex was much in its infancy, with the homes just barely starting to show their final form. However, the outlines of a few larger buildings were visible.

She pointed at them, and he stopped. "I hope those will prove to hold a grocery store, a post office, and a beauty salon."

Roger laughed. "And a barber shop and hardware store." Frances laughed with him.

"What do you think?" Roger asked. "Is it a place you'd want to live?"

Frances was startled. Why was he asking her that? But his expression was innocent, devoid of any ulterior motive.

"I suppose anything is better than barracks. I bet Verja Duke would love to live here." She quickly described for him the tiny trailer Verja was currently in.

He nodded. "The damned base is being built too fast, and the community can't keep up. At least the Navy is attempting to do something about it."

Remembering a memo she had typed, Frances said, "The Navy is going to take applications for these houses. I bet they are all taken the day the application period starts."

"Without a doubt," he said.

Gunney whined as Roger started to drive away. "What's the matter boy? Would *you* like to live here? Not as much room to roam as we have on base."

The dog woofed softly in reply. As softly as a dog that must weigh at least eighty pounds could, anyway.

They re-entered the base, with the Marine guard on duty hailing Roger with a salute, followed by a glance at Frances and a quirked eyebrow. "Mind your business," Roger growled, but it was so mild that the other Marine laughed.

They drove some distance onto the base, ending up along some farmland that, unlike the field where they had seen the movie, was clearly still in agricultural use. "What is this?" Frances asked. "I thought the Navy had taken over everything."

Roger turned down a narrow dirt road in the middle of the field. "They did. But it helps them to leave some vegetation growing. It encourages the birds and wild animals to congregate here, rather than on other properties, particularly the landing strips being constructed. A propeller is no place for an osprey. It'll take an aircraft right down. And, of course, the bird does not come out well from the encounter."

He slowed down as they approached a shallow wooded area near the water's edge. "Funny to think that, until the Navy took over all this property, it was just farmers and subsistence workers living along the shore. Rich people find it distasteful. I love the water. It's so serene and a joy to watch the birds and other sea creatures that live here. I'd be very happy to live along a waterfront piece of property, away from the irritants of life."

Roger was so wistful that Frances blurted what was in her mind. "Then why don't you do that?"

He seemed to consider it, then shrugged. "Hard to imagine doing anything that permanent while wearing a uniform. But there certainly is a lot of shoreline around St. Mary's County, so maybe I will do just that when the war is over. Here we are."

Roger had pulled up in a small clearing next to a dilapidated shack that was well-hidden by the vegetation. He got out of the driver's side and came around to let Frances out, then to open the door for Gunney.

The dog bounded around joyously. This was obviously a familiar spot for him.

Roger opened the trunk and, to Frances's surprise, pulled out both a faded olive-green blanket and a substantial two-handled hamper. He held the hamper up and grinned. "Lunch. Courtesy of a woman named Maisie in your barracks."

Had the entire barracks been working in the background on her date?

***

Roger placed a hand to the small of Frances's back to lead her through the thicket to the shoreline. His touch was gentle but strong.

Her shoes, however, were wholly inadequate for shuffling through old, dead leaves and stepping over branches. What had she been thinking to put these pumps on for a picnic?

But she soon forgot about her disastrous fashion choice. "Oh," she breathed as they exited the woods and reached the water's sandy edge.

It was as if a painter had taken a brush and stroked it against the landscape in order to create a canvas entitled "Serenity." The sky was lapis blue, with random white puffs of clouds lazily making their way across it. The sky met the water, which was an unusual olive shade—not quite green and not quite brown, at a distance that seemed impossibly close and impossibly far away at the same time. Frances put up a hand to shield her eyes from the sun and thought that she could just make out a faraway land mass.

Enhancing the scene was a small rowboat that had been dragged ashore and was partially in the water. Streaks of red paint still showed through the old wood and the boat creaked as it rocked back and forth against the gentle waves rolling in.

Completing the landscape was another dilapidated building. Except this one wasn't covered by vegetation but stood proudly in the water a short distance from the shore. It was tall, made of wood and brick, and had a square tower at one corner. The wind and waves had clearly been attempting their best at destroying the edifice. "Just try and beat me," the building seemed to whisper.

Roger followed her gaze and said, "That's the Cedar Point lighthouse. Where she sits is where the Patuxent River meets the Chesapeake Bay.

I've rowed out there numerous times. I believe she was built late in the last century, but seems to have been abandoned decades ago. In any case, no one claims her. Looks like she's been done in by erosion and the weather, in addition to mining that supposedly went on somewhere nearby. I bet she was a beaut in her day."

Frances nodded. "She's beautiful now, in a proud but faded and forgotten sort of way."

Roger stared at her as if seeing her for the first time. "Well said. I view the lighthouse as though she needs protection. My protection. Silly, I know."

They stood together in silence for several moments, gazing at the old building as the water lapped lazily at the shore. It was bucolic, but Frances's heels were sinking into the sand.

She reached down and removed her shoes, letting her toes curl around the cool sand. It might be November, but it still felt wonderful out here. She dug her feet in even deeper, giggling at how marvelous it felt.

No wonder Roger liked it here.

"Tide's low, so we should eat now before it comes in," he suggested, snapping the blanket out on the ground with military precision and then rummaging through the basket.

Frances wondered if it was the blanket from his own bed that he was risking ruin on for this picnic.

The thought warmed her toward him even more.

Gunney was pacing back and forth along the sand, sniffing happily at everything in his path—

shells, vegetation, an old, waterlogged stump. Nothing was too minor for the dog's attentions.

Roger invited her to sit down next to him on the blanket and offered her some cheese and the ubiquitous Spam. Maisie had at least added a mason jar with what appeared to be a sauce of some sort and they dipped slices of the meat into it. There was also a small loaf of French bread tucked in the basket with a small knob of—oh, what heaven—butter.

Roger cut a couple of narrow Spam slices for Gunney, who devoured them before Frances could finish placing a small slice of cheese on top of her first piece of Spam.

However, the dog didn't beg for more and, instead, curled up on the blanket next to Frances.

"I guess he likes you," Roger observed. "Ungrateful wretch."

Gunney thumped his tail on the blanket twice.

Roger shook his head. "I'm lucky to have him on my night duty walks. He hears things long before I do and has helped me run down many locals trying to sneak onto the station from the water. Can't say as I blame people— they're curious about what's going on here. But they cannot be permitted aboard under any circumstances. There are a couple of exceptions, of course."

Frances thought of Verja. "Like military wives?"

He nodded. "If they have been granted living quarters on base, yes. We keep a list of them. And then there are a couple of farmers remaining who grow the crops and vegetation the Navy needs for the wildlife. The Navy turns a blind eye if they also keep a few cattle and pigs, although once more airplanes start coming in, the animals will be terrified of the constant noise. Wouldn't surprise me if their cows stop producing milk and their chickens refuse to lay eggs."

He changed subjects. "Sometimes I fish out here. My Uncle Nathan taught me when I was a kid, and it's part of why I love the water so much, although I grew up in Michigan on Lake Superior, not on a river. Unbelievable fishing there, something like eighty species that can be caught. Do you fish, Frances?"

Frances shook her head. "No. I wouldn't know the first thing about it. Although Freddy—my brother—enjoys it. I sometimes wonder if he is somewhere that he can fish to have a little pleasure in his life."

Roger was silent for several moments. "Still haven't heard from him recently?"

"No. Like everyone else, I pray and hope."

They ate in silence for a while. When there was no food left, Roger said, "Would you like to row out to the lighthouse?"

Frances agreed, taking his proffered hand to rise from the blanket. Roger helped her into the boat, and she sat on one of the two worn, wooden boards that stretched across the beam of the small craft, while he held it steady from the ground.

"Gunney, wait here," Roger commanded the dog, who had seemed ready to step into the boat, too.

The dog whined, and Frances was about to suggest that they bring him along, but Roger knelt and addressed the dog. "We discussed this. You don't get to go everywhere, right, pal?"

The dog lay down on the sandy beach and stared morosely over to Frances. She wasn't sure whether to laugh or weep for the pup.

Roger maneuvered the boat backward into the water, then hopped in, seating himself facing her on the other wooden bench.

"I found this old boat inside that shack that has not yet been torn down. It must have belonged to one of the farmers who owned property along Cedar Point. I imagine the Navy ran him out before he could properly collect everything. If I knew who it was, I'd get it back to him, but I like to think he'd be glad to know the Navy didn't toss it into a burn pile."

He bent over for one of two oars that lay on the bottom of the boat and began rowing in silence. The sound of the oar dipping into the river then coming up again to let water drip off it and back into the river was mesmerizing for Frances, particularly after a nice meal.

"The water is such a murky color," she observed, hugging her arms around her. Lillian had been right about the sweater. It was much colder on the water than it was on shore.

"Yes. There's a lot of silt in the water here that gets churned up, so it's not as blue as the Atlantic, but it's still beautiful to behold."

"It is," Frances agreed.

"Shall I take us around the lighthouse?" he asked.

She nodded sleepily despite the chill in the air, as Roger piloted them toward the crumbling structure.

The building was both more decrepit and more stately than Frances had realized from the shore. "Have you ever gone inside?" she asked.

"No. It would be very dangerous in there. It's impossible to know in what ways the tide and weather have battered her. Besides, it would seem...disrespectful...to intrude on her. She deserves her privacy."

Frances nodded as they rowed around the opposite side of the lighthouse, not visible from the shore. It was in even worse condition than the other side.

But it had stopped holding interest for her. How intriguing and unique Roger Douglas was. A hardened Marine Corps exterior with a soft interior, like an M&Ms candy.

CHAPTER 22

FRANCES WONDERED WHAT it was like to be a U.S. Marine. "You talked about the lighthouse being dangerous in its condition. Your work must be dangerous on a daily basis."

He shrugged. "Comes with the job. Catching criminals is a risky business. Although sometimes leadership is more dangerous than the criminals."

"What do you mean?"

Another shrug. "The higher up in leadership a Marine goes, the more he is concerned with what politicians think than what is best for the men. Sometimes political circumstances prevent you from doing your job. Or, at the least, instill fear for your future employment. Suppose that's true in all branches of the armed forces."

Roger seemed pensive about this.

Frances had seen enough Navy messages to understand this. "Have you been involved in political circumstances?"

His expression went from pensive to hardened. "Afraid I have. As you know, our job is protecting the base from anything that affects not just the base and its people, but our ability to win this war." Roger drew the oar up into the boat and laid it across his lap. Water dripped from the paddle onto the floor of the boat, but he didn't seem to notice.

"A few months ago, I arrested a hooligan who was breaking into a building site's storage shed. No doubt trying to steal equipment to sell somewhere so he could purchase a bottle of rotgut. I had no idea who the kid was, nor did I care. But it turns out he was a friend of the commandant's son. Instead of the boy going to jail, I received a lecture from my boss that I needed to watch myself, or I could have 'problems.' I also had some sort of 'note' added to my personnel file that I wasn't permitted to see."

How unfair. But so much of life during this war was callous. Sometimes you just had to cling to whatever mental life preserver you had and pray for an end to it all.

Roger wasn't done. "My boss wouldn't permit me to nab Kenny over at Solomons Island. Apparently, this would have also led to unidentified 'problems.' Why have Marines if they aren't permitted to do their jobs, even the simplest parts? As far as I know, Kenny isn't related to anyone important, so what made him untouchable?"

He grabbed the oar and thumped the paddle against the ledge of the boat. The bang of it caused Frances to jump. "Sorry, I shouldn't have done that," he said.

She ventured forth an opinion. "Is it possible that, in Kenny's case, every man is valuable in the fight so that his occasional unreliability is something the Marine Corps is willing to overlook?"

He shook his head. "It goes against everything we are trained to be. We are an elite fighting force. Discipline and loyalty are our most important traits. Kenny displays neither. I don't understand it. But I–" Roger stopped.

Frances waited, but Roger wasn't completing his sentence. "But you…?"

"But I can't let it go. The only solution is for Kenny to be forced to quit the Marines. He isn't deserving of the uniform."

Frances was alarmed. "What do you mean? Roger, please don't do anything foolish."

He grunted. "I would never do anything foolish. I must deserve the uniform, as well."

Roger was so committed as a Marine that Frances immediately believed that he wouldn't go so far as to…hurt…Kenny and thus tarnish his own brass buttons.

"But I need to expose Kenny to my leadership so that they can themselves witness how unfit he is for the Corps. Witness it such that it is impossible for them to cover it up. Kenny is so irresponsible and careless that it shouldn't be difficult to do."

Frances was in a terrible quandary. Although she didn't think he would do anything violent, she absolutely believed Roger intended to bring Kenny to heel to prevent him from doing something that would impact the war effort.

Was she going to have to warn Sophie to prevent her friend from being heartbroken when Kenny was eventually caught in a transgression?

Of course, that would just provide warning to Kenny. Or did justice need to prevail, no matter the cost?

CHAPTER 23

FRANCES VENTURED FORWARD again. "I'm sure that deep inside Kenny is as patriotic as we all are." She lightly touched Roger's knee. Immediately realizing how bold she had been, she quickly retracted her hand.

Roger stared at where Frances's hand had been and sighed. "I suppose I should warn him one more time that his actions are dangerous for himself and the country. Truly, though, I don't hate Kenny, I just want what's best for the Marine Corps and the country."

"I know."

He was gazing at her now with an intensity she couldn't quite understand. Frances had little time to contemplate it, for suddenly the boat was rocking from side to side. "Oh!" she squeaked involuntarily, grasping the bench beneath her with both hands to stay steady.

Cold water splashed into the boat, hitting her feet and causing her to shudder involuntarily.

"It's getting a little rough out here. Let's go back." Roger confidently steered the boat around and made his way back to shore. It wasn't a long distance, but it was very unsettling to be jostling back and forth as he maneuvered the little craft back to shore.

How did sailors manage the enormous swells, winds, and even hurricanes that they faced while at sea? Granted, their vessels were enormous and made of steel, but surely, they weren't immune to the effects of wind and tide.

Frances shuddered again at the thought.

"Are you okay?" Roger asked, reaching out a hand to touch her knee as she had done to him and just as quickly retracting it. He flushed red.

"I'm fine. Just happy we are almost back." She smiled to let him know she wasn't upset, although she was secretly pleased at his touch.

Back on shore, Gunney had made himself at home on their picnic blanket. He sat up and thumped his tail against it as the boat lodged into the sand. Roger jumped out, dragged the boat up onto the beach a little more, and offered Frances a hand out.

Together, they returned to the blanket. "Good boy," Roger said, reaching down to scratch Gunney behind the ears.

They sat, whereupon Gunney flopped back down and put his head in Frances's lap. She ran her hand along his muzzle, and he licked it.

"You really *are* a good boy."

"He's usually suspicious of strangers, but he can sense that I like and trust you, so he's fine." Roger reddened, so Frances chose to pretend she hadn't heard what he said.

"What makes the water suddenly get so rough?" she asked.

"Good question. On Lake Superior, the same thing happens. It can be perfectly calm one minute, then choppy the next, then back to calm right after that. During storm season, bad weather rolls in quickly from nowhere, and we can get very large waves. I'm glad we were close to shore when the water reared up. Frances, I-I need to talk to you."

"Of course." They were sitting so closely together that Frances could have easily rested her head on his shoulder. Instead, she pulled away to face him, tucking her bare feet under her in as ladylike a fashion as she could muster.

"I am involved in a project that may take me away for a while. If I go, I might not have much occasion to write to you as I will be very…busy. I-I just want you to know that it won't reflect my great esteem for you."

Every time he spoke to her like this, she found herself falling a little more for him.

He continued. "I know I have no right to ask it, but I hope that—if I should have to go away—that I might find you…available…upon my return."

His words were so unexpected and touching that Frances was speechless. It seemed everyone was waiting for someone to come home—even she was already anxiously awaiting the day her brother would return. It would be no great burden to wait for a man like Roger Douglas.

"I will wait for you."

Roger smiled. "I was hoping, but didn't really believe you would say those words. Come."

He stood and held out a hand to help her up. To Frances's surprise, Roger put his hands to either side of her face and lowered his lips to hers. The electricity of a thousand lightning bolts shot through her.

"This seals the deal," he murmured, placing his lips against her forehead.

Next to them, Gunney thumped his tail on the blanket and panted.

"That reminds me," Roger said, keeping an arm around her shoulders as he turned to face the dog. If—when—I go away, Gunney will need a friend. One of the guys in my barracks will take charge of his basic daily care, but I'd like to arrange permission for you to walk him, if you wouldn't mind doing so."

Frances nodded. "I will walk him as often as I can."

Roger visibly relaxed. He pulled her close, kissed the top of her head, then broke away.

"What is your favorite flower?" he asked, ricocheting off to another topic.

"I like lilacs, but they're impossible to find now. They only bloom in the spring."

"I'll find them." His expression was determined. "I hear there's a hothouse in the county, so maybe I can find them there. You should have lilacs."

Frances was so inordinately pleased by what had transpired between them she felt she might break out giggling like a child at any moment.

But her tranquility was broken in an instant by a booming male voice.

"What the hell are you two doing?" A man in dungarees, a long-sleeved, threadbare thermal shirt, boots caked with old mud, and wearing a wide-brimmed, straw hat emerged from the woods, carrying a shotgun.

Frances admired whatever training the U.S. Marines experienced, for Roger's first reaction was to step in front of Frances and put himself between her and the shotgun while maintaining utter calm. He also placed a hand on Gunney's head, saying quietly, "Stay." That seemed to also keep the dog in check.

"I'm stationed here and was just visiting this little beach with my girl. Who might you be, sir?"

"Not that it's any of yer business, but I'm Harold Johnson and this here's my property. And yer trespassing." The man spat on the ground and kept his shotgun trained on Roger.

Roger remained respectful. "I believe all of the property belongs to the U.S. Navy now."

"Yeah, well, I have rights to it. I've got thirty acres I'm still farming, and I have the Navy's signature on that. Least they could do given that they practically stole the land from the families who lived here."

"I wouldn't know about that. I was assigned here last year and found this nice fishing and picnicking spot. No signs telling me it's not Navy property."

"Don't get smart, boy." He squinted as if to get a better look at Roger. "You Navy or Marines?"

Roger stood tall. "U.S. Marines, security detachment at Patuxent River Naval Air Station."

The farmer harrumphed. "I've seen other uniforms down here where they don't belong, too. Gettin' tired of chasing you buzz cuts off. You keep coming back and I'm gonna do worse, just see if I don't."

With that subtle threat, the farmer stomped back off into the woods and out of sight.

The intrusion had completely broken the spell of their date.

CHAPTER 24

ROGER HAD BEEN away for more than four months on his secretive mission when Frances received one of her own.

"Yeoman Parker," Lt. Cmdr. Mackey barked as he passed by her desk one day. "Come to my office in ten minutes."

Frances jumped at the sound of his voice and turned to where Dottie was seated. Dottie shook her head before mouthing, "You'll be fine."

Frances stopped what she was doing and went to the bathroom to freshen up. It was pointless to sit down and be berated with a full bladder.

She arrived at Lt. Hall's desk at the appointed time and was, as usual, made to wait for several minutes. This time, though, Mackey didn't come barreling out of his office. Instead, Lt. Hall escorted Frances into his private office. The lieutenant then sat in a chair off to one side of the office, which was kept as messily as the outer sanctum was kept tidy. Mackey had stacks of folders and correspondence everywhere—on his desk, on a credenza behind him, and even propping up one of his desk's corners that was missing its leg. Interestingly, the walls were devoid of any pictures whatsoever.

Catching Frances's visual survey of his office,

Mackey barked at her again. "No judgment from you. I know where everything is."

Knowing how foolish it was to argue with him, Frances merely nodded and waited expectantly.

Mackey cleared his throat. "So, Lieutenant Hall here tells me your work is exemplary, and you certainly carry yourself in a manner befitting a trustworthy member of the U.S. Navy."

Frances had never received this level of praise from him before. She hoped this wasn't a precursor to bad news.

"As such, our department has been given an assignment, and I've decided to put you on it. Mind you, there are men in the department who might like to have this job, so I will expect the utmost discretion from you."

Lt. Hall was nodding, so apparently his assistant knew about whatever this assignment was.

"Yes, sir, how can I help?"

"I need you to go to Solomons Island."

<hr>

The bus deposited Frances and Dottie at the entrance to the amphibious base, then belched its way back up the Dowell Peninsula. Frances had convinced Mackey that she needed assistance on her mission, so he had granted permission for Dottie to accompany her.

"This place is so…primitive," Dottie observed. "I'm glad we were able to borrow some boots to wear. The mud here reminds me of a pig farm. What do we do next?"

Frances's instructions were simple yet might be impossible to execute. Mackey had told her that the commander of the air station, Capt. Stricker, had heard rumors of poor conditions at Solomons. Within the captain's own chain of command, he had been shut down when he attempted to find out details.

Concerned for what service men might be enduring but unable to go there himself lest his leadership discover his poking about, Stricker had sought advice from various members of Navy leadership at the air station.

It was Lt. Cmdr. Mackey who had suggested the plan that Stricker approved, which was to have someone pose as part of a USO tour advance team, seeking venues for shows at Solomons and at Patuxent River.

"They will be suspicious of you, of course," Mackey had said of the finalized plan. "But you will produce a letter from Capt. Stricker stating that he has welcomed your team in its effort to bring some sorely needed relief to our boys. It will be difficult for them to argue against such a proposal."

She had interrupted her supervisor's train of thought. "But sir, if the conditions are terrible there, why would they even let us aboard the base? Why not just tell us there is no possible location for a show and then turn us away?"

Mackey had gazed at her hard for several moments. "You'll figure out a way to charm them or terrorize them into doing what you want. From there, make sure you aren't escorted around so that you can traverse the base yourself and get an idea of conditions. As detailed a map layout as you can create of the buildings and their conditions will also be helpful to Capt. Stricker, as the maps he has are from the initial construction plan. Work has continued apace there with no real accountability. Any other details you can manage to ferret out about how the boys are doing there would be helpful. Capt. Stricker will then send over whatever aid he can, likely under cover of night by boat."

It was a shame Sophie had transferred out of the department. She would have been so much better for this assignment. Although given how much Lt. Hall despised Sophie, it likely would have never been offered to her under any circumstances.

Frances had never met Capt. Stricker, but she could only imagine how good a man he was, to undergo this much subterfuge to help the men who weren't even directly under his command.

Now she and Dottie stood at the ramshackle entry to the amphibious base. A disheveled-looking, uniformed guard exited his shack, eyeing them with interest. "Well, aren't you a couple of lookers? What can I do for you? Most everyone is away at Red Beach on training, so if you're looking for your boyfriends, or are interested in finding boyfriends, I'm afraid I can't let you in."

Dottie shuddered and stepped behind Frances, who ignored the man's comment. "We are with the USO and have been invited by Captain Aaron Stricker to seek out a good venue for putting on a show for all of the boys in Solomons and at Patuxent River." She held out a folded piece of paper that was the good captain's "invitation."

The guard's expression was incredulous as he came closer, took the sheet from her, and unfolded. "You're looking for that *here*?"

That was when Frances realized that the man had clearly not bathed in many days. He stank of sweat and grime. Was it an anomaly that he was permitted to keep himself in this slovenly fashion or where there something behind it?

Was Roger not bathing, as well?

The guard shrugged as he glanced at Frances's letter and handed it back to her. "Go ahead, ladies. And good luck. I'm certainly not escorting you around. Try not to get buried in mud and be careful of the convicts."

With that, he opened the gate to let them through and disappeared back inside his shack. Had it really been that easy?

⚍

Frances and Dottie spent the next several hours plodding through muck and mire as they surveyed the various buildings on the tiny base. Dottie had turned out to be a good choice to accompany Frances, as she had considerable skill in drawing. Soon she had mapped out the enlisted barracks, officers' quarters, an administration building, an air raid house, a tiny dispensary, a drill field, and a total of ten piers, in addition to other random structures. They also made their way along the beach facing Mill Creek and outlined the shoreline.

Everything was just as deplorable as Capt. Stricker had imagined it to be. Few buildings even had coats of paint on them. Even to the naked eye, it was obvious that they were haphazardly constructed. Many needed repair, either missing windows or with damaged roofs—no doubt from one of the storms that Roger had said could quickly arise on the water.

They also managed to ascertain that the water supply was inadequate, thus pipes were shut off several times a day to control usage.

The smell of sewage hung in the air no matter where they went. Attempts had been made at sidewalks and streets, but nearly everything was just mud and puddles, punctuated by patches of concrete.

The multitude of piers seemed well-made, although Frances could imagine that a different, more specialized construction team had likely built them. A Higgins boat, a landing craft with a drop-down ramp used to transport men quickly from a larger ship to shore, was moored to one of the piers.

She and Dottie were challenged several times, but Frances became quite skilled at airily proclaiming that she was there with the USO under Capt. Stricker's orders. Shockingly, other than to make suggestive remarks or glance at their mud-spattered legs, the men there provided no impediment.

It was as if they didn't realize there was a war on, and they should be greatly suspicious of two women parading around the grounds.

As they stood outside what Frances had ascertained as the brig, based on the heavy vertical bars inset against small openings in the building, she saw a man striding toward them from a distance.

"Uh oh," Dottie breathed from next to her, folding over her sketch pad so that what she had been drawing was not visible. "I think our luck has run out."

It was almost worse than having run out. "Hiya, ladies, what brings you to my house?" the man asked. He was rail thin, unshaven, and wore an Army uniform. What should have been closely cropped hair was growing out in strange patches.

"Your house?" Frances repeated as she tucked her own small notepad in her jacket pocket. What an odd turn of phrase.

He pointed at the brig. "Seems a strange place for you to be. You got a fella in there or something?"

"No, we are with the USO and—I'm sorry, are you the warden?" she asked.

"What? No sirree, I'm not. I'm waiting my turn to be held here. Name's Charlie. Charlie Skinner." The soldier laughed, exposing crowded teeth, some of which appeared to need serious dental work.

Now Frances was completely flummoxed. "I–I don't understand. You're waiting your turn?"

"Got caught pilfering some cigarettes. Guess they take that right seriously here. 'Cept there's no room in the brig right now, so I hafta wait until someone is released before my turn. 'Course, I'll likely be sent outta here to fight before that happens." His tone was breezy. Apparently, he was completely unconcerned about his looming prison sentence.

"Anyways, what's this about you being with the USO? Why would the USO want to perform in a swamp like this place?"

Frances repeated what had become a rehearsed speech. As with everyone else, Charlie took her story without question. "Seems to me the best place for your show would be on a stage on the beach. There's not a building here on base fit for entertainment."

With that, Charlie Skinner sauntered off, whistling until he stumbled into a small sinkhole. With a great deal of cursing, he pulled himself out and continued to parts unknown.

Frances turned to Dottie. "I think we've done as much as we can. We need to submit a report to Lieutenant Commander Mackey. Let's go see if the bus has returned for us."

She hoped Capt. Stricker would be pleased with her work.

CHAPTER 25

MACKEY HAD OFFERED rare praise for what Frances and Dottie had done. "Captain Stricker says he plans to write a letter of commendation for you both. Even said he might actually contact the USO to do a beach performance over there, if he can pull it off. Which means my idea might merit a promotion, hah!" Mackey snapped his fingers. His good mood lasted for weeks.

Despite Frances's successful mission and the frenetic activity in the administration building, time was dragging by.

Frances met some of the girls at the canteen one evening as a distraction. Contrary to Lt. Hall's admonitions, it was a safe, lively place. Verja Duke had easily come aboard the station to join Frances, Lillian, Sophie, and Dottie after working hours to listen to music and talk about their workdays. Other women from the barracks had also wandered in for fun, including Lt. Wallace and Maisie.

But Verja soon had everyone's attention, as she had had a letter from her husband, Walter, and was clearly bursting at the seams to share its contents. Even the quartet playing in one corner quieted down to listen to Verja.

She unfolded two pieces of paper that were scrawled on front and back. "He says that he only had five hours of training on his P-38 aircraft before he began flying combat missions with the 459th squadron. Can you imagine? I bet no one else could do that." Verja was flushed with pride, and Frances could hardly blame her.

Verja then began reading straight from his letter. "'We started operations primarily as escorts for bombers striking targets in Rangoon and Meiktila. But I've secured my first official victory. I shot down two enemy aircraft and, sweet darling, I received the Distinguished Flying Cross and have been promoted to captain. They tell me it's a rare thing for someone my age to achieve this. I'll be 23 soon, so I guess I'm not *that* young.'"

Everyone in the canteen burst into laughter at his modest observation about himself. "He deserves kisses from every dame in this place," Sophie shouted, to which all the women raised their glasses in a toast to the newly minted Captain Walter Francis Duke.

"But there's more," Verja said from her spot atop an old, scratched, gray metal swivel stool with a wood seat and a wide strip of metal for the back. They were far more comfortable than they appeared to be.

Most of the furniture in this "new" canteen looked as though it had been dragged out of someone's shed after being left there for decades. Not that it mattered, just having somewhere new to go within walking distance was marvelous.

Verja continued reading. "'I get a little scared

in the tough spots, but I am doing okay. I haven't even received a scratch yet. I have fifty-two missions completed and have also received the Air Medal. They give that one out for meritorious achievement while participating in aerial flight, but it's nothing. Out here, they are a dime a dozen."

More modesty that elicited laughter and whoops from the women in the canteen.

"And the rest is personal," Verja said, folding up the sheets and tucking them into her purse.

"Oh, sweetie, I bet it is," Sophie said with a wink.

Verja blushed furiously and shrank back on her stool.

Frances reached across the table and patted her hand. "What a wonderful husband you have."

There was no other discussion to be had, for the canteen door opened and in piled Roger, Billy, Kenny, and George.

"Ladies, your fellas are on leave!" Kenny pronounced loudly. "One at a time, no rushing, no crowding. There's plenty of Sergeant Campbell to go around."

Sophie squealed in delight and ran toward him, but at the last moment, she flung her outstretched arms around both Kenny and George.

Roger was glancing around until he saw Frances, then broke out in a beaming smile as he approached her.

He was back. And, even better, he seemed inordinately happy to see her.

"Frances Parker, may I speak to you in private?" he said, his tone very formal.

"Of course." She slid off her barstool and followed him outside.

⚓

Roger had managed to borrow a car again. "I thought we might go back to Cedar Point. It shouldn't get dark for at least an hour or two."

"What about your friends?" Frances asked, curious as to what was so important. "I imagine they are counting on you to drive them back to your barracks."

"Those knuckleheads can walk; they don't mind."

Roger drove back to the beach area where they had eaten their picnic lunch and taken a boat ride. The decaying lighthouse stood in the water just as Frances remembered her, faded yet vigilant.

Roger parked, got out, and came around to let Frances out of the car, an older model than what Sophie drove. It smelled of must and stale beer. "Let's walk along the beach," he said. "This time we don't have Gunney for protection, though, if the farmer decides to come back."

He took Frances's hand in his and led her along the water's edge. The sun was dipping in the sky to their left, creating a pretty palette of pinks and oranges along the horizon. She stopped to remove her shoes, carrying them in her free hand as she tucked her other hand back in his.

"I'm not afraid if I'm with you," Frances said. She sensed his chest broadening next to her.

He spoke quietly as they walked. It was always good policy to be cautious about your words, no matter how isolated you thought you were. "I've been leading some Army troops in training exercises at Solomons," he said, his voice barely audible. "They are destined for an important mission. I have experience in the type of training they need from my time at Guadalcanal and other places. The Marines understand certain… maneuvers…that the other branches don't. So, I was called in for it. Kenny, George, and Billy recently joined me to help."

Frances felt a catch in her throat. Had she been no more than yards away from him during her own mission? If he'd seen her there, her pretense would have disintegrated. But based on what she'd learned after sitting in on so many meetings, she knew exactly why he was training these men.

She was both relieved and surprised that he had been so close by. "Say no more, I understand completely."

Roger nodded. "I wasn't sure how to tell you without revealing anything."

"It's a constant topic in the administration building."

"Do you know when they might go?" he asked. "All I've heard is 'soon.'"

"They will probably head over in the next couple of weeks. Then it will depend on the weather. They say General Eisenhower smokes three to four packs of cigarettes a day, worrying about the exact date."

Roger cleared his throat. "That's all right then. Let's speak no more of it."

They were nearing the end of the beach, and

the tide appeared to be coming in. When they could no longer walk, Roger turned Frances to face him and dropped to one knee.

"I know we haven't known each other long, Frances, and in normal times, you might cast me off as an idiot. But these aren't normal times, and I am hoping that you would consider me as perhaps a guy who could eventually earn your respect and love. Would you do me the honor of marrying me?"

Frances was stupefied. This was the last thing she had expected. She hadn't known Roger Douglas for very long, but what she knew, she liked. He was warm, fun, and a perfect gentleman. He was also genuinely patriotic. Whether he remained in the Marine Corps or not, he surely had a bright, successful future ahead of him. There was just one thing…

"I want to say yes without reservation, but–" she began. His gaze upon her from his kneeling position was full of hope and anxiety, making her feel terrible for placing a condition on him.

"Yes? What? Anything," he said, taking her shoes from her other hand and dropping them to the ground so that he could have both of her hands in his.

Frances finished her thought in a rush before she lost her nerve under his intense scrutiny. "The great nurse, Florence Nightingale, rejected a suitor whom she had loved for something like seven years because she was worried that she would have no ability to be a good nurse if she were married. That society would frown upon her, and she would eventually have to take a traditional homemaker's role. I like my job with the WAVES—a lot of us girls do—and although I realize my position will likely be eliminated once the men come home, I do like having a useful occupation."

Roger slowly nodded. "I understand. My mother—whom you will meet—has always had a hard edge to her, and I've always thought it was because she has never felt very useful in life."

"If—when—we have children," Frances said, feeling heat creeping up her neck, "I would stop to raise them, of course. But until then, and particularly while you're off on missions, I don't want to stay at home staring at the draperies."

Roger broke out in a grin. "Then we have an accord, as the pirates would say. But unlike a pirate, I don't have much treasure. And so…" He dropped her hands to unbutton his shirt pocket and retrieve something.

It was a thin gold band with a tiny diamond on top, flanked by two small pearls. He held her left hand and slid it onto her ring finger. It fit perfectly.

"I know this isn't much, but it was all I could find at the pawn shop. I promise I will do something much better when the war is over. You will have a ring so stuffed with diamonds you'll hardly be able to hold your hand up."

Frances smiled, gazing down at the circle around her finger. She knew she would never want to wear anything else. "I don't care about that, as long as you come through the war safely."

Roger stood and wrapped her in his arms,

kissing her with a fervor that took her breath away. She knew she was now keeping secret from him her visit to Solomons. He no doubt had military secrets of his own.

Frances vowed to herself that once the war was over, she would tell him about it.

Roger broke away, placing a kiss on her forehead. "I will. I promise. Now, I'll have to return to Solomons soon, so what would you think about getting married this week?"

CHAPTER 26

ROGER WAS MIRACULOUSLY able to pull off a ceremony within a week, and their wedding day dawned gloriously, a sunny and warm Saturday in late April 1944. Kenny stood in as his best man, while Frances asked Sophie to be her maid of honor. George had agreed to care for Gunney for the next few days. Frances's parents had not had the resources to make the trip but had sent a gift—the silver teapot they had been given at their own wedding nearly thirty years earlier.

All four members of the wedding party wore their dress uniforms for the ceremony, and Frances carried a bundle of sunny yellow daffodils that Roger had managed to obtain. Her new husband seemed to be able to accomplish anything to which he set his mind.

They were married by John McHenry, one of the two chaplains at Saint Nicholas Chapel on base. It was a lovely church, originally started by Catholic Jesuits in the late 18th century, with the present building having been constructed at the turn of the 20th century. The Navy had taken it over last year and re-designated it the Base Station Chapel.

"Repeat after me," the minister intoned. "I,

Roger William Douglas, take you, Frances Evelyn Parker..."

McHenry stood in white robes before them, next to an enormous pulpit that had been recently donated to the chapel by the U.S. Naval Academy, which was performing its own chapel renovations. It, too, dated back to the early 1900s.

"*...to have and to hold from this day forward...*"

Even with such short notice, Frances's co-workers and some of the other WAVES in the barracks had thrown a simple bridal shower for her in the dining hall. Roger had declined his friends' attempts for a bachelor party.

"*...until death do us part in accordance with God's holy law...*"

Lt. Hall had even surprised her at the bridal shower by giving her a pair of white pillowcases with a "D" embroidered on the cuffs in cornflower blue.

"*Repeat after me. I, Frances Evelyn Parker, take you, Roger William Douglas...*"

"This color is a symbol of loyalty and trust," Lt. Hall had told her as Frances ran her hand over the design.

Frances was touched, especially given how quickly the lieutenant must have worked to have obtained them and then done the thread work.

"You may kiss the bride," McHenry said, closing his thick minister's book.

After the morning ceremony, the assembly of around fifty guests filed outside for an informal celebration with cake and champagne.

"I guess we'll both be brown baggers now, sweetheart," Roger said loudly for all to hear. "Capt. Nickerson says he will help me get quarters at the Cedar Point trailer park off base, so no more mess hall chow for us."

"Already taken care of, Douglas. Come see me for the key," Nickerson replied just as loudly, waving a brass key in the air.

If she were lucky, Frances would be neighbors with Verja.

Sophie had disappeared briefly from the outdoor gathering but reappeared shortly, driving her car, honking the horn as she approached where everyone still stood. She jumped out of the vehicle and saluted. "I'm your driver, here to escort you to your new quarters, Master Sergeant and Mrs. Douglas."

Walking through the assembly of cheering guests, Frances and Roger went to the car. Sophie returned to the driver's seat, while Roger ensured Frances was seated on the rear bench before going around to the other side and joining her.

Sophie slowly drove away while Frances waved at everyone through the open window. This was only going to be a five-minute drive, but it felt vitally important. As if she were being driven from one life into another.

Roger brought her attention back to him. "Now, Mrs. Douglas, I need to write a letter to my parents to let them know of our nuptials. We will plan to have them visit us when I return from mission. For now, though, I want you all to myself."

Frances blushed under his suggestive gaze. Yes, she was being driven to a completely new life.

CHAPTER 27

"SWEETHEART, WHAT'S WRONG?" Frances had awoken in fright over Roger's thrashing back and forth. She rose to one elbow and laid a hand on her new husband's shoulder.

"Huh? What? What?" Roger slowly came out of whatever nightmare he was having. "Sorry. I was just seeing—never mind. Nothing to worry about."

He patted her hand, shifted around under the coverlet so that he faced away from her, and returned to a fitful sleep.

This was the third time in the past few days he had had some sort of nightmare, and the third time he had dismissed it.

What demons controlled his dreams? Roger's work locally was relatively sedate, but she wondered about his service at Guadalcanal for six months in '42. Roger had made references to the taking of the series of islands in the British-controlled Solomon Islands in the Pacific as having been unexpectedly harsh.

Frances was certain his mind was taking him back to that six-month period.

Roger had been granted two weeks of leave after their wedding, and now was days from having to return to Solomons Island, Maryland, to continue beach landing training. It was so strange that he would literally be so close by—just a couple of miles as the crow flew—but they would have no physical contact with one another until he was done. Not only was he required to stay at the amphibious base for the nearly round-the-clock drilling he was conducting, but getting from the nearby island back to St. Mary's County was a protracted affair involving watermen ferries and hitched rides, or else—as she well knew—a very long drive up the St. Mary's County peninsula, through Charles and Prince George's County, and back down the Calvert peninsula.

Roger had spoken vaguely of his time at the Solomons amphibious base, mostly in terms of the local infrastructure not ready for the influx of thousands of soldiers descending upon it. They had no gym, no commissary, not even a chapel. Frances had bitten her tongue on her firsthand knowledge of it all.

"Almost as bad as the conditions at Guadalcanal," he'd said, "except no Japanese around every corner. The Japs fight like banshees, and they never surrender. At most, they will pretend to surrender, using it as cover to lob grenades at you. I've spent enough time in the Pacific to admit that I don't care to ever go back."

That was as much as he'd had to say on his time overseas. But his nightmares told a far more harrowing tale.

Frances had performed her own research on Guadalcanal. The campaign—called Operation

Watchtower—was the first major land offensive by Allied forces against the Japanese Empire. Conducted predominantly by U.S. Marines, the campaign had completely derailed Japanese expansion attempts in the Pacific.

The Japanese had had possession of a group of islands consisting of Guadalcanal, Tulagi, and Florida, but the Allied forces had swarmed them and forced their retreat, although not without considerable casualties and loss of ships and aircraft.

The Japanese were still a dangerous force, but they no longer had total control over that strategically important chain of islands that was serving as a base of operations for them to reach targets like Australia, Hawaii, and the U.S. West Coast. Another step closer to the war's end.

Roger seemed reticent to talk about his battle experiences, forcing Frances to infer much about what he had endured.

One day, he dropped an enormous duffle bag by the door. Had he carried this around with him everywhere overseas?

"I want to show you something. It means a lot to me." He went to his stuffed bag, knelt down to loosen the knot at the top of it, then dug around until he pulled out a black, zippered case about twelve inches square.

He brought it to where Frances sat at their tiny dining room table and set it before her. "Open it."

Curious, Frances lifted the case, which was scratched and embedded with dirt, and unzipped it. Both sides lay flat against the table, and the case's contents were remarkable.

Under sewn-in loops against completely unblemished, cushioned red damask fabric were a priest's tools. A crucifix, a round gold plate, a purple stole, a white napkin with a gold cross embroidered on it, a tiny brass communion cup, and a tiny vial of clear liquid.

Frances gently withdrew this vial. "Holy water," she said.

Roger nodded. "A priest had probably been administering communion to whomever wanted it, in addition to extreme unction."

She replaced the vial under its loop. "What happened to the priest?" she asked, not sure she wanted the answer.

Her husband shrugged. "I don't know. A lot of priests never go deep into the battlefield. This fellow followed the troops deep ashore. I'm guessing he was killed. It seemed disrespectful to leave this behind in enemy territory, so I took it."

Frances zipped up the case. "One day, when we have our own home, we will put this on the mantel to honor that priest."

Roger's smile of appreciation made her glow.

"Let me help you unpack." Frances put a hand to the duffel bag with the intent of picking through it for unwashed clothes. A new Wash-a-teria had opened in Lexington Park, and she was interested in trying it out. The facility charged by the hour, so she intended to get full use of an hour.

"No, there's no need to–" Roger had put an arm out to stop her, but Frances's hand had already found another box. This one was smaller than the priest's traveling communion kit.

She withdrew her hand with the flat box in it. It was slightly larger than her open right palm where it rested. "What's this?"

"Nothing," he mumbled.

The box had a hinged top and opened smoothly. Frances couldn't believe what lay inside.

"This is a medal," she said stupidly. Of course it was.

"It's nothing," Roger repeated.

The round bronze medal was attached to a pinned ribbon with three vertical stripes of navy, gold, and red on it. Frances fingered the bronze and turned it over. "You were awarded a Navy-Marine Corps medal. When did this happen? How did you earn it?"

For a third time, he tried to brush it off. "It was just a silly thing. Helped a few fellows escape from a hidden water trap that was set for us when we took the airfield on Guadalcanal. The men nearly drowned, but I swam them out. The brass thought it was noteworthy, but it wasn't anything any of them wouldn't have done for me."

Frances turned the medal back over and gently shut the box. "You never cease to surprise me with your bravery and your humility, Master Sergeant Douglas."

"Oh yeah?" Roger said, taking the duffel bag from her and searching around in it himself. "How about this for a surprise?" In his hand was a wilted bunch of wildflowers, tied together with string.

He frowned. "They looked much better this morning."

Frances smiled. "They are the most beautiful flowers I have ever seen in my life."

PART 5:
DIANE

Present Day

CHAPTER 28

FRANCES HAD MARRIED Roger Douglas. I found myself mentally cheering her for that. Yet I had so many questions, chief among them was the existence of Billy Alvey. Was this the same Billy Alvey who was my distant uncle? Although the name itself wasn't that unusual, it was certainly coincidental in the extreme. The Marine in Frances's journal just had to be my distant relative. Except…

I wasn't sure how many "greats" back Uncle Billy was. I just knew that he had worked the family tobacco farm and joined the Navy the moment Pearl Harbor had been bombed. By great fortune, he ended up back in his hometown. Perhaps his injury had landed him the fortuitous posting. Would the papers and photographs my family held give me more information about what had occurred at Pax River during that time?

I vaguely recalled that he had served overseas, as most service members had. I also knew that he had survived his time in the war, returning to start a large family, of which I was a distant relative today.

But if Uncle Billy had been in the Navy, that

couldn't be the Marine named Billy Alvey in Frances's journal.

I shut the diary and put it away again. It was time to get more answers.

I arrived unannounced at my aunt's house on the following morning, a Saturday. Aunt Poppy lived in Ridge, way south of the base. She had several acres left of what had been a family farm. Like so many others, it had been cut up and sold off in parcels over time, but she still had a private lot with an old, two-story brick home on it.

The house had several odd wings covered in white siding, designed by farmers, not architects.

"Well, as I live and breathe, what brings Diane to my house today?" she said as she opened her door to me. Aunt Poppy was around seventy years old, probably five feet tall, and ninety pounds soaking wet, but she had the endless energy of a bird pecking around for food all day long. She baked, cleaned, and volunteered her way through each and every waking minute. Her church loved her.

The aroma of baking wafted over me. "Hi, Auntie Poppy, that smells like your famous almond crescents." I stepped over the threshold and back several decades. This side of the family didn't believe in getting rid of anything. Any pictures, furniture, clocks, vases, or figurines that had been purchased generations ago were held, tended to like delicate orchids.

There were curio cabinets everywhere along walls smothered in old cabbage rose wallpaper. The cabinets displayed everything from baby spoons to crocheted doilies to porcelain wedding toppers. Many of them had tiny little cardboard signs propped next to them, with hand-written explanations such as "Caroline's tooth fairy box, 1968," or "John III's favorite pocket watch, ca. 1924."

It was both overwhelming and comforting to have that much family history surrounding me.

"Yes, Deacon Cole just picked them up for Mrs. Norris, who's been feeling poorly. I thought she might like a little treat. I'm also putting together a coffee cake. It's just about done; would you like a warm piece?" my aunt asked.

That didn't require a second offer. I cast my glance at another baked dish, blueberry cobbler, if I wasn't mistaken, cooling on the old white enameled, cast-iron stove she used. The old Magic Chef was enormous and full of drawers and burners. How it still operated decades and decades after it must have been new in the 1950s was a testament to how appliances were built then.

While we sat over cake and freshly brewed coffee in her kitchen, which was full of kitschy, country decor, I gave my aunt a modified reason for my visit. "I'm working on a History Hall for the base's administration building, and I've found some old ephemera related to some Marines who were on base, including a Navy-Marine Corps medal. I remember that Uncle Billy had earned one of those, and it got me to wondering what you might have on his time in the Navy."

Aunt Poppy shook her head as she sprinkled some artificial sweetener into her cup of coffee. "Honey, Uncle Billy was in the Marine Corps, not the Navy. Someone who owned a hardware store down here—it's long gone—had fought as a Marine in World War I. Billy admired the man, who had been gravely injured at the Battle of Belleau Wood yet returned and started a successful business, and Billy decided that only the Marine Corps would do for him."

I was stunned into silence.

Aunt Poppy sipped her coffee, then smacked her lips and frowned. She sprinkled yet more sugar substitute into her cup. "Billy was wounded at Midway in 1942 while defending *Yorktown* with anti-aircraft fire. He was responsible for taking down quite a few planes. He suffered burns before the ship was torpedoed. It must have been quite terrible, for he ended up losing a couple of fingers. He came home, and they stationed him in the Marine security detachment at Pax River. He was lucky they put him close to home." She sipped again and smiled, apparently satisfied now with her coffee.

I knew my jaw was hanging open, but I couldn't help it. "Are you serious?" was all I could manage.

Aunt Poppy looked at me curiously. "Of course. Why? What's the matter?"

"Um, I, er–nothing. I was just doing some research on the Marine security on base during

World War II. What a coincidence that Uncle Billy was one of them." I stuffed a piece of coffee cake in my mouth, hoping Aunt Poppy would accept that answer.

She did. "Do you want to see Uncle Billy's things?"

"I do. I can climb into the attic if his things are up there."

Aunt Poppy laughed. "Sweetie, I pulled all the family memorabilia out of the attic a long time ago. Well, except for that hideous old fox stole that belonged to Aunt Erma. She was, let's see… my second cousin twice removed. Or maybe she was three times removed? Never saw much of her, so I don't remember." Aunt Poppy rose from the table and indicated that I should follow her.

I had never heard of Aunt Erma and had no idea what her relationship might have been to me. I grabbed the last piece of my coffee cake between finger and thumb and popped it into my mouth before getting up from the table to trail after Aunt Poppy.

My aunt led me down the right-hand hallway of her house. There were two hallways that jutted out the back of the house, each ending at its own covered porch. I think the original point had been two wings to provide bedrooms, one wing for children and the other wing for family visitors, but I wasn't entirely certain.

Most of the bedrooms still existed, all to the right side of the hallway with a bank of windows to the left, although there was a new-ish bathroom or alcove cut out here and there.

Aunt Poppy led me to the last room in the hallway.

She opened the door into a room full of more curio cabinets and pictures hanging from the walls. "Here we go. I call this the 'War Room.'"

As I closely inspected the room, I saw that, indeed, it was chock-full of ribbons, medals, folded flags, knives, official papers, framed photos of people in uniform, and other military memorabilia.

Aunt Poppy stepped over to a green trunk on the floor and pointed down. It was one of few things too large to be contained within a curio or bolted to the wall.

"This is Uncle Billy's trunk. It went all the way to the Pacific and back with nary a scratch on it. Have a look."

I knelt in front of it and stroked the top. What a piece of history. There was no lock on it, so I gently lifted the hinged lid.

Aunt Poppy stepped back, as though to give me space to pay reverence to the trunk.

Inside were a variety of items, presumably all Uncle Billy's. I gently picked up and examined each one in turn. There were his discharge papers from the Marine Corps, all typed in that peculiar typing font of the time. Inside a yellowed cardboard sleeve was a photo of my distant uncle in his uniform, shorn, smooth-faced, and staring intently at the camera.

It reminded me of those I'd seen in the Morgue.

Even more interesting was a one-page front and back, handwritten letter to Uncle Billy, dated July 1942 and signed by "Rosie." This must be the same woman Frances had mentioned in her diary. The page was fragile, appearing to have been creased and re-creased many times. I felt like a voyeur reading the love letter from a girl to her deployed boyfriend.

I glanced up at Aunt Poppy, who shook her head. "No, he didn't marry her. She found someone else before he returned home. He married Helene Pippin and was reasonably happy, but I think this girl, Rosie, was the 'one who got away,' as they say."

Reasonably happy. I suppose I was reasonably happy, too, and that wasn't such a bad place to be, was it?

And I was now positive that my uncle was the same Billy Alvey whom Frances had known. How ironic.

Also in the trunk were a pitted helmet, a compass with a cracked top, a dented canteen with a fitted cup on it, and a thin, sealed envelope marked *"Open only in case the Marines need me again."* World War II GIs were known for their ability to find humor in almost any dire situation. I smiled to think of Uncle Billy writing a missive as to why he should be excused from ever seeing combat again.

It was all fascinating.

And then, buried beneath it all, instead of resting on top of everything, it lay gleaming at me. Uncle Billy's Navy Marine-Corps medal.

Not in a presentation box, as was the medal in the Morgue, but pinned to an old piece of black velvet. Pinned next to it was a scrap of paper. "William Alvey, 1942."

I hesitated to reach in for it.

"I think he got it for the number of enemy planes he shot down at Midway despite being under fire himself," Poppy said without my having to ask. "Such bravery."

I nodded, still hesitant.

I finally pulled out the piece of cloth to look at the medal more closely. It looked just like the one I had held in the Morgue.

"Do you mind?" I asked Aunt Poppy, holding it up to her and miming removal of the medal from the cloth.

She gestured to me to go ahead.

Taking a deep breath, I unpinned the medal. The clasp was small, and it was difficult to undo, but with some minor maneuvering, I did so.

I laid the cloth onto the ground next to me, where it rested amid everything else I had pulled from the trunk. I spread the medal out in my left hand and closed my fingers around it.

I swear I almost felt a psychic connection to the past. It both electrified and terrified me and made me eager to jump back into Frances's story.

Saying my goodbyes to Aunt Poppy, who insisted that I not leave without a heavy helping of coffee cake in a plastic container, I slid into the driver's seat of my SUV and drove north on Route 235, eager to get back to my office and the diary. The base gate was always open and manned, so I knew I could get access to my building, yet few people would be working on a weekend in the administration building, and I would hopefully be alone.

Just to prove me wrong, there were barriers at the gate preventing any admittance while some sort of security breach was being investigated.

Such things happened all the time. Typically, it was some lunkhead trying to get on base to use shopping or gym facilities without having the privilege to do so, but sometimes they did catch someone unsavory trying to breach Navy security.

I sighed, turned around at the next light, and headed home. Gus was coming by this afternoon, anyway. I may as well play in my garden and think until then.

<hr>

I loved the times when I could play in the dirt—moving bulbs around, setting up decorative flowerpots on my front porch, and coming up with yearly color schemes for my annuals. This year, I was working in purple, which looked great against the backdrop of the house's cedar siding, which was painted a dark chocolate brown. I tried to spend time working on it every Saturday in good weather.

By noon, I was weeding in and around the flourishing pansies I had planted near my porch back in the spring. I owned a small rambler near Pax River's Gate Three. It was very basic, with three small bedrooms, a modest kitchen, and a one-car garage, but I was proud of having saved enough to put a substantial down payment on it, which made my monthly payments very reasonable.

What I loved most about my little house, though, was the very cute front porch that ran the length of it, with a classic-looking white rail enclosing it. I had picked up a couple of cheerful yellow wood rockers, and they made a sweet addition to it.

I managed my ever-rotating flower garden to complement my porch, pulling some of the plants from the beds for transplanting into large round pots for an explosion of colors on the porch.

It was soothing to me to sit on the porch with an audiobook in my ears and a pitcher of sweet tea at my fingertips, distracted by butterflies and hummingbirds and never actually listening to more than a few minutes' worth while rocking for hours at a time.

I knew people who loved vegetable gardening—"Diane, there's nothing like having food that is the product of your own labor"—but I was never drawn to that type of gardening. All the neat rows which must be ever purged of invading insects, plus the endless harvesting…it seemed too much like toiling and not enough enjoying.

It made me realize how spoiled I was, imagining Frances Parker—and everyone on the home front—and their victory gardens, which were crucial for survival, while I dallied about with floral color palettes.

I rocked back on my knees and glanced down at my watch. Four hours had passed, and Gus was scheduled to come over in about an hour. I rose from what I was doing to clean up, change into fresh clothes, and pull out a pitcher of sweet tea I had made that morning.

I was sitting in one of my rockers when Gus pulled up in his silver Toyota sedan. Ever the practical one, he always drove a reliable vehicle in a muted color that would have the best resale value. Not that he often sold cars. He had once told me that he typically drove cars until parts were falling off as he puttered down the highway.

I smiled as I considered that image.

"Hey," he said as he climbed onto the porch and sat on the other rocker. He eyed the pitcher on the small wicker table between the chairs. "That looks good."

Gus was clean-shaven, as always, and wearing his customary polo shirt, shorts, and grubby tennis shoes. It was almost an off-duty uniform for him. He certainly wore the uniform well with his lean but muscular build.

He poured himself a glass, and we talked idly of the week at work. Any two people who work at Pax River, no matter if on opposite ends of the base, had plenty in common to discuss.

I let him chat about his week, then dropped my important news. "I had an experience in the Morgue this week."

Gus knew all about my History Hall project and the time I was spending on collecting ephemera from it.

"Did you find Moses's tablets?" He laughed at his own joke.

But I was too tense to enjoy his humor. "No."

I briefly told him about my discovery of the

print shop behind the bookcases, the mysterious photos and documents, Frances Parker's diary, and the connection to my Uncle Billy.

At this, he was interested, leaning forward in his chair, the glass forgotten as he held it on his knee. "What great finds. Don't let Facilities know about the print shop, though. They'll wall it up like it's a plague town."

I laughed, totally agreeing with his assessment. Everyone knew not to trifle with the Facilities people.

But he just as quickly lost interest when I said, "I think there may be a mystery to solve between the mysterious documents and the pages of Frances's diary. In fact, I–"

His eye roll annoyed me. "A mystery?" he said. "Like in one of those books you're always listening to on your tablet? Diane, you've been doing tons of research back to that time period and beyond. You've probably let yourself get over-tired and are taking some of this way too seriously." He removed the glass from his knee, set it on the table, then turned his chair sideways to face me. "Hell, Di, I'm a programmer, and when I get on a roll, it's easy for me to go way too deep in what I'm doing, gold-plating my projects and adding in way more functionality than what the customer has requested. I seriously doubt there is a 'mystery' in what you're reading and discovering. It's all just 'history.'"

"Okay," I said, noncommittally, my stomach plunging in disappointment.

His sermon over, Gus returned to his tea and

discussing inanities, as though I'd never brought up unusual findings.

I found a strange emotion rising to the surface of my soul, though. I was irritated, yes, but soaring over that was something else. Longing. A desire to continue discovering what may or may not have happened all those decades ago. And to have my partner support me.

I realized that I wouldn't be able to discuss it ever again with Gus. I'd have to keep it between Mary and me. Although I didn't like the idea of being secretive with him, I also couldn't bear the thought of not following through on what I had discovered thus far.

I was certain there was much more to learn. As it turned out, I was right.

CHAPTER 29

ON MONDAY MORNING, I reached my office and spent a few quiet hours researching D-Day and Pax River's involvement in it. There was no question to me that the invasion at Normandy was what Frances and Roger were involved in, in their different ways.

My fingers flew over my keyboard as I dug up online sources. I learned that there had been a training area built near Solomons specifically for invasion training, but it had been dismantled long ago. I beheld a photo that made me laugh out loud, for it was clearly taken by a farmer from his front porch as the troops "invaded" his land.

I printed the photo. It might make a fun addition to the History Hall.

Interestingly, the Marines were involved, but only in training troops. Apparently, the largely unseasoned Marines, part of the Army's 2nd Infantry Division at the 1918 Battle of Belleau Wood in France, had fought ferociously under horrific conditions that included mustard gas, endless machine gun fire, and a lack of supplies. However, the Marines had bested the Germans and decisively took the area, greatly improving Allied morale. Although the Army had also suffered great casualties in the battle, it was the Marines who were covered in glory, and the Army didn't want a repeat of that. So, the Marines were invited to help out with training at Solomons and then to climb into the back seat and be quiet while the Army managed invasions.

No doubt that activity would have been kept very secret by everyone involved, even Capt. Stricker was in the dark—yet it had seemed simple enough for Frances to make her way onto the base. No wonder Roger was so upset by Kenny's seeming carelessness about the activities there.

But perhaps Roger had taken it a step further…

My research so occupied me that I didn't have time to return to Frances's diary before I needed to leave the office at four o'clock to get ready for another impromptu date with Gus. I had agreed to meet him at Bollywood Masala, a local Indian restaurant, for dinner, as he had said he had a surprise for me. As Bollywood was casual, I just wore a loose, long-sleeved floral print dress and ankle boots.

I had a hankering for Chicken Korma and was happy when the steaming hot plate, along with a bowl of fragrant Basmati rice and a basket of decadent garlic-butter Naan bread, was set before me. "So, what's the surprise?" I asked.

"I got a promotion to Senior Technology Scientist," Gus said triumphantly, and I have to say, it was the most emotional I had ever seen him. He's usually like a duck on the water. Maybe there's some furious paddling going on beneath, but he's barely moving above the waterline.

"That...that's great," I said, still astounded by his animation. "I hope you got a great raise to go with it."

"I did. But I'm mostly glad for the new work I'll be doing on a new classified weapons system project. It's going to be a challenge. Although I can't really talk about it."

Of course not. Every base employee had to be cautious about what they said, even to close friends and others who also worked on base. I was secretly glad, as it saved me from a long conversation about computer coding.

"Perhaps we should go on a getaway vacation to celebrate," I suggested.

"Yeah, okay. Maybe a weekend in New York City?"

"Well, I was thinking something...bigger. What about a cruise? I've never been on one."

Gus looked at me as though I had just handed him a piece of three-day-old fish. "A cruise? Why would you want to do that?"

I was stunned. "What? I don't understand. Cruises are supposed to be fun. You know, getting away from it all, lying around on a Caribbean beach, swimming with dolphins, eating your own body's weight in food in five days, and drinking frou-frou drinks with umbrellas in them."

I can only describe Gus's expression as aghast. "Why would I want to float around for a week with two thousand other people? What if I get on the ship and don't like it? I'm stuck and can't go anywhere else. We can go to Solomons Island, and you can have all the frou-frou drinks you want."

Once more, I was utterly deflated by his dismissal of an idea of mine. "Okay."

"So, let's plan a trip to the Big Apple. We can find out what's playing on Broadway."

I didn't respond. After his reaction to the cruise suggestion, I was absolutely not going to New York. Was I being childish and petulant? Maybe, but I thought he had reacted insensitively to me.

I was quiet the rest of the meal, although Gus didn't notice as he was busy talking about how he was going to outfit his new office. It was a plum to transition from a cubicle to an office, so I did understand his excitement.

I drifted into my own thoughts as he prattled on about his new position. My cluttered musings ran the gamut from my History Hall research to my growing dissatisfaction with Gus to what else I might learn from Frances. I hardly heard a word my boyfriend said.

Once Gus ran out of steam and had paid the check, we stood to leave the restaurant. In that moment, I had the painful realization that I wasn't particularly in love with Gus. I liked him a lot, but he wasn't very…stimulating.

I felt a pang of guilt over that traitorous thought. He was nice, he was intelligent, and he was generous. So I didn't feel fireworks when he kissed me, and we weren't lockstep in our interests…so what? Perhaps that was the trade-off one made for stability.

But if that were true, why were my insides

gnawing at me? Why couldn't I just be *satisfied* with him?

Maybe I was spending too much time with Frances in her romantic marriage with the handsome and rugged Roger Douglas.

CHAPTER 30

THE REST OF the week was so busy with impromptu meetings and the hosting of Maryland legislators that I had no time to return to Frances's world.

On the following weekend, I found myself on a group date with Gus, Mary, her boyfriend, Brad, and another couple, Jinx and Maggie Jarrett, having agreed to join in for a trip over the Thomas Johnson Bridge to Annmarie Garden in Solomons for one of their periodic outdoor markets. The markets were always popular and featured unique artisans from the area, in addition to being an opportunity to wander through the Garden's open-air displays.

We all meandered through the outdoor sculpture garden that wound its way through calm and serene woods. Gus walked alongside me, hands in his jacket pockets, while in front of, us Mary had her arm entwined in Brad's.

It made me both sad and irritated at the same time to know that Gus was vehemently opposed to "PDAs," or public displays of affection.

We all stopped at an interesting stone grouping. It was sort of like a mini-Stonehenge, except with stone seating arranged in a semicircle in front of it. For contemplation, I guess.

As the six of us relaxed in front of this sculpture, Brad began rambling about his latest inventions and patent applications.

Like any quintessential mad scientist, Mary's boyfriend dressed acceptably but frequently wore a stained t-shirt or mismatched socks. He was exceedingly intelligent but awkward in group settings.

Hence, he merely began enumerating his projects with no preamble, so that the rest of us had to catch up with what he was talking about. He made no mention of his recent unemployment, but who could blame him?

Jinx, whose real name was actually Carl, was the complete opposite of Brad. Where Brad was tall and handsome in his own oblivious way, Jinx was short and balding. His looks were compounded by a wrinkled forehead earned by too many days on sunny tennis courts.

Yet Jinx, ironically nicknamed because he was famously known for being ridiculously lucky in life, had a magnetic personality, which probably had more to do with his "luck" than anything else.

He'd had a successful career in the Navy as a pilot, retired very young, and five years ago started his own defense contracting company, which of course had also been successful. All of this by the age of forty-six. Now he was running for county commissioner and by all accounts, stood a very good chance of winning.

It was through his contracting work that Jinx had met Gus, who had done some sort of consulting for Jinx. The two had both discovered a mutual love for competitive tennis despite their fifteen-year age difference and regularly met up at one of the local county parks to slam the ball around on the court.

Jinx's wife, Maggie, spent her time raising their three perfect children. As in, they were the politest, most well-behaved, perfectly groomed set of three kids all under the age of twelve that I had ever seen. Maggie was a veritable kid whisperer.

"…and it will be something homeowners can use to transform the look of their homes with the click of a button," Brad was saying, swiping some of his shaggy, curling hair out of his eyes.

I had only been paying partial attention to Brad but noted that Jinx sat up straight in full alert. "Wait, what?" Jinx asked. "What does this device do?"

"It paints murals, photographs, and the like. It's sort of like a printer for your wall."

Gus laughed. "Aren't murals what rich people do to their walls? They want hand-painted work they can show off to their friends, don't they?"

Brad's expression was pained. "Yes. But with this, you don't have to be rich to have that hand-painted look."

"Isn't wallpaper simpler and less messy?" Maggie asked. "I know you can buy wallpaper in the form of murals. That seems easier than spray painting a wall inside your home."

"It's just one of many patents I've applied for," Brad said through gritted teeth. "One of them will end up a million-dollar idea."

Jinx, though, was thoughtful. "It could be a

new home option for builders. With the price of a new home, the entry hall receives a mural painting of the buyer's choice."

Brad shot Jinx a look of gratitude. "Yes."

"Good luck, man. If you can make it work, that's great."

Mary seemed relieved that the conversation had ended with a bit of support for her boyfriend. Once again, I began doubting myself. Gus certainly didn't float from one invention to the next, tinkering away for days at a time, oblivious to the outside world. Wasn't I lucky compared to Mary?

"So, who's tired of looking at these blank stone walls?" Jinx asked. "What's next?"

I had an idea. "I'd like to go see where the Solomons amphibious base was."

"The what?" Maggie asked.

"There used to be a base on Solomons that was used to train soldiers for the invasions at Normandy and other places during World War II. I don't know what might be left of it, but I'd like to see it."

"Why the interest in that?" she questioned.

"I'm working on a History Hall project for my building and want to include a wall panel on it. It was a very important part of the Allied success in finishing off the war. The Solomons base was referred to as the 'Cradle of Invasion.'"

Gus frowned. "Does this have anything to do with your Nancy Drew sleuthing?" he asked quietly.

"No," I said flatly.

"I don't think there's anything left of that but

a road marker," Jinx said. "I'm pretty sure it was located where Calvert Marina is now, at the end of Dowell Road past Annmarie Gardens. They dismantled the base at the end of World War II."

I didn't realize Jinx knew so much about local history but given his illustrious naval past as well as his interest in local politics, it shouldn't have surprised me.

"Eh, I'd rather go get a beer," Gus said, standing.

"Yeah, me too." Brad also rose.

"I'd like to go see the amphibious base remains," Mary said, frowning.

"Go ahead. We'll meet you guys at the Ruddy Duck in an hour." Brad was surprisingly uncurious about it. I guess a passion for science didn't necessarily translate into a passion for history.

And I knew Gus didn't care about it because it was linked to my presumably overtired fantasies.

Jinx, Maggie, Mary, and I jumped into Jinx's spacious SUV and headed down Dowell Road, coming upon a historical road marker near the end. Jinx pulled off the road and we all clambered out of the vehicle to read it.

This nation's first naval amphibious training base was established here at Solomons, where between 1942 and 1945 some 68,000 Sailors, Marines, Coast Guardsmen, and Soldiers were trained. They formed the major components of the amphibious forces that landed at Guadalcanal, North Africa,

Sicily, and Normandy. Ironically, some of those trained here at Solomons, Maryland, participated in the landings in the Solomon Islands in the Pacific.

This lined up with Frances's diary. I grabbed my cell phone out of my purse and did some quick research. "Solomon Islands in the Pacific is named for the Biblical King Solomon, whereas our Solomons Island is named for Captain Isaac Solomon, who started an oyster cannery on the island, which basically founded the village. The cannery failed, but Solomons Island lives on."

We got back into Jinx's SUV and drove into the marina, but it was quickly evident that there was no trace of the old base remaining, although we did find a bronze sculpture entitled "On Watch," that commemorated the amphibious base.

"I think we should visit the Calvert Marine Museum," Jinx suggested. "I bet they have good historical information there."

Off we went to the museum, which was located just a couple of miles away in the opposite direction.

As a group, we got completely distracted by the museum's displays, including visits with the stingrays and the museum's two resident otters in their indoor-outdoor tanks.

Finally, though, we found an exhibit on the amphibious base which included photos— several of which I had already found—and a map of the practice operations.

I pointed to the map. "So, in their trial runs,

they didn't invade here at Solomons, they set off from here," I said with realization. "They piloted around to Drum Point and Cove Point for their practice invasions, which can't be far away by boat."

Jinx seemed just as excited about this as I was. "If Solomons was rural back then, imagine what Drum and Cove Points were like. It must have looked like Armageddon occurring to those poor farmers. Wow."

"I appreciate your enthusiasm," I said. I really did.

"Yeah, this stuff is fascinating. I've got relatives in my past who fought in the war—who doesn't, right?—and it makes you feel sort of…connected to them in a weird way."

I couldn't have agreed more.

During the ride back to meet Gus and Brad at Ruddy Duck, Mary whispered quietly to me in the back seat, "I have an idea. Why don't I visit you at work next week, and you can show me the print shop? I'll be quiet as a lamb about it, I promise."

I nodded. It felt odd to think that Mary would "share" in what was happening, but I would look forward to Mary's visit the rest of the weekend.

However, Sunday turned into one of the worst days of my life.

CHAPTER 31

GUS CALLED WHILE I was re-framing some old family photos that I intended to put in a collage pattern on the wall leading to my bedroom. I guess all the History Hall work was impacting my own personal activities.

He wanted to stop by with something important. I really just wanted to finish my home project but agreed to see him.

I soon wished I hadn't done so.

He arrived in business attire: charcoal gray dress pants, checked sport jacket, white collar shirt, and a muted, dusky blue tie. He had taken care with his black Oxfords, which were burnished to a deep glow.

As for me, I was in sweatpants and a t-shirt, my usual style for housework. I had at least put on a little makeup and had brushed my hair out before the doorbell rang.

Tobias hissed at Gus from atop the refrigerator, one of his favorite napping places, but quickly lost interest in Gus's presence and curled back up for more sleep.

Gus made no comment regarding the photos and frames spread all over my dining room table and sat down in my living room rocking chair.

My living room was cozy, and I loved it.

The room contained a small leather loveseat, a recliner, and a rocking chair over a thrift store-purchased carpet that lay atop old cherry hardwood flooring. On the long wall across from the furniture were built-in shelves containing books and decor, plus an open space for my television in the middle of it.

I sat on the loveseat and curled my legs under me. "Everything okay?" I asked.

"Yeah." Gus glanced up at the ceiling and rocked back and forth, as if gathering his thoughts. He finally stopped rocking and faced me. "So, I was thinking that it probably makes sense for us to go ahead and get married. In fact—" He reached into his sports jacket, pulled out a key, and held it up. "—I thought you'd like to have a key to my house. We should exchange keys."

Exchange keys? *This* was his marriage proposal? Wasn't a marriage supposed to be the merging together of two lives? This was more like neighbors agreeing to keep an eye on each other's places.

I admit I just sat there, shocked, my mouth hanging open.

"Do you have a ring for me?" I finally asked.

"Oh, I was thinking you could go to the jewelers, pick something out, and I'll go get it. Or you could buy it and I'll reimburse you. That would be easier."

I remained stupefied. Perhaps I had never been proposed to before, but I was quite certain it was supposed to be a little more romantic than this.

"We need to work out a few things, of course," Gus said, placing the key on the arm of his chair. "Pets, children, vacations, that sort of thing."

I knew I could strike "cruise" from the list of potential honeymoons.

As if reading my mind, Gus said, "Maybe we can delay going to New York and make it a honeymoon trip."

No, no, no, my brain screamed.

I had many thoughts in the moment, none of them good. But the strangest, most overwhelming thought was, *Why isn't he more like Roger Douglas?*

What a crazy notion, comparing my boyfriend to someone from the distant past.

But what did it say that I was making that comparison? That a Marine from another era held more appeal to me than the living, breathing man across from me?

Gus was looking at me expectantly. I swallowed, knowing what I had to do and dreading it.

"I don't think it's a good idea," I said. There it was, I'd said it. It had to get easier from here.

"What? Going to New York? That's fine, it was just a suggestion. We could go somewhere else. Boston, Newport. Maybe down south, Charleston or Savannah."

I shook my head. "No, the marriage itself isn't a good idea. I–I don't want to marry you, Gus."

Now it was his turn to be shocked. "I don't understand. Why not?"

"I just don't think you are the right person for me." How could he argue that?

"That's ridiculous," was his response. "We've

been together for over two years. The natural outcome of our relationship is marriage. I think I know what the problem is."

"You do?" I was gripping the arm of the loveseat, worried that maybe he had gained powers of extra-sensory perception.

"You're just stressed over that stupid History Hall project you're working on. It's made you a little off-balance lately. Once you're finished with it, you'll be fine."

I swear, that statement made me so mad that if someone had waved a red cape in front of me in that moment, I would have charged it.

"No, Gus, I'm not refusing you because of my workload. I'm refusing because I don't want to marry *you*. We aren't well-suited to one another. I need someone who is more affectionate and less…robotic."

I couldn't be much clearer than that.

He shook his head. "It's my fault. I wasn't keeping an eye on things like I should have been. We should have been taking more vacations. You've been overwrought by too much on your plate. Let's plan to go to New York soon, and then we can take a longer honeymoon vacation somewhere else."

Did he realize how condescending he sounded? "Gus, you're not listening to me at all. I'm not overworked and I'm not overwrought." Overwrought? What ridiculous phrasing. "I simply do not want to get married. To you. Now or ever." I said it with as much finality as I could muster.

Something I said must have penetrated his

brain because he became quiet and still. His typically bland expression took on a hard edge as he contemplated me, as if seeing me for the first time.

His gaze glittered to such an extent that it made me nervous. "You realize that with my promotion, I am really on my way now. My salary will keep climbing, and I could have provided you with a very comfortable life. But you've ruined that for yourself. You'll just be nobody now."

This was the second time in a very short period that I had witnessed Gus show actual emotion. It was unnerving.

"I don't want to get married just to be comfortable," I said. "I have my own home and career for that. I want to be *happy* when I get married."

"Some career. Writing a newsletter and making fancy event signs."

"I like my work. I make a difference in employees' lives."

Gus rolled his eyes. "Yeah, planes will roll off the flight line much faster with Diane Alvey on the case, scribbling out articles on when the swimming pool is opening and what movie is playing at Center Stage."

He was being downright mean to me, but I mentally shrugged. I had broken up with him, so at some level, I decided to endure the berating without comment. Perhaps once Gus had gotten it all off his chest, he would be calmer.

But he wasn't done. "Is there someone else?"

I shook my head. "As I said, this is purely my

decision that we simply aren't right for each other."

"I think there's someone else. What about Patrick Barry? You're awfully friendly with him."

"What?" I said in disbelief. "He's my *boss*. You're grasping, Gus."

"Well, there must be some good reason why you're acting deranged. I just have to figure out what it is."

"There's nothing to figure out. I—"

Gus rose abruptly, grabbing his key and tucking it back into his jacket pocket. He strode to the door and walked out without a word and without even shutting the door behind him.

I rose and went to close the door, ensuring that I turned the deadbolt as Gus spun his tires in my driveway like a petulant teenager. I certainly hadn't expected his visit to end up that way. Strangely, I felt a mingled sense of guilt and relief at his departure. Although I would never say he *deserved* what I had just done to him, I was also glad I had stood firm and ended it. I had hurt him, but in the long run, he deserved someone who loved him without reservation. That was never going to be me.

I wondered if Gus would be back to once again convince me that the problem was my own.

For his part, Tobias jumped down from the refrigerator and came to me, weaving in and around my ankles while mewling at me. Apparently, I was too wrapped up in myself and not paying attention to the far more important matter of my cat's dinner service.

With Tobias's needs met by a can of tuna morsels and unsure what to do with myself in the aftermath of the breakup, I did the only thing I could do in the moment. I finished my framing project.

CHAPTER 32

I WOKE UP MONDAY morning with my stomach somersaulting. Had I done the right thing in breaking it off with Gus?

I showered and got ready, then made a pot of coffee. I typically drank a cup at home and then took an insulated cup's worth for the drive.

While sitting at the kitchen counter, I once more contemplated what had happened with Gus. Downing another gulp of black fuel, I came to the same conclusion. *You were never going to be happy with him.*

Which led me to the second conclusion. My upset stomach wasn't because I missed him, but because I felt guilty.

Enough of that.

I headed into work, where Patrick hailed me down as I walked past his office.

"Just wanted an update on where you are with the History Hall," he said. "What's your estimated date for showing me the mock-ups?"

I hadn't picked up Frances's diary in days and needed to finish it, to see what sort of information it was going to provide and how it was going to impact the World War II story of the hall.

"A month from now?" I ventured.

He nodded. "Let's go downstairs, and you can at least show me how you generally plan to lay it out."

I dropped my purse off in my desk, then followed Patrick downstairs. I showed him my basic thoughts as we stood inside the reception area. Ellen Pope, the receptionist, was already answering call after call, completely ignoring us. Mondays were busy in the administration building. It's like everyone rejuvenated after a weekend away. Or else they were worrying through problems over the weekend and wanted to fix things first thing at the start of the workweek.

"I want to start with this wall to the left next to the entry as a starting place, giving a quick history lesson on how a tribe of the Piscataway nation lived here before giving Jesuit missionary Father Andrew White two thousand acres of land. Then I'll use a space to discuss Mattapany, the home that Governor Charles Calvert built for his wife in the 1660s, and Susquehanna, an estate with a sordid history involving the murder of three royal customs collectors in the 17th century. Then I will talk about how this area was known as Centerville until 1878 and was predominantly farmland, being renamed to Jarboesville in 1878 after its first postmaster, Jefferson Jarboe. I have a photo of him we can put right here." I pointed to yet another location on the wall.

Patrick frowned. "Mattapany is now Quarters A. I don't think I know Susquehanna."

"No," I said. "Henry Ford dismantled

Susquehanna and had it reconstructed at his Greenfield Village open-air museum in Dearborn, Michigan."

Patrick's jaw hung open. "I didn't know that."

I nodded and continued. "Then I'd like to move to the next wall, which is a nice length, to discuss the Navy's acquisition of 6,400 acres from the businesses and farmers here."

Patrick nodded. "It's going to be hard to tell that story without talking about how the Navy bullied everyone and gave them less than a year to vacate."

I sighed. "I know. But the story must be told. Then I will spend a few paragraphs talking about the actual construction of the air station, the influx of building contractors, and the introduction of WAVES onto the base. I've even found an old typewriter that I can use to create a World War II office vignette. I'll also discuss how the surrounding area coped with it all, to include how the Navy solved its housing crisis."

I pointed to another location. "I think it will also be important to highlight important people from Pax River's history." I intended for my spread on Frances Parker Douglas to be a surprise for my boss.

I stepped to the other side of the reception area. "Picking up the story on this wall, I want to talk about the 'Cradle of Invasion,' and how this was a critical point from where the D-Day invasion was practiced. Natalie has a great background photo for this. Then out here—" I stepped into the hallway with Patrick right behind me. I pointed to the left wall and started walking slowly down the hallway. "Out here, I want to show how the test pilot school was developed and discuss some of the famous astronauts that came through here. John Glenn, Alan Shepard, Scott Carpenter, and so forth. I'll also include photos of the long line of commanding officers on the base. Further down the hall, I'll show the important aircraft and technologies that have been developed and tested here on base."

Patrick continued to nod. "There's a mural of them at the Pax River Naval Air Museum."

"Yes," I replied. "That mural used to hang in the officer's club that was demolished in 2018. I might see if I can get a photo of it to include here." I moved away from where we stood.

"Then, coming around to the opposite hallway wall, I'll discuss the challenges the base has had over the years. Base realignments, closure threats, terrorist threats, Congressional maneuverings. You know, all the rotten stuff. Plus, some good stuff, such as how the community has developed a close relationship with the base and how it has handled base expansions subsequent to World War II. Then I'll end up with a big feature on the future of the base. I'm thinking of doing some comparative statistics of the base from 1943 versus today, as well as including photos of experimental aircraft and defense-related technologies."

I had brought us back to the reception area. "Anyway, that's the general plan. I'm sure it will modify somewhat as I create it. Particularly as I pick and choose which past employees should be highlighted." I wondered whether I could—

or should—make the diary itself part of the display.

"This looks great, Diane. Can't wait to see Natalie's artistic work on this." Patrick turned to go back upstairs, and I was about to follow him when, to my utter shock, Sophie Russell stepped out of 1943 and in through the entry door.

CHAPTER 33

I BLINKED FOR SEVERAL seconds and reached for the wall for support. How was this possible?

"I'm here as promised," she said.

That's when I realized it was just Mary entering the building. She had her platinum curls tied up in a red bandana with white polka dots and wore a blue denim long-sleeved shirt over casual pants. She looked like a World War II "We can do it!" poster.

"What's the matter?" she asked, rushing to me as I exhaled loudly.

"Nothing. I—you look like—um, I must tell you that, that, you very closely resemble Frances's description of her friend, Sophie Russell. Especially with what you're wearing today. You look you've just stepped out of an airplane factory."

Mary giggled. "What can I say? I'm a classic."

She struck a pose and pouted her lips, which were painted a cherry red, flawlessly matching her bandana.

I stood upright. "Okay, Rosie the Riveter. Come on upstairs."

I introduced her to Patrick as we went past his

office. Fortunately, he didn't question why my friend was there.

We stopped in my office so I could get the key to the Morgue. I had intended to just grab the key from my desk and go, but Mary plopped herself in the chair across from my desk.

"So, you're not going to believe this," she said without preamble.

I shut the door to my office and sat behind my desk. "What's up?"

"It's Brad. He did it. He just called me to tell me that he obtained his patent for that wall painting device. He's going to offer it to some national printer companies. Can you believe it?"

I was speechless for the second time in a few days. "Wow. Well, congratulations to him."

Mary leaned back. "Just imagine. Brad might be rich one day soon."

"Anything is possible. He's lucky to have you. While we are on this topic of our men, I need to tell you something..."

I outlined my breakup with Gus.

Her mouth formed an "O" as I told her about his reaction. "Well, you seem okay with your decision. And Gus really was sort of boring. No offense. But...you don't think he will retaliate against you, do you?" she asked.

"No offense taken, and no, I don't think he has the sort of personality. He's mad, but he's more likely to take it out on an inanimate object. Like a tennis racket. I'm sure Jinx will get an earful the next time they're together." It was amusing to think of Gus bashing an expensive tennis racket against a tennis court fence post. Poor Jinx.

"Well, we are having opposite days, aren't we?" Mary said, rising. "Okay, I'm dying to see the old print shop."

Grabbing a flashlight from a desk drawer, I walked her down to the Morgue and locked the door behind us.

With Mary's help, I went through the process of removing the shelves and the items on them, then pulled open the wall, taking a moment to show her how the diary had been lodged in the wall.

"Holy cow," Mary said, stepping into the old room, which was just as frozen in time as it had been when I first found it. "This is remarkable. Truly a find."

She helped me hide the print shop again, then we went to the ephemera box.

"Is this where the diary is?" she asked.

"No, I keep that in my office." I reverently pulled out the items for her to examine. Mary held the Navy-Marine Corps medal in her hand. "I feel like I'm in a museum right now. A special one. And you—" she glanced up at me "—you are the curator, with a responsibility for telling the story. So, are you done reading Frances's journal?"

"Embarrassingly, no, there's been so much going on that I temporarily put it aside."

Mary shook her head. "Snap to it, woman! There's a mystery to solve, remember?"

I smiled. "You're right."

"I'll run down to Center Stage theater and grab us some coffee. I know how much you like your peppermint mochas. When I get back, you should have Frances's story all figured out."

As soon as Mary left the building, I settled back down to Frances's writings.

PART 6:
FRANCES

June 1944

CHAPTER 34

"DID YOU HEAR? Bell Motor Company has a 1942 Chevrolet Fleetline in its showroom, never driven. Let's go take a look at it." Sophie stood on Frances's stoop, holding up the key to her government-issued car late one afternoon.

Taking a ride to town wasn't a proper use of the vehicle, but life was so mind-numbing these days that Frances readily agreed. She was grinding her way through her daily routine in the administration building. The chaotic days were followed by lonely evenings in her marital trailer, doing things like inventing exotic menus she would cook when rationing was done, writing letters to her husband in hopes that they might eventually reach him, and applying needle and thread to repairing clothing, in hopes that they might make them last another season.

The only relief consisted in sporadic letters from her beloved. She was glad she knew he was safe, or else the lack of contact would have driven her insane by now.

Frances kept his letters stored under her mattress, tied with a hair ribbon. Overly sentimental, she knew, but there was a pleasure to be had in retiring each night to withdraw the growing stack, untying it, and re-reading one or more of them.

The postmarks on his letters came from locations such as Baltimore, Detroit, and Washington, D.C. Roger had been very careful in his correspondence not to reveal anything too sensitive and had clearly extended that secrecy to having the letters posted and re-posted by acquaintances across the country so that their origination was indecipherable.

Reading between the lines, she knew that Roger continued having an exasperating time of training the troops under his care. Although he was ably assisted by many of his fellow Marines from the air station, some of his exasperation came from Kenny, who continued to behave like, well, Kenny. And Kenny seemed to be needling poor George every chance he got.

The Army troops Roger led were miserable, and some amused themselves with petty—and sometimes larger—crimes. As Frances already knew from her clandestine mission to Solomons, there was no adequate jail on the base for holding the miscreants, so arrestees were permitted to wander around until such time that they were brought to trial.

Poor Roger.

But if Frances was interpreting some of Roger's cleverly written words correctly, even worse was that he was receiving distressing orders from his superiors. He offered no detail on it, and she hoped the orders wouldn't result in anything dangerous for her husband.

Frances sometimes thought that the home

front had similarities to the war front—days of endless boredom punctuated by moments of sheer terror. The terror at home occurred when bulletins were issued regarding Allied casualties in a specific location, causing people to fret over whether a husband, son, cousin, or other relative was among their number.

Getting accurate casualty reports was so difficult. They were agonizing for both those who thought a loved one had died who, in actuality, had not, as well as for those who thought their beloved was safe, only to find out later that he had been killed in action.

Thank God, she didn't have to worry about reports from the Pacific or European theaters with Roger's name on them. Which meant everything and yet nothing to her, given that she still scanned for her brother's name and shared her relief that she didn't see it whenever she corresponded with her parents.

Yes, taking a ride to Leonardtown, the place where the dealership had been relocated after being evicted from its original location on now-government property, was just the thing to shake off Frances's malaise in Roger's absence.

She and Sophie sought out Lillian and Dottie at the barracks to join them. Dottie was out—no doubt with Ira Reed—but Lillian enthusiastically hopped into the back seat of the car.

"We are going to be murdered if we get caught at this," she said, throwing back her snood-covered head in laughter before opening her clasp purse and pulling out a shiny new tube of lipstick. "Look, girls, Regimental Red," Lillian said. She removed the cap and twisted up the richly dyed stick. "Maisie managed to get a dozen tubes. It's the latest Helena Rubenstein color." Lillian applied it ostentatiously to her lips. It was rare to see Lillian carefree and not in total, reserved possession of herself. She was likely as bored as Frances, who joined her friend in laughter.

"Very classy," Sophie observed after a quick glance at the back seat. "I've got to make my own appointment with good ol' Maisie."

But Frances was much more concerned with where they were headed than with their barracks. "To think that we are excited to see a two-year-old car. But I bet it's far nicer than this poor old bumbling bug, which has seen better days. What year do you think this is, Sophie? A 1929?" Not that Frances cared. It had been the car in which she'd had her first date with Roger, as well as the vehicle in which she had been driven away from her wedding at St. Nicholas Chapel.

"Probably. But it doesn't matter, we can have a grand ol' time no matter how old the bug is. Remember, it's like Mae West said, 'Well-behaved women do not make history.'" Sophie turned the key, and the car roared to life. Sophie guided the car sedately off the base, then stomped on the gas once they were on the relatively quiet country roads toward Leonardtown. The sedan initially lurched forward but eventually engaged in response to Sophie's heavy foot.

To Frances's surprise, there must have been a lot of bored people in the county, for there was a crowd out to see the glossy, army-green Fleetline sedan, which the dealership had driven into the middle of the town square so that onlookers could more easily ogle at it.

"Isn't she a beaut?" Sophie breathed. "Imagine driving that instead of this old hearse."

They climbed out of Sophie's car and joined the other onlookers. A salesman stood by the driver's side door, extolling the vehicle's virtues.

"This 1942 Fleetline is a Special Deluxe Coupe. She's got a 216 cubic inch inline-six Blue Flame engine. At ninety horsepower, she can easily reach speeds of eighty miles per hour. Note her smooth curves and stainless-steel trim."

Except for the tires, the metal trim work, and the split front windshield, the entire car was the same olive color, down to the large round hubcaps covering the centers of the tires. There were "oohs" of admiration in the audience, which consisted of men, women, and children. In fact, the atmosphere was so festive it was as if the car was a prize-winning bull at the county fair.

The salesman opened the car door to further boast about the Fleetline's interior. "Note the luxurious cloth bench seats and the metal dash accented with a simulated burl woodgrain. Why, that dash is so sparkling you'll need to purchase a sunshade for the hood to protect you from the glare!"

There was a smattering of appreciative laughter. Frances couldn't imagine owning *any* car, much less worrying about dash glare.

"Don't worry, don't worry, friends, everyone

will have an opportunity to sit in the front seat and experience this fine piece of machinery before she goes to her final destination. She's got a radio with a built-in speaker, as well as an ashtray on the right side of the dash. You'll notice the clock integrated into the glove compartment door. The clock will last seven days on a single winding, so you don't have to constantly attend to it. Have a look."

At that, he stepped aside from the car and let people individually slide into either the driver or passenger side to experience the feel of the car. Frances observed that hope seemed to be attached to each person who exited the vehicle, as if they had just touched their own futures.

The salesman clearly noticed it, too. "One day soon, this type of car will be back on the assembly line for anyone to purchase. And what a grand day it will be. Come back to Bell Motor Company when that happens, and we will get you seated behind the wheel of the best car at the best price."

A farmer in coveralls and caked work boots said loudly, "My people have been buying from the Bells for twenty years now. Not likely that we'll be going anywhere else."

The salesman beamed. "And we thank you for that, Mr. Abell. Make sure you get something new for your wife when the war is over, she deserves something nice for putting up with someone as cantankerous as you are."

The townspeople, including the farmer, laughed at that.

The salesman turned serious again. "Meanwhile, as all of you are well aware, there hasn't been a new car off the line since February 1942, as we are all doing our part for the war effort. But that doesn't mean there wasn't a stockpile of about a half million cars that dealerships were authorized to ration out for sale to essential drivers, both civilian and military. This particularly gorgeous lady is destined for such a driver, but I can't reveal who it is." He let that statement hang in the air.

Next to Frances, Sophie squealed. "Maybe it's for someone famous," she said.

"Here in the backwoods of Maryland?" Lillian replied. "Are you aware of Dinah Shore or Marlene Dietrich stopping here on their USO tours? Honestly, Soph. Besides, the color suggests it is intended for military use."

Sophie rolled her eyes. "You never know what can happen. Who would have thought we'd ever have a Fleetliner sitting here before us in the first place?"

Now it was Lillian's turn to roll her eyes.

"Who wants to take a turn sitting inside?" Frances said to distract them. The crowd was beginning to thin out, so they were able to get much closer to the car. As they waited, Frances noticed the marquee for the new movie theatre Sophie had mentioned. She wondered how much tickets cost, but immediately forgot about it as it was now their turn to experience the Fleetliner.

As a trio, they slid in, Sophie and Lillian in the front and Frances in the rear.

The car must have been stored lovingly under blankets in a building, for it was in brand new, immaculate condition. The seats, which smelled reminiscent of Cashmere Bouquet, that perennially popular fragrance by Colgate, were finely stitched and smooth—no rips with stuffing poking out of it like in Sophie's military car.

Not that she had cause for complaint. Both she and Roger had benefitted greatly from that car.

Perhaps the storage facility had been full of dust, for Sophie started coughing, gently at first and then building to a crescendo. Her face grew scarlet beneath her blonde hair as she worked to catch her breath.

"You okay?" Lillian asked her from the driver's seat. Frances reached a hand over the seat to rest on Sophie's left shoulder.

Sophie nodded, her closed fist to her lips as the coughing finally subsided. She shook her head. "Sorry, I don't know what that was about. Something in this car, I guess. I think I'm tired now. Can we go back to the base?"

"Sure," Frances said. "Can we stop by the general store in Lexington Park first? I want to buy some seeds for the new garden I've started behind my trailer."

"Only if you promise to come help the garden at the barracks once you have it in order," Lillian said. "It looks like an abandoned town from the Old West without you there tending it. I think everyone is tired of playing farmer in addition to working endless hours for the war."

So true. Frances leaned back against the luxuriously stitched seat a final time. The war had dragged on for far too long, as had the sacrifices made by every American citizen. Surely good times were coming.

Her fanciful dream was shattered by the boom of an explosion.

Although Frances, Sophie, and Lillian jumped out of the car to run for cover, it was obvious that the other townspeople were unconcerned.

"Just the ordnance testing in Newtowne Neck," a woman with a toddler in her arms told them. "Nothing to worry about. Goes on all the time."

How had the country reached a place where a mother was unconcerned for her child's safety during the detonation of explosives?

"We've got a history of strange doings in St. Mary's County," the woman continued, likely in response to Frances's incredulous expression. "Why, we're home to Moll Dyer, dead now nearly two hundred and fifty years."

Sophie perked up at this. "Was she a gangster's girlfriend?"

Lillian snorted. "Sophie, there weren't gangsters in the seventeenth century. I'm sure Moll was short for Molly or Martha."

The mother nodded and switched her now-sleeping child to her other hip. "She was a witch. Legends say she was responsible for some crop failures and disease that ran through the county. Locals chased her from her home, and she died on a rock in the woods. The rock has never been found."

"Ooh," Sophie said. "Wouldn't that be a wonderful movie plot? A witch who flies to Germany and ruins all of Hitler's crops and gives him smallpox!"

CHAPTER 35

BUNDLES OF NEWSPAPERS crowing about the Allied victory had been dropped off all over the base, and nearly everyone had a copy in his or her hands.

Stars and Stripes
June 7, 1944
ALLIES DRIVING INTO FRANCE
Opposition Less Than Expected;
Troops Are 10 Miles In

The front page included a map showing where the invasion had taken place the previous day, although Frances had already known that they were crossing the English Channel into Normandy.

Armadas of Allied Planes Hammer Nazi Targets! one article boasted.

Armada Moves Within Firing Range of French Coast! proclaimed another.

She flipped the paper over without opening it. A tiny article on the back page caught Frances's eye.

JAP DESTROYERS SUNK IN PACIFIC
Nazis Fear Blow from East Next

The Allies may have had a great victory, but it wasn't over yet. Thus, Roger wasn't going to be finished with his troop training here anytime soon.

She sighed.

There was little time to consider it, though, for Lt. Hall came to her desk with an instruction.

"Captain Stricker wishes to have a memorandum created to be distributed to all station personnel." Lt. Hall dropped two photo negatives and a sheet of onionskin on Frances's desk. It was covered in tight, cramped writing. Frances lifted each of the negatives up toward the light so she could see them. One picture was of President Roosevelt, the other was of a P-38 Mustang.

Verja had said the P-38 was the plane her husband was flying.

"He doesn't want it to lag too far behind *Stars and Stripes*, so it needs to be done right away. After approval, we will need copies run out of the print shop."

Frances sat down at her typewriter, rolled in a sheet of paper, and got to work, starting by counting the characters in the title, aligning the type guide to the center of the page, and counting backward for half the characters before striking the keys.

A MIGHTY ENDEAVOR HAS BEEN WON!

June 7, 1944

Attention Sailors, WAVES, and other workers aboard Patuxent River Naval Air Station!

As many of you may know, yesterday saw the tremendous victory of our troops during their invasion of Normandy. It took time for accurate reports to be released, as the news media outlets were suspicious of it being a German trick.

But the Allied forces have been triumphant...

The memorandum went on to praise the air station's involvement in the victory.

Once she had finished her typing, Frances quickly turned the platen knob to enable the feed roller to push the sheet of paper up and out of the typewriter. She presented it to Lt. Hall, along with the original missive by the base commander, to have her work checked.

Lt. Hall nodded. "Go straight to Yeoman Blake so he can typeset it and get copies off the press by lunchtime."

Frances hurried to obey the order, telling Blake what was required.

"Can you help me with this print job?" His apron was already smeared with black ink early in the day, an indication that he was very busy. "I'll need you to do this one start to finish if it's going to be done by noon."

Frances had never managed an entire print job by herself but grabbed another apron from a hook on the back of the door to the print shop and got to work, performing the tedious work of setting type for a page-long memorandum to go out to all personnel.

Occupied with getting her task done in time, the time flew until Dottie rapped on the door frame. "I'm headed out to the canteen to meet Ira for some lunch. See you in a bit."

Frances glanced at the wall clock, which showed that it was just past noon. How had three hours passed so quickly?

Completely absorbed in the work, she felt no hunger and continued working to print as many copies of the flyer as she could and put the freshly printed sheets on every available space to dry.

"Good work, Yeoman," Lt. Hall said later, when they had been bundled up and given to a courier to distribute around the base. "Lieutenant Commander Mackey will be pleased, and so will Captain Stricker."

Frances glowed at the words. It felt like she was finally becoming a valuable asset to the Navy.

She had little time to contemplate it, though, for at two o'clock, the building's loudspeaker crackled on and then boomed with an announcement.

"ALL HANDS. REAR ADMIRAL JOHN TOWERS IS ARRIVING AT PATUXENT RIVER NAVAL AIR STATION THIS AFTERNOON AT FOUR O'CLOCK AND INTENDS ON SPENDING TIME HERE WHILE HE REVIEWS ACTIVITIES ON STATION AND AT NEARBY LOCATIONS. THE UPSTAIRS

ADMINISTRATIVE OFFICES WILL BE COMMANDEERED FOR USE BY THE ADMIRAL AND HIS STAFF. WORKERS CURRENTLY IN THESE SPACES ARE TO BE ABSORBED DOWNSTAIRS OR IN OTHER LOCATIONS."

Rear Adm. Towers, Chief of the Bureau of Aeronautics, had been the one to request approval to begin construction at Patuxent River, so he was an exceedingly important visitor.

Just like that, Frances's life was turned upside down. In a mad dash, everyone in the Nursery packed up their desks and looked for accommodations elsewhere. Lt. Cmdr. Mackey attempted to bring order to the situation, but it was nearly impossible. He did at least secure help in moving furniture and equipment, although he did so by getting permission to drag in Marine security guards to perform the work, none of whom were happy about it.

Yet, within a couple of hours, Frances was seated at her desk in a downstairs hallway, along with Dottie and many others from the Nursery. At least the hallway was wide enough to accommodate them and still permit passage past them.

Lt. Hall waved everyone off early to return to their quarters. Frances folded the Stars and Stripes paper, which was just a few thin pages, and slid it into her handbag to finish perusing later.

She stopped in at the telephone office to see Lillian, who sat before a large bank of wires and plugs. Two other women also sat behind similar machines. Lillian was removing her headphones and smoothing back her hair.

"Have plans tonight?" Frances asked her friend, who whirled around on her stool and frowned at seeing Frances there. The other women glanced back over their shoulders at Frances, then turned back to answering calls and patching them through to their respective recipients by plugging wires into holes marked with indecipherable numbers and letters over them.

Lillian unplugged her headphones from the unit and tossed them onto the small ledge that protruded from her switchboard. "How did you get in?" she said without a greeting.

Frances shrugged, taken aback by the response. "I walked in. The door wasn't locked."

"How long have you been standing there?" Lillian seemed agitated.

"Perhaps two seconds. Whatever is wrong with you?"

Lillian visibly calmed. "Nothing. Sorry. I guess it has been a long day. You asked about plans. Want to drop by the canteen for a while together?"

"Exactly what I was thinking," Frances said. "You probably heard the announcement that Admiral Towers is on his way down. Haven't seen him yet, but we were chased out and have set up camp in a hallway downstairs. I'm just beat from the day's events. A beer and some music would be just the thing to relax me. Plus, I hear the canteen is featuring crab soup today."

When Dottie had returned from lunch, she

had raved about the thick, tomato-based soup, which was full of tender, locally-caught meat.

"Sounds wonderfully sudsy," Lillian said, slipping off her stool and waving goodbye to the other two operators in the room and tucking her arm inside Frances's for the walk to the canteen.

Two hours later, completely sated on bottles of Ballantine's, crocks of surprisingly delicious soup, and the sounds of brass music playing on repeat in their heads, Frances and Lillian parted ways in front of the WAVES barracks. Once ensconced into her trailer, Frances opened and smoothed out the copy of Stars and Stripes atop her small dining table. The interior of the paper contained a special message from President Roosevelt's wife, Eleanor. It was intended as an encouragement to Americans to keep going, fighting, as the war pushed into what was a turning tide. One piece of it was dramatically striking to Frances.

> *The time is here, and in this country, we live in safety and comfort and wait for victory. It is difficult to make life seem real. It is hard to believe that the beaches of France, which we once knew, are now places from which, in days to come, boys in hospitals over here will tell us that they have returned. They may never go beyond the water or the beach, but all their lives, perhaps, they will bear the marks of this day. At that, they will be fortunate, for many others won't return.*

Frances sent up a quick prayer for her brother. *God, please, let Freddy return from whatever hospital, beach, or battlefield he might be on. And let everyone around me see their loved ones home safe.*

The First Lady's message inspired her to write a letter to her brother. She wrote at length on a wide range of topics—her job, her WAVE friends, and, of course, her marriage to Roger. How embarrassing that she hadn't written to Freddy straight away after the wedding.

She was just getting to the part about learning how to operate printing equipment when she heard an insistent rapping at her door.

Frances put down her pen and answered it. Verja stood there, her face streaked with tears.

CHAPTER 36

"HE'S GONE," VERJA said, trembling at the bottom of the two metal steps that led to the door.

"Oh, my dear," Frances responded, ushering the other woman up the steps and into the trailer, then wrapping her in a hug.

Verja broke away, pulling an embroidered pink handkerchief from her purse and dabbing her eyes with it.

"Two men in dress uniforms and white gloves showed up here; one carried a large envelope, and the other had a flag. I knew, I *knew*, Frances, why they had arrived, and I just screamed at them to go away and slammed the door before they even got a word in. I thought–I thought–" Verja stopped to blow her nose. "I thought that if they weren't able to speak, it wouldn't be true."

Frances breathed heavily. This story was so common, but it didn't make it any less terrible each time it happened. "He didn't...suffer?"

Verja shook her head. "I don't think so. He knew he was coming home, just as we were all anticipating his return. He and his squadron had been given one last assignment to sweep the western edge of the Burma valley. He lost sight of his wingman, radioed it in, and went in search of him. The wingman eventually returned to base, but Walter never did, as several Japanese Zeros that had been lying in wait went after him. Walter got three of them before going down himself. In the P-38 he named for me."

Frances hardly knew what to say. "And tomorrow is supposed to be Duke Day in town to celebrate his homecoming. How awful for those who love him."

"Yes, everyone who knew him loved him." Verja sniffed back a tear. "Colonel Duke, his father, was the chairman for the event, which was to coincide with the county's fifth war bond campaign. The colonel refuses to leave his bedroom now."

"Oh, my dear," Frances repeated, hugging her friend again while her own thoughts skittered through her head.

God, thank You for keeping Roger healthy and whole. And nearby.

Verja broke away, clearly intent on talking. "He wrote to me every week without fail, did you know that? Sometimes I wondered if he wrote from inside his cockpit."

What a devoted man Walter Duke was.

"His squadron referred to him as the 'dragon with the sharpest claws.' I'm told that he destroyed 119 enemy aircraft between March and May of this year. My husband is a hero." Verja attempted a smile, which quivered on her face. "I am supposed to be receiving all his medals. He apparently has many that I don't know about—a distinguished flying cross, a

Purple Heart, I don't remember the others. I can't believe he didn't tell me about them."

Just like Roger, hiding his valor away so as not to seem pompous.

How this war spun people's lives around in dizzying circles. All one could do was pray, breathe deeply, and hope not to see anyone familiar on a casualty report.

CHAPTER 37

FRANCES SPENT THE next days in emotional conflict, both overjoyed with the rest of the country over the successful D-Day landing and devastated over Verja's loss.

But another event soon took her mind off both happiness and sadness, replacing them with unexpected irritation.

As Sophie dropped her off from work one day—an occurrence that was becoming more frequent these days, Frances was embarrassed to admit—she saw an old, faded blue Ford roadster sitting in her driveway.

"That better not be the Navy coming to visit you!" Sophie had blurted, echoing Frances's own sinking thoughts.

Frances stepped out of the government car and waved Sophie off, determined to face whatever this was on her own.

Exiting from the car were an older couple, both tall and elegantly dressed. In fact, the woman, whose gray-streaked dark hair was swept up and set in place with enameled hairpins, wore a fox stole around her shoulders over a chocolate and black striped dress, which seemed odd in the middle of summer.

As Sophie drove off more slowly than she had

ever driven in her life, looking back over her shoulder, the man called out, "Are you Frances Douglas?"

Who were these people?

"Yes. I don't believe I've had the pleasure…"

The man, whose faded blond hair was thinning and swept over to one side, approached, shook her hand vigorously, then grabbed her in a quick bear hug before releasing her. "I am Arthur Douglas, and this is my wife, Genevieve. We are Roger's parents. Welcome to the family, my girl."

Genevieve Douglas extended her hand as though she expected Frances to kiss it. "Arthur, really, so uncouth," the woman said before addressing Frances. "And it is Zhan-vee-ev."

She pronounced it in the French manner, as opposed to how any normal American would say it, Jen-eh-veev. Frances's neck prickled at the pretentious new mother-in-law she had inherited.

"We received Roger's missive that he got married," Zhan-vee-ev said. "We are quite shocked that he would do so without even informing us that he had a fiancée. Or a steady girl, even. Did you two get married because you were in a troubled way?"

Roger's mother glanced pointedly at Frances's midsection as Arthur stared up toward a passing cloud, apparently chastened into silence.

Frances was mortified by the implication. "Of course not. We were married because we wished to be. It happened quickly because Roger didn't want to wait, and I agreed with him."

Her mortification was quickly replaced with irritation. Why were they here?

Mrs. Douglas arched an eyebrow. "Will you be inviting us into your little home?" She nodded toward the trailer.

Roger had spoken little about his parents, and it was easy to understand why. Although he hadn't told her that his family was seemingly well off.

Frances walked up the two steps to her new home and placed the key into the lock, feeling that irritation build as she pushed the door open and walked in to hold it open for her new in-laws.

Mrs. Douglas swept in and had taken in the entire place within a few moments. "I suppose you keep it tidy enough, and this is the most we can expect from the Navy, what with the war going on and all."

Roger's mother hadn't been in her house two minutes and already all of Frances's poise and conduct training was flying away like a Wildcat coursing off an aircraft carrier catapult.

"In fact, the war has made housing *very* scarce here in Lexington Park, Mrs. Douglas. We were fortunate to be granted this private married housing, and I will never sneer down my nose at it because I know how lucky my husband and I are." She hoped Roger's mother caught her emphasis on *my husband*. "May I offer you a beverage? I'm afraid we don't have much, but the water is cold."

Mrs. Douglas's expression was one of utter

disdain with just the tiniest hint of respect. The respect didn't last long.

After pouring glasses of tap water from a pitcher that had been chilled inside the refrigerator, Frances invited her in-laws to sit at their tiny dining table. She also offered to take Genevieve Douglas's stole but was rebuffed.

Frances noted with satisfaction that the fur wrapped around the woman's shoulders had bald patches. Mrs. Douglas wasn't so fine that she wasn't making do with worn, repaired clothing like everyone else.

The air in the trailer was suddenly and uncharacteristically stuffy and heavy.

"Have you no ashtray?" Mrs. Douglas asked, sweeping her glance around the room.

"I—no, we do not smoke. It is an expense we cannot afford. But I can provide you a makeshift one." Frances rose, went to the trash can, and pulled out an emptied Spam can. With a quick rinse to it under the kitchen faucet, she presented it to her mother-in-law, laughing inwardly to herself.

Mrs. Douglas licked her lips as if about to let loose with invective, then apparently thought the better of it. Instead, she pulled a packet of Marlboro Silhouette cigarettes from her purse, removed one, and put it between her lips as she tossed the ivory-colored package onto the table. The cigarette tip was dyed a red brighter than the woman's lipstick.

Mr. Douglas, well-trained, pulled out his own pack of Chesterfields and a pack of matches, first lighting his wife's and then his own.

Mrs. Douglas closed her eyes, inhaled deeply from her cigarette, then slowly blew out a stream of smoke.

Frances had to admit she was fascinated to watch the other woman's actions, as it made her seem so…modern. Although servicemen smoked so much that cigarette packs were part of their rations, it had just started becoming fashionable for women to do so. Lt. Wallace had strongly discouraged it, though. "Not ladylike. You're WAVES, not actual sailors," she'd said, so few women in the barracks had responded to the barrage of Philip Morris magazine ads encouraging them to smoke.

Except for Sophie, of course, who had practiced with an unlit cigarette in front of one of the bathroom mirrors, striking poses in an effort to imitate actress Lana Turner's seductive look. But even she hadn't dared to light one and come under Lt. Wallace's scorn.

Mr. Douglas opened with a friendly statement. "We understand you are a WAVE here on the air station. I'm sure your work is interesting. And of such help to the boys overseas."

"I am. I work in the administration building's communications department, typing up memos and reports, as well as helping in the print shop. I operate the—"

"What is your intention once the war is over?" Mrs. Douglas was obviously not the least bit interested. "Will you ignore your duties as a wife to continue in this role, taking away a job a returning soldier might want?"

Frances stared at her new mother-in-law.

This wasn't just an inauspicious start to their relationship, it was downright hostile. She took a deep breath and chose not to answer the question, which wasn't really a question at all.

"Mrs. Douglas, may I ask what I have done that so offends you, other than marrying your son?" Frances kept her tone even, despite wanting to rip the fox stole from the woman's shoulders and shove it down her throat.

Arthur Douglas shifted uncomfortably in his seat, but he didn't try to save his wife, who proceeded on. "It's not so much that we are offended, my dear—although it was *quite* rude of Roger to simply tell us after the fact—it's that we envisioned our son's path to be a bit different once the war is over. His ship veered off course, so to speak, by marrying you. Don't worry, I am not gossiping about my son. I plan to tell him this very thing when he returns home this evening."

Frances narrowed her gaze. Nearly every man desired to get married, as did every woman. Not to mention that all parents wanted it for their children. "You're a grown woman now, sweetheart," her mother had said on the phone call where Frances had shared her joy.

Even if Roger had wed quickly and unannounced, how could they view this as a detriment to his future?

"What do you believe he will be unable to do now that he is apparently burdened by me?"

Arthur Douglas continued to be conciliatory. "All my wife means is that we know Roger is passionate about whatever he does, and she wants to know that he will have the right time to devote to a new wife, what with the demands of the Marines. Isn't that right, Genevieve?"

The disdainful glare Mrs. Douglas gave her husband made Frances feel quite sorry for the man and his unforgivable mispronunciation of his wife's name. "That is *not* right, Arthur. You must understand—" she turned her attention back to Frances, "—that there are multiple problems at work here."

She put her right elbow on the table and held up a hand of manicured nails. In doing so, her stole slid off one shoulder and Frances understood why she hadn't wanted to remove it.

Genevieve Douglas had an enormous, bright plum-colored birthmark starting midway down her neck and reaching across her shoulder, disappearing somewhere beneath her dress sleeve.

The elder Mrs. Douglas began ticking off reasons as to the grand problems Frances was creating, striking her left index finger against a separate, glossy-polished nail on her other hand as she did so.

"First, you must understand that we didn't want Roger in the Marines at all. He was to enter war service through the Army, like his father did in the Great War. But he didn't respect our wishes."

Frances failed to see how serving in the armed forces via the Marines versus the Army was disrespectful, but there was much she was not understanding at the moment.

Mrs. Douglas tapped another fingernail.

"Second, his father had a position at the ready for him at Chrysler when the war is over. A ready-made, important career awaited him just as soon as their factory got re-tooled for automobiles again. But now, with this marriage, who knows what he will choose to do instead?"

Roger hadn't mentioned this to Frances. But if he was trying to stay completely away from home, she could well understand *that*.

But it was Mrs. Douglas's next statement as she tapped a third nail that had Frances on full alert. "Finally, there is Roger's, shall we say, mental state."

Frances straightened in her chair. "His what?"

"Now, Genevieve," Arthur said. "No need to dredge up the past."

Genevieve Douglas clearly wanted to dredge up the past, but on her own terms. She dropped her finished cigarette into the Spam can and picked up the pack to withdraw another slim stick.

Mr. Douglas threw his own cigarette into the can and quickly struck a match to light his wife's second one.

Frances knew that Genevieve was making her wait in a perverse game of cat and mouse in which her mother-in-law was determined to make Frances the mouse.

She watched Genevieve calmly as the other woman again took a deep drag from the cigarette, held it, then slowly exhaled toward the ceiling, as if deep in thought.

As Frances suspected, Genevieve Douglas was anxious to drop her little bomb. "You see, my dear, Roger isn't like other men. He has always had a…brutish tendency…toward other men. Oh, I'm sure he would never harm you, but when others go against what he considers his code of honor, he is quick to dispatch them with word and fist." Her lips curved into a smile, a strange reaction to her own words about her son.

Frances remained still as her thoughts raced. What Genevieve was saying was completely preposterous, of course, but…what about Roger's nightmares, which Frances had attributed to his harrowing experiences in the Pacific?

Was there more to it than that? Was it possible that Roger had a strange, violent streak to him?

She felt a chill run up her spine when she considered how angry Roger had gotten at Kenny over the other man's foolishness. But that surely didn't mean anything. After all, everyone got righteously angry at some point.

Still…

"In fact," Genevieve continued, breaking Frances out of her reverie, "we've always had to keep Roger under close supervision because of his temper. Once, as a boy of about twelve, he nearly killed another boy because there was a rumor that that other boy—what was his name, Arthur? Henry, wasn't it?—had stolen a bicycle from another neighborhood boy that Roger knew."

"What did Roger do to him?" Frances asked, dreading the answer.

"Beat the boy senseless is what he did." Arthur seemed to have found his voice. "Prattled on about honor and decency, but the other child did end up with bruises, stitches, and a hospital stay."

Was there a hint of pride in Arthur's tone? If so, Frances was certain he wouldn't dare be obvious about it.

What was also obvious was that if Roger had attacked another boy, it was likely that the other boy had started an altercation or there was more to the story than what his parents knew. "I'm sure it was just an accident of some sort."

Mrs. Douglas once more tapped her cigarette against the edge of the makeshift ashtray. "An accident," she repeated, as though Frances was an idiot.

"Yes. If Roger was unstable, I'm sure he wouldn't have been accepted into the Marines. Moreover, I would have seen evidence of it by now."

If anyone was unstable, it was the woman sitting before Frances.

"You! You hardly know him. I'm telling you that Roger needs some sort of supervision. His father and I have been scrupulous about this, as my dear, dead brother's will stipulated a trust fund to be held for his nieces and nephews until they individually reach the ripe old age of thirty. Trust monies cannot be doled out to any of them not leading exemplary lives at that point and instead must remain with the trustees until their lives are turned around. We want to ensure Roger can receive his inheritance when he turns thirty."

This conversation was abominable. Roger's parents' disloyalty to their son was shocking. "Well, I regret to inform you that Roger will not be home this evening. He is away on a training mission and will likely not be home for weeks."

"Away!" Genevieve Douglas exploded. "We drove here from Michigan and won't even be able to see our son at all?"

Did the woman think Frances was at fault for this? "A telegram might have saved you considerable trouble." She wasn't about to tell her new mother-in-law that Roger was close by.

Mrs. Douglas drew again from her cigarette before tapping the long ash against the edge of the Spam can. The ash hissed as it hit the bottom of the can, still wet from being rinsed.

"I suppose we will have to head back home. We are fortunate that your father-in-law is a very important man at Chrysler, so we are able to drive here instead of getting mixed up in unreliable train schedules."

"Indeed," Frances murmured, standing to indicate the visit was done. "May I pass on a message to Roger for when he comes home?"

The Douglases stood as well. Arthur Douglas reached out and arranged the fox stole around his wife's shoulders. Genevieve ignored his ministrations, leaning down to grab her cigarette pack and dropping it into her purse. "Yes, tell him we are very disappointed."

Frances remained at the window long after her new in-laws had departed, staring at nothing and wondering how she was supposed to be a good and dutiful daughter-in-law to Roger's parents.

CHAPTER 38

A COUPLE OF DAYS later, Frances was especially happy. Her in-laws were forgotten, the cigarette smoke was almost aired out of the trailer, and she had been able to secure a nice beef joint for five ration points. A local butcher had set up a lean-to tent just outside the base gate, which she had discovered while borrowing Gunney and taking him on an extra-long walk.

Roger always talked about his family's Sunday roast tradition and wanting to do the same with Frances when rationing was finally over.

She wanted to re-create this pleasant memory for him, despite believing that most of his other childhood memories must be brutal, based on her hour-long interaction with Mrs. Douglas.

Frances hummed as she flipped through her copy of "Macy's Cookbook and Kitchen Guide for the Busy Woman." It had been Lillian's wedding gift to her, given with a card that said, *"Imagine what you can create when the war finally ends."*

Frances almost felt guilty breaking the cookbook open now, as if it were somehow wrong to be enjoying a nice piece of meat. But most of the existing wartime cookbooks only offered suggestions on how to make "mock" versions of everything, in addition to describing how to make various foods last.

It was that last bit that she was exploring now. Perhaps a pot roast with vegetables for dinner—hmm, the recipe called for a sprig of parsley, could she just skip that?—then she could use the leftovers in a stew, removing the bone and saving that for a beef broth and future soup.

Satisfied with her choices, she browsed her dessert choices. A frosted raisin spice cake looked lovely. Oh, but it required both a cup of sugar and two-thirds of a cup of molasses. Could she substitute applesauce for the sugar? Would it make the cake too runny? Maybe a little extra flour to thicken it…

She had sprinkled the meat with salt and pepper, dusted it with flour, and was about to sauté it in a heavy pan when there was a knock at the trailer door.

She smiled. Probably Verja stopping by for coffee. They had gotten into a regular routine of spending an hour or so together on Saturday mornings. Frances didn't think Verja was ever going to recover from Walter's death, but it was nice to see that she occasionally found things to smile over.

It was gratifying to be a supportive shoulder for her friend.

Wiping her hands off on her white apron decorated with lemons, limes, and cherries, Frances walked the few steps to the trailer's entrance and opened the door.

Standing there were two men in military uniforms, wearing gloves. One held a folded flag, and the other held a large envelope, which he opened and from which he withdrew a sheet of paper.

"Mrs. Douglas, it is my sad duty to inform you—"

She slammed the door and collapsed on the floor.

CHAPTER 39

FRANCES HAD NO idea if days or weeks passed after the Marines came to deliver the news that Roger's body had been found at Cedar Point.

It wasn't possible. Not Cedar Point. That was their little hideaway place. How was it possible that he had been there without her?

Various images passed through her mind, thick with grief.

George Somerville, his eyes rimmed in red, bringing Gunney for a visit.

Gunney, slobbering kisses on her as she sat listlessly in a chair.

Kenny Campbell and Billy Alvey, hats in hands, making weak attempts to joke with her.

Lillian, Sophie, and Dottie, coming through to dust, clean, and straighten the trailer up.

Frances had sat listlessly through that, too.

Lt. Cmdr. Mackey and Lt. Hall arriving with a small bouquet of flowers. They were now limp and brown on the center of the kitchen table. "His dedication likely prevented many deaths in ways you can't ever know about on this side of heaven," Mackey had said.

Nauseating.

Then there was a nasty encounter with Roger's

parents, who had rushed back into town. They had insisted on their son's body being taken home to Michigan instead of being buried at Arlington National Cemetery.

Frances had roused herself enough to fight furiously on that. In the end, they had attended a service at St. Nicholas Chapel—an event Frances didn't believe she could endure after having just been married there—and then immediately departed for home with hardly a word to Roger's widow. They didn't even wait for his body to be taken to Arlington, but coldly shook her hand after the service and took their leave. Roger's mother, her lips pinched together so tightly they were white, leaned into Frances as she held Frances's hand with a grip so fierce she felt like the mouse again, only this time trapped in an eagle's talons. "Roger was an excellent swimmer and boater. *What happened to him?*"

They were absolutely right.

They had stalked off before Frances had had time to formulate a response. She wished she could have told her in-laws that she agreed with them. There was something very, very wrong about Roger's death.

Despite all that had happened since Roger's death, the absolute worst thing of all was that Frances had not been permitted to even see him a final time before the casket lid had been closed. It felt as if she had no confirmation that it was really him in there.

The funeral director at W.C. Mattingley Funeral Home had been kind to her, but also appeared to be taking direction from the Navy. Not only was the casket closed and placed in the front of the chapel before she had an opportunity to see Roger, and not only had a variety of lilies been selected and placed everywhere in vases and an enormous spray of lilies and carnations spread over the closed casket, but the funeral director had met all of her suggestions for the service with, "It's all taken care of, Mrs. Douglas."

It was infuriating, but events were moving faster than lightning bolts in a summer storm, and she was ill-equipped in her grief to spend time questioning it all.

Verja, though, had been a constant, protective presence. She chased away people she deemed to be gossipers, cloaked as sympathizers paying their respects. "I'll not have you endure their phony dour faces. They just want all the juicy tittle-tattle about Roger's death so they can strut it around to their friends. I quickly had enough of them, I can tell you."

But in the end, it was Roger's supervisor, Capt. Nickerson, whom the others often called Sparky, showing up to offer condolences days after the funeral and to explain Roger's death, that was the most painful of all.

His expression was troubled as he sat across from a lifeless Frances. "I think you should know the truth of what happened," he began.

"That would certainly be a change in the course of events, given that I wasn't even permitted to see my husband after he died." Frances bit the words out sharply.

To his credit, Capt. Nickerson reddened in embarrassment. "Yes, well, it came from higher up that it would be unseemly for you to see Master Sergeant Douglas in his…condition."

"How very kind of the Navy to attend to the affairs of its employees so benevolently." She knew she wasn't making Capt. Nickerson's visit easy for him, but she was so exhausted from crying and grief that it was difficult to care about others' feelings.

"I understand your anger, Mrs. Douglas… Frances. If it brings you comfort, I don't think Roger suffered for long."

That pierced Frances's fog, and she laughed mirthlessly. "For long? How very reassuring."

Nickerson cleared his throat. "An investigation was conducted. There was a small rowboat along the shore with fishing gear in it. It is believed that Roger—your husband—took a boat out from Solomons, was fishing, and fell out of the boat, hitting his head on some rocks."

She remembered her in-laws complaining that Roger was an excellent fisherman and swimmer. She herself had witnessed his expertise with a boat. "That seems highly unlikely. Roger was very experienced on the water. He wouldn't have done anything foolish enough to topple him out of it. Besides, why would there be some random rowboat sitting at Solomons?"

And how would Roger have gotten to Cedar Point? That would have been a dangerous crossing in a mere rowboat.

Nickerson nodded somberly. "It's always hard when the inexplicable occurs. But the winds can whip up without warning on the river. He might have gone out too far, and the waves may have gotten too rough for him to maintain control of that little craft."

Frances realized this was even more unlikely. A rowboat was far too small a craft for Roger to have attempted rowing down the Patuxent River, even if he was hugging the shoreline. It didn't make any sense.

"I don't believe it," she said.

Nickerson patted her shoulder as though she was a little girl whose puppy had been run over. "There, there. All will be well. It will just take time to accept this tragic event."

Frances had turned away from Capt. Nickerson at that point, not trusting herself to remain civil.

❧❧❧

It was Verja who sat at Frances's bedside one day and suggested she return to work. "The war might be winding down, but you are still needed in service to your country. Roger would be upset to think you weren't giving your all for the cause."

It was that statement that finally drew Frances from the bed and into the bathroom to confront herself in the mirror.

She was a sorry sight.

After a long soak in her tiny bathtub, followed by some half-hearted arranging of her hair and some strokes from a tube of Elizabeth Arden Montezuma Red, courtesy of Maisie, Frances returned to the administration building and was welcomed back with great enthusiasm.

It was gratifying, and she endeavored to focus on her work, but her world collapsed again when she received an official letter that she would only be permitted to stay in her married quarters another thirty days. She had the choice of moving back to the barracks or attempting to find lodgings in town—still a near impossibility despite how much work had been done to create more housing in St. Mary's County.

Back to the WAVES barracks, she would go. Maybe it would do her good to be with the girls again.

<hr>

Frances sat before Lt. Cmdr. Mackey and Lt. Hall, enduring a litany of platitudes.

"Your husband is a hero."

"Try to get your mind off your sorrow. Your country needs you."

"A Marine's life is a risky one."

"He will always be remembered for having done his duty."

It was exhausting. She just wanted to escape them and bury herself in the mountains of typing awaiting her. She trudged her way through the days, willing herself—and failing—to find some modicum of happiness.

She packed up her goods in a near-trance-like state, although she was heartened by the idea of being housed with her old friends again instead of living alone in her tiny trailer.

She stood in the middle of her trailer a couple of days before she was to depart, surrounded by borrowed pieces of luggage filled with her meager belongings, when there was a sharp rap at the door.

To her surprise, it was the farmer who had yelled at her and Roger down at Cedar Point. Today, his expression was much softened, and he held his straw hat in his hands. "I'm Harold Johnson. 'Member me? Just wanted to extend my condolences, ma'am."

Frances was suspicious and did not invite him in. Discomfited, he twisted the hat around until it was in danger of coming apart.

"Um, I know you're not as likely to want to see me, missus, but I thought it just weren't right for you not to know."

"Not to know...what?"

The farmer glanced around furtively. "It was me who found your husband, missus. There on the point. Go down there a lot, you see, what with the nighttime explosions in the sky usually resulting in some sort of trinkets floating in that I can sell. Went down with Red, my dog, and there your man was. On the shore. I—I—reported it to the Navy. They came and picked him up straight away."

The farmer was causing Frances to relive the horror. *Why is he doing this to me?*

She remained very still in her doorway, continuing to gaze at him, two steps down. "But, um, later, when I saw the newspaper article about him, I noticed there was something missing. Something important."

Frances was even more guarded. "What do you mean, 'something missing'?"

"Yes, ma'am." He was twisting the hat so hard

it looked like an airplane propeller warming up. "When I found him, it looked like he had a big stab wound in him."

CHAPTER 40

FRANCES SAT IN Capt. Nickerson's outer office, simmering. Unlike Lt. Cmdr. Mackey's outer office's austere walls, Nickerson's was full of Marine Corps memorabilia and photographs plastered everywhere in an overenthusiastic attempt to shout OORAH to the world.

She was eventually invited back to meet him and was surprised that, although he was very trim and muscular, he was quite small. She hadn't noticed that when he had visited her before. Not that she had paid attention to much of anything. Frances towered over him in her heels. His close-cropped hair was very dark and his eyes were a shade of copper that was strangely mesmerizing.

"What can I do for you, Mrs. Douglas?" he said kindly, indicating that she should sit down on the wood chair across from his desk. "I'm going to guess the Navy wants you to leave your quarters. I have some pull there and can at the very least get you a postponement so that–"

Frances held up a hand. "I'm moving back to the WAVES barracks and prefer to do so, sir, thank you."

"Of course. Time spent with your friends will bring you round again, right?" He offered an encouraging smile, which served to infuriate Frances more.

"Captain Nickerson, I am here to ask you a very direct question."

He folded his hands on his desk. "What is that?"

"Was there anything unusual that you noticed on Roger's body when you found him?" She had decided in advance to ask a leading question, to see if Roger's supervisor would offer information unbidden.

He shook his head. "Unusual? I mean, it was certainly unusual to find one of my men dead from an unexpected accident like that. Tragic as it was, though, I don't think it was *unusual.*"

"I see." Her blood had gone from simmering to boiling and was nearly blocking her vision. She took a breath. "So, you do not believe that Roger's stab wound was anything out of the ordinary?"

Nickerson stilled except for a small tic in his cheek. "Who told you that Master Sergeant Douglas had a stab wound?"

"I'm not sure that matters, sir. I'm just curious as to why his death would have been declared accidental when he was clearly murdered by someone." Frances felt her tone rising but breathed to maintain control.

Nickerson considered her for several long moments, clenching and unclenching his fingers on his desk but otherwise maintaining his prior demeanor.

"Mrs. Douglas—Yeoman Douglas—you of all people should realize that we are fighting to win a war. Both men and women are working tirelessly to ensure that all our fighting boys return home safe."

Frances was confused. What did this obvious statement have to do with anything? Roger had died off the American shoreline not in the enemy territory of the Pacific

"In addition, you of all people—you work in the administration building, helping to churn out Navy propaganda, right?—must know that it is of paramount importance that we not alarm others. Keeping calm is the byword, is it not?"

"Sir, of course we are to keep calm, but in this case, a man—*my husband*—was murdered. The Navy and the Marine Corps should investigate his death."

Nickerson offered her a sympathetic look. "I'm not sure you'd like to see where that leads. We have worked very hard to keep your husband's post-mortem name clean."

Dear God, he was implying that Roger had done something to get himself killed.

Her temples throbbed with anger. She ignored the man's cruel insinuation. "Also, why do you imagine his body washed up at Cedar Point when he obviously must have been killed at Solomons? He's been there without returning home for months."

"That may or may not be true, madam. What we *can* be sure of is that you should not step into official Navy business, or else you–"

"Official Navy business!" Frances exploded, rising out of her chair and pointing at the man. "First, you tell me it was an accident, then suddenly it's official business. Which is it, Captain?"

Nickerson rose, as well. "Whether it is official Navy business or not, it is most certainly not *your* business. Good day, Mrs. Douglas."

CHAPTER 41

FRANCES ENTERED HER compartment in the barracks at the end of a particularly trying day. Regaining your footing after losing someone cherished was difficult, and in Frances's case, it was made more so by the new flurry of activity at the administration building. With D-Day successfully accomplished, it was clear that the war would be over soon, which was now changing the nature and tone of communications across the Navy. Instead of propaganda extolling people to save, conserve, and silence their way to victory, now the government wanted the populace to tamp down its exuberance over what was certain to be victory.

Sometimes Frances felt like she was the only person on station who wasn't bursting with joy.

Even the small ceremony in which she and Dottie received commendations from Capt. Stricker for "duty beyond the call of service" did little to improve her saddened state.

There were rumors that the government was working on a way to finally and completely end the war, but rumors and bluffs were a regular part of the daily propaganda being churned out.

Besides, hadn't Roger told her that the Japanese

never surrender? Even if Hitler did, what about the Axis forces in the Pacific?

A new WAVE had her old compartment, and Frances had been assigned to the other side of the hall, closer to Sophie, whose cough had persisted for far too long after their visit to Leonardtown. Frances planned to recommend that her friend see the base doctor right away. Maybe Sophie had bronchitis and required some penicillin injections before it turned into pneumonia.

Frances's new compartment looked much like her old one, which looked like all the others. The only difference in hers was that she had brought over the bedspread she had shared with Roger in their trailer, one of the few new possessions that she had acquired in their short marriage. The bedspread contained a profusion of cream, orange, and yellow flowers against an emerald green background, a stark contrast to the drab coverlets in most of the other compartments. It was far too big for her little bed, but she didn't care.

On her chest of drawers, she had a framed wedding photo that she put next to the photo of Freddy, as well as the communion set that Roger had found on the beaches of Guadalcanal.

As she stepped out of her heeled shoes to the relative comfort of her bare feet against the floor, she noticed that at the foot of her bed was a folded sheet of paper. Probably a note from Sophie about plans for the evening. Lifting it to her nose, Frances sniffed the paper. No perfume scent, so it wasn't from Sophie. Lillian or Dottie, then.

She opened it up and was surprised to find a masculine scrawl inside.

Frances,
We know you don't think Roger's death was
an accident. We don't, either. We'd like to
talk about it with you. Meet at the canteen at
seven o'clock?

George Somerville
Kenny Campbell

Did they truly agree with her? Finally, a show of support. Frances glanced at the clock on her chest of drawers. If she hurried, she'd just make it.

She quickly changed into simpler civilian clothing and ran out to meet Roger's friends.

The two men appeared to have already been dousing their feelings in brown bottles of Ballantine's beer as they sat on stools at a round wood table.

The canteen was the only location on the air station—except for the officers' club—where alcohol was permitted, and the Navy was very strict about it. Even ships out to sea carried only the barest minimum of alcohol, to be used for medicinal purposes if someone experienced a great shock or for crews who were out at sea more than forty-five days. Even then, the limit was two beers.

That made canteens like the one at Patuxent River even more popular, since the service members could essentially drink what they wanted, needing to just avoid getting caught drunk until they could sleep off their inebriation.

Tonight, the air was heavy with smoke, and a cigarette girl wandered about the canteen in her blue and gold, above-the-knee dress and matching pillbox hat perched jauntily on one side of her head, offering packs of smokes and matches from a tray supported by a strap around her neck.

There was no live music in the canteen this evening, but she could just make out the scratchy strains of music coming from a phonograph player perched on the bar. Vera Lynn's voice warbled out unevenly from it, but the lyrics were still poignant.

We'll meet again
Don't know where, don't know when
But I know we'll meet again some sunny day…

Both men slid off their chairs as Frances approached, standing until she sat on a bar stool that George had pulled out for her. A bottle of Ballantine's and a glass were already waiting for her at the table.

"Good to see you both," Frances said, eschewing the glass and raising the bottle in a salute to them before taking a sip of the malty brew. It flooded warmly through her, making her understand why it was called "liquid courage."

"Hope you're feeling okay, Mrs. Douglas," George said. "We've been worried about you."

Frances smiled wanly. "So formal now, George?"

The Marine's blush was evident even beneath his chocolate skin. "Just paying respect, ma'am. Frances, I mean." He shifted uncomfortably on his stool.

His discomfort endeared him to Frances. As had his willingness to care for Gunney after Roger's death. Or maybe the beer was relaxing her.

"I know that. I just wouldn't like to think that we are no longer all friends just because…just because–" She swallowed. "Just because I'm alone now."

Kenny sat up straight. "You'll never be alone, Frances. Not with Sergeants Somerville and Campbell at your service."

Kenny's swagger and grandiosity never waned. "Thank you for that," she said. "Roger would be so pleased to know you were looking out for me. But from your note, it sounds like you are looking out for him, as well…?"

Both men started to speak at once, then George inclined his head toward Kenny so that the other man could talk first.

Kenny dropped his voice, so it was barely above a whisper, making it difficult to hear him above the din of bottles clanking, the roaring chatter, and Vera Lynn's voice. "We've been talking and think you're right. Roger's death was not natural."

It was gratifying that they agreed with her, but did they have an idea of what to do next?

However, what Kenny said next electrified her. "We suspect Captain Nickerson might be involved."

Now it was Frances's turn to sit up straight. "Why do you think so?" she asked, pushing the half-empty bottle to one side.

The two men glanced at one another, sharing a message Frances couldn't fathom. "He called us in and told us you came to him about Roger's death," Kenny said. "He was…dismissive… about your concerns. But he also told us why you thought it was impossible that Roger had died the way he had, and we agree with you."

George nodded animatedly next to Kenny. "But Captain Nickerson doesn't. He said you were just reacting emotionally to your husband's death. Said you might have been experiencing some 'female hysteria.' But Kenny and I don't think you were, and we think it's very strange how insistent the captain seemed to be to convince us that you were barking up the wrong tree."

That didn't seem like much to establish Capt. Nickerson as somehow culpable in her husband's death.

"Why in the world would he want Roger dead?" Best to start with the most obvious question. "He was a valuable, decorated Marine. So brave." She choked on the word "brave" and cleared her throat, blinking back tears that threatened to spill.

"We've thought about that," Kenny said. "First, we think Sparky either did it or is covering up for whoever did it."

"But why would he do that? If he was covering for someone, couldn't that get him into considerable trouble?"

"Not if he was covering up for someone above his own station." Kenny looked at her bleakly.

CHAPTER 42

TEN THOUSAND THOUGHTS WERE competing inside Frances's head, and she was unsure which one to expel first. "Are you saying…are you saying that Roger's death was initiated by top brass within the Navy? But again–why?"

George spoke up. "We were with Roger at Solomons, helping him train, but got sent back here directly after his death. There was no reason to send us back; we were helping Roger lead training teams over there, and the training effort is short-staffed as it is. We think we were sent away on purpose." He nodded as though thoroughly convinced of the truth of it.

"Cigarettes? Gentleman and the lady?" The cigarette girl had approached their table. "I have unfiltered Camels, Lucky Strikes, and Chesterfields here. I also have one pack of Philip Morris left."

Kenny purchased the Philip Morris cigarettes, and the girl continued on her path through the now-crowded canteen. "I don't know why, but I like to smoke when I have beer."

George laughed. "I like to smoke when I have bullets cracking past me."

George's joke lightened the moment, but the

"why" question continued to repeat in Frances's head.

Kenny picked up on the story. "There's a lot going on at Solomons that I don't think brass wants anyone to know about. Mostly, their mismanagement of the base. It's run almost like a prison camp over there, all deprivation and no freedom. Roger tended to be a thorn in their side, constantly going up against them and demanding fixes for the men. All the incoming soldiers respected him, knowing that he would charge into the officers' quarters to right any wrong, and there were plenty of wrongs to be corrected."

Realization was dawning in Frances's mind, and it was frightening. "You're saying that Roger was killed to cover up his knowledge of conditions at Solomons?"

My God, had she somehow been responsible for her own husband's death by submitting her report to Capt. Stricker?

"No. We think he was killed to cover up his willingness to go public over those conditions and embarrass the Navy," Kenny said.

Frances's heart plummeted as she tried to absorb their theory. "But they didn't kill either of you, and you presumably know as much as Roger did."

George shook his head. "No. Men went to Roger privately all the time. And we didn't stay in the main barracks with the troops. We had our own Marine quarters—hardly more than a shed—away from them, where we could go over the day's training and Roger would prepare us for the next day."

Frances searched her memory for where the Marine barracks were at Solomons. They were at the south end of the base, while regular barracks were at the north end.

Kenny slid out of his seat. "I need another beer. Anyone else?"

Frances needed many more beers to numb her brain. She nodded at Kenny, as did George. Kenny returned momentarily with three more bottles of Ballantine's dangling from the fingers of one hand. He put the bottles on the table, pulled a bottle opener from his pocket, deftly popped the tops from all of them, and handed them round.

He was uncharacteristically silent while he smoked and made his way through his bottle in deep gulps. Eventually, Kenny propped his elbows on the table and dropped his forehead onto the palms of his hands. "Sometimes I thought Roger was an ass—pardon my language—but he was just keeping me out of trouble."

He looked up again. "Roger knew I was planning to take Sophie over to Solomons to show her around and stopped me. I ended up just showing Sophie the edges of the base and some of the fishing boats around the other side of the island so that she'd think I had done somethin' special for her.

"If I'd been caught on base with her, I would have ended up in the brig for sure. I should have thanked Roger instead of ignoring him. I guess I was the ass."

Despite how dejected he looked, Frances still couldn't discuss her secret trip to Solomons and how she herself was largely responsible for Navy brass learning about conditions there. She simply said, "I'm glad Roger was such a good friend to you."

"Yeah," George said. "He always looked out for me, too, even when I thought I didn't need it. I usually did. He was the Marine that every other Marine should look up to." He rubbed a fist against one eye, then downed the rest of his bottle.

"Oorah," Kenny said morosely, holding up his half-drank bottle and clinking it against George's empty one.

As George repeated the simple Marine Corps phrase that solidified all Marines with one another, Frances was distracted by motion at the canteen's front door.

Dottie had just entered the canteen with Ira Reed. Together, they sought a table along a far wall away from most people. Dottie hadn't noticed Frances, and Frances decided not to bring attention to herself, for clearly the two of them wanted to be alone.

In fact, as they sat down, Ira took Dottie's hands in his across the table.

Frances's innards twisted, and she had to turn away from that romantic gesture.

Would there ever be a day that this felt better? Maybe it would if she, with George's and Kenny's help, could bring resolution to Roger's murder. And hopefully prove to herself that she had nothing to do with it.

"Hey, Francie," Kenny said, using Sophie's term of endearment. "You won't tell Sophie about my trip to Solomons with her, will you? That I didn't really show her anything? I'd hate to have her disappointed in me."

George rolled his eyes from where he sat at Kenny's side.

"I won't say anything," Frances promised. There had been enough pain and disappointment to go around without ruining Sophie's impression of her beau.

Kenny rose from his seat. "Need to go visit the johnny house. Be right back." He must have had quite a bit to drink before Frances had arrived from the canteen, for he staggered before catching his balance and walking away.

Once Kenny was out of view, George leaned across the table conspiratorially.

"I have a second theory that you might find crazy, but here it is. I think maybe Kenny was the target," George said. "Someone killed Roger, thinking he was killing Kenny."

This was outlandish. "How would someone mistake Roger for Kenny?"

George pressed his point. "In the dark, it's hard to tell one uniformed Marine from another. And although it's true that Roger was creating a lot of problems for the higher-ups at Solomons, *so was Kenny.*"

Frances clutched the clear, squat Ballantine's bottle. "What was Kenny doing?"

"Constantly pranking the recruits. Laxatives in food, scrambling up boots so that no one had his own pair next to his bunk, just dumb stuff.

But that started to bore him, so he came up with plans to prank the officers. You gotta understand, it is dull as dirt at Solomons. You can almost get why Kenny was doing it. But one of them was a hothead and had threatened Kenny more than once against his antics. His threats were not of the formal disciplinary kind."

"No," Frances breathed. Some officers enjoyed being "one of the men," but many did not. If Kenny had pranked the wrong officer…

"You think an officer went after Kenny, mistakenly got Roger, and now there is a cover up over the entire thing?" Frances could hardly believe her own words. "I can't believe because of a few pranks they'd want to kill someone."

George shrugged. "That's my theory. But I haven't told Kenny because he feels bad enough about Roger as it is."

Roger may have died because someone was trying to kill Kenny to stop him from his own stupidity.

That seemed too farfetched…didn't it?

CHAPTER 43

FRANCES WAS PENSIVE the next day in the Nursery, hardly able to focus at typing up correspondence. Fortunately, everyone was still giving her a wide berth, so she was able to remain immersed in her thoughts.

Those thoughts had grown dark and terrible as the day went on, for truly evil concepts had entered her mind and given her chills.

It was clear that George was jealous of Kenny's relationship with Sophie. A dreadful, unthinkable thought darted around in her mind.

Could George himself have accidentally killed Roger, thinking *he* was killing Kenny?

Had she been sitting casually with a murderer at the canteen?

She shook her head. If a fellow Marine had killed her husband, surely Roger's supervisor would have had him immediately arrested.

The interminable workday finally ended, and she returned to the WAVES barracks. She considered climbing straight into bed to hopefully go unconscious and forget the past couple of days, but Sophie popped in, buoyant.

"Hey Francie, they're going to do a girls' sing-along tonight in the dining hall. Who knew that Lieutenant Wallace was bangers on a piano? I'm going all-out for the gals. You're gonna be there, right? Oh, and Maisie is going to be offering lyric sheets for sale. It'll be loads of fun." Sophie acted excited, but there were dark circles under her normally sparkling eyes.

Frances stifled a yawn, glanced longingly at her bed, but agreed to attend.

"It's gonna be a real pip. The monkey's eyebrows, as they say. Ta-ta for now." Sophie scampered off, presumably to convince other women in the barracks to attend. Frances closed her curtain but heard Sophie coughing as she walked away. It was a rattling, syrupy cough.

Frances drew the curtain back and stepped out of her compartment. Sophie was already at another compartment, animatedly talking to another WAVE, but Frances noticed a wadded-up handkerchief in her friend's hand. Whatever Sophie had was not going away, and she had not heeded Frances's admonishments to visit a medic. Frances would again urge her to do so after the sing-along.

Frances busied herself with examining her limited wardrobe and stitching fixes where she could. When the war was over, the first thing she would do was buy some new skirts. If there were any to be had.

While sewing, she debated with herself whether to talk to her friends about her conversation with George and Kenny, as well as her devastating thoughts regarding her own possible responsibility in Roger's death.

In the end, she decided to keep everything to herself. No sense agitating Sophie about Kenny, and she didn't want to risk revealing anything about her and Dottie's time at Solomons, which was still a secret.

Three hours later, she was seated in the dining hall next to Dottie and across from Lillian. They had just concluded their suppers of corned beef fritters and potato biscuits, finished off with an apple crumble. Sophie was already at the front of the hall, waiting her turn to belt out lyrics while Lt. Wallace fingered out the music. The poor piano was badly out of tune, probably an instrument that someone had decided to donate instead of smashing up for kindling, but it still produced recognizable sounds.

Now, another WAVE was rifling through a box of sheet music, while Lt. Wallace waited impatiently.

"How was your week in the telephone room?" Frances asked Lillian, knowing that soon the air would be too filled with discordant music for conversation.

Lillian flashed a smile and reached a hand back to pat her snood. Frances noticed that it was an affectation Lillian seemed to have, patting her bundled-up hair as if to assure herself it was still there.

"Very busy. The switchboard buzzes all day long. They've given us a bicycle to use to deliver telegram messages around the station, which I do in the afternoons. The other girls run messages in the morning, so it's just an overwhelming flow of communications. Some of it encouraging, some of it…" Lillian let her voice trail off.

Frances knew that, despite the tide of the war turning, it was more important than ever to keep quiet about anything you knew.

"I know," she said quietly.

Lillian offered her a strange expression, as if considering telling her something but then thinking the better of it.

"How is it for you being back in the barracks? Is it difficult?" she asked.

"With Roger gone, I'd rather be around everyone than be by myself, so I suppose it was a blessing to be evicted from our married quarters."

Lillian nodded and touched her snood-covered hair again. "It's much safer, too."

That was an odd statement. "What do you mean?" Frances asked.

At that moment, Lt. Wallace started banging on the piano and the WAVE standing next to her began singing, curbing the conversation. After a few lines, Frances recognized that the woman was mutilating *Don't Sit Under the Apple Tree*. The beloved Andrews Sisters had had a great hit with it.

> *Don't sit under the apple tree with anyone else but me*
> *Anyone else but me, anyone else but me*
> *No, no, no*
> *Don't sit under the apple tree with anyone else but me*
> *Till I come marching home.*

The WAVE—Madeline was her name, as Frances recalled—sounded like a cat trapped in a room full of dogs. Waiting her turn in line, Sophie's expression was one of satisfaction, like another cat, this one preening over her whiskers as she observed the one cornered by dogs.

The WAVE finally finished. Two other girls sang romantic tunes of longing and loss. Then it was Sophie's turn.

Lillian, who was facing away from the makeshift stage area, turned around to watch their friend. Frances, who had fully expected Sophie to sing something sultry and befitting a movie star, was completely surprised by her friend's song choice, a rousing ditty called, "In der Fuehrer's Face," made popular in a Donald Duck cartoon film short a couple of years ago.

Sophie had a tiny kazoo in her hand that she brought to her mouth and through which she blew a raspberry every time the lyrics reached the words "Heil!"

> *When der Führer says we is de master race*
> *We heil (pffft) heil (pffft) right in der Fuehrer's face*
> *Not to love der Führer is a great disgrace*
> *So we heil (pffft) heil (pffft) right in der Fuehrer's face*

Sophie marched around as she sang, making comical faces and exaggerated arm swings. The women in the audience responded wildly to Sophie's comic interpretation of the song.

Frances realized that Sophie wasn't interested in singing as much as she was in *performing*. Once Frances understood that, it all made sense.

She also realized that as Sophie performed, she didn't seem ill at all. Her face was aglow with pure joy.

The next verse was dedicated to the two most detested men in Germany after Hitler: Joseph Goebbels, Hitler's Minister of Propaganda, and Hermann Goering, commander-in-chief of the *Luftwaffe*, or air force.

> *When Herr Goebbels says we own the world and space*
> *We heil (pffft) heil (pffft) right in Herr Goebbels' face*
> *When Herr Goering says they'll never bomb dis place*
> *We heil (pffft) heil (pffft) right in Herr Goering's face*

The women in the dining hall laughed uproariously at Sophie's antics.

Frances turned to make a comment to Dottie about Sophie's comedic talent, but Dottie wasn't paying attention. Instead, she was glancing around furtively.

"Is everything alright?" she asked her friend.

Dottie turned her attention to Frances and smiled wanly. "Of course," she mouthed.

Sophie finished her musical routine to great cheers, accepting accolades as she made her way back to where Frances and the others sat.

She plopped down on a chair next to Lillian, red-faced and sweating, her hair stuck to the sides of her face.

Frances started to offer congratulations to Sophie on her performance, but Sophie interrupted. "Where's Dottie?" she asked.

Frances turned again. Dottie was nowhere to be found. With Ira Reed again, no doubt. What a shame that she couldn't be open about it.

She quickly forgot about Dottie's ill-fated love affair, for Sophie began coughing violently.

CHAPTER 44

FRANCES WAS GRATEFUL that Lt. Wallace had allowed her to resurrect her work in the garden. Rooting around in the soil, dropping in seeds–some as large as peanuts and others as small as nits, moving seedlings around, and pulling weeds, were activities even more relaxing than sitting at the canteen with Lillian.

"You're one of us, my girl, so you're welcome to run the garden as you see fit, even if you're just a mature older woman now," Lt. Delores Wallace had said with uncharacteristic warmth.

Frances particularly needed the relaxation now, as Sophie had told her privately that she had been diagnosed with tuberculosis, a grave diagnosis. Tuberculosis was also contagious, so Sophie had been sent to St. Mary's Hospital for quarantine. The base hospital was still in its infancy and couldn't accommodate a quarantined patient yet. Meanwhile, the rest of the women in the barracks had submitted themselves to TB skin tests, which all came back negative.

It just wasn't possible that fun, vibrant Sophie was so ill.

All of Frances's gardening supplies had been saved, so she gathered them together, tied a scarf around her head to protect her hair, pushed sunglasses up over her nose, and gloves over her hands, then got to work in the garden.

Thinking it was much too big an implement for what she was doing today, Frances tossed the long shovel to the ground behind her and just kept her small hand tools nearby.

It didn't take long before she was in near perfect communion with the vegetation in the warm sunshine. She spaded, plucked, and planted with gusto in the hot sun, trying to forget Sophie's doleful expression at delivering the news the previous day, as well as her own weepy reaction to hearing it.

Wasn't God satisfied with taking youth from those dying in the war? Did He also require sweet young women who had done nothing wrong?

But no one had ever said that dying was only for the old.

Eventually, Frances sat back on her folded legs for a break. She closed her eyes and leaned up toward the sunshine, observing with wry amusement that she probably looked a little like one of Sophie's movie stars, what with her billowing head scarf and old Bakelite sunglasses.

The sun felt good against her face, like a warm caress. An assurance from above that all would be well.

Roger was gone, but maybe Sophie would get better. It was a hope she would cling to like a life preserver.

She opened her eyes at the sound of a seagull squawking overhead, hoping it wouldn't send any droppings her way. The bird made a graceful arc as it turned back in the other direction.

With the peaceful moment broken by the bird, Frances resumed her gardening, picking up a spade to dig around and soon coming across old garlic cloves that had never sprouted.

She bent down to examine the cloves as she dug them out, brushing the soil away from them. She wrinkled her nose. Not only had they not become bulbs, but they were moldy and soft. Had someone planted them like this, or had they simply gotten too wet underground?

Frances wondered who had overseen planting garlic this year. Not that it mattered, given that it was frequently difficult to get high-quality seeds and bulbs, anyway.

She would wait until there had been a good frost on the ground before bringing some new cloves to plant. She had kept a small bag of them in her possession, leftover from the refrigerator in her trailer, and could plan to spend a Saturday planting them here at–

Frances suddenly felt a chill run up her spine. The sort of someone-stepped-on-your-grave chill. She sat up and shivered with the useless garlic cloves in her gloved palm.

What had caused that? She shrugged. Grief, worry, fear…she no doubt had all manner of gremlins eager to wreak mayhem in her, as they were rumored to do in aircraft.

Well, she owed it to the country to keep moving forward, no matter what her personal sufferings were. Dottie had lost her brother and soldiered on, even finding a secret romance with her civilian worker, though she was risking exposure by constantly disappearing to see him. Lillian had lost her fiancé and soldiered on, passionately—if not downright protectively—embracing her career.

Everyone else had loss and pain, and soldiered on, Frances would do the same.

She bent down again, dropping the cloves to one side as she continued digging out more.

All her gardening was forgotten, though, as she heard an object swishing through the air. Suddenly, a thousand stars burst inside her head as she experienced the worst, most instantaneous headache of her life. She sensed herself pitching forward into her garden. It was surreal, as if she were individually counting seeds, cloves, and weeds as she went down on top of it all.

The sunlight was blotted out by a figure stepping into view, but the light was too bright and her senses too rattled to make out who it was.

The last thing she remembered was a deep male voice growling from above her. "That will teach you to nose around, woman."

PART 7:
DIANE

Present Day

CHAPTER 45

I SHUT THE DIARY at the sound of Mary's return from the coffee shop, my mind whizzing in many different directions.

My God, it wasn't Kenny who was killed, it was Roger. And someone had attacked poor Frances, presumably for questioning her husband's death.

"Girl, are you okay?" Mary's disembodied voice came from somewhere near me. I nodded, although I wasn't sure I was okay at all.

She handed me a warm paper cup, complete with paper sleeve and a domed plastic lid.

I took it from her, realizing that I was shaking from what I had read. Poor Frances. And poor Verja.

After I regained my senses, I outlined for Mary what I had learned.

She stared at me, silent and wide-eyed, while I talked. "This is your mystery," she said. "I'm certain of it. You have to resolve her husband's murder for her. That's why there are all those papers and photos with notes about 'the incident' in that box. She never knew who murdered him, although it sounds like it was Captain Nickerson. Even if you can just besmirch his supervisor for posterity, that would at least be something to honor Frances. And how amazing is it that you read about Captain Duke, the county's most famous resident?"

I had not only read about him, I felt like I had actually seen him—along with Frances, Roger, Sophie, and everyone else—with my mind's eye. I nodded. I was having an idea. I should immortalize both Walter Duke and Roger Douglas on my building's History Hall.

First, though, I had to figure out a way to get information that Frances had no way of knowing. "I think it's time to do a deeper dive through some of the records here in the Morgue."

Mary clapped her hands together in anticipation. "Let's go. How can I help?"

Fortified with some of the coffee, my first stop was the box of items containing the service members' photos with dates and "Just before it happened" written across the back of each of them. With Frances's descriptions, I was able to confidently identify who was in which picture. Roger, George, Kenny, and Capt. Nickerson all passed before my view, and I pointed each man out to Mary. I determined that another photo was of Frances's department head, Lt. Cmdr. Mackey, with his tell-tale eyebrows, although I didn't see one of Lt. Barbara Hall.

But as interesting as the individual photos might be, they didn't tell a story.

I also now knew for certain that the photo of the women in uniform were WAVES, who had newly arrived on base. The picture was grainier than the other photos and there was nothing written on the back of it.

"Oh, look!" I exclaimed and tilted the photo

toward Mary, pointing at two women. "I think that these two are Frances and Sophie."

"Amazing. And the image you think is Sophie does sort of look like me, doesn't it? But do the pictures give you any information?"

"Not really." I put all the photos back. I wondered if it was possible for me to find employment records of people from so long ago, before digitized files.

Maybe the files of everyone concerned would reveal some secrets.

I drained my coffee cup in several long gulps.

———✺———

With Mary close on my heels, I sought Leila out, completely unsure how to frame my question. In the end, I decided to be mostly honest.

"Howdy," I said, standing in her doorway and tossing my now-empty cup into a round waste basket by the door. I was surprised by how much better I felt. "I'm thinking of running out for more coffee with my friend. Want anything?"

Leila looked up from where she was typing into her computer. "Yes, something dark and strong to get me through this project. Basically, order me the opposite of whatever you just drank." She grinned at me.

"I'll have what she's having," Mary piped up, pointing at Leila. "Except with lots of cream and sugar."

They both laughed.

Mary and I drove the short distance to the base movie theater, which had a coffee bar. The employee behind the counter offered Mary a curious glance, no doubt because Mary had just been there a half hour earlier. The girl behind the counter then shrugged as we ordered three wildly different coffees but quickly prepared them so we were able to return to the office quickly.

Back at the building entrance, Mary's phone buzzed. She glanced down and grimaced. "Sorry, I need to get back to my office. Good luck and keep me posted." She saluted me and returned to her own car.

I made my way back to Leila's office. Once she had taken a few appreciative sips of her caffeine-laden drink, I ventured into my question, having decided in conversation with Mary during the quick drive how to frame it.

"I was wondering if you could help me with my History Hall project," I began.

Leila took another sip. "Of course. What do you need?"

"I'm looking for information about employees from the beginning days of the base. I found some old photographs and thought it might be fun to do profiles on World War II era workers. They don't have to be in great condition, as Natalie can work wonders with them in her software."

"That sounds fun." She frowned. "Those would be some really old paper records, though. There's nothing in the Morgue?"

I shook my head. "No, just some photos. I do have names."

"But no dates of service? No birth dates? I don't think they would have been tracking by social security numbers then as they were just being rolled out for federal agencies in the 1940s. I think the military began using them in the late 1950s." Leila was warming up to what I would have considered a daunting project.

"Regardless, I have none of that info. Just names and photos. Oh, and all the photos were taken in 1944, if that helps."

She pursed her lips. "Okay, get me those. I'll see what I can do. I've got an idea or two."

To my surprise, Leila was in my office, sitting in a chair across from my desk, when I arrived the next morning. On my desk was a beaten-up, cracked plastic tub overflowing with papers. It looked immensely heavy. How had she even carried that thing around?

She was grinning as though she had just won the lottery as she nodded at the container. "I stopped in at the Pax River Naval Air Museum to see what they might have."

I shook my head. "Don't they just have old aircraft and equipment over there? And the Cedar Point lighthouse bell, of course."

"Primarily. But they are always receiving donations, sometimes from people who have items in their possession that perhaps they shouldn't. I figured they might have some personnel records tossed in with some old maps or aircraft drawings. And today is your lucky day. Didn't get a chance to go through this in detail, that's for you to do. The museum had a surprising number of old papers having nothing to do with their naval aviation exhibits." She rose from the chair. "Have fun."

She left my office, and I went straight to work on the box, sorting and organizing. It was a fascinating trip through the history of the air station from a human perspective.

As Leila had indicated, it was indeed my lucky day. By lunchtime, I had separated out a stack of what I thought were relevant file packets and photos to examine in depth. To enhance that luck, I loaded the stack of files in my arms and carried them to the Morgue with me. Maybe the atmosphere there would somehow help me.

I dropped the stack on a table in the Morgue, pleased that it didn't topple. I locked the door and got to work, standing as I went through the files as quickly as I could, discarding to one side papers that didn't seem as relevant as I had hoped.

Several groupings had cover sheets on them, with markings such as, "From the Test Ranges Department," or "Donated by Test Pilot School." There were also smaller bundles of documents that were donated by various individuals. Names such as "Bunky Harper," "Desmond Smith," and "the Clifton Family," passed before my eyes.

After an hour of careful sorting, my hand touched a large manila packet marked, "Provided by the Jarrett Family."

Jarrett. That was Jinx's name.

How curious.

Before I could unravel the twine closure on the back of the envelope, my phone rang.

CHAPTER 46

"IT HAPPENED!" MARY was breathless on the call.

"What happened? Are you okay?" I had to jostle my mental state to the present.

"Brad sold his patent to a printer manufacturer. He says it's completely under wraps for now who it is, but they are apparently excited about it and, get this, he sold it to them for two million dollars!"

I sat back down in shock. Brad was so...Brad. But Mary's faith in him wasn't misplaced, after all. He really did know what he was doing.

"Wow, that is amazing," I said. "He's the first person I've ever known to accomplish such a feat."

"But there's more," Mary said, dropping her voice even more.

"What?"

"I'm getting married!" her friend squealed. "He gave me a ring as soon as he was done telling me about the patent purchase. So, I'll be getting married in the spring. Are you ready to go bridal dress shopping with me?"

I couldn't help it, I started laughing at the irony.

"What's so funny?" Mary asked.

"Nothing. I'm very happy for you, my friend. It's just ironic that it's on the heels of my breakup with Gus. And of course I'll go shopping with you. Whatever you need."

"I need you to hurry up and figure out who killed Roger Douglas so you can fully focus on my nuptials!"

I laughed again. "I'm not done with the diary yet. Frances may have figured it out for herself."

"Nope, I don't think she did." I could imagine Mary vigorously shaking her head as she disagreed with me.

With that humorous image in my mind, I clicked off the call and finished sorting the various stacks of papers I had, leaving the Jarrett envelope until I had a more complete pile of documents to review.

I finally decided to call it a day and wait to finish work on the stack, as I didn't think it likely that there was anything earth-shattering in the collection of papers.

I was wrong. I couldn't believe what I found buried inside the multitude of documents and photos the next day.

CHAPTER 47

THE NEXT MORNING, I rose two hours early, completely unable to continue sleeping. I sat in front of the television with an extra-large bowl of Cheerios for fortification and spent about an hour watching a shopping channel. I polished off the cereal and ordered a brightly colored jacket with red and blue parrots on it that called out seductively to me with its easy payment plan and quick shipping offer.

That accomplished, I fed the ever-disagreeable Tobias, got a large thermos of coffee made, and got ready for the day. After showering, I donned leggings, an oversized, plum-colored sweater, and boots. It was casual yet dressy at the same time.

Back in the Morgue, I went through several groups of donated papers and saw nothing of interest, save some formal military photographs. One was of Lt. Cmdr. Mackey and was attached to a promotion announcement from lieutenant commander to full commander in November 1945.

Hmm. Good for Lt. Cmdr., I mean Cmdr., Mackey.

I also found another photograph of the man I was sure was Roger's supervisor, Capt.

Nickerson. Surprisingly, it was a casual, outdoor photo of him surrounded by other Marines under a pavilion. They were seated at a long picnic table that was covered in beer bottles, cigarette packs, and what looked like the remains of a barbecue, although who knows what meat they may have had access to for their meal. Maybe a local hunter had provided some game.

Capt. Nickerson stared seriously at the camera while the Marines around him appeared to be reacting to a good joke. It was difficult to tell who else might be in the photo. One of the laughing Marines looked to be Roger, but I couldn't be sure.

Maybe I just wanted it to be another photo of Roger.

I finally opened the Jarrett envelope, which contained mostly inconsequential photos of base construction, but also contained a document that I had to re-read twice.

By the third read, my hands were trembling.

CONFIDENTIAL MEMORANDUM
Date:May 17, 1944
From:Sparky Nickerson
To:Lt. Col. Clasen
Ref:Personnel Concerns, Sgt. Kenneth Campbell

Sir,
I am increasingly concerned about the impact of Sgt. Campbell on the reputation of the Corps.

Witnesses attest to seeing Campbell initiate altercations with other Marines, specifically, but not limited to, Sgt. George Somerville. He has also proven himself unable to control his drinking habits. I have enclosed more thorough details of Campbell's malfeasance and behavior unbecoming of a U.S. Marine.

Recommend his dismissal from the United States Marine Corps. Await your response on how to best accomplish this, given Campbell's unfortunate connections.

We may be able to organize a situation that places guilt on him and leads to a court-martial for which no one can argue. His posting at Solomons helps make that possible.

Perhaps Capt. Stricker can be read in for assistance.

Would like to meet on Thursday, at the usual place, to discuss.

The enclosure Nickerson referred to was not there. It was also not typed on any sort of official letterhead, but it was clear that Clasen was someone high up in the ranks.

I laughed in disbelief. Had Jinx's family been related to Capt. Nickerson or this Lt. Col. Clasen to have been in possession of this memo? Or had it passed into their hands accidentally?

My phone buzzed on the table, and I picked it up.

"Good morning. Am I bothering you?" Ironically, it was Jinx.

"Not at all. Just working on some World War II research. Get this, some of the files I came across at the naval museum showed that they were donated by the Jarrett family. Relatives of yours?"

"Really? I imagine so. We've been around a long time, and I know there are members high up in the tree who were in both world wars. Let me know what you find out. Maybe there's something illustrious in my background that my future constituents would like to know." He laughed at himself.

"Anyway, just wanted to see how you're doing," he continued. "I played tennis with Gus Thursday afternoon, and he told me what happened between you—the rejected proposal and all. I wanted to be sure you were okay."

Jinx was really Gus's friend, not mine, so I appreciated the call of concern.

"Thanks. I'm fine, really. I'm sorry that I hurt him, but it was for the best."

"Sure." Jinx was silent for several moments. "Meet for a quick lunch? I'm a little embarrassed to be the middleman here, but Gus passed me a few of your things and I'd like to give them to you."

I doubted it was anything of significance, but I agreed to meet Jinx at Salsa's in Leonardtown at noon.

I returned to my office to sweep through e-mail prior to lunch. As I was about to leave, Ben Tennyson appeared in my doorway.

"Just checking in. You wanted to talk about my family's history, so I thought we could agree on a day and time to meet—" He quirked an eyebrow at me. It was so cute, I felt terrible for having to reject him.

"I'm so sorry, I've been really busy. And now I have a lunch meeting that I'll be late for if I don't leave soon…"

He gave me a thumbs up. "No problem. We'll try again another day." Ben-Ten winked as he walked out.

Just before twelve, I slid into a booth across from Jinx. He had already ordered a large bowl of guacamole and chips. There was a paper-handled grocery bag on the seat next to him.

It had been hours since my cereal, so I dove in with gusto. We ordered chimichangas—mine chicken and his beef—then settled down to chat.

"Might as well give you this now," Jinx said, lifting the bag and setting it on the table.

I pulled it toward me and went through it. It contained an old photography magazine, a toothbrush, a half-used tube of toothpaste, a pair of winter driving gloves, and a wool scarf that was unraveling along one edge.

Jinx's expression was one of embarrassment. "Maggie said you wouldn't care about any of it."

I smiled at him. "It's fine. I can't promise to keep any of it—except maybe the gloves—but I appreciate you bringing it all to me."

Jinx seemed relieved. "Beyond Gus, how are things? How's your Solomons amphibious base research going?"

"I've learned quite a bit," I said. "To include that

there were some, shall we say, very interesting Marines at Pax River at the base's beginning."

"How so? Who were they?"

Our steaming plates of food arrived. I took an appreciative bite and swallow of my fried tortilla meal before continuing. "Pax River's origins were not as…peaceable…as you might think. The Marines came through and cleaned up a lot of corruption on the base. But I believe one or two of them were corrupt themselves. A Marine was found murdered at Cedar Point in 1944, and I think another Marine may have done it."

Jinx's mouth hung open. Fortunately, he had not yet touched his food. "Truly? You've come across a real murder case at Pax River? Have you figured out who specifically did it? It wasn't some relative of mine, was it?"

I shook my head no. I wasn't ready to discuss my suspicions.

He took a sampling from his plate and swallowed. "Man, imagine the headlines once you do. 'Pax River Communications Official Solves Cold Murder Case.' The article just writes itself. Oh wait, *you* could write the article. Maybe you could publish a book about it and make millions." He laughed again.

Jinx was getting way ahead of things. I guess that was how thoughts raced through the mind of a public figure.

"Mary says the same thing about the fame and fortune that would follow me if I figured it out." I laughed with him.

His tone turned serious again. "I must admit, when Gus told me about the breakup, I got concerned that he might say or do something public against you. He's generally mild-mannered, but he can display an odd temper, as I'm sure you know."

"Yes, I know," I murmured.

"In fact, after he had finished telling me what happened, he took his tennis racket and beat it against the court until it completely broke apart. Then he simply walked to his car, opened the trunk, and took out another one, as if nothing had occurred." Jinx shook his head at the memory.

"Gus tends to take things out on inanimate objects, not people," I assured him, inwardly amazed that Gus had done exactly what I had imagined he would do.

"Yeah, let's hope so. I would be less than truthful if I didn't tell you that witnessing him do that made me worry that he might do something in public that might, um, hurt my campaign if people were to learn that we were tennis partners. I'm sorry, that sounds so selfish." His ears reddened.

"Don't worry about it. I seriously doubt Gus would do anything drastic. And you can always count on my vote." I smiled at the man I hoped was a future county commissioner.

I also hoped that I was right, and that my breakup with Gus wouldn't derail Jinx's political career.

I returned to the Morgue, put aside the piles of documents Leila had found, and picked up Frances's diary again. It was time to find out the rest of the story.

PART 8:
FRANCES

August 1944

CHAPTER 48

FRANCES AWOKE TO Maisie, the barracks purveyor, standing over her. "Whatcha doin', Miz Parker? I mean, Mrs. Douglas?"

Frances's entire cranium throbbed as though Lt. Wallace was continuing to beat a metal spoon against a metal pan that was attached to the side of her head. She attempted to rise, realizing that her mouth was full of soil. She spat it out.

"I-I—" Frances stopped. Even in her foggy condition, she realized she had made a terrible enemy on base. It was a man, of that she was sure, but who was it? Capt. Nickerson's visage loomed in her mind.

In this moment, she trusted no one, male or female, other than Sophie, Lillian, and Dottie.

Maisie knelt and helped Frances into a seated position. "Didja faint or somethin'?"

"I guess I must have." She touched a hand to the side of her head. It came away with blood.

"Oh!" Maisie exclaimed. "I couldn't tell you was bleeding with all that dark hair of yours. We gotta get you to a medic."

"No, no, I just need to clean up and go to bed," Frances said. She glanced around. The shovel was gone.

Maisie was also looking around. "How could

you have gotten such a big bang on the head out here? It's like you've been conked by an anchor or somethin'. We should tell the lieutenant that you—"

Frances held up a hand. "No, please. If you could just help me to the bathrooms…"

Maisie shook her head but did what Frances asked.

But now what was Frances to do?

<hr>

Thank God Maisie had found her and helped her get back to her compartment. The bump on the back of her head hurt like the devil, but a few aspirin, a shower to clean up the blood, and by the next morning, Frances felt reasonably human again.

As if her own brush with death weren't enough, she now stood trembling at Sophie's bed at St. Mary's Hospital, clasping the other girl's hand between both of her own, despite the great risk to her own health it was to do so. In fact, she had had to argue hotly with the nurse to be allowed into Sophie's room, which was overwhelmed by the odor of Lysol disinfectant.

Standing over her wan and fading friend, praying, Frances's thoughts wandered, wondering how death could be happening again so soon.

Sophie's tuberculosis had been much further along than anyone had realized, whether that was through Sophie not getting a diagnosis soon enough or her simply hiding it from others, Frances wasn't sure.

It didn't matter now.

Sophie was ashen but awake. At Frances's touch, she struggled into a more upright position against her raised bed. Despite her weakened state, Sophie had managed to ensure she was wearing a sweet, adorable, apple green seersucker bed jacket.

"Oh, Francie, you shouldn't be here. I know I'm contagious. But I'm so glad you're here. I haven't seen anyone since my parents left last week. I've wanted to talk to you."

That simple statement seemed to wear Sophie out. She leaned back against her pillow and closed her eyes for several seconds. Her lips were colorless, and tiny veins were visible beneath her papery skin.

Frances swallowed. How close was Sophie to death?

Sophie opened her eyes again. "How are things with that old battle axe, Lieutenant Hall? Is she still a terror?"

"Not much. She mostly leaves me alone because she doesn't understand the print shop."

Sophie nodded. "That old battle axe," she repeated. "I was thinking, when I get discharged from here, I'm going to do a photo spread on the grass and trees being planted on the base. I miss green things after being in here. All I have is this jacket."

"I think that's a wonderful idea. I bet most people don't realize that the Navy is trying to clear the dust and make the place hospitable for its workers." Frances gently squeezed Sophie's hands between hers.

Another nod. "I have other plans, too." Her voice was a whisper now.

"With Kenny?" Frances asked.

Sophie frowned, seemingly puzzled. "No, he doesn't…care…about this. He finally made a visit. He stood over there at the door, and I told him about it. He said I should forget about what he says are 'fancies' and just focus on getting better because he doesn't want to propose to an invalid."

Kenny was certainly able to make light of the most wretched situation.

"I'm sure he didn't mean anything by it, Soph. He cares about you and looks forward to your getting well."

Sophie lifted her shoulders in a shrug. The effort appeared to be monumental.

"Truly, Francie, I'm not sure if I care about wearing Kenny's ring anymore. He's swell fun, but…I have dreams beyond the Navy. I'm going to go to Hollywood when the war is over. I'm going to meet Charlie Chaplin and Paulette Goddard and Joan Fontaine and, and…" Her voice drifted off, and she fell asleep for a few moments.

Sophie blinked awake. "What? Oh, yes, I'm going to Hollywood. Can you imagine? With the war ending soon, I'll be able to buy my own car, afford gas to go across the country, and be surrounded by famous people. *Movie Life* magazine says most starlets start off in menial jobs before getting their big breaks in motion pictures, but I figure that with my photography skills, I can start right out working for a studio in that capacity."

Frances was heartsick. Sophie was never leaving this bed.

"Maybe I'll go with you and become part of your entourage," she said, teasing her friend.

Sophie smiled. "You would make a great member of my entourage."

Frances stayed and listened to all of Sophie's dreams as the other woman drifted in and out of sleep. But those dreams were not to be. Sophie was gone four days later.

———— ❧ ————

It seemed as though the entire base turned out to pay respects at Sophie's funeral. In addition to Sophie's parents and most of the Marines, all of the WAVES were there. Each woman had taken a movie star magazine from Sophie's compartment and held it up as they all stood around the coffin, as if to give Sophie one last glimpse of what she had loved so much.

Kenny rubbed his fists against his eyes as if to erase what he was witnessing.

Through brimming tears as she half listened to the same minister who had married her and Roger drone on about Sophie's entry into the Kingdom of God, Frances caught sight of someone skirting along the edges of the mourners.

It was George Somerville. He had Gunney with him.

When the burial was over and people were trudging away, Frances walked hurriedly over to where George was moving away to escape the crowd.

Frances caught up to him and placed a hand on his shoulder, causing him to start and turn around.

"George, why were you hiding from Sophie's funeral?" she asked.

"Aww, Frances, I think we both know Kenny didn't want me here. No need to upset him any more than I probably already have." George's eyes were red and swollen. Gunney sat patiently next to George, happily wagging his tail and accepting Frances's head pats and scratches.

"Was there something between you and Sophie?" she asked.

"No. Maybe. Not enough that she woulda stepped out on him. She was too sweet and good to have done that." He choked on his last words.

"Well said." Sophie could be silly and obsessed with Hollywood, but there had never been a mean bone in her body. Other than her low opinion of civilian workers, of course.

"I sometimes used to think that…that… one day after the war, she and I would go to California. We would make movies together, me the director and her the star. A foolish notion, I know, because she was surely going to end up marrying Kenny. Besides, look at me. No one would have ever accepted us together."

Frances sighed. "I think Sophie would have liked going to California with you very much, George. Much more than the idea of marrying Kenny."

George looked at Frances as though she was tossing him a life preserver. "You really think so?"

She nodded. "I really do. Sophie told me a week ago that her dream was to go to Hollywood and get into motion pictures. She no longer cared about marrying Kenny."

George's expression was anguished. "I should have asked—what if I had only—but I wasn't good enough–" He sighed, too. "Your husband warned me that nothing good would come of pining for Sophie. But Sparky—I mean, Captain Nickerson—said to ignore Roger, that I was a U.S. Marine, and taking territory is what Marines do. He said that Kenny could fight for Sophie if he loved her. I mean you no offense, Frances, but I wish I had listened to Sparky instead of Roger."

Frances felt his pain, even if his position had been pointless. "Sophie would still be gone, George," she said simply.

George gazed at her with sympathy. "And so is Roger," he said before turning away with Gunney.

CHAPTER 49

June 1967

TWENTY-THREE YEARS later, Frances wore a midnight blue skirt and jacket over a snowy-white blouse, topped with a matching blue pillbox hat with netting covering the front of her face. Thus attired, she laid the small, store-bought bouquet on her husband's grave.

She'd had the florist tie the stems together with a white ribbon, as usual. White was such a happier color than black, the color of death and despair.

Frances bent her head and murmured a quick prayer for his soul, then held out her free hand toward the handsome young man who had accompanied her. Together they walked away from the grave and toward another.

At this new gravestone, Frances pulled another bouquet from the worn leather tote she had carried since her later WAVES days. Kneeling again before a stone engraved with Sophie Russell's dates of birth and death, she said another prayer.

After this, she rose and, not seeking his hand, walked slowly toward a small monument, an obelisk four feet high. There was no one buried here, yet she knelt again and withdrew the final bunch of flowers from her tote bag.

Frances reverently laid the wildflowers at the base of the obelisk, whispering softly as she did with every visit, "I'm so sorry I wasn't unable to find the beast who murdered you, my love. Please forgive me. One day, the truth will come out. I pray for it every day."

The florist had frowned the first time she had presented these flowers to be tied together with white ribbon. "Are you sure you wouldn't rather have a nice array of roses or carnations?" he'd asked.

Frances had just smiled and shook her head. "No, please. I want these flowers that I picked myself."

Eventually, the florist had gotten used to her periodic requests for two small bouquets and a ribbon for whatever wildflowers she'd picked or obtained from a greenhouse and no longer questioned her.

But the young man standing beside her now did. "Mom, you always stop at this monument. I've never felt like I should ask, but it's really bothering me. What is the significance of it?"

Her son was right, he had politely never questioned this. But he was a grown man of twenty now, so it was time he knew.

She stayed kneeling. "I put this monument here to remind me of someone buried in Arlington. His name is—was—Roger Douglas."

"Roger? But that's my name."

Frances nodded. "Yes. You were named after him."

She brushed away a tear that had sprung from her eye. Funny how time never put an end to some grief.

She held out a hand once more, and he helped her up. "So, who was this fellow?"

Frances began walking again toward young Roger's car, her arm linked in his, and told her son everything—in a rush before she lost her nerve—including how Roger had died mysteriously and no resolution had ever been had. It felt cleansing to share her deepest secrets with him, particularly since he would be on an airplane soon, and God only knew if she would see him again.

Her son was her life's breath. But the Army owned him now.

"Did Dad know about this?"

How could she even explain the aftermath of Roger's death to her son? She knew that Capt. Nickerson had put Henry Lake directly in her path and encouraged her to accept Henry's pursuit of her.

Henry had been a nice man—pleasant, accommodating, generous—just a bit boring. As an accountant working for one of the myriad defense contractors that had descended into St. Mary's County post-war, he had made a decent living and offered no resistance when Frances had stated that she intended to remain in the Navy until having a child. He also made no comment to her insistence that their child be named Roger.

He'd made a weak effort to have her get rid of Gunney. She had "inherited" the dog after

George Somerville left the air station at the end of his tour. Frances had not even entertained the idea of giving up Roger's beloved dog, who lived about six years past his master before succumbing to an intestinal disorder.

George had purchased a farm, got married, and had fourteen children. Many of them were still in the area.

Kenny Campbell had continued escaping any formal trouble for his antics until one day he took up with a fellow Marine's girl. The resulting fight had ended with Kenny in the hospital and the other Marine hanging on by a thread. As usual, Kenny's luck persisted, and the other Marine recovered. Kenny ended up punished but not jailed and offered an honorable discharge, which he greedily snatched before heading to parts unknown.

Despite his admirable qualities, Henry had never filled the bleeding wound in her heart, that neither time nor distractions nor even a cherished child had been able to staunch. He wasn't a terrible man, he just wasn't Roger Douglas.

"Generally, yes. He knew about my marriage to your namesake, of course. Everyone in the county knew about it, given that his body was found at Cedar Point. It wasn't too difficult for your father to figure out why I wanted to name you for Roger."

Frances paused to turn to her son and put a hand to his cheek. "You don't know how much it meant to me to have you. You gave me purpose and meaning."

Roger blushed. "Were you visiting his grave while Dad was still alive? Did he know about the monument?"

A pointed, direct question. No sense in lying to her son now. "He didn't know about the monument. I know it was a secret I kept, but I didn't think he would be happy about it, and I was determined to memorialize Roger locally somehow. Driving up to Arlington to his official grave site didn't seem…appropriate. When I visited Sophie's grave, I visited the monument."

"Does Uncle Fred know about this?" Roger was clearly bursting with questions.

"Yes, of course." Freddy had returned from the war missing his left arm from the elbow down. He had remained good-natured about it, saying that it was just a scratch compared to what other fellows had suffered. It had reminded her of Billy Alvey's cheerfulness.

Her brother had reunited with an old girlfriend from high school, married, and went on to have six children and a successful business. He had eagerly accepted when someone offered him a restaurant franchise in Chicago for only $3,000. The restaurant chain, called McDonald's, had been expanding across the country after the McDonald brothers had installed a man named Ray Kroc to lead the company's franchising efforts.

It had been a wise move on Freddy's part. The strange little hamburgers being promoted by the strange little clown named Ronald on television were a hit with American consumers, and Frances's brother was quickly becoming wealthy, having invested most of his early profits into two more franchise locations in the Chicago area.

She rarely saw him anymore.

"Your Uncle Fred knew how feelings ran long and deep during the war years. During the other war, I mean." How had America reached a place where it was embroiled in another conflict just twenty years after World War II? And that didn't even include the Korean "police action" that took place not five years after the end of the war.

"He understood why it was important for me to keep Roger's memory alive, even if I was starting over in a new life."

Frances had felt pressured into the relationship with Henry by everyone around her, who had meant well but simply didn't understand her desire to be alone. He was a nice-looking man, kind and full of good conversation, but he just wasn't Roger. Reluctantly, she agreed to date Henry and allowed him to woo her into marriage.

Her parents had expressed doubt about Frances's plans but had eventually offered their blessing and sent along a gift. She and Henry had visited the Parkers only twice before her parents died together in a car crash while driving to Colonial Beach, Virginia, for a weekend getaway.

Lillian, Dottie, and the other WAVES had been concerned for Frances's living circumstances after Roger's death. The girls had been worried that returning to the barracks had been too much of a step down in Frances's life. For her part, Frances couldn't have cared less if she ended up living under a tree.

What no one knew was that, deep down, she figured that marrying Henry would keep her safe. It had been months since the attack in the barracks victory garden, but she thought they'd not try to do so again if he had to get past her husband first.

CHAPTER 50

ALL THIS CONVERSATION with her son got Frances to thinking about her old friends and old life during the war. Verja had eventually remarried, too, and moved away with her new husband. They'd exchanged letters for a while, but things naturally dropped off as Verja started having children and became absorbed in her new life.

She wondered what Verja looked like now. Was the gray creeping into her hair, as it was Frances? Did Verja also need glasses to read recipes and the latest issue of *TV Guide*?

Lillian and Dottie still worked on the air station, both retiring from the Navy and transferring into civilian service, which had become a respectable institution over the years.

How shocked Sophie would be to know that.

Lillian had found her way into operations management, and Dottie and taken over as head of communications for the air station, replacing Mackey upon his retirement six years ago, in 1961. A small ruckus had occurred at Mackey's retirement party, for while he was on his fifth or eighth glass of wine, he admitted that he and Lt. Hall had been in a relationship for the past two decades, never revealing it for fear that they would be disciplined—or worse—for fraternization. But with his retirement, the two planned to get married and move to be near his family in California.

The "old gang" from the communications office had gotten together and thrown Lt. Hall a bridal shower. Frances returned the sweet deed Lt. Hall had done for her years ago and gave the woman a pair of pillowcases with an "M" embroidered on the cuffs. Frances's needlework wasn't nearly as good as the lieutenant's was, but the other woman wept in joy over them, nonetheless.

A few years after Dottie took over Mackey's office, she had adopted the recommendations of Robert Propst, a forward-thinking inventor who had come up with an "action office" system that eliminated the rigid rows of desks that defined most office layouts. Propst's system created modular cubicles that provided workers with flexibility, privacy, and ownership over their spaces. So devoted was Dottie to the concept that she had even demolished the office suite in favor of cubicle walls and furniture.

Dottie's beau, Ira Reed, had moved back to Florida after the war to resume his place in his family's pre-war, thriving construction business. He'd proposed to Dottie and begged her to go with him, but she had tearfully told him no; both the Navy and St. Mary's County were in her blood now. She had never married.

Lillian, on the other hand, had made more than one disastrous marriage decision, with one husband running off with another woman and another running off with her retirement nest egg. It was ironic, given how thoughtful and level-headed she'd always been. She had lived out of wedlock with another man now for more than a decade. Everyone in their social circle had chosen to ignore the societal impropriety, given what she'd been through. She had never pursued her teaching dreams.

It had taken Frances some time to forgive Lillian, though, after discovering that she had been privy to some correspondence surrounding the Navy cover-up of the Solomons base conditions prior to and after Roger's death. Lillian had, of course, never known that Frances had been there herself. Lillian had pleaded for forgiveness, citing her restriction to secrecy. It had certainly explained some of Lillian's strange behaviors. Frances had eventually granted the forgiveness, knowing that it hadn't really mattered–Roger's murderer was still unknown, and it was impossible to know how it might have related to his death, anyway.

Several years ago, Dottie had helped Frances gather the meager documents surrounding Roger's murder. Together, they had boxed them, and Dottie had ensured they were stored on shelves in the Nursery.

The print shop had been covered over because the facilities people hadn't wanted to take care of disposing of the mammoth pieces of printing equipment, as technology had greatly reduced the size and cost of the machinery, while improving quality and speed. The Navy moved on by ignoring what was old and inconvenient.

Henry had died after a shocking series of strokes three years ago. Frances missed him, as one might miss a pair of comfortable shoes or a warm blanket, but deep down she had never felt the keening grief she had felt—still felt—over Roger.

Marrying Henry Lake hadn't been a terrible decision, she supposed. He gave her a son she loved and adored. In addition to providing well and not interfering with her job, Henry had largely paid no attention to anything she did. She sometimes wondered if Henry had expressed an interest in her because it meant obtaining married housing.

Regardless, his inattentiveness permitted her long hours to simply *think* without his asking why she was so preoccupied.

Frances had spent years thinking about Roger's death, knowing that it was no accident. Her thoughts always came around to believing that his supervisor was somehow involved, but for what reason, she couldn't fathom.

She had been so lost in thought that she hadn't realized that her son had escorted her a distance away from the cemetery to a local diner.

Frances smiled in appreciation at her son as he held open the door for her, and they sat at a booth next to a window overlooking the sidewalk.

"Diner food is the best food," she declared, picking up the extensive menu and perusing it.

"They have grits," her son observed from behind his menu. "Your favorite."

Frances ordered a large bowl of grits, loading

them up with salt, pepper, and butter, as any good Southern girl would do. Roger seemed bemused by her as he picked up half of his Reuben sandwich, dipping it into a container of extra Thousand Island dressing and eating it in large bites.

Frances refused to contemplate what sort of rations he might be eating a month from now.

Thus fortified—and after ordering chocolate shakes to finish off their wholly unhealthy eating—Frances continued her thoughts. "I have always thought—hoped—that one day someone might figure out what happened to Roger. A foolish notion, I know. He's already been gone more than twenty years, and so few people even remember him now, except me. Most people believed he was the victim of an accident, but I know better."

"What sort of accident?"

"His body washed ashore at Cedar Point one day while he was on duty at Solomons, where there was once a training base. A local farmer found him. Roger really knew that area. He had fished from there, rowed around on a skiff, taken his dog with him there. It was at Cedar Point that he proposed to me." Frances brushed away a tear. It had been decades, so how was it possible that she still felt the loss so acutely?

A loss she didn't sense at all was that of her former in-laws. Genevieve Douglas had ended up institutionalized at the Wayne County Infirmary in Eloise, Michigan, several years ago. All her claims of Roger's mental instability were just products of her own fantastical imagination. Frances had no idea if Genevieve and Arthur were still alive. Truthfully, it didn't matter much to her.

Her son made sucking noises as he attempted to get every last drop of his shake from the bottom of his glass. With the drink now gone, he said, "Mom, just because he knew the area doesn't mean it wasn't an accident. Most people who die in accidents do so within a few miles of their homes." He was gazing at her sadly.

"You sound like everyone else," Frances said. "It just simply wasn't possible that it was an accident because he was found with, he had a kni—never mind, I think perhaps I'd like to stop discussing it." She rose from the table.

"I'm sorry. Of course, whatever you wish." Roger tossed down some money, joined her, and wrapped an arm protectively around Frances's shoulder as he walked her back to his car. He drove her home in silence.

"You're still beautiful, Mom," Roger said as he pulled up in front of the home. "You could find someone else. I wouldn't mind. It might even bring you comfort while I'm gone."

Frances certainly didn't need to be reminded of the fact that her son had been drafted and was headed to Vietnam, a thought that not only turned her insides watery, but also reminded her of her first love's time in Guadalcanal and how it had affected him.

Roger Douglas had returned from the Pacific… would Roger Lake?

PART 9: DIANE

Present Day

CHAPTER 51

ICLOSED THE DIARY. I was fascinated that Frances had amended her journal decades later. How had it ended up in the print shop wall?

Her friend, Dottie Morgan, had worked in the Morgue for many years and had also helped Frances bundle up some papers. It must have been Dottie who had hidden the diary. I contemplated why and concluded that Frances had made some damning statements within its pages. Perhaps I needed to credit Dottie with trying to ensure Frances's plight received future attention.

I sat in my chair, still reeling from the notion that Frances Parker had been hoping for the rest of her life that someone—anyone—would take up Roger Douglas's cause.

At least she and Roger were reunited now.

I closed my eyes to focus. With Frances's story jumping more than twenty years into the future, I was certain I had seen all there was to see from the past. Could the answer to Roger Douglas's death have been presented to me somewhere along the way?

I remained perfectly still, letting Frances's memories wash over me. Except for random chatter in the hallway, all was quiet.

Eventually, I opened my eyes, feeling a sense of "coming to."

It seemed to me there were three possibilities regarding Roger's death, and I needed to ferret out which solution was correct.

First, and, in my opinion, most likely, was that Roger's supervisor, Capt. Nickerson, had caused Roger's demise, either intentionally or accidentally, as part of getting Kenny drummed out of the Marines.

Kenny was apparently "well-connected", and thus his leadership found him to be untouchable. I wish I knew how Kenny was connected.

Could Roger's superiors have had him killed to make it look like Kenny had done it, thus giving them a reason to drum Kenny out of the Corps over which no one could argue? Roger was known to be agitated over Kenny's behavior, so a report of Kenny killing Roger might be believable.

My God. Of all the inane things the military was capable of doing, surely they wouldn't have done this to one of their members, let alone a decorated war hero?

And wouldn't it have been simpler to have just directly killed Kenny and made it look like an accident?

Of course, Kenny had never been accused of it.

My second theory strained credulity a little, but it was possible. Given Roger's disgust with Kenny, he was no doubt further irritated by the jealousy transpiring between Kenny and George. If George and Kenny had ended up in a violent altercation and Roger had intervened, it was possible that Roger had been accidentally killed in the fray.

That would have made George and Kenny complicit together in Roger's murder and performing as remarkably agile liars when they went to Frances about it. But if they had accidentally killed Roger and no one was the wiser, why go to Frances at all? They would have just let the proverbial sleeping dog lie.

Unless they were trying to cast aspersions at Capt. Nickerson in hopes of—what? Getting him court-martialed? But Diane had seen no evidence that Roger's supervisor had done anything hostile toward either George or Kenny.

Then there was the third possibility, the most outlandish of all.

In fact, I felt icy tendrils wrap themselves around my heart, freezing it and refusing to let it beat as I played this thought out in my head.

Roger's parents hadn't seemed to be overwhelmingly affectionate toward their son, and they certainly were not toward their new daughter-in-law. His mother, Genevieve, was particularly hostile toward Frances.

Excuse me, *Zhan-vee-ev.*

There seemed to be some sort of inheritance over which they were concerned about losing control. But surely…

Surely, they wouldn't have committed filicide and murdered their own son over some money.

Would they?

It was unthinkable.

My thoughts drifted to the topic of family

relations and how they are sometimes far more fragile than anyone outside the family can imagine. My mind then went backward to my visit to Aunt Poppy.

I stilled.

Uncle Billy's belongings had included an old envelope that admonished the holder to open it only if and when *"the Marines need me again."*

At the time, I had assumed it to be a funny way of saying, "Don't let the Marines draft me again."

But what if there was something in that envelope that had nothing to do whatsoever with Billy's draft potential? I had been so focused on his medal that I had disregarded everything else in his trunk.

I had to visit Aunt Poppy again right away.

CHAPTER 52

I WAS BREATHLESS BY the time I was banging on Aunt Poppy's storm door. My thoughts were a veritable tempest, and I could hardly contain myself.

But by the time she opened the door, wearing her familiar old ruffled white apron with cherries, lemons, and blueberries printed all over it, I had regained my composure.

"Hi, Aunt Poppy. What's cooking?" I asked casually. "Need some company?"

Aunt Poppy's puzzled expression immediately cleared. "I just tried my hand at making beignets. My friend, Shirley, just came back from New Orleans, and she said they are all the rage down there. They are quite easy to make. Come in, come in."

I followed Aunt Poppy inside, remaining calm as we went to the kitchen and sat down. Aunt Poppy put a plate of powdered sugar-coated sweet biscuits in front of me. They were still very warm to the touch, and the first bite had powdered sugar literally melting inside my mouth.

"I also made some chocolate sauce for dipping." She placed a small bowl next to me, and I dipped the remainder of the square confection in it.

It was so delectable that I almost forgot about Uncle Billy.

Almost.

I polished off both beignets on the plate and pushed it aside. "Hey, Aunt Poppy, remember showing me Uncle Billy's World War II memorabilia?"

Her puzzled expression was back. "Of course I remember. I'm not senile, you know."

"Sorry, I know. I was just wondering if I could see it all again."

She nodded. I admit that I licked my powdery fingertips before wiping them on a napkin and following her down the hall again. Once more, I knelt next to Billy's trunk and opened it, this time going straight for the envelope, which was still there.

I pulled it out reverently and read the blue scrawl across the front. *Open only in case the Marines need me again.*

"That's what interests you? Why? I never opened it because it was sealed, and I didn't want to destroy it. Seemed like it would be a little sacrilegious." There was a warning in Aunt Poppy's tone, but I wasn't going to be stopped.

I turned to my aunt, who slowly got down on her knees to join me. "Auntie," I began. "I must open this envelope. It's hard for me to explain right now, but I think the contents are very, very important."

"Important? After all this time? To whom?"

As quickly as I could, I told her about finding Frances's diary and the contents of it.

Aunt Poppy didn't interrupt, she only nodded

at various points of the story. When I finished telling her that I believed Billy's envelope to be important, she nodded a final time. "Okay, my girl, let's see what we've got here. But first—"

Aunt Poppy scrambled up to her feet. "Wait here."

I felt a little foolish remaining on my knees in front of the trunk with the envelope laid reverently in my palms, but my aunt returned momentarily with an ivory-handled letter opener. I imagined it to be as old as she was. "Try to be as neat as you can. Respectful."

I understood her perfectly. I gently put the tip of the opener under the envelope flap. It cut through the paper like butter. Aunt Poppy took the opener from me as I opened the envelope to remove its contents, which amounted to two thin, yellowed sheets of lined paper full of even tinier writing than what was in Frances's diary.

CHAPTER 53

AUNT POPPY TOOK the envelope from me, and I'm pretty sure we were each holding our breath. I carefully unfolded the pages. The cramped writing covered both sheets, top to bottom and front to back.

I read aloud.

> *Mom and Dad,*
> *I sure hope that you don't ever see this while I'm still alive, coz for sure you'd be disappointed in your only son. A decorated hero, they call me, who's got a lot of shame to bear.*
> *No, I'm no hero. Maybe I took care of some of the enemy, but I couldn't help my comrade when he needed me, and that makes me a cowardly schnook. I need you to know about it, but I can't bring myself to tell you about it face to face. I can stare down a thousand Japs, but I couldn't bear to see you disappointed in me.*
> *While I was with the Marine detachment at Patuxent River Naval Air Station, I had a gas with some of the other fellas. There was Roger Douglas, Kenny Campbell, and sometimes a black fella named George*

Somerville. Some folks were pretty mean to George, but he never flipped his lid or got mad about it.

Kenny was sweet on a WAVE named Sophie Russell, and George was, too. Of course, no one was ever going to accept her going 'round with George, although I think she was sweeter on him than she let on.

But Kenny knew it and was none too happy about it. Him and George were helping Roger with troop training over at Solomons, with Kenny always causing some kind of trouble. Not that he cared, he had cover from somewhere up on high.

I'd almost say he was on the sauce and that's what made him act the way he did, but he never did seem to be buzzed or on a bender. At least, not until that one bad night. No, I think it's just how he was—a crummy leatherneck who was doll dizzy for that Sophie Russell and a fat head when it came to anyone or anything else.

I'd bet money Sparky knew who was covering Kenny, but he never let on. I think he was hoping to move him out of the Marine Corps without it looking suspicious. Roger thought the Marine Corps was trying to have him take care of Kenny permanently and take the bum rap for it. Roger wouldn't do it and that's why he died.

I stopped for a moment, rereading the last sentence. Had the answer to his death been in my uncle's letter all along? How strange to find out this way—

I hurriedly read on.

You see, Kenny was not just a disgrace to the uniform; he was able to get away with murder. The wrong murder.

I don't know when his cap snapped and he decided he was going to remove George as his rival for Miss Sophie's affections, but I caught him polishing the blade of his K-bar one day in the barracks. He was alone in there, sitting on his bunk, and had a map of the amphibious base next to him. I asked him what he was doing, since he was mumbling to hisself and seemed to be short-circuiting between his ears.

He told me to mind my own self. But I had my suspicions about him and started keeping my peepers alert to his movements.

I soon knew Kenny was after George because he kept suggesting that they volunteer for duty over there together. He wanted to catch George unawares at Solomons—the place was the latrine of Navy bases, and you probably coulda dumped a body in a ditch there and no one would have been the wiser.

So, I got lucky when Roger requested my presence at Solomons. I followed Kenny everywhere that I could. One night, all the fellas got together, bought some beer, and met down along the shore for a bonfire and some hijinks. Like I said, I was keeping close watch on Kenny and made sure to sit next to him on a blanket. He proceeded to drink a month's worth of brew that night, no doubt liquid courage for what he planned to do. But he was too soused to pay good attention to what he was doing.

George was sitting with us and said he was going to go find some cigarettes for all of us and walked away. There was nearly a full moon but a lot of cloud cover, so George disappeared from sight pretty fast. Kenny waited about a minute, then told me he had to relieve himself at the latrine.

That was, of course, an obvious lie, so I waited a minute and went after him. I was about twenty yards away from him when I saw him approaching another man walking along the shore's edge. Kenny suddenly ran at him, as though possessed by the worst demon hell had to offer. The man turned toward Kenny, and at that moment, the clouds parted to reveal that it was Roger there, not George. But Kenny was too far gone and plunged his K-bar into Roger.

I'm not proud to say that I turned tail and ran. If he would do that to Roger, what would he do to me? And he had enough protection that he would never be punished.

I vomited my guts out in a trash barrel and tried to hold myself together. Kenny came back to the bonfire like nothing had happened. All the play acting with George that came after was sickening. But Kenny never tried to get George again, as far as I know. Maybe he got scairt hisself. I was never so glad to see someone's backside as when Kenny left the air station.

I swear, I wish Roger had taken care of

Kenny personally. Then he'd still be here, and Kenny would be in hell, where he belongs. At least that louse moved away after the trouble with that other gal. Don't know what mighta happened to him and don't care.

All I know is if Kenny were to find out that I know what he did, he would blow for sure and come after me. And he's such a conniving cheat that he would never face me man-to-man but would most certainly ambush me somewhere. I'd end up with a knife in my chest while sitting on the toilet, you know?

I hope that in the event of my demise, someone will think to open the envelope containing this letter.

As God is my witness, this is the entire truth.

And if the Marines ever come looking for me, it can only be to make sure I never breathe a word of what I know.

———— ✖︎ ————

So, there it was; my very own family had the answer the whole time.

I quietly folded the letter. Next to me, Aunt Poppy let out her breath in a great whoosh. "I can't believe I never opened that. Not that I would have even understood what he was talking about without your story. Well, you know what you need to do now, right?"

I was hoping she would tell me to go home and sleep on it overnight. I was suddenly exhausted.

"You've got to figure out how to tell Frances's son that you solved it. And that begins with figuring out what eventually happened to her and where she's buried. You should visit the St. Mary's Historical Society to get those answers."

Yes, my aunt was right. I dashed out of her house.

CHAPTER 54

MAYBE I COULD spend some time at the historical society before it closed for the day. It was going to be at least a thirty-minute drive to Leonardtown from Ridge.

As I drove, I made a mental list of questions to be answered, hoping that the historical society had possession of extensive birth and death records, as well as area newspapers going back to World War II. I knew they had digitized much of their collection, as I had accessed it during all my History Hall research, but talking to an actual archivist would make my pointed research so much simpler.

Some of my questions were to solidify my answers about Roger's death, while some were just to satisfy my own curiosity. Had Roger Jr. returned from Vietnam? When had Frances died? Had Roger's death ever been investigated by the local papers? Were there any historical records on Sgts. George Somerville or Kenny Campbell? What about Capt. Nickerson, or even Lt. Colonel Clasen?

Moreover, I wondered if the historical society could help me track down records from further afield. Had Roger's parents ever come into a vast sum of money? Could I learn what had happened to them? Frances had seemingly lost all contact with them, but maybe I could create a paper trail to the past.

I made a quick stop at Pax River to pick up Frances's diary and the box of old documents. It might all come in handy. I continued my journey, my thoughts scattered from Billy's letter to Frances's diary, to the multitude of other documents I'd found. Something wasn't sitting right with me about Uncle Billy's letter. But I couldn't put my finger on what was bothering me.

As I entered Leonardtown, I dialed Jinx's number.

"Diane, your ears must have been burning. Gus is here and—"

I had no interest in anything Gus was doing. "Hey, Jinx, no time for that, sorry. I wanted to let you know that I have some evidence on that cold case murder from World War II. I didn't want to wait until your next visit to tell you about it. I have a document stating that Kenny Campbell murdered Roger Douglas in 1944. I think he might be a relative of yours."

There were several seconds of silence on the other end. "What? How do you know this? I'm aware of Campbells in my ancestry, but what you're saying would be common knowledge in my family if true."

I shrugged, not that he could see me. "Remember I said I found documents donated from your family? I think they prove a cover-up the military was doing to protect Kenny from—" From what? Based on Uncle Billy's letter, I wasn't sure anyone, but he was witness to what Kenny had done. "From himself," I finished up lamely. "I'm on my way to the county historical society to conduct a little more verifying research, but I thought you'd want to know right away what I learned."

Jinx's voice was now distant and sad. "Yes, thanks. I just—wow, this is going to make for an interesting conversation at the dinner table tonight. Keep me posted on what you find."

I clicked off, parked on a side street, and hopped out of my car, only then realizing I had no pen or paper with me. Hopefully, the historical society could help with that, too.

As I crossed the rear of the property toward the entrance, I saw a small, plexiglass-covered monument. It appeared to be a weathered, oblong rock, protected from the elements by its encasement.

I approached the metal placard standing nearby and read it.

> *Approach the Moll Dyer Rock with caution!*
> *Its curse is whispered to linger, causing injury,*
> *illness, and even camera failure if touched*
> *by any mortal…all because of Moll Dyer's*
> *vengeance on that cold night in February*
> *1698.*

I laughed at the humorous admonition.
But "vengeance" was certainly an apt term. According to Uncle Billy, it was Kenny's desire for vengeance on George Somerville that led to

Roger's death. But was it? I was troubled by my distant relative's "confession."

I read on. This rock, which claimed to have Moll's handprint gouged in it, had been found in 1968 by someone named Philip Love. It had been moved to the grounds of the Old Jail in 1972 and then to the grounds of Tudor Hall in 2021.

I bent down to gaze more closely at the rock, which was more aptly a small boulder. I could see where there was an indentation that might have been construed as a handprint, but it was hard to tell. I wondered how Mr. Love had determined that he had found the rock that Moll had flung herself upon.

Hadn't Frances and her pals gone to Leonardtown Square to see a Fleetliner and run into a woman who had talked about the Moll Dyer legend? The woman told Frances that the rock had never been found.

I rose. I didn't have time to wonder about this for long, as I had other research to conduct.

Inside the historical society building, I found a helpful volunteer who set me up with a comfortable chair and table with a computer linked to their considerable database of digitized records.

The volunteer also proceeded to bring me volume after volume of paper artifacts and records after I said that I preferred to flip through paper rather than making pointed searches through digital records. Sometimes you come across the most interesting things by simply browsing and immersing yourself in tangible bits of the past.

I was absorbed in research in no time. Although I started with dry census and statistical records, I quickly moved on to more interesting newspaper articles. One from 1945 caught my eye. The article was a fluff piece, detailing the departure of many service members from Pax River to their homes in states across the U.S. In addition to a photo of a line of men holding duffel bags, there was a list of sailors and Marines who were leaving service and returning to their homes. I caught Kenny's name and that he was returning home to "the Midwest." I could imagine him being slippery with the reporter about where he was specifically headed.

A special inset showed that local service member, George Somerville, was being bussed a short distance to his home in St. Mary's County.

I knew Somerville was still a prominent name in the area. In fact, there was a road named for Joseph Lee Somerville, Sr., who had been the first black sheriff in St. Mary's County and the state of Maryland in the 1970s.

Another inset listed all the service members who had called St. Mary's County home but had never returned home from the fight. It would be interesting to compare the list to the monument in Leonardtown Square.

I discovered a June 1961 wedding announcement for Cmdr. Edward Mackey and Lt. Barbara Hall. Mackey towered over his slight, severe-looking bride. They were just as Frances had described them.

The paragraph below the posed wedding

shot stated, in part, "…the blissful couple will honeymoon in the Poconos, Pennsylvania. Both the bride and groom were repeatedly recognized by the U.S. Navy for exemplary, sometimes dangerous, beyond the call of duty service during the war."

Hmm. I rolled my eyes at the exaggeration. Hadn't it been Frances—and Dottie—who had served in an exemplary manner?

Higher-ups had taken credit for their subordinates' actions since time immemorial, I supposed.

I froze. I heard a small clicking in my brain, like gears falling into position.

Roger worrying over Kenny's unbecoming behavior.

Uncle Billy confessing to having witnessed Kenny mistakenly attack Roger instead of George.

Capt. Nickerson's clandestine memo to Lt. Col. Clasen, considering a request for help from above to eliminate the Kenny problem.

My God, I knew what had happened! I couldn't prove it one hundred percent, but I could most certainly do something about it.

With my heart pounding, I looked at obituaries to see when Frances, Lillian, Dottie, Kenny, George, and even Roger Jr. had died. I didn't find anything immediate in my pile of documents and knew that would require searching some sort of database. With staff help, I was able to learn that Frances had died first, in 1986, followed by Lillian in 1998, and Dottie in 2001. George had had remarkable longevity, living on until 2012 and leaving behind dozens of grandchildren and great-grandchildren.

Roger Jr. had indeed returned from Vietnam. It looked like he had stayed in St. Mary's County until his mother's death, and then he disappeared from the record.

Nuts. I couldn't tell him personally what I knew. But maybe with social media I could find him and at least tell him via a message.

I couldn't find anything on Kenny Campbell other than the article showing that he had returned to the Midwest. Once more employing staff help, I was able to access other databases, and that's when I discovered a shocking revelation.

The *Kansas City Star* had published an article in 1992 regarding the death of a World War II "hero," Kenneth Campbell, a loner who had no known relatives in the area.

Sgt. Campbell had apparently taken his own life, leaving behind a cryptic note that the article's author stated: "...*made no sense and might have been the product of dementia, God rest poor Sgt. Campbell's soul*".

CHAPTER 55

ICOULDN'T BELIEVE MY luck. The paper had included Kenny's note, primarily because the police had sought the public's help in deciphering it, as the sergeant had left behind no known relatives, and, in fact, had been discovered after his death by a paid caregiver making daily visits to his tiny home in the seemingly depressed area known as Ivanhoe.

So much loss, so much waste. I'm sorry, Roger, I wish it had been George. I'm sorry, Sophie, you should still be here. Nothing ever went my way in life, thanks to all of you. You each had a part in ruining my life, but none of you cared. At least I never suffered the indignity of a jail cell thanks to dad's connections. But no one ever understood how George had insulted me.

I know everyone thought I was a clunkhead, but that insult didn't mean that I harmed anyone. But I know who did it. A brown-noser who even got rewarded for it.

I also knew Billy always suspected me of it. He thought I was the one in the shadows that night, when all I did was go to the latrine for a few minutes.

*My conscience is clear, and I am innocent
of wrongdoing, yet my mind troubles me
sometimes. I don't understand it. How I still
miss Sophie.*

Yes, I understood it all. Uncle Billy had been quite mistaken in his assessment of whom it was he saw on the shoreline that night.

A photo of Kenny in his later years accompanied the article. The photo showed a man to whom time had not been kind. It showed him hunched over on a cane, with wisps of white hair combed over a head dotted with liver spots.

So much duplicity. I considered how Capt. Nickerson had acted suspiciously, being dismissive of Frances's fears as well as being cagey toward her about Roger's death. He must have known Kenny was the target and that Roger's death was an accident. He had obfuscated everything from Frances to protect her—and himself—from the consequences that the truth would bring.

I scrambled backward to look for Frances's death notice. She had died six years prior to Kenny's suicide, so even if she had known to look for this newspaper, she was sadly gone before its publication.

Frances had been buried in a local cemetery, Charles Memorial Gardens. Why not visit her grave and tell her that I now knew the truth behind Roger's death?

I stretched, exhausted from both being hunched over research and making such alarming discoveries.

I looked around me for the first time in hours and realized I was the only visitor there and that it was near closing time. In fact, it was dusk outside.

I visited the restroom, then thanked the remaining staff member on my way out the door. The sun had all but disappeared, and the air was chilly. I pulled my inadequate jacket around me, glad that I was wearing long pants today. I walked along the brick path and rounded the corner to the rear of the building, my heels tapping out a rhythmic beat as I did so and bringing calm to my whirling mind. It seemed as if my brain was constantly in overdrive these days, leaping from one situation to another and—

I felt a tap on my shoulder. "Diane," murmured a low male voice.

"Gus?" I said, turning. "How did you know I was—?" But before I could complete my thought, I felt pain exploding in my left temple as I stumbled to the ground.

"That will teach you, woman," a man's rough male voice growled at me.

CHAPTER 56

MY GOD, THE words uttered to Frances in her garden. Words that I now knew belonged to Roger Douglas's killer. The pain made me confused—had the man come back from the grave to attack me like this?—but I flailed, reaching out for anything I could grab. That turned out to be the leg inside a pair of men's slacks.

The owner of that leg grunted as he pulled away from me. I was dazed and confused, but held onto cloth and bone with both hands like it was a life preserver. The man started uttering expletives at me as he tried to shake me off, but I managed to get my hands around his ankle, further anchoring him to me.

"Let go of me, you idiot." That voice didn't belong to Gus.

It was Jinx.

"Why are you attacking me?" I gasped, still refusing to let go of him even though he was giving it all he had to shake me off. He was pulling me down the walkway in the direction of the Moll Dyer rock. The brick beneath me was rough and uneven and scraping my skin through my clothes. But I was determined not to let him go.

"You couldn't just be satisfied with some historical tidbits, could you? I was patient when you started snooping around Solomons, and even tolerant when you showed me all your little findings—damn, woman, let go of me—but if you think I'm going to let you go public about my ancestor's misdeeds, you are sorely mistaken. I haven't come this far in my career to be derailed over a piece of ancient history. You know how people talk in this county. Kenny's sins will become my own. I'm taking care of you before you do anything to ruin me." His speech was labored as he dragged me along. I realized that he was headed not just in the direction of the Moll Dyer rock but was aiming for it.

I wondered if he realized how stupid he sounded. He didn't need to worry about Kenny's actions tainting him. In this moment, he was quite full of his own sins.

And those sins included "taking care of me." Did he plan to bash me against the plexiglass enclosure? I would be seriously injured if he did.

"Jinx," I gasped. "It wasn't Kenny who did it. Do you hear me? It wasn't Kenny!"

I wasn't sure what to do. If I let go of him, he would then be free to just hook his arms under my own and carry me wherever he wanted. I'd never be able to get up on my feet and get away from him before he had me in his grasp.

I wanted to scream, but it was impossible to catch my breath enough to do so.

If only someone were leaving the historical society building right now. However, we seemed to be alone together in the twilight. I would have to take care of myself.

I grabbed around his ankle, squeezing as hard as I could and digging in with my nails, hoping they were penetrating the fabric of his pants. He howled in pain and paused to bend over and pull at my wrists, cursing me volubly as he did so.

I used the moment to roll away from him.

Jinx attempted to reach for me but instead slipped and fell. I watched as his head struck the Moll Dyer placard and, with a loud grunt, he collapsed to the brick pavers below. I dragged myself into a seated position, panting heavily from fear and exertion. I then leaned over Jinx's sprawled body, staring into his face. I was utterly disgusted.

"Who knew that you were just as stupid and self-centered as your ancestor, Kenny Campbell?" I shook my head and got to my feet. Within a few moments, my head cleared, and I was ready to act, ignoring the various points on my body that promised to make me beg for mercy later.

I ran faster than a rocket boat crossing the Chesapeake Bay—in my own mind, at least—leaping headfirst into my car, locking the doors, and dialing the police.

I met the sheriff's deputies, who were on the spot in minutes, and followed them to watch as Jinx, the golden boy of St. Mary's County, was led away in cuffs in the deepening twilight. He seemed to have recovered from knocking himself out on the Moll Dyer placard. In fact, to my shock, Jinx sneered and spat in my direction as he walked past me. How could this possibly be the fun, happy-go-lucky man that I knew?

He was no longer a favored son, though. That status remained Captain Walter Francis Duke's.

Now I could visit Frances's grave and set her mind at rest, finish my History Hall, and focus on Mary's wedding.

CHAPTER 57

I PLANNED A GRAND unveiling of the History Hall, replete with local news coverage and attendance by all the area's naval leadership, to include not just Pax River, but Webster Field, Naval District Washington, and other regional sites. There was more brass wandering through the first-floor exhibit than might have been found at the Pentagon.

Mary—who had been stunned into silence when I told her about Roger's true killer—was there to congratulate me. "What a triumph!" she exclaimed, as did other occupants of the building.

I was pleased by the reaction to it, particularly after everything that had happened over the past few weeks. I noted many people were lingering to read the walls in depth. I was even more pleased that Leila shoved a warm cup of coffee into my hand to have while meeting and greeting visitors.

Patrick was all smiles. "I knew you and Natalie would do a great job," he said. "You're the finest PAO I've ever had." Then he moved off to be interviewed by a local news affiliate.

I was quite aglow with that praise and wrapped Natalie in a hug of thanks. She, too, was radiant from the warm reception the project was receiving.

I was even more aglow when the news reporter came to interview me, asking lots of interesting questions about the base's history. I led the reporter to the wall section about World War II to show him Roger's story and death, my hope being that the tale might get traction and people around the country would know about him and Frances.

I briefly described to the reporter Mackey's betrayal and murder of a fellow service member he had hardly known for a mere promotion.

A brown-noser who even got rewarded for it, Kenny had said. He knew that Frances's own supervisor had killed her husband. I was thankful he didn't know what role she had inadvertently played in it herself. Her mission at Solomons had provided Capt. Stricker with what he needed to try and improve conditions at the amphibious base… but had also inadvertently provided Lt. Cmdr. Mackey with the information he needed to travel there and attempt to take Kenny out.

He had done it for the notion that taking care of Kenny would shower him with glory and guarantee a difficult-to-get promotion. No doubt the idea of such glory was intoxicating to someone who would never see combat duty.

Uncle Billy thought he had seen Kenny mistakenly attack Roger instead of George that night on Solomons, but, in reality, it was Lt. Cmdr. Mackey who had stepped out of the shadows at the same time Kenny had gone to the latrine.

Except that Mackey wasn't looking for Kenny. He was seeking Roger, who had become a thorn in the sides of both Marine Corps and Navy leadership. A thorn both for bringing attention to the conditions at Solomons and for refusing to take personal action against Kenny.

Mackey, who no doubt believed his behavior to be noble and righteous, even if he had made a heinous error, had been promoted to commander less than two months following Roger's death, for "non-combat service that likely prevented many deaths," according to the promotion announcement. What a cretinous, inane statement.

I had gone back to Frances's diary. Mackey had made the same comment to her when visiting in the aftermath of Roger's death. "His dedication likely prevented many deaths in ways you can't ever know about on this side of heaven."

It was a seemingly kind statement that Mackey had no doubt come up with and provided to Nickerson for the promotion write-up. It wasn't unheard of for a promotion candidate to write up his own accomplishments.

Mackey must have had lots of cooperation from above to have avoided any sort of scrutiny and to have instead been rewarded. Capt. Nickerson was certainly involved, potentially telling Frances that Roger's death was none of her business. Stricker must have approved the promotion.

Roger was a whistleblower and suffered the ultimate penalty for it. Lt. Cmdr. Mackey was a self-centered brute and had gloried in praise and reward.

It was all sickening and heartbreaking. The military killed one of their own, and this bothered me on a personal level. I supposed this could happen today, too, if someone deemed someone else was not towing the line. The whole revelation gave me chills.

I wondered, without answer, if Lt. Hall had known of her future husband's perfidy. I couldn't even contemplate the proposition that she might have been part of it.

In addition to Roger's death, I did devote a small section to Frances's and Roger's tragic love story near my WAVES vignette. That vignette included a desk, a typewriter, and other old office supplies I had found in the Morgue.

I included a few snapshots of Frances's diary, both Billy's and Freddy's letters, as well as Roger's Navy–Marine Corps medal, the WAVES bus photo with Frances in it, and Roger's formal portrait. I added Mackey's photo, but made it as small as possible. Was it petty? Maybe, but it seemed like the right thing to do in my quest to bring Roger and Frances at least a little bit of justice.

Once the crowds had thinned out, I headed back to my office.

As soon as I stepped over the threshold, the heady smell of lilacs was overpowering.

There, in the center of my desk, lay a sweet little bundle of purple and white blooms, tied together with a piece of old twine. It reminded me of the bouquets Frances had described receiving from Roger.

There was a knock on my office door, and Ben Tennyson entered.

"Hey, really great job on the History Hall," he said. "I hope you like 'em." He nodded toward the flowers.

"Are these from you, Ben-Ten?" I asked more sharply than I intended.

"Yes. I'm sorry, do you not like lilacs?" His cheeks reddened as he reached out to take the flowers.

I instantly regretted my tone, as I had clearly embarrassed him. "No, I love them. I just wasn't expecting such a great…kindness…from anyone in the office. Which reminds me," I added, changing the subject, "I'm afraid I've been so busy with the History Hall that I haven't had time to meet you for the article write-up on you that I promised." My coffee was getting cold, so I placed the cup on my desk near the aromatic bundle.

"What?" His brow furrowed. "Oh, that. Not to worry, you can immortalize me another day. But you did promise to have coffee with me to talk about my family history. So, um, hey, I'm wondering if you'd like to refresh that cup of coffee. With me. At the coffee shop of your choice."

I was both inordinately pleased and shame-faced. Because of my forgetfulness, I hadn't been able to include anything from him in the History Hall. Too late now, and he didn't seem to care. "Why, Ben-Ten, are you asking me out on a date?" I could barely remember Gus's face at the moment.

"That depends on how likely you are to say yes."

I considered him carefully. "Tell you what. I have a story to share with you, and your reaction to it will determine whether I say yes or no."

He raised an eyebrow but took a seat in the chair across from my desk. "Color me intrigued. Shoot."

And so, I told him all about Roger and Frances Douglas, their friends, and what I had done to figure out that Lt. Cmdr. Mackey had killed Roger. I told him about how and why Jinx Jarrett, St. Mary's County's darling, had attempted to kill me himself. I finished up with how important it had been to me to memorialize Roger and Frances, to bring their story to light.

To his credit, Ben-Ten just nodded at my account of the past few weeks, only interrupting to suggest that he go to the jail, where Jinx was awaiting trial, to eliminate the trouble of a trial.

And so, we went on a date.

And on many more after that, until one day I became Diane Tennyson.

Of course, I named my three children Frances, Roger, and Sophie.

Every year on the anniversary of the invasion of Normandy, June 6th, I visit Frances's grave, laying a wreath there to honor her World War II service. My children and husband go with me, and it has become a tradition for me to remind the kids of Roger's and Frances's story and how they got their names.

I'm sure my children are bored of the story after so many years, but if I have learned anything, it's that knowledge of history is vital for forming an educated future, and I want my yawning, impatient teenagers to understand how important St. Mary's County's past is to their generation and the generations to come.

I'm even hoping one of them might name a child Lillian or George or Dottie.

THE END

AUTHOR'S NOTE

MY REGULAR READERS know that I like to write a detailed author's note to explain some of the history behind my books. Buckle up, this is a long one.

The idea for this story came when someone in casual conversation said to me: "Did you know that training exercises for the D-Day invasion of Normandy took place down here?"

Upon hearing it, I was at full alert. How had I not known about this in all the years I had lived here? I immediately began digging into the World War II history of St. Mary's County, not realizing that my little community was such an important player in the war.

The Navy viewed the area as a good, centralized aviation testing site in the general Washington, D.C., area that was large enough—and reasonably isolated enough—to allow for exhaustive aircraft test and evaluation. At the time, test facilities were divided across several stations located in Hampton Roads, Virginia; Dahlgren, Virginia; and Anacostia, Washington.

As a former Navy civilian, I can say that when the U.S. Navy decides something, it is decided. The same was true in the 1940s, when the area known as Cedar Point saw itself torn up, to be quickly replaced by a naval air station.

Although the Navy initially called it Cedar

Point Naval Air Station, it was determined that "Cedar Point" sounded too much like "Cherry Point," the name of a U.S. Marine Corps air station in North Carolina, so eventually the Navy commissioned it as **Patuxent River Naval Air Station** in April 1943.

Jarboesville, the area just outside of Pax River's main gate——at the time (now "Gate 2")——was indeed renamed **Lexington Park** in honor of USS *Lexington*, a battlecruiser-turned-aircraft carrier originally built during the 1920s. *Lexington*, nicknamed "Lady Lex," was the sixth ship to be christened with this name, in honor of the Battle of Lexington and Concord during the Revolutionary War.

Lexington was at sea in the Pacific when Pearl Harbor was bombed on December 7, 1941. Five months later, on May 8, 1942, she was crippled by Japanese forces during the Battle of the Coral Sea, located between Australia, New Guinea, and the Solomon Islands (not to be confused with Solomons Island, Maryland!).

Lexington was scuttled by an American destroyer to prevent her capture. A total of 216 crewmen were killed and 2,735 were evacuated from the ship. Also lost were 42 planes that went down with *Lexington*.

In June 1942, shortly after the Navy publicly acknowledged the ship's loss, Navy Secretary Frank Knox agreed to a proposal to rename a new carrier under construction from *Cabot* to *Lexington*. The Frank Knox building, which sits just outside Gate Two and is today used for training and other administrative purposes, is named for Secretary Knox.

Lexington's wreck was discovered off the coast of Queensland, Australia, in March 2018, during an expedition funded by Microsoft co-founder Paul Allen.

Speaking of wrecks, the **Cedar Point Lighthouse**, a cottage-style wood and brick edifice with a square white tower rising above one corner of the roof, was completed in 1896 on an acre and a half of land. It marked the southern point of the confluence of the Patuxent River and the Chesapeake Bay. By the 1920s, the lighthouse was completely surrounded by water due to nearby mining operations and natural shore erosion. It was abandoned in either 1924 or 1928.

The Navy purchased it in 1958 but performed no maintenance, and the building continued to deteriorate.

After damage by Hurricane David in 1979, the Friends of the Cedar Point Lighthouse initiated an effort to preserve the lighthouse's cupola. In 1981, just prior to the lighthouse being demolished, the cupola was removed and, in 1983, was given to the Patuxent River Naval Air Test and Evaluation Museum.

The image of the Cedar Point lighthouse remains an enduring symbol of St. Mary's County.

The **D-Day invasion at Normandy** on June 6, 1944, code-named "Operation Overlord," is today recognized as the crucial turning point for the Allies. France was occupied by Nazi

Germany at the time and the amphibious assault required some 156,000 Allied troops to be landed across the beaches of Normandy in a single day.

At the time, the D-Day invasion was the largest naval, air, and land operation in history. Within days, approximately 326,000 troops and a multitude of vehicles and equipment had landed.

By August, all of northern France had been liberated, and by the spring of 1945, the Germans had been defeated.

The attack required months of planning and considerable cigarette smoking and coffee drinking on the part of the Supreme Commander of the Allied Expeditionary Force, General Dwight D. Eisenhower. It is shocking to think that the U.S. was able to keep the secret of it, misleading the Germans into thinking the Allies were intending to land at Pas-de-Calais.

Instead, the Allies selected a 50-mile stretch of Normandy coastline, with the first phase to be a naval assault, followed by a larger invasion along five separate beaches, code-named Sword, June, Gold, Omaha, and Utah.

There were many Allied successes during the war, both on land and at sea, but D-Day is largely recognized as the beginning of the end of World War II.

To support this invasion, there were indeed beach landing training runs at the **Naval Amphibious Training Base Solomons**. Imagine being a farmer going out to collect eggs one morning and facing a small flotilla of

Higgins boats dumping men in full military gear onto your property in order to "take" it and quickly set up a base of operations. No doubt the farmers received warning of the training exercises, but it would have been a terrifying sight to behold.

As how beaches were named at Normandy, the mock landing sites at beaches along nearby Cove Point and Drum Point were given code names: Red, Blue, Yellow, and Green.

The amphibious base was riddled with problems from its inception in 1942. Constructed to be temporary, as it was believed that all training demands would be satisfied by July 1943, the initial design called for a base that would accommodate 500 men. That estimate was raised to 1,000, then to 2,000, and then again to 3,500.

Construction of the base was done with an austere approach, eliminating any "extravagant luxuries," such as a chapel, married quarters, theaters, gymnasiums, swimming pools, ball fields, and the like.

But the Navy skimped on basics, too. There were no sidewalks, mud was prevalent everywhere, and water only flowed for a half hour each morning and night. There were no laundry facilities, no ship's store, and little response to requisitions for supplies.

This meant that the troops stationed there had literally nothing to do when not training, and their living conditions were spartan at best. The Navy compounded this misery by severely restricting liberty. Ultimately, Solomons was so rural that there was nowhere to go anyway, but Uncle Sam made sure the troops had no chance at it.

Furthermore, the training—which should have been extensive and well-organized—started off haphazardly. New Army recruits were sent to Solomons for eight weeks of training on a topic that was only deeply understood by Marine Corps personnel. These recruits were frequently loaded onto boats and expected to figure it out for themselves.

As if all that weren't enough, the base's brig (jail) had a long "waiting list," so that many prisoners wandered about the grounds at will.

In time, conditions improved, and training became more methodical, which led to an improvement in morale, but housing and facilities never really caught up to the numbers of men passing through.

In all, nearly 68,000 troops were trained at Solomons by the time the base was closed in April 1945. The site is now occupied by Calvert Marina.

The Solomons amphibious base became known as the "Cradle of Invasion" for the impact that its training had on successful beach landings in both the Pacific and the European Theater. It was in a nod to that moniker that I named Frances's offices "the Nursery." That, and when I worked for the Navy at Webster Field, we called an old, high-ceilinged room full of abandoned junk and files in my building "the Morgue," which I always found funny and is a term that seems like the opposite of "Nursery."

I also have Roger showing Frances a priest's travel communion kit that he picked up in the Pacific. The idea for this came from a dear widow I met years ago in England. Her husband had gone to Dunkirk, and while on the beach there, he had come across a priest's communion cup and plate. Having no idea what may have happened to the priest and assuming he had been killed trying to deliver solace to the troops, the soldier picked up the items and brought them home, where they maintained a place of pride on their fireplace mantel.

Capt. Walter Francis Duke was a St. Mary's County resident who was a highly decorated fighter pilot during the war. He had received flight training, was assigned to the 89th fighter squadron of the 80th fighter group at Mitchell Field in Long Island, and had become a second lieutenant...all by his 21st birthday in August 1942.

Eventually, he would join the 459th fighter squadron of the 80th fighter group, then marry his high school sweetheart, **Verja Graham**, in April 1943, before shipping out to India a week later. In the story, I have them married in November 1943 to fit my own timeline.

Between March and June 1944, he was credited with destroying 19 enemy planes and becoming the squadron's—and Maryland's—leading war ace.

On May 27, 1944, Duke received word that orders were being cut for his return home.

St. Mary's County planned a "Duke Day"

celebration for the return of its favorite son. Alas, it was not to be.

On June 6, 1944, ironically the same day as the Normandy invasion, Duke flew what was to be his last mission. His squadron had divided into two groups and performed a sweep over Rangoon, Burma. Duke's plane was shot down and lost. He reportedly shot down three enemy planes before disappearing.

During his short life and career, Capt. Duke earned the Silver Star, Distinguished Flying Cross, the Purple Heart, the American Defense Medal, the American Campaign Medal, the Asia/Pacific Area Service Medal, the Canadian War Medal, and the British Burma Star.

Capt. Duke's remains were finally located in Burma in 2012, 68 years after he was killed. He was a couple of months shy of his 23rd birthday at the time of his death.

Duke named his P-38 "Miss V," in honor of his beloved wife, with whom he spent a single week of marriage before being shipped off across the globe, never to return.

Today, a local elementary school and a regional airport are named for the intrepid pilot. He is also included on a war memorial in Leonardtown, Maryland, as well as at the Walls of the Missing in the Manila American Cemetery in the Philippines.

The war effort made supplies of basic materials, such as food, metal, paper, and rubber, very scarce as there was great demand for them not only by American troops, but our Allies overseas and our own home populace.

Rationing was the government's attempt to control demand and ensure crucial supplies were available to everyone. The resulting rationing system, run by the Office of Price Administration, or OPA, set limits on purchasing certain high-demand items and impacted nearly every family in the United States.

Rationing involved issuing booklets to every person—even babies—that contained stamps worth various points. A shopper would not only have to pay cash for food or other restricted items, but also turn in the appropriate number of stamps. Thus, if bacon was 30 cents per pound and meat was rationed at seven points, the shopper would have to pay 30 cents and turn over seven points' worth of ration stamps.

Tires were the first consumer good to be rationed, starting just weeks after Pearl Harbor. Every day, consumers could no longer buy new tires; they could only patch them or have treads replaced. Exceptions were made for medical and emergency personnel, while bus, delivery truck, and farm tractor owners could apply for approval of tire purchases. Tires became so valuable that automobile owners were advised to keep track of their tire serial numbers in case they were stolen.

By February 1942, automakers were converting their factories to produce jeeps, tanks, and ambulances, making cars scarce. In May 1942, gas rationing began.

The year 1942 also saw food rationing, starting with sugar. I'm not sure I could have survived without my beloved flavored coffee creamer, but it wouldn't have mattered because soon coffee was added to the list, followed by meats, butter, cheese, and canned milk and fish.

As with most government programs, rationing started with good intentions but was fraught with inefficiencies and unintended consequences. For example, the moment the OPA announced that an item was to be restricted, shoppers stampeded into stores to buy up as much of that item as possible, creating immediate shortages.

As you might imagine, rationing also created a black market for many items, resulting in headaches with the government trying to tamp down that activity. Some people were even jailed for it.

I try to imagine Americans agreeing to a rationing system today and it seems like an impossible idea to implement.

The war came to a close in 1945, and rationing ended, except for sugar, which continued to be rationed until June 1947. Many other goods did remain in short supply for several months after the war ended because of years of pent-up demand.

Related to rationing was the government's push for everyone to have his or her own **Victory Garden**. This was the government's effort to reduce the burden on commercial food production by having citizens grow and can their own food so that commercially produced foods could be diverted to the troops. By doing so, the populace would help win the war, thus they were "victory" gardens.

I came across multiple pamphlets and posters issued during the war that covered topics such as how to grow vegetables from seeds and how to stretch a single piece of meat into multiple meals. Newspapers, home economics classes, and various government organizations published recipes for stretching rationing points by creating meatless meals, such as walnut cheese patties and creamed eggs over pancakes.

Kraft Macaroni and Cheese, a staple for kids even today, became immensely popular because it was cheap, filling, and, best of all, required few ration points. Kraft sold more than 50 million boxes during the war.

The Women Accepted for Volunteer Emergency Service, or **WAVES**, played an important role in keeping the base operational while so many sailors were overseas during the war.

Eight days before the commissioning of Patuxent River Naval Air Station, the first WAVES arrived—one ensign and twelve yeomen. By January 1, 1944, the total number of WAVES was 127, and a new WAVES barracks was opened for them in May 1944. For the pacing of my own story, I had the barracks open in 1943.

By the summer of 1945, there were 550 enlisted WAVES and 35 WAVES officers aboard the air station, an enormous swelling of personnel.

Black women were not allowed into the WAVES ranks until October 1944, when the war was nearly over. Notable among these new enlistees were Lt. Harriet Ida Pickens and Ensign

Frances Wills, the first two black officers to be commissioned into the women's reserve.

Speaking of WAVES, I have Sophie observe how inane the building numbering system is on base, asking the others to imagine how confusing it would be if homes were addressed in such a fashion.

Base building numbers are indeed assigned based on their completion date; thus, a lower-numbered building is an older building. It also means that Building no. 1 could be next to Building no. 300. It seems illogical unless you understand how it's done.

And even then, it's still just a wee bit illogical.

However, for Sophie to imply that homes at the time were numbered rationally isn't quite true. At the time, with St. Mary's County being entirely rural, most addresses were based on postal routes—literally, the number of a route assigned to an individual mail carrier plus the number assigned to your box. Thus, most addresses were something like, "Route 2, Box 281," with the "Route 2" being meaningless to anyone except the post office since it didn't indicate any specific road or street.

In the 1990s, St. Mary's County shifted over to a five-digit grid addressing system, so it now not only makes sense to everyone, but emergency personnel can figure out where someone in distress is located.

Today's **civilian service** is not what it was during World War II. While current civilians are selected and promoted based on a combination of merit and experience, the civilian workforce of the World War II era was largely comprised of either people who couldn't serve due to some sort of disability or who were conscientious objectors.

Civilian service today can be a good career, consisting of jumps through a series of responsible positions. During World War II, however, civilian workers were largely given very undesirable jobs, such as trail building, pest control, and dam construction. Frequently, the work was forced and could also be unpaid. Why? Because the draft number for a conscientious objector would come up, and the idea of such a belief system was viewed as unpatriotic and cowardly, particularly by those families who either had fathers, sons, and brothers serving or who had lost a relative to the horrors of war. Thus, the objectors would still be drafted into service but would be placed into the worst of jobs.

I am not aware of how many civilian service members would have been involved in constructing Pax River, but I imagine there would have been quite a few among the thousands of hired building contractors.

For a great movie on a World War II conscientious objector, Desmond Doss, see the Mel Gibson flick, *Hacksaw Ridge*. Doss was a remarkable, patriotic man who saved around 75 men in Okinawa without firing a shot.

Although men still need to sign up for the selective service, we have been a volunteer force for many decades.

Pax River today is predominantly made up of

civilian service personnel, with relatively few career Navy members aboard the base. When the base was officially commissioned on April 1, 1943, there were a mere 173 civilians. By July 1945, there were a whopping 2,414 civilian employees, a growth rate of 14 times what it had been two years earlier. As of the early 2020s, there were approximately 10,000 civilians at Pax River and thousands more contractor personnel also support the base.

By contrast, the military populace on board the station at the end of 1942 was 168. By June 1945, that number had grown to 3,802. Today, there are only around 2,400 military personnel on the base.

As I said, when the Navy decides something, it is firmly and irrevocably decided. The Navy acquired the property in 1941. A construction camp was started on the base in the spring of 1942. By June of 1942, a contract was let for a railroad from Pax River to connect with the Pennsylvania system at Brandywine, Maryland, to haul freight, and was put into use by April 1943. Station security was in place by November 1942. Flight tests were transferred from Anacostia in June 1943, armament testing transferred from Norfolk that June, and by August 1943, radio test and aircraft environmental test had reported aboard from Anacostia.

Anyone working for the government today knows that this is a nearly impossible speed, what with the number of regulations to be followed and approval processes that have to be conducted to make such enormous changes.

In the story, Sophie Russell is enamored of the movie stars of the time. The 1940s were known as the **Golden Age of Hollywood**, not without reason. The movie industry was just a few decades old, and "talkies" had only been popularized starting in 1927. Without the unrelenting and intrusive presence of social media, movie studios could carefully craft the personas of their brightest stars. Movie stars such as Clark Gable, Rita Hayworth, and Judy Garland were elevated to cult status despite tragic personal lives

Cinema was an extremely popular pastime in the war era, and the war itself became a significant theme in many films, with depictions of characters navigating through the love, loss, and chaos of the times. Between 1939 and 1943, many films were propaganda-based and dealt with portraying an evil enemy. They were designed to help Americans view the troops as brave and selfless, an important purpose for a populace that was eaten by grief and worry. Examples include *Sergeant York* (1941), the documentary series *Why We Fight* (1942-1945), and *Guadalcanal Diary* (1943).

Later films would focus on the home front, and the deprivations and longing experienced by Americans at home (*Since You Went Away*, 1944, is an example). These could be very syrupy movies, but they were deeply felt by citizens who were sacrificing mightily in hopes of bringing loved ones home.

Other, later, war-based movies become more realistic in their portrayals of the horrors of war, such as *Sahara* (1943), *Thirty Seconds Over Tokyo* (1944), and *They Were Expendable* (1945).

Overall, the movie industry provided both escapism and reassurance at a time when Americans desperately needed both.

It wasn't uncommon during World War II for residents on the East Coast to see night explosions in the distance, then find life jackets, dead birds, and other flotsam along the shoreline the following morning.

German submarines, or U-boats, were perpetually testing the waters, so to speak, and American forces spent a great deal of time repelling them, leading to frequent clashes.

I'm not sure that things would have floated as far inland as Cedar Point, given that the Eastern shore of Maryland and the Chesapeake Bay lay between the Atlantic Ocean and St. Mary's County, but it suited my story to have it so in the novel.

The construction of Patuxent River Naval Air Station created two enormous problems for the area. First, with the chaos that naturally accompanies such a great upheaval of people, criminals began to ply their trade. It is true that many of the Pinkerton Detectives who were brought in for station security were themselves robbers, liquor smugglers, confidence men, and other felons. There was also a prostitution problem on station. The Marine security force that was established in September 1943 made quick work of cleaning out the bad apples.

Second, and with greater long-term impact, there simply wasn't enough housing in rural

St. Mary's County to accommodate the unprecedented influx of workers. The landscape became littered with small trailers, with local residents renting out parts of their properties to them. Of course, a lack of housing also led to a lack of everything. Restaurants, laundromats, barbers, doctor offices, clothing stores, and so forth were all in short supply.

Many farms located in Cedar Point and Jarboesville were forcibly bought out, and businesses along the 6,400 acres either went out of business or relocated themselves. For example, Bell Motor Co. moved to Leonardtown, becoming a landmark there until selling out to another dealership in 2008. The building was finally given over to shops in the early 2020s.

The Navy developed the area immediately just south of its main gate and across Three Notch Road into an area of small family housing units that was quickly nicknamed "the Flattops" because of their unusually slanted roofs. The streets were laid out and named for World War II battles in the South Pacific, a lasting reminder of the U.S.'s presence there. Before the housing was ready for occupancy in late July and August 1944, it was fully applied for.

The duplex homes were considered very modern for the time, with their tall banks of windows and odd roofs.

Once the county started catching up on services and housing, the homes were no longer needed, and, in 1962, the government sold them. They eventually went into such disrepair that they were leveled in 2005. Today, no trace of the Flattops exists except for one remaining structure that was formally dedicated as the U.S. Colored Troops (USCT) Memorial Interpretive Center in 2014.

As a related aside, in 1947, another housing project known as Patuxent Park was initiated along Great Mills Road near the first main gate, this time with 14 streets named for aircraft carriers, such as Yorktown, Saratoga, Midway, and Enterprise. That development still exists.

Sharp-eyed local readers will note that there are many buildings and significant people associated with the early days of Pax River that received little or no attention in this novel. For example, actress Helen Hayes spent summers at a cottage on base that became "Quarters R."

Also, Mattapany Mansion, eventually "Quarters A" and home to the base commander, is an 18th century structure that has a rich history connected to the prominent Calvert family.

As mentioned in the story, the historically significant Susquehanna home was eventually moved to Henry Ford's open-air museum in Michigan.

Because my story was predominantly concerned with the activities surrounding the construction and early build-up of the base, I chose to omit a plethora of details to keep the book to a reasonable page count.

The idea for Diane to construct a History Hall in her building came from reality. As PAO for several years at Webster Field, in St. Inigoes, Maryland, I worked on an identical project in the administration building there to commemorate

Webster Field's 80th anniversary in 2023. It was great fun sifting through 80 years of Webster Field photos, documents, and other ephemera.

But I never found an old diary to read!

Today, Lexington Park is the most populous area of St. Mary's County, and Pax River is the area's largest employer. The U.S. Navy's impact on the county cannot be overstated. In 1940, the county population was 14,626. By 1950, there were 29,111 residents and by 1970 there were 47,388 residents, more than triple what it had been 30 years previously. More than 50 years later, in 2023, the St. Mary's population had more than doubled again to over 115,000.

St. Mary's is a growing, vibrant community that still retains its rural flair. I love the idea that you can stand in a field full of cows and watch state-of-the-art fighter jets roar overhead, then jump in your car and be catching crabs from a pier along the Patuxent or Potomac rivers within ten minutes.

There's nowhere in the world like St. Mary's County.

SELECTED SOURCES

Blauvelt, Christian. *Hollywood Victory: The Movies, Stars, and Stories of World War II.* Philadelphia: Running Press, 2021.

Chambers, Mark A. *Images of Aviation: Naval Air Station Patuxent River.* Charleston: Arcadia Publishing, 2014.

Cole, Merle T. Cradle of Invasion: *A History of the U.S. Naval Amphibious Training Base of Solomons, Maryland, 1942-1945.* Solomons: Calvert Marine Museum, 1984.

Gilman, John and Heide, Rober. *Home Front America: Popular Culture of the World War II Era.* San Francisco: Chronicle Books, 1995.

Grubber, Karen L. *St. Mary's County (Postcard History Series).* Charleston: Arcadia Publishing, 2015.

Hammett, Regina Combs. *History of St. Mary's County, Maryland.* Ridge, Maryland, 1977.

Klotzbach, John. *A Sentimental Journey, America in the '40s.* Pleasantville: The Reader's Digest Association, Inc., 1998.

Reno, Linda Davis. *St. Mary's County (Images of America).* Charleston: Arcadia Publishing, 2004.

Making for fascinating reading was a series of "America in WWII" magazines I found. Published from 2005 through approximately 2017, they provided me with an in-depth understanding of not just what was going on for the military men fighting both in Europe and in the Pacific, but also how the war was dealt with on the home front.

I also stumbled upon a 1949 Patuxent River Naval Air Station yearbook, which was chock-full of photos and descriptions of the base in the years right after the war. It was fun to flip through and see all the faces that once traveled the same base streets that I myself have driven.

Although I always make my best efforts at research and try to respect the past as much as possible, this novel is ultimately a work of fiction. Any historical errors are mine alone.

ACKNOWLEDGMENTS

I AM COMPLETELY INDEBTED to the late Regina Combs Hammett, a St. Mary's Countian who was a local schoolteacher and self-taught historian. Her considerable work, *History of St. Mary's County, Maryland*, first published in 1977 and undergoing several reprintings and a revision, reflected a Herculean effort in compiling the history of the county from the time of its English settlement in 1634 through the time of its publication. The work is very readable and provided me with a captivating trip through time.

Ms. Hammett spent her early teaching career at St. Michael's School in Ridge, Maryland, and later taught at Frank Knox Elementary School. This school was housed in the same Frank Knox building mentioned in the story which was named for the World War II era Secretary of the Navy.

Ms. Hammett was a life member of the St. Mary's County Historical Society for decades. The St. Mary's County Board of Commissioners asked her to write a county history book to commemorate the St. Mary's County's 350th anniversary in 1984. The result was the aforementioned book. Ms. Hammett received St. Mary's College of Maryland's Distinguished Alumni Award in 2006 and was the county's official historian from 1988 until her death in 2010.

As an author, it intrigued me to see that Ms. Hammett self-published this considerable, 500+ page work, in hardback, in 1977. The cover flap even shows how to order it from her via a "general delivery" address. What a publishing trailblazer she was!

I wish I had been able to meet this intelligent woman who made an indelible mark on St. Mary's County.

As mentioned, I am a former PAO who served at Webster Field in St. Inigoes, Maryland. It was a job I stumbled into with nothing but some writing skills and an exhausting gift of gab. I had the great fortune to meet Mr. Patrick Gordon, the PAO for NAS Patuxent River, who graciously and effortlessly mentored me through some sticky public affairs situations. Although many other PAOs across Pax River were of great assistance to me, it was Pat who taught me how to deftly and gracefully handle delicate situations. I'm indebted to you, Pat.

Nicki Strickland, whose graphic design talent is unparalleled, was instrumental in helping me bring the design for Webster Field's History Hall to fruition. In a sense, she helped to inspire this story.

I spent a pleasant couple of hours one day at the Calvert Marine Museum in Solomons, Maryland, to research the amphibious base that was once nearby. The museum has a very nice exhibit of it. The museum also famously has otters, and who doesn't want to see otters at play? Calvert Marine Museum seems to get better every year and is well worth a visit to learn about the history, wildlife, and water-based industries associated with the area.

I am also grateful to the shops in St. Mary's who enthusiastically carry my books and sell them at an incredible pace. Marie & Nash, Cecil's Country Store, Fenwick Street Books, Keepin' it Local, and the St. Mary's County Museums—you all are the best!

Also among the best are my lovely editor, Sue Grimshaw; my talented cover designer, Kim Killion; and my wonderful copy editor and book formatter, Jennifer Jakes. Thank you all so much!

I would be nowhere without the love and support of friends and family who, for some reason, seem to enjoy listening to me babble about my latest research nuggets.

And, of course, I would be lost without Don, the best thing I never planned.

Dominus vobiscum.

OTHER BOOKS BY
CHRISTINE TRENT

HEAERT OF ST. MARY'S COUNTY
St. Clements Bluff
Three Notch Safari

THE ROYAL TRADES SERIES
The Queen's Dollmaker
A Royal Likeness
By the King's Design

THE LADY OF ASHES MYSTERIES
Lady of Ashes
Stolen Remains
A Virtuous Death
The Mourning Bells
Death at the Abbey
A Grave Celebration

FLORENCE NIGHTINGALE MYSTERIES
No Cure for the Dead
A Murderous Malady

SHORT STORIES & ANTHOLOGIES
A Death on the Way to Portsmouth (eBook only)
A Pocketful of Death (The Deadly Hours)
*Mrs. Beeton's Sausage Stuffing (Malice Domestic
Presents Murder Most Edible)*

ABOUT THE AUTHOR

CHRISTINE TRENT IS the author of the *Royal Trades* historical series, the *Lady of Ashes* historical mystery series, and several other historical novels.

St. Clements Bluff is the first in a new series, The Heart of St. Mary's County, set in her beloved, wonderfully history-rich home community in Southern Maryland.

Want to read more samples of Christine's work and learn more about her? Visit *www.ChristineTrent.com*.